SINK OR SELL

SINK OR Sell

MARGARET ROSE

HP HUDSON PRESS

For Jeff, my hero.

CHAPTER
One

SHARP, sterling silver scissors are cold in my hand. Gran would kill me if she knew I was using her embroidery tools for this, but I've got to stop thinking about the *kiss*.

Outside, a winter moon is high but mostly hidden from the window by camellia bushes that grow wild in Seattle. I tilt my head toward tulip-shaped sconces casting a glow overhead. "Come on, Stewart," I murmur, as if I'm gearing up for a battle.

Around me, baby pink tiles I've warred with since grade school mock my inability to make a decision. For example, are said tiles ugly? Or full of cottage charm?

Is this a good idea? Or a colossal mistake?

Leaning in toward the mirror, careful not to knock my precariously perched laptop with a paused tutorial, I pull a chunk of hair between two fingers.

Drastic times, desperate measures... is that how it goes?

And then I do it. Someone should be filming for Nike while reading my internal monologue aloud. I just do it—*snip!*

It's exhilarating, thrilling, and downright cathartic. I'm on my own for the first time in my life. Scared? Um, *yes*. And in desperate need of a power move.

I don't have the relationship I want, I don't have the job I want, and now Gran's left me in this house all alone. She's probably already snoozing through a post-welcome wagon martini buzz in her new retirement home. Living a more complex and inspired life than I ever have. The place sounded like Walt Disney World meets the Playboy mansion meets *The Golden Girls*.

But what was she thinking, leaving her tools and the cottage in Capitol Hill in my possession?

"A woman has to have something of her own, always!" she used to say while cleaning her dentures each night. She doled out the really important advice at bedtime and I've never had the heart to tell her it's impossible to take her seriously in a semi-see-through cotton gown with no teeth.

My fingers tense and I go again, trigger happy now—*snip, snip, snip!*

Pieces of wavy hair fall to the sink. Suddenly and without warning, my endorphins go with it, down a proverbial drain. My heart stills to the point of chest pain. I glance at vanity drawers wondering how I'm going to remedy what I know is fast becoming a style crisis.

Maybe I need to walk away and come back with fresh eyes?

Padding down the hall in Wonder Woman slippers, I search the living room for the remote. That fantasy series I want to finish might help me stop thinking about *the kiss (and now my hair)*. But as I toss a button-down I'd been adorning with sequins to a corner and reach under chintz-covered cushions, my traitorous brain flips back in time to replay the holiday party kiss-capade *again*.

The DJ, set up in our office playing Ariana Grande. George in a corner near a tree decorated with dreidel ornaments. His eyes meet mine. I saunter over to him as if there's a breeze blowing my hair in slow motion, and I go for it. He tastes like scotch and soda. But the song changes seconds after my lips —still salty from the pretzels I'd knocked back while trying to act casual— land on his. The glaring silence gives him a chance to break away, sparkling blue eyes wide, pulling at his chin in shock and smile-laughing.

But he kissed me back, for a liquor-soaked split second before he pulled away to make a toast. A snake coils in my belly just thinking about it.

After the holiday party there were a few busy days where it was all-hands-on-deck just to get through shipping deadlines. Then I took the week after Christmas off so I have no idea what George is thinking. I haven't seen him in—I stop searching for the remote to count on my fingers—eight days.

"Enough!" I wander out to a large gold mirror in the entryway for another look in better light.

It's not that bad.

My eyes narrow and I'm horrified when I see a hint of the General looking back at me. The daughter Gran raised, the woman who half raised me, is ferocious and never makes mistakes.

Maybe water will help?

I run the tap to fill Dad's old mug with the anatomical heart diagram, and smash frizzy curls against my forehead with damp fingers. My heart rate kicks up and my armpits start to sweat. If it's possible for my skin to get paler, and my smattering of freckles to stand out more, they do with dark brown bangs.

Deep breath, Holly, it's just hair.

But I haven't changed one thing about myself since I can remember. The fact that I *haven't* changed sticks out more than usual where I work. Where I have to return to work tomorrow and tell my crush, once and for all, I think he walks on water. Lorden's department store, known as America's largest retail flagship on Pine Street. The sleek, shiny escalators, every level curated, dripping with consumerism at its most glorified, and quoted as being a goddamn *Seattle Treasure*. And I've just gone and chopped off my hair. Customers are going to stare as I make my way around the store doing daily tasks and employees are going to wonder if I'm finally having my quarter-life crisis!

I look down, dumbfounded, into the water in my cup and my throat runs dry. My slippers look back up at me and like a true Wonder Woman, I realize I need my trusty sidekick, my wingman, my *bestie* with a heart around our initials.

What *would* Lenny do?

I text him quickly—*click, click, click.* His response uncorks bubbles in my chest.

> **LENNY**
>
> What lengths are you willing to go for his attention?

> **ME**
>
> OMG, ARE YOU MAKING A HAIR PUN RN?

> **LENNY**
>
> Send me a picture.

I do—*swoosh!*

> **LENNY**
>
> Didn't your mother tell you nothing good ever happens after midnight. It applies to haircuts and tattoos. Unless you're a rock star, and you're no Lady Gaga.

> **ME**
>
> I'm freaking out. And you know my mother will hate this. Maybe that's why I did it!!!!

I drain the mug in one glug and deposit it in the kitchen sink. I don't think twice about putting it in the dishwasher. *Take that, General!*

> **LENNY**
>
> Don't bite the hand that's going to help you…

> **ME**
>
> I just acted. Out of desperation. My lovesickness has turned lethal, my heart is gangrene.

> **LENNY**
>
> Do we need wine?

> **ME**
>
> No more booze. I'm sticking to my New Year's resolution and telling him how I feel. Tomorrow. I want to arrive stunning and impossibly fresh-looking.

LENNY

Did you just quote SATC to me?

I ignore him and pace my little cottage made for two, wondering why I feel like my grandmother dumped me to be a geriatric party girl and I can't even ask my crush out on a date.

LENNY

And wasn't that the purpose of the make out sesh?

ME

I finish what I start. And he liked it. Right? Has he said anything to you?

LENNY

Go buy a straightener, they sell them at the twenty-four-hour drugstore. See if that helps, and meet me in the morning in the spa room. We need to talk.

Oh shit, what does that mean? I grab my keys and text with one hand as I drag my sweatpants-clad body to the car.

ME

K.

The temperature is below freezing and I see my breath as I turn the key in the ignition, realizing and not caring that I'm still wearing my slippers. Bangs were definitely a bad idea.

Stark halogen lights sting my eyes as I breeze through automatic doors and scan aisles until I spy hair care. The entire store smells like plastic and bad decisions.

Dashing down rows of shower caps and bobby pins, I come to hot tools and feel a sigh of relief escape my lips. *Everything is fixable.*

"Um, excuse me." The voice startles me, but I keep my head down, my eyes on the prize, *no time for distractions!* I've narrowed it down to two different straighteners. One is pink, one gold; decisions, decisions.

How do I feel about gold today? How will I feel tomorrow?

Still, I can feel the presence of a warm body hovering and I just want them to shoo.

"Hmm?" I finally mumble, managing a glance at shiny black shoes —nice shoes, expensive. But my eyes quickly go back to scan the fine print on each straightener. They both go up to four hundred and ten degrees, though why this is necessary eludes me; that's more heat than you need to cook meat.

My knees hit the floor, this is going to take a minute, and my enormous handbag that I use to carry everything I need on the daily for work flops open next to me as if saying, *this is an emergency situation, every man for himself, there's just no time!*

"Sorry, but do you know where the, um—"

The guy sways, I can smell liquor rolling off him and detect a slur in his words. He braces slightly against the shelves above me, encroaching on my personal space.

Undeterred by my ignoring him, he clears his throat and starts again. "Do you know where the *condoms* are?" He uses the loudest whisper known to man when he says *condoms*. "I can't find anyone who works here," he follows up with a snort.

I clutch the gold flat iron to my chest—you can never go wrong with metallics—and pull myself to my feet as he dips down and grabs my abandoned bag. We barely avoid a forehead collision as he hands it to me, and that's when I finally get a look at him. Our eyes lock, our tongues tie.

Momentarily stunned, smelling like a medieval tavern, is my boss.

"Holly?"

I slap a hand across my forehead, nearly dropping the straightener. "George, oh! Hi. Um…" My bag slides down my other shoulder and I shrug uncomfortably to keep it up while clutching the box. A muscle in my neck spasms and I wince.

"Sorry," he chuckles. "I don't usually do these kinds of errands, but it seems I found just the person I need."

Guaranteed, George Lorden has never set foot in a twenty-four-hour drugstore or maybe he has, but it's been a while. I know this because in addition to managing all administrative departments at Lorden's, I've been running errands for him for a little over three years under the unofficial guise of "store manager's assistant."

"Aisle three, I think," I say, nodding toward a sign a few aisles down that reads Family Planning.

He winks. He actually winks. I don't think he's ever winked at me. And God help me, my heart flutters even though I know what he's here for, which means I know what he's doing, which means he's not planning to do it with me. Even after I Ariana Grande'd him at the holiday party.

"Thanks." He pulls himself up to his full height, a tree at six foot three. "Can't wait to have you back tomorrow, it's been rough without you."

At first, I think, *Aw poor George! Has he not taken any time off after the gut-punch that is holiday retail?* But then I quickly remind myself, he's the *boss*. Mr. Three-Hour Lunches, Mr. Work Trip to L.A. to court vendors, Mr. *It's Product Research, Gotta Take the Company Jet to Coachella to See What the Kids Are Wearing!*

With a shake of my head and a smile, I say, "Yep. See you tomorrow, George."

Is he thinking of the kiss, right now? Like I am? I turn and drop the hand that was hiding my wild woman hair. Why did I not wear a hat?

A clerk appears to ring me up—thank you, retail karma—because I need out of here, now. But apparently, George is on a mission, moving fast and possibly not as drunk as I thought. After fumbling down aisles in my peripheral, he appears behind me with a box of condoms in hand. A big box.

"Have a nice night," the sleepy clerk says to me; a teenager with a thoughtfully placed eyebrow stud and a red apron-type vest hanging off one bony shoulder.

"Thanks, you too." Over my shoulder and running toward the automatic doors, I toss, "See you in the morning!"

But George is tapping the pockets of his cashmere coat, then his Canali suit pants that I pick up weekly from the cleaners. He looks up at me sheepishly and the pink of his cheeks warms my heart. I love this adorable man. He manages to look like Superman and a fumbling, good-natured bear clutching a jar of honey at the same time. Who wouldn't gush over that? And how is it a thirty-year-old man can't find his wallet and buy himself condoms? Still, even if I know he's about to sleep with another woman, my gut drops when he flashes perfect white teeth at me.

Maybe she doesn't matter? Maybe she's a one-night stand? I'm pretty sure he hasn't been seeing anyone serious, hence my attempt to finally tell him how I feel. I usually know, because I shop for and wrap all the gifts, but it's been a while.

"I can't find my wallet." His watery blue eyes dance as they ask me what I know he won't actually say in words because he knows he won't have to.

I backtrack. "Here," I say, handing the clerk my debit card. His eyes move between us, trying to assess the situation as he rings and bags the box of Trojans.

"Oh man, thanks a lot, Holly dolly. You. Are. The. Best." He always says it staccato.

My body melts at the nickname he's had for me since I was sixteen — that's a solid eight years of swooning so far.

Throughout my teenage years at Lorden's, George never really saw me. His horrid little devil brother did, but to George, I was just another employee at the store. Still, I clung to that nickname like a girl's first love letter. Until now. I'm determined to make him see me now, and remind him that there's more where that first, albeit sloppy, kiss came from.

Just maybe not tonight.

"Sure, George. You, uh, be safe." Oh God. "And I'll see you tomorrow!" I run out the door and leap into my car, letting out a long, hot breath that turns to smoke. The car smells like cold air as I wrap my bare fingers around the frigid steering wheel.

Then I make the fatal mistake of turning my head and looking at the parked car to my left.

A beautiful blond with a cut jaw and rugged five-o'clock shadow is sitting in the driver's seat of George's Range Rover—the same car I've ridden in exactly three times for off-site annual reviews—smacking his lips and applying gloss.

CHAPTER
Two

AFTER A RESTLESS NIGHT sleeping alone in the house, the straightener barely makes a dent in the bird's nest that has taken up residence on my forehead.

I'm heading into work wearing a beret, my hair knotted to the side, with a chunky sweater. The cream fisherman's knit pairs nicely with slim leather pants that Lenny made me buy on Christmas Eve, when all the designer markdowns go through the system but aren't actually marked on tags or live on the website. Being part owner of the biggest retail company in the United States has perks, like the inside track on everything designer. Lenny's world revolves around *stuff* and my capsule, *girl on a budget,* wardrobe thanks him.

In addition to my sorry excuse for a disguise, I'm late. So, instead of parking in the employee lot, a good million years from the building, I park front and center. And instead of taking the employee doors, which lead to a cement tower filled with stairs and pee smells, I skate through glass doors that open automatically for me and deposit me safely in Cosmo—the land of cosmetics, floral scents, color, glitter, and streakless mirrors.

Holly with bangs is a rule breaker. Or maybe it's that I'm going to tell George I love him today and rules don't apply to grand gestures.

Maybe Gran's absence is making me so lonely I no longer care about consequences. It's anyone's guess.

Music filters through store speakers as my heels clack across gleaming marble floors. I doubt there was much to hear in the morning announcements. These are the cold, slow days of January retail. I pass a wall of perfume bottles, angle down aisles of makeup, and make it to two heavy double doors with large gold pulls. Nodding my hellos to the fine jewelry and handbag department openers on either side of the spa, I enter the calm, dimly lit room full of eucalyptus mist and pampering devices I can't afford.

"Morning, Len." It always smells like heaven and money in here.

"Let's see it." He turns from white lacquered shelves meticulously stocked with product, no doubt rummaging for samples for employees having a bad day. "Please, remove the cat from your head. The bangs can't be worse than that."

"It's mohair."

"It's abhorrent."

"You gave it to me two years ago for my birthday!"

"I love it," he snort-laughs. "Sit." He motions to a tall chair reserved for high-rolling clients who get facials with their skin care purchases. A straightening iron is in my hair along with his long capable fingers—this one has tilting plates, better to grab the hair, he explains as I discreetly adjust a wedgie. My leather pants are sticking together at every point of contact; today's just going to be one of those days.

"Why do you own such a fancy straightener?" I ask, settling in and letting my foot bob while dangling a heel off my toes. His floppy blond hair is clearly unstyled yet always in place. It's annoying. Lenny is the perfect combination of a man who takes care of himself but also looks natural and unaffected in his own skin. He's never touched Botox or fillers as a matter of personal principle.

"Do you think the girls manage themselves?" The girls, of course. Lenny's alter ego adores wigs of all kinds and colors. When Lenny does drag, he is totally *extra* about it and insanely talented.

"Thanks for the 911 appointment."

"What were you thinking? At the very least you should have come to me. I would have helped," he says, as if I've gone to the black market for a fake Fendi.

"I was just restless, I guess. Couldn't stop thinking about—"

"Granny O. moving out and leaving you alone with all your sequins and glittery puff paints?"

"No—*the kiss!*" I should have spent my college years learning to flirt instead of earning a textiles degree, up to my elbows in Rit dye every night.

He gives me a discerning look then asks, "How's she settling in?"

Everyone from Lorden's loves Gran. She was the head tailor for nearly twenty years and is as much a legacy at the Seattle store as the corn chowder in the café.

"Living her best life. I talked to her on the way in this morning. Last night at happy hour she met some guy named Bernie. She's going to live the geriatric version of *The Bachelorette*, I guarantee it."

"She's a lover; someone who believes in true love and all the gooeyness."

I scoff dramatically, but he pins my head in place and I still. "A romantic in hard-ass clothing! You know when I told her I kissed George she made me Zoom the General. They both told me what a colossal mistake it was and made me swear it wouldn't affect my making it to Corporate." My dark eyes meet his bright baby blues—an aggressively recessive Lorden trait—in the mirror.

"You run this whole store. You can love who you want and it won't affect your productivity, your résumé, or your reputation but, is that still what you want? A Corporate desk job? I thought you liked being on the floor, around the merch, in the mix?"

"Getting to see what designers are doing, having my hands on all the fabrics, and checking the construction of the seams all the way to how brands are marketed is great but Corporate's been my plan all along. You know that."

"I hope she finds a man." He ignores my comment about climbing the ladder of the company he owns with his brother—family owned for generations that will poetically pass to the next set of brothers one day. He could probably get me any job I wanted, within Lorden's or otherwise, but he wouldn't do that. And I'd never accept without knowing I'd gotten there myself, even though I'm sure the General would call me a fool. "Your Gran's a lover deep down. Totally a hard-ass too, you're right. She's both, in impeccably tailored clothing." His eyes turn wistful as he continues working through my hair. "God, I miss her. So does my wardrobe. Tom tries, but he's no Granny O. Remember when I was styling Mrs. Smith, after she had that melt-down and refused to work with anyone else?"

"So, they had to pull out the big guns, a Lorden!" I fan myself, both because I'm hot from the heat on my head and because I like to give him shit about being part of the royal family. He puts the straightener down.

"Thankfully, I was able to pass her off to Jenny when she became the stylist manager. Anyway, your Gran about chopped my head off when I promised Mrs. Smith a twenty-four-hour turnaround on her Jason Wu. Remember when Michelle Obama put him on the map at the swearing in—"

"So, realistically, Mrs. Smith had to have a Jason Wu *STAT*."

"She is related to Michelle, honey. Second cousin, and she won't let you forget it," he says, arching a brow. "But oh, the miracles your Gran could work. She did it. After Louie and I, both of us, had a conference call with the Wu team. We got the dress, and she turned out the alter-ations in less than a day."

"She's a talented woman."

"You are too, you know—"

"No, I'm not. I've got hobbies, I like clothes and aesthetics. Knowing how they're made and how they end up in people's closets is fascinating, but sewing beads on vintage jackets with shiny threads isn't a career. Gran's a master seamstress. An artist. That's something to be proud of."

He rakes his hands through my hair, turning my chair and allowing me a look at myself full-on in the mirror. "Actually, it suits you, you just needed to tame it."

In this case, not having the guts to *make a decision* and lop off my hair in one chop worked out for me. Now that he's properly pressed them, I have shaggy bangs that cover my eyebrows and tickle my lashes.

"Holy hell, I'm good. You look like Jane Birkin," Lenny appraises.

"Who?" Every once in a while, our fifty something, twenty some-thing age gap shows and in cases like this usually leads to a long-winded answer about an old Hollywood starlet that Lenny worships. I act like I hate it but secretly I love it.

"Listen, Holly..."

Uh-oh.

"If you're going to lecture me about George, don't." I pop up from my chair with more thrust than necessary, it continues to spin. "I'm doing something about it, Len. I made my move at the holiday party. It could have gone better, sure, but I'm glad I did it. No more sitting and waiting for him to come around—*that's what you said*. And—" I hold up a hand before he can protest. "I'm going to tell him I'm in love with him. And if I lose him, I'll deal with it. But what if he loves me back, Len? I have to know. I have to."

He shakes his head, eyes contemplating more than I can make out. "Don't ever let your mother tell you you're not an optimist."

Lenny always has my back. My relationship with the General is tumultuous at times, but when I became an adult—e.g. started paying Gran rent—we found common ground, as long as I stick to her five-year plan for my future: work, work harder, climb ladder, take over world.

Lenny opens the door, ushering me into a day I'm not fully ready for. He's wearing a tartan kilt that he bought in Scotland during his *Outlander* obsession, a black tuxedo jacket, and a thick white T-shirt. "I wasn't going to bring up George—though that's a concern. There're some changes coming down the pike, big ones, and I want you to know that whatever happens, we'll make sure you're taken care of. Remember, you're family."

I most certainly am not family. The family consists of two sets of brothers from the past two generations of Lordens: Louie and Lenny, and Louie's offspring, George and Declan. But I've been here long enough to know that whatever is coming will blow over and become the new normal in a matter of time. New tag guns, mobile checkout, changing the gift wrap from classic navy to recycled brown paper that made us look eco-conscious—Declan's idea. If I had a dollar for every time the company rolled out new protocols, I wouldn't have to be George's assistant in addition to running Customer Service.

"I can handle whatever they roll out. When are we hearing?"

"Weren't you here for announcements? We've got a store meeting tomorrow, 7 a.m."

"*Whomp-whomp*," I sing. "That's going to make for a day of general grumpiness." Customer Service has recently dwindled to me manning the desk most days while one guy putting himself through college takes the night shifts. Stocking coffee and bagels for the entire store tomorrow will probably fall on me. "Remember when they stopped doing quarter coffee for the openers? I wish they'd bring that back. People are working here a full two hours before the store opens. We need caffeine, Len!"

He rolls his eyes. "Will we *never* hear the end of quarter coffee?"

It was a nicety, a tradition since the flagship opened in 1901. Of course, then it was nickel coffee. A thank you of sorts to the openers, the employees who trudged in early and loaded the registers with cash before the overhead lights were even on. It was a shock when the company did away with it last year.

Lenny walks me to the shiny first-floor escalator that will take me to the second floor and then to the third. The café and a few departments are on the third floor with the support offices tucked behind where most customers have no idea they exist.

"Bring it back, Lenny! You have the power. You're an owner. Why'd they get rid of it, anyway?"

"I'm brother to the king. No better than the royal jester. I have no power, you know that."

"You have stock, don't sidestep."

"Not enough, I assure you. Why don't you ask your beloved Georgie? He's firstborn, the eldest being groomed to take over when Louie finally steps down."

"I'm supposed to do things for *him*, not the other way around."

"Ask Declan, then. The resident ballbuster. What would that equate to in royalty—the king's guard?"

I make a face as if I've just had the first inkling of food poisoning. "I would rather sell quarter coffee on a street corner than ask Declan Lorden for anything."

"Meow. You two. You know everyone around here is placing bets on which one of you will *finally* grab the other by the neck and—"

"Yuck, stop!" He gets the full-on, hand-over-mouth, I'm-going-to-vomit-I'm-so-disgusted-with-what-you-just-said gesture from me, but he rolls his eyes and shakes it off as I continue, "I'm determined to have a good day with my new hair and my planned declaration of love for the *nice* brother." I check my watch—I'm very late. "Do not sully my good mood with talk of swine." I will not chicken out today, I will not stop halfway, I'm going to tell him everything.

Let the chips fall where they may!

Stepping onto the escalator, I give him a small curtsy. It's an effort because my leather pants stick together at the calf and I almost tumble down the metal mountain.

"Wait, are you the princess now? I'm confused," he hollers loudly through the immaculate store. Employees dressed as if they're going to a club opening even though it's barely nine in the morning stare, some roll their eyes, and some ignore us altogether because they're accustomed to our antics.

My mountain rises, taking me right along with it. Sometimes, when we're joking like this—and because this is the only job I've ever had and this place feels just as much like home as Gran's cottage in Capitol Hill—I do think I'm one of them. "Yes! Just call me Princess Holly!"

Our offices are not posh by any stretch; I like this about the Lorden building. They put all their money where their mouths are, the Lordens. Everything is for the customer: the fixtures, the lighting, the cash wraps complete with tissue, and navy boxes (only the bags were switched out for eco paper—we do have a brand to protect), and glossy bows. Most of these things don't exist anymore, a brick-and-mortar consumer is hard-pressed to find gift wrap in any major department stores these days.

An assortment of Valentine's Day gift cards fill a small box I use to cart them around the store, stopping at each cash wrap to fill plexiglass holders with choices. Foot traffic isn't what it used to be and I have to scoop out most of the Hanukkah, Christmas, and Kwanzaa cards destined for the shredder.

"Morning, Holly." Callie is a newbie in Lingerie, just outside Customer Service and the support offices on the third floor. She's bright, but not exactly a born salesperson. It's not likely she'll make it; fresh out of college and trying to pay rent on an entirely commission-based paycheck, which sounds absolutely terrifying.

"Hey, Callie." I blow my bangs out of my eyes and smile at her. "Any traffic this morning?"

"Zero, we're already"—she leans a hip into the counter and checks a smart watch on her wrist—"an hour in. Geez, I'll be lucky if I make a sale before my shift's over."

"Sorry, it's the winter lull. Things'll pick up." I give her my best hang-in-there smile.

The next department is aptly called Active, where all women's swim and workout gear are housed.

"Morning, Holly. Cute hair." Alice, a middle-aged mom, is wrestling with the receipt tape. "This one always jams," she says into the machine.

"Thank you." I beam. *See, taking chances pays off!* "Here, let me." We trade spots. She takes the box of gift cards, emptying and filling the slots at her register while I peer into the bowels of the machine.

Alice is old-school. She's worked here part-time while raising four kids and her youngest went to college last year. I know she wants more hours now that she's an empty nester but lately, departments have been downsizing—swimwear and women's athletics being two of them combined to form Active. Jobs seem to be dissolving every day but Alice is a lifer, when something opens she'll be the first up for it.

"Got it!" I announce, pulling the guts of an old receipt roll out and popping a new one into place.

"You're a lifesaver, thanks. That would have taken me an hour," she says, pushing readers up her nose.

Rounding an escalator that will take me to the second floor with my box of gift cards in tow, leather pants sticking about every ten steps, I greedily inhale smells from the café. Easily the best part of working here. The corn chowder is hot and ready daily, an absolute legend of Lorden's. They bottle it and sell it, it's such a fan favorite. Also, the chef has regular specials that rival Michelin star restaurants in town. Most Lorden's across the country have cafés now, a multimillion-dollar arm of the business.

"Dawdling? Daydreaming again, Holly?" His voice is steak knives down a chalkboard.

Declan.

He's popped up from the shadows of the still darkened café, which doesn't open till closer to the lunch hour, Dixie cup of scavenged coffee in his hand; essentially quarter coffee the kitchen brews just for him and he doesn't pay a cent. Why would he? He's a Lorden. The little prince. The second son. The rule breaker. The ballbuster. I could go on...

"Nope," I say, as cheerily as I can. "Especially now," I add, after quickening my steps.

He follows behind me, hollering, "I heard that."

We don't exactly have the most professional interactions, Declan and me. It's as if we're still sixteen years old instead of mid-twenties, meeting for the first time, and hating each other on the spot every single day.

I pick up the pace. If I don't, he'll question me until my brain bleeds. It's always the interrogation from him: What are your tasks, where will you be after lunch, how many hours have you worked this week?

And why? Just to make me answer him. A power play, that's why.

"Holly, a moment, please?"

And I hate it—he's not my boss. So, I keep moving even as he's calling my name to stop.

I risk a glance over my shoulder. He's still on my heels, moving fast in Nikes compared to my pumps.

George wasn't in his office when I popped in to stow my things and grab the gift cards, but his coat was on the hook so I know he's here somewhere. If I'm going to declare love for the store manager — first-born son at the helm of the $1.2 billion-dollar company I work for — I may as well start by being a star employee. It would be smart to hold back from firing off a four-letter expletive at his little brother.

Still, Declan follows me toward the escalator. His eyes squint behind large burgundy frame glasses, wavy strawberry blond hair on top of his head, and an angry vein popping in his neck. I freeze and fake right, but he isn't fooled. *Damn*, for a pretty big guy, he can move fast. I commit to the escalator and pick up the pace, taking really large steps so my pants don't stick. This is like a scene from Animal Planet, except with leopard print dresses instead of actual leopards.

The escalator is within reach. I will jump on it like a woman hurling herself at the last summer sale Chloé bag. *Evade the predator at all costs!*

"Holly, a word—" His deep voice echoes through the third floor. Employees are smirking.

Thing is, we have nothing in common. Are nothing alike. George is sweet, kind, and thoughtful. Declan is prickly, grumpy, and self-absorbed. He will stop me to tell me I've missed a spot with my gift cards, he will say I need to double-check every slot to make sure there's not one free space.

Nope. You are not raining on my parade today, Declan Lorden, bane of my existence.

Two steps in, and I risk another glance. He's still moving toward me, muscles flexing under a thin cashmere sweater and collared shirt, so I move even faster down the escalator. But then my damn pants snag at the ankle, the leather sticking together like cling wrap, and it's either grab the black tar railing or face-plant into metal grids that I'm sure will shatter every tooth in my mouth.

At the last minute, I grab the rails and realize there's nowhere for the box of gift cards to go but cascading down the moving stairs. Hundreds of tiny plastic rectangles fly—branded for Valentine's Day with hearts and cherubs and the shiny Lorden's name. Some find slots and crevices to get stuck in, and some go over the sides and fall on heads like rain. Their metallic hologram faces wink at me as I struggle to get my heels back under my feet.

I do not fall. A bead of sweat rolls down my cheek as I push sweaty bangs to the side of my forehead and breathe. *Phew!*

Just as I'm getting my wits back and feeling damn grateful I still have all my teeth, the escalator chugs and racks itself to a slow, snail's pace. Gears grind from the underbelly and—

Oh. My. God.

Smoke begins to seep and bloom from gaps in the metal. The whole thing jerks to a stop and I'm almost pitched over the side. The unidentified sounds emitting from the underbelly of the beast are prehistoric and the reek of hot metal permeates the air.

Tiptoe, tiptoe; I make it to the middle. A damsel halfway across a drawbridge, and tentatively taking another step. From this vantage point, almost every floor of the store has a front-row seat to my situation.

"Holly Stewart, stop!" Declan's voice bellows through the store as he glares at me from the top of the escalator. He's got a walkie-talkie in his hand and speaks into it as smoke causes me to lose track of him.

I continue to sneak down, moving slowly because I can't see through the smoke and the whole escalator is shaking. Then, over the speakers, interrupting a Death Cab for Cutie throwback, I hear the page:

Kelly Bear, five-five. Kelly Bear, five-five.

Declan has ratted me out. He's called the operator and now she's announcing a code loudly through the sound system. The code for store emergencies.

CHAPTER
Three

WHEN KELLY BEAR is called for the third time to the second floor, I know I'm screwed. Every manager in the store will respond to Kelly Bear, in addition to the entire Loss Prevention team (LP is our own version of a Lorden police force) and the actual police will be called after the store operator has finished her announcement. I know the protocol because as the Administrative General Manager, I wrote every word of it and trained the operator myself.

The escalator is still smoking, and the few morning customers I can see from my perch are being escorted to exits by department managers —calm, trained faces reassuring curious, concerned mugs. At the bottom of the escalator, on the second-floor landing, George appears, sliding to a stop in Gucci loafers, his red tie catching up with him a split second later.

Our eyes lock, both of us squinting through smoke, and I can't read the look on his face but it's entirely possible I'll get fired by the love of my life today.

Declan materializes on the escalator at my side. "Hang on to me."

A visceral reaction rolls through my shoulders, and my hands automatically shove against the soft knit of his sweater. He teeters as if losing his balance and the escalator chooses that moment to lurch.

Immediately, I cling to him, pressing the length of my body against his rough, raw denim, pulling him back because I'm not trying to get his head cracked open, no matter how much I loathe him and his bossy glasses. Who choses *burgundy* frames?

He inhales a sharp breath, then exhales slowly and way too close to my ear. My skin crawls.

"Chill, Holly." The disdain in his voice makes me reconsider pushing him to his death.

Instead, I attempt to turn and climb back to the top because he's gotten in the way of me going down, using his body as a shield, like when a driver puts his hand out for the passenger when he breaks too hard. The show of concern is for the watching employees' benefit. Declan's not even *close* to that chivalrous.

"Not today, Lorden. You are not going to pin me here just to embarrass me more than I already am, you egomaniac."

A surprisingly strong arm wraps around my waist and stops me. "You can't go back up. We have to go down—and I don't think you used that word right."

Excuse me, sir!

Through the smoke that admittedly is spewing mostly from the top of the escalator, I manage to glare at him over my shoulder. "You only care about yourself, I used it right." My gaze drops to his hand as if it's the tentacle of an alien that's somehow suction-cupped itself way too close to my butt. "Let go."

"Oh, sorry." He drops his hand immediately.

As if on cue the machine jolts back to life and I go flying back into him. "Ah!" I yell.

He catches me easily. "Oof," he grunts as his legs brace against my weight. He doesn't budge, a pillar of strength, balance, and agility. *Annoying* is the first thing that comes to mind. "Gotcha. Is this okay?"

"Put me down!" Without thinking it through, I kick my feet, which only makes him grip me harder.

"It was either catch you or let you plummet. I swear, you've been a brat since the day I met you."

"Declan Lorden, *I swear* if you don't put me down—" I break off when he lets out a large cough from smoke inhalation. The escalator shudders and instead of finishing my sentence I wrap my arms around his neck, holding on for dear life.

It's unfortunate for me that he smells nice, like fresh water, the outdoors, and clean sheets all rolled into one. The laundress at his castle must use some really fancy dryer sheets.

Muscles in his jaw flex. I've pressed my face—*out of fear*—against his and he pulls me closer, his biceps curling so I'm cocooned against his chest. He begins taking tentative, slow steps down.

Fine, he's strong and carrying me in a bridal hold that is totally unnecessary. Yes, I like the way he smells and might be taking advantage of face-to-face contact so I can feel the slight scrape of his five-o'clock shadow—it's been a while. He's still an entitled dictator and probably uses one of those military trainers who yell like jerks so their jerk clients can achieve maximum levels of buff.

"Can you walk?"

I huff, "Of course, I'm fine."

For a moment, he eyes me as if he's got a question on the tip of his tongue, then sets me on my feet. We're not quite at ground level yet. "Hold on, this beast could come back to life any minute and I don't want to deal with skyrocketing insurance fees because an inept employee decided to off herself on company property."

I would rather burn every article of clothing in my closet then hold on to him, again. "I didn't trip on purpose—"

"I know, you were running from me. The egomaniac who followed you into this mess."

"Can you blame me?" I don't bother waiting for his response and instead take in the general calamity blanketing the store as we carefully finish our descent, but I'm pretty sure he grimaces. Serves him right. You can't live as a miscreant your whole life, then expect to be a prince and save the day.

He grasps my hand, pulling me gently over the final step to solid ground. But just as quickly, I detangle my fingers that had laced with his because now I'm in George's embrace—kind of. He's holding me at arm's length as I stare into the chest of his asphalt-colored shirt.

"Jesus, Holly," George says over the top of my head.

"You're Jewish, George," I say, looking up at him.

"I can still—" He begins moving my arms, squeezing my shoulders. I think this is George checking me for injury. "Are you okay? What happened?"

Declan fidgets beside us, watching all of this go down. "She tripped, probably couldn't see with all that hair in her face. Gift cards slipped between the inner and outer rails in the escalator, blocked the continuous chain, and halted the drive wheel—what?"

Both George and I are staring at him with open mouths.

"How do you know the inner mechanics of the escalator?" I'm hyperaware of George's hand now, patting my back. It appears Declan is too, his eyes lazer focused on the movement.

"When the maintenance team comes every month, I pay attention." He's a dad, annoyed with his kids for not understanding how our own home functions. "Tell her to take the day off—"

"But I just got back!"

"What's wrong with her hair?" George looks at me curiously. I wilt a little because he clearly doesn't notice the change.

"You're done for the day," Declan says. "Go home and cool off."

Cool off? I'm perfectly cool. "You're not my boss, it's not your call."

Technically, his name is on the door and it most definitely is in the realm of his call but semantics. Also, I clearly shouldn't be talking to him in front of other employees like this, but this is how Declan and I operate. He called me a brat on company property, I'm entitled to buck his authority. We are dog and cat, little sister and big brother, high school bully and hero of the day—in that last scenario he's obviously the bully, even though he technically just rescued me.

Instead of answering, he does this thing that I hate—he takes a long, deep breath. Exhales through his nose as if totally exasperated and chews his bottom lip. "Meet me in my office," he finally says to George. "We'll both need to sign off on the police report. Dad will get a notification, so you're in charge of talking him through it. Managing this"—he motions toward the smoke that still billowing up three floors —"is going to set me back today."

"You're going to have to start standing up to him, Dec," George says.

"Not today, and not for this." With that, he turns on the heel of a retro Air Jordan and walks away.

I have to fill out a report and speak to the police—who continuously refer to me as the *gift card girl* when they can't remember my name—before I'm cut and forced to clock out for the day.

It's no secret I'm irate. Really, I'm mortified, but it's coming off as pissy as I pound my seven-digit employee code into the computer to clock out: 8229742. George tells me it's extra vacation, but I know they're doing damage control. The scene I made this morning might be over now, and it may go completely unnoticed, back to normal tomorrow, business as usual. But we all know Declan Lorden is never going to let me live this one down.

And Mr. and Mrs. Lorden will definitely be notified. Declan wasn't exaggerating. Which is why, when I get Lenny's text that afternoon while curled up with a cup of loose leaf tea and an embroidery project I've been tinkering with, I throw up a little in my mouth.

> LENNY
>
> I'm doing Lady Gaga tonight, not meat dress or McQueen platform Gaga, Joanne bring-a-tear-to-your-eye Gaga. Everyone's going to shit themselves when they see me in a pink Stetson. You in? Dinner before?

> ME
>
> That may be the only thing that can pull me from the death spiral I'm descending RN. Time?

> LENNY
>
> I heard. 7:00. Death spiral indeed. You could have knocked your teeth out, isn't that your worst nightmare?

I've had recurring dreams about my teeth
falling out for years. I was terrified.

LENNY

Means you're sexually frustrated, everyone
knows that. BTW—staying at mansion while
my apartment is being staged for a photo
shoot with Architectural Digest. Use the front
door.

The last thing I want to do is grace the Lordens with my presence,
but Lenny has always been sensitive because of who he is, what he
comes from. He's well into his fifties, single, and has been out almost
his entire life. Over many, many bottles of red wine I've come to understand what a tough, brave, and extremely sensitive man he is.

If I cancel now, he'll know it's because I don't want to go to the
mansion. It's not that the Lordens aren't nice people—surprisingly,
they are—it's just they're on another planet entirely and you can't hold
it against them. They live in a jewel-encrusted version of the Upside
Down. Their life, inherent wealth established three generations back, is
nothing less than charmed. As much as we joke, it is almost royal the
way they interact with celebrities and politicos. They are the beautiful
people, the dream, impeccably dressed with first choice off the
runways each season.

Of course, I have always wanted to see the mansion in person.

The historic lakefront house is located on Laurelhurst Drive near
the University District. Nestled in trees and topiaries—the finest
Seattle suburbia has to offer—and an easy fourteen-minute commute
to the store. It boasts five bedrooms, five bathrooms, a little over eighteen thousand square feet, and costs a little over fourteen million
dollars. I know all this because I Googled it after my first day working
at the store, trying to figure out why Declan Lorden was such a
conceited prick. He barely acknowledged me the day we met, let
George shake my hand and do all the talking, sticking to a corner and
scowling all the while. Growing up in a house like that, it'd be hard not
to be a bit affected, I'll give him that, but George managed it.

While I've seen every photo the internet has to offer, have imagined myself walking down the dark wood staircase covered in swirling carpets of red, navy, and hunter green, I've never actually been inside. They've hosted lavish parties over the years, which have afforded me a visual tour reading soapy blog posts. Often, I fall asleep at night dreaming of being George's date at one of these parties, dazzling his parents with wit and charm so that he has no choice but to propose to me on the spot, stopping only to ask for his grandmother's ring. Sometimes, these dreams feel as close to reality as playing Lenny's VR.

But blogs and Google have not properly prepared me for two-story gates, meticulously pruned boxwoods that could rival the Queen of Hearts's garden, or the Trevi Fountain reproduction in the circle drive —all touched with a bit of January frost that looks like a fine sheen of glitter. The house itself is unassuming, Kennedyesque tradition with muted red brick, diamond-soldered windowpanes, and the peak of a whimsical turret poking up from behind the roofline.

A maid, pink-cheeked and looking like she's been plucked from a movie set answers a lion-knockered door and ushers me up a winding staircase—the one with the red, navy, and green swirling medallions. I let my hand slide up the banister and shiver.

While leading me like a tour guide, she smiles kindly, then motions down a fat hallway and says I'll find Mr. Leonard in the east wing. Pushing my shoulders back and ignoring the itch to take my shoes off, I pretend I'm the sister in *The Royal Tenenbaums*–I've seen richer.

I knock, he answers. "Enchanté, Ms. Stewart."

He's in character, the expressive, artistic side that lights him up, ready to pounce.

"Hi, Len." I pat him on the arm and push through, I can only humor him so much.

Lenny leads me through a sitting room with tastefully preppy furnishings and a useful kitchenette that leans just French enough to be chic. We walk through another hallway that could double as a room, with mirrored closets running along each wall and reflecting multiple chandeliers.

In the sleeping quarters, Lenny perches at the edge of an unmade satin mountain.

My hands itch to touch all the crystal and polished wood. Cream walls shine as if coated in silk. "Why are you living here, again?"

"This biscuit, David, is photographing my apartment for the April issue of *AD*. He insisted I repaint beforehand, a bit domineering, but I like him. After two dates, he convinced me. My apartment will now be awash in chartreuse." He gestures with an intentionally exaggerated ballerina's arch of an arm. My face must betray I'm unconvinced as he concedes, "The sacrifices we make so cute boys will love us."

"So, you're here."

"For the month, at least. Could be worse. I'm driving Louie even more batty than he already is. Mira loves me more than him, always has, and he can't stand it." He crosses his legs and pulls a mischievous face. "Reminds me of our days at Vohs."

"It's still hard to imagine Louie as the wild one. And it's impossible to imagine you in high school."

"He made me look tame, gave me a lot of shit too. But if anyone else gave me trouble, Louie Lorden would pulverize them. No matter what our parents would do to him as punishment. My nephews followed in our footsteps in that way."

It's easy to ignore that last part, I don't want to think about either of the Lorden boys at the moment. Declan because he's the ultimate pest. George because I didn't get my chance to finally, finally profess my love today. Now that I've decided to tell him how I feel like a grown-up the suspense is killing me.

Len's changed from his kilt and now sits in his tux jacket, T-shirt, stiff white boxers, and sock garters wrapped around his calves holding up black socks. Behind him is a red feather boa that I'm sure was recently wrapped around his lean shoulders. Beside him on the floor, a few empty wine bottles poke from underneath the bed. On an adjacent poof sits a picked-at charcuterie.

"Looking forward to the show tonight? I can't believe you're doing Joanne—our personal drinking album. Remember when your neighbors called the police with a noise complaint?" Lenny has a real affinity for Gaga, has even met her a few times. The best memory of his life is sharing a smoke with her in an alley outside the underground club he performs in—his words.

"I believe the complaint was something to do with screeching cats." We both share a laugh and a memory like the old friends we are, happily unconventional. "We had some good times, but I think we're both due for a change, don't you? I feel it coming. David might be the one…"

If he is, I'll be the first in line to offer congratulations. But we've had our fair share of relationships gone wrong—his because they never stick, mine because they're mostly fantasy.

"I just made a change." I point to my shaggy bangs, proud of myself for taking a chance and liking the outcome.

"Holly, bangs are not a life choice."

I sniff, annoyed a little that my breakthrough isn't enough for him. "Sounds like I need to meet this guy sooner rather than later, you're getting all serious on me." I motion to the half-eaten food and the silver tray. "Are we eating in?"

"Heavens, no. Mira would have my head if I didn't show for dinner." He checks his Cartier and pulls on a pair of creaseless silk pants covered with the Chanel logo. "And it's time to go."

"They're home?" They're usually jet-setting, yachting, carrying on like the rich people they are. "I didn't really dress…" I motion to my sweater and chinos I swapped out for the death pants. Mom's old Bass loafers from when she was my age are on my feet instead of heels; tarnished pennies look up at me.

"Did you do that?" he asks, poking a finger at the grosgrain ribbon I've added down each side of the pants.

It's sort of a nod to the Gucci I can't afford, deep green and burnt red. I shrug.

"And you hand-embroidered flowers through it," he says approvingly.

"Yeah. Gran and that textiles degree I don't use taught me just enough to be trouble."

"You've got a natural eye, natural style." He makes a face, I know he wants to say more. Press me to pursue a more creative career with my degree, but we've been down that road before. I can't afford not to be practical, I was raised to be practical. The General made it clear early in my childhood that *fashion designer* was not a job title she'd recognize.

Instead he says, "Before we go, I need to tell you what's going down at tomorrow's meeting." He takes a breath and lays a hand on my shoulder as we stand. "Support is getting cut—Customer Service, all of Admin. Across the board, including you. Marketing is spinning it that we're moving to AI, which is bullshit, but—I thought you should at least hear it from me."

"Wh-what?" I stammer. This is the last thing I expected. I never thought they would fire me. Never. "Tomorrow? Why?" I sputter on, "George needs me. Is it because of today?"

"You're not listening." He taps me gently between my eyes and I blink. "The entire company is making huge cuts. We're a sinking ship, Holly."

"You can't be serious. I know retail has been suffering, for a while —" I break off as my brain stutters. Hasn't the General been telling me to find a new business for years? That brick-and-mortar retail are about to become cement dinosaurs? Vacant malls are the new black eye of America? That I'll never have a dependable job in *"fashion!"*

"Two-day, hell, same-day, shipping is eating everyone alive. We've been trying to compete, upping our internet business and adding things like the Stylist Program to try to get a bigger piece of the pie but—"

"George hasn't said anything."

"George is scared. I told him to sit down with you a month ago, but you know him. He's making the announcement tomorrow."

"But you said—"

"I said we'd make sure you have a place in this company, and we will. Let's just leave it at that, okay? There's still a lot of moving pieces."

"What do I do when I get fired tomorrow? What about telling George how I feel about him? I can't really respond to him saying 'you're fired,' with 'okay, thanks, and by the way I love you!'"

"You need to think about what you want, Holly. Is George what you want? Is there anything between you other than friendship, or are you trying to manifest something that's just not there?"

It almost feels like I've been smacked in the face. "I know how I feel about him." At least, I think I do. It's possible it's been easier loving him from afar, fantasizing about what we could be. Living in my head, living out my own versions of conversations and kisses.

Maybe I've been waiting for him to make a move? And if I'm really black-and-white about it, minus the friendly embraces and inside jokes, he hasn't, has he?

"There'll be an offer for you and I'm asking you now to keep an open mind."

Maybe this could be a good thing.

Lenny's eyes spark with mischief. Maybe this is my chance at Corporate, at a title, at really *being* somebody. I've been telling the General for years that I'm climbing the ladder, investing my time in the company toward a future payoff, when *really* I've been stagnant, playing it a little safe, and yes, making googly eyes at George. At least I can admit it.

This could be my chance to make her proud.

He offers me his arm, "I can see the wheels turning but put a pin in it. It's time for dinner."

CHAPTER
Four

MY MIND IS RACING when I enter the Lordens kitchen, trying my best to compartmentalize while taking in a spacious nook for dining the size of my bedroom. It's never been photographed as far as I know, and it's full of layered fabrics and warm colors. There's a rustic china cabinet on one wall with a display of expensive dishes. Adjacent, a healthy fireplace burns at full roar. The mantel is taller than I am, and I'm an above average five foot eight. A harvest table sits elegantly in a wide bay window and I get a chance to run my fingers along the chilled metal between diamond panes before I take a seat.

This is like getting a glimpse at the First Family behind closed doors. I hate to admit it's a little thrilling.

Lenny and I are the first to arrive at the table set with chintz china. Our elbows rub as we sit close and a knot catches in my throat. What would my life look like without Lenny? If we no longer work together, will we stay close? It's an odd friendship already, our age gap making us an unlikely pairing, but I push the ugly thought down before it can take hold.

Seconds after we sit, Mira pops through a swinging door with a platter of cheeseburgers. "Hey, Len. Holly, so nice to see you again. It's past time you joined us for a family dinner. I feel terrible it's taken this putz living here for the month to make it happen." She sets the platter in the center of the table, and I worry for the grease stain that will surely be left on the lace tablecloth.

Pressing a touch screen near the door she says, "Iris, can you please bring two bottles of Chateauneuf-du-Pape—anything after 2000 is fine —to the house kitchen. Thank you."

"Nice seeing you again too, Mrs. Lorden—"

"Oh, stop that. Mira. You know better. I've known you since—well, since before you could drive, right? When you started in your grandma's tailor shop?"

I love that she calls the alterations department Gran's tailor shop. They were tight. Mira had Gran on speed dial for wardrobe emergencies. I assisted on many occasions and have seen Mira Lorden's beauty displayed equally in denim, pantsuits, and Oscar de la Renta gowns. "Yes. Thanks for having me, Mira."

A car door slams just outside, though when I turn to look out the window all I see are gray skies, evergreen bushes surrounding the fountain, and a bare gravel drive.

Mira glows like a punk itching for a firework. "Now which of my boys will that be?"

In total and complete horror, I hold my napkin up to fake cough and whisper to Lenny, "Boys?"

"Did I fail to mention this is a family dinner?" he asks. I make a beseeching face. "Sorry, I needed moral support," he whines. "It's hard moving back in with your big brother. And I wanted to tell you face-to-face—"

"That my days are numbered, I know." I'm running on adrenaline now and pushing that freak-out deep down.

"George is a shit for not telling you sooner."

Mira coughs lightly, and I drop my napkin for fear of appearing rude. Her features are sharp and elegant. Her hair ombrés from silver to dark and black at the ends, complementing dark eyebrows that frame a commanding but kind face. Bronze skin looks sun-kissed even at the end of a Seattle winter—that's the Greek blood that didn't affect the Scandinavian in George but pulls pretty strong in Declan.

Who, thank the Lord, does not walk through the door.

Instead, it's George. "Brace yourselves, family—we made the five o'clock news, but we came out on top." He drops an enormous smartphone on the table as punctuation.

Heat blooms in my chest but not the kind I usually harbor for George. I *am* mad at him for not having the guts to tell me I'm getting tossed out on my ass tomorrow. After all these years, he owed me at least a warning. A chance to prepare.

"Goddamn it, I heard that." Mr. Lorden, Louie, barrels through another set of doors wearing a plaid robe with boxer shorts and a T-shirt that says Canali Suits Co., Italy. He's carrying a golf club like a baseball bat over his shoulder. "You said it'd fly under the radar." His hair is slicked back, well dyed, and he's wearing athletic socks with Adidas slides.

"Please tell me"—I start another whisper behind my napkin— "they're not talking about me."

Mr. Lorden sits at the head of the table and looks directly at me. "Holly, what the hell did you do to my escalator?"

The room goes silent and I hear my own gulp. "I—"

"And how's your grandmother? She was the finest tailor I've ever had, an artist—"

"She's f-fine," I sputter, as if I haven't spoken to this man a million times before. It never gets easier, Louie Lorden is a legend. When he comes to the store, slackers stand straighter, go-getters grovel and gofer for him as if they're dogs fetching slippers.

"Lay off, Dad. It was a three-minute piece about a mechanical failure."

"Thanks to Dec—" Lenny says.

"You knew about this?" I demand.

He shrugs.

Everyone sits unceremoniously and begins passing food around the table while I hold my breath and wish for my little granny cottage and a lonely dinner for one.

George pushes on while he loads his plate. "The reporter interviewed Dorian—"

"Who?" Louie puts three deviled eggs generously sprinkled with paprika on his plate and hands the platter to me.

I hate eggs, of any kind, but I put one on my plate anyway and aggressively wipe my fingers on my trusty napkin. I breath through my mouth so I don't have to smell the yolk.

"Dorian, our department manager in Designer. He was praised for ushering out an old lady who was on the second floor trying to find her teenage daughter a birthday present. He sold her a T-shirt by The Great, somehow managed to add on Air Pods and teach her how to use them, gift wrapped them, and had her safely out the door just as a news team showed up. Anyway, Dorian spoke well, stuck to protocol, made a joke, and peacocked a little with his usual swagger. We came out looking great."

"I'm so sorry, Mr. Lorden."

"Mistakes happen—glad you didn't break a bone. Declan said it was due for maintenance, anyway. Where's the ketchup?"

"Here." Lenny hands over a bottle.

I have an out-of-body experience, like déjà vu—both the normality and the insanity of sitting at this table. It makes my head spin. I know this family so well, but office well, not eating cheeseburgers and passing the Heinz well.

The swinging door opens again and it's a woman dressed all in black with two bottles of red wine. The Lordens drink good wine—I've been on the receiving end on numerous nights out with Lenny and also while traveling with George for business.

"Thank you," Mira says, after every glass has been filled with the decanted vintage.

The woman bows slightly, then attempts to leave but the door swings on its hinges once again.

"I fucking love burger night." Declan walks in, tracking wet across the floor in a pair of lace-up Danner boots that look like they've been passed down. "I saw Mom's Swiss in the staff kitchen, but did they do any cheddar for me?"

So, that's how this kitchen looks like a page out of *Southern Living* but still manages a hot meal on the table.

He reaches over Mira's shoulder to grab a burger covered in orange cheese, oblivious to the rest of us. "Ketchup?" His eyes begin a scan of the table that is downright methodical. I watch as his free hand snatches a deviled egg. He eats it in one gulp, he doesn't even chew.

Louie hands his son the bottle and Declan proceeds to load his cheeseburger with every accoutrement available before taking a bite. He looks like he's in a commercial. It's statistically impossible that nothing falls from his burger but nothing does, and the way he chews around it all almost looks…primal; all white teeth biting, plump lips chewing, tongue licking his bottom lip clean. He's going after this burger like it's his *job*—not going to waste one bit.

Then he grabs a napkin from the open seat. "Thanks, Mom, I'd stay…" he says while swallowing the last bite. I watch his Adam's apple bob between the half-zipped anorak he's wearing, still dotted with drops of rain that must be falling now outside.

He struggles to find the rest of his words as his gaze lands on mine, darts to his brother, then lands back on me. If I didn't know his face so well I'd question it, but there is most definitely loathing in his glare. My face trips him up so entirely he just stands there until finally he clears his throat and speaks without looking away from me, "I had to stay late at the office, and I'm behind on the boat."

"Honey, please sit. Holly's here…"

But he's already turned and gone, the swinging door sweeping closed slowly on thick hinges.

"Let him go," Louie says. "I didn't realize we had guests, but you'll be privy to this sooner or later, Holly. We've got business to tend to."

"Not at the table, Louie," Mira chides.

Am I going to get fired at the dinner table?

But Louie nods at his wife, his eyes smiling sadly at her. "Okay, Mirabelle. Family first, family business second. Everyone, finish up and meet me on the putting green." He stands and picks up his plate.

"But it's freezing out!" Lenny protests.

"I won't keep you long. Since no one wants to make a decision about Hawaii, I've figured out a way to get it done. Fair. Square. You may want to stretch. See you out there."

We all bundle up. I didn't wear a coat fit for extended periods of time in thirty-degree Seattle drizzle, so George offers me his puffer and borrows another from his dad.

His coat falls almost to my knees and smells like the latest men's fragrance with Robert Pattinson in the commercial. It's nice, but he changes his cologne every time a new movie comes out so nothing ever really smells like *George*.

Louie has added his own knee-length Canada Goose coat to his socks and sandals ensemble. He's bent over his golf club, intently putting on a manicured green tucked into the side of their property. Beyond, down short stone stairs, is the lake, the dock, and Declan's boat. I can faintly see him doing something with a hammer on the deck while the hull gently rocks back and forth.

"Dad, what are we doing out here?" The wind blows at George's perfectly combed dark hair, it doesn't move an inch. Tiny snowdrops, bluebells, and crocuses are popping up all around us as spring tries desperately to show herself.

"Hawaii needs an answer. Since the three of you can't pull your heads out of your hind quarters, this is what we're going to do." He hands George the putter and my heart drops. The Hawaii store numbers have been low for months, everyone's been saying it needs new management if it's going to make it in this market. There've been murmurs about closing it all together.

"Best handicap wins. The one with the most strokes takes the job."

I grab Lenny by the shoulder, his Dolce poncho blows fringy on a gust of wind.

"Someone has to go manage store twelve. We've got too many big salaries here," he says. "We haven't been able to decide who should go."

Louie cups his hands around his mouth and shouts, "Declan! Get up here and take your shot, son! Youngest to oldest." Then he chuckles to us under his breath, "Shortest to tallest."

Declan is not short, he falls just under his brother's colossal six-three. And just a hair under Lenny's six-two. It must be Louie projecting some unresolved self-loathing because he seems just barely taller than me.

Louie speaks pointedly to George and Lenny while I hover beside Mira. "You know your little brother never had a lesson, much as I tried to get him to the club as a kid. Should have listened to his old man."

"My God, Louie. Have you lost your mind?" Mira gives her husband a pained look. Her dark eyes pool with water. "You said you were going to help them settle it *fairly*. They all have a reason they want to stay, as well as reasons it'd be good for them to go. I won't be part of this." She stomps her way back to the big house. On her way, she kicks at a pile of bocce balls and sends them flying across a combed sand court before slamming French doors behind her.

My chest is an empty balloon. Hollow is the feeling, because they've all been working together at the flagship—store one, the store their great-grandfather founded—since I've known them. There's been many business trips, new store openings, extended stays in every big city on the map to train staff, but they've always worked as one. This family is far from perfect, but they at least stick together.

Declan jogs up the stairs two at a time. "Is it time to putt?"

"You knew about this?" George asks his brother, incredulous.

Declan grabs the putter and without breaking eye contact, answers, "Let's get it over with." The pain in his eyes isn't as well hidden as he seems to think it is. He must feel me watching him because his gaze cuts to me sharply. "Why are you still here?"

"I didn't know," is all I can manage. It appears to be enough when Declan merely nods.

Lenny is a wilting flower when I turn to him.

"I know I should step up," he says. "Don't make me feel worse than I already do."

"That's not what I was going to say." I'm not sure what I was going to say. Standing up for Declan feels wrong, but so does banishing him to Hawaii because he's a weak golfer.

"You're a coward, by the way," Lenny says, looking at George. George's eyes go wide until he adds, "For not telling her."

George pulls a hand down his face. "Holly, I'm—" He looks truly stricken and I feel bad for him when it's a real toss-up if I should.

Declan breathes in deeply through his nose, exhales, and bites his bottom lip. "Don't throw me a going-away party, Stewart. Much as I know you'll want to celebrate."

He makes it sound like he knows he's going to lose.

"We can talk tomorrow," I say to George.

Declan begins taking practice swings and even I can tell he's holding the club all wrong.

Oddly, I'll be devastated no matter who goes. Each one of them has been an everyday part of my life since I was a kid—since I stopped moving around the country with the General and came to Seattle to live with Gran. Nothing has been very solid in my life, except Lorden's department store and the people in it.

I can't watch and slink up the stone steps and around the side of the house to my car, still in George's coat, bracing against the chill in the wind and the gray in the sky.

CHAPTER
Five

RALLY DAYS MAY START EARLY, but you know by the end of George Lorden's speech you're going to be inspired. Well, most of the employees feel this way—there are bad apples in any bunch. But this morning, I know what's coming, and it's less than inspiring. A lot of people are losing their jobs today. I'm still hoping George saves me. All night I ran through reasons why he wouldn't have told me I was losing my job. My conclusion is that he must have plans to find a way to keep me.

Because Declan is head of Operations and totally addicted to punishment, LP and Maintenance got here even earlier than the rest of us and set up a state-of-the-art sound system on the second floor. Our largest women's department titled Point of Power has been pushed to the side so folding chairs can stand at attention in rows before a small podium.

He's been stomping around glaring at everyone including me. I've just finished struggling with one of the four folding tables I'll have to set up for breakfast when I come face to face with him over a bag of bagels. He's staring.

"You're here early," I mutter, my throat still froggy from early morning.

"Did you buy bagels?"

Fresh smells of asiago, poppy seed, and blueberry waft between us. My gaze drops to the bags on the table in front of me and then slowly, I look back up. "Clearly. Did you fall down and bump your head this morning? I get bagels for every company meeting."

"There was an email, no bagels."

"I didn't see any email about bagels?"

Finally, he looks away. "It went out last night."

"Oh, well, I missed that. But everyone loves the bagels, and the smear, and the coffee." I begin unloading, not even sure if I believe there was an email or if he's just winding me up per usual. "Besides, George would have told me. Lorden's may have done away with quarter coffee but a continental breakfast with company meetings is still par for the course."

"For now," he says cryptically. "Hand me those?"

"The tablecloths? Why?"

"Because," he shifts on his feet, hands in pockets then out, nervous energy running through him. That's new. "I want to help, okay?"

"Since when do you want to help? Me?"

"You know, Stewart, we don't have to be enemies."

"Since when?" I half bark, half laugh.

"Since now. Hell, I don't even remember why, or how we ended up like this."

"Because you're a peculiar pest who's never been nice to me."

"Maybe I've been waiting for you to be nice to me, ever think of that?"

Before I can sling a comeback at him, he quickly pops up the remaining tables, then begins trying to smooth the tablecloths over, making a mess of things but getting it done nonetheless.

My gut reaction is to run him off, tell him I don't need his help. But he had a rough night last night, and maybe he is just trying to help. Maybe his big move to Hawaii is causing him to turn over a new leaf, to settle his debts and befriend his enemies before his departure.

I continue down the table putting out the spread while he stomps off and murmurs to himself about diaphragmatic breathing.

Behind the podium a banner reads Lorden's State of The Company: The Next Generation and How You Can Be Part of It!

As employees trickle in to load their plates with bagels and fruit, the smells and vibes of an all-you-can-eat buffet permeate the second floor. They stop to fill coffee cups and use generous amounts of creamer after I've scrambled to refill it.

Speakers crackle and scramble to life as "We Are the Champions" begins the chore of waking everyone up and setting the tone for the meeting—a meeting where everyone is going to realize the strain internet businesses and two-day shipping guarantees have taken on brick-and-mortar retail. It's hard to believe it's finally hitting the juggernaut that is Lorden's.

First up, Lenny takes to the podium and welcomes everyone with a wide jester smile. Today, he's laid-back Len in a tracksuit, but makes it fashionable with jeweled sneakers and a mesh fanny pack. He pulls it off well, like a fifty-year old Bowie. I know this look for what it is, hungover Len. His performance last night must have rolled well into after-hours. I catch a stern look from him and know I'm in trouble for missing it.

He brings us up-to-date on sales numbers—they are grim. The company's still owned by the Lorden family, but rumor has it the board has been pushing to go public. So far, they're keeping it a family affair and I can't imagine things any other way. It's poetic that Louie and Lenny will pass it down to a second generation of brothers in George and Declan one day.

But as I look around the room, the crown molding needs a fresh coat of paint, the brass fixtures could use updating, and quite a few pieces of marble tile in the aisles are chipped. It's as if I'm seeing the store for the first time without rose-colored glasses and puffs of designer perfume wafting up my nostrils.

Grim, indeed.

George takes the stage in a pinstripe suit that is my least favorite and makes me think of a nicely dressed telemarketer and, with little ceremony, drops the bomb that companywide we'll be incurring layoffs.

I haven't even gotten a bagel and shit gets real—fast.

Alice discreetly shimmies out of a back row and comes to stand next to me. I'm dumping plastic platters full of crumbs into trash bags when she says, "What does this mean, Holly?"

George is still speaking and probably about to cover the fine print, but I understand why she's asking me, she's scared. And I'm usually the person employees come to about these things. "It's only going to affect support for now, as far as I know," I whisper.

"Oh." She looks relieved and I stop to rub her shoulder lightly. "Wait, what does that mean for you? Surely, the family won't let you go?"

My *fears*, exactly. I hadn't even been able to stay and watch the end of the most gruesome round of miniature golf in history, last night. Afraid Louie might turn around and hand me the club next.

The more I think about it, I know George will find a way to keep me. It's not as if he's just any store manager, he's a Lorden. And it was clear who was going to lose the putting contest. Declan is destined for Hawaii, and they're going to need someone to run the office *and* pick up the slack when all support staff is gone. It'll be me.

"They won't." I'm sure of it, and give Alice a smile and a nod that I hope communicates, *all is well, we're on the inside, you and me. Lifers. Indispensable!*

George clears his throat and the microphone reacts with a high-pitched shriek. "Sorry," he says, "as I was saying, this is the final announcement today. Stick with me, guys, I know it's been a long one this morning. It's with a heavy heart that I announce I'm transferring to Hawaii, to store twelve in Ala Moana Center, as the store manager effective immediately. It's been an absolute delight to work with all of you, some of you since I spent my high school summers breaking down boxes in the warehouse."

Wait, *what?*

My gut plummets. His words, though I'm aware they're still coming through the sound system, fade.

I take deep breaths so I don't hyperventilate.

No. No. Triple no. This is not how this is supposed to happen.

A montage of memories floods my brain as if I'm in a death scene on the Hallmark Channel: sweeping floors, running tailoring to and from departments for Gran, digging through boxes of mannequin parts, hanging holiday bows and candy canes over the doors, training young kids with stars in their eyes and dreams of a job in *fashion!* as they complain about sore feet.

I do not want to resurrect my résumé and go on interviews. I never had to do that in the first place, my high school job parlayed into my adult job. I've never been on a proper interview in my life!

"And I want to thank you," George says, his voice coming back to me as I desperately try to surface from drowning thoughts. "I know we say this, but I mean it, without you this company would not be what it is today." His eyes drift to me for a second. "We will persevere. We will thrive. Now, go out there and make a sale today!"

No!

There's a smattering of applause but no one moves, the shock in the room palpable. This sort of thing has been in the news for a while now. Other companies have been struggling for years but not Lorden's.

And no one ever thought George would leave. *I* never thought George would leave. What the hell happened on that putting green?

We will, we will, rock you. We will, we will, rock you pumps through the speakers as he all but drops the mic.

Seconds later, before I've registered a thought, Declan's voice booms over the music and chatter, "Please stack your chairs and drop your trash in the bins. Maintenance is not here to clean up after you."

Pushing past Alice, I run to the second-floor ladies' room, lock myself in a stall, and burst into tears.

It's happening. The only job, the only company I've ever worked for is firing me. *George* is going to fly to Hawaii to become the world's richest businessman turned surfer dude and probably marry the first person who makes a joke about getting laid with a floral necklace. The General is going to *I-told-you-so* me so hard.

I wince, knowing what's coming and that I'll have to tell both the matriarchs in my life I can't make rent next month. If we lose Gran's cottage, where she spent her life with my grandpa and raising my mother, she'll be devastated.

But I don't get a minute's peace to think what I might be able to do about it when the door opens. Muffled music swells in the bathroom until it closes and I'm ensconced again in mint walls and silence.

Peeking through a crack in the stall I hear footsteps coming at me, and then I see the soles of vintage Air Jordans.

This cannot be happening.

Snot rolls down my face and I can't hold back a sniffle as I frantically pull tissue from a metallic dispenser.

The sneakers turn, coming to a stop right in front of my butter yellow stall door.

"Get out of here, Declan!"

Nothing.

"Get out of the women's bathroom!" The rest of the store is breaking down and breaking off to do opening tasks, but at some point, someone's going to come in here and find him.

What will they think?

He sighs, his feet shift slightly. "I don't have to tell you—my whole family knows I can't putt for shit—"

"Then why is it him?" I sob-moan. I take back what I thought about wanting everyone to be able to stay. I want it to be Declan who's leaving, and not George, so bad I'd trade teeth for it.

"I did lose the putt, but we got drunk on my boat after and he offered to go. I was resigned to going myself, knew Dad wanted it to be me. He's never been happy with my trajectory here. He's wanted me to be more like George since forever. But then George said he *wanted* to go. It's not landing well with my parents and what they had planned for him. I think that's the point."

He wants to go? That means there's nothing for him to stay here for. Of course, there's not. Did I think I would be something that would affect George Lorden's life choices? Had I been that delusional only a day ago?

"I'm really fired now. As if cutting support wasn't enough, there's no saving my job *now*." A desperate light bulb bursts in my mind as I taste salty tears on my tongue. "Wait, would he take me with him? I don't know who's going to do the day-to-day tasks here, but I'm still his assistant in addition to office manager. Maybe—"

"You want to move to Hawaii? What about Granny O.?" She is the store grandmother, they will probably erect a statue outside the main entrance one of these days.

"The cottage is my responsibility now, and I love it, but I've always wanted to travel." I think out loud, ignoring him and wiping at tiny balls of toilet paper sticking to my face. "Sandy beaches, little umbrellas in coconut drinks…" If I made enough and lived cheap traveling with George, I could still keep the cottage and my job.

"He's not taking you with him, Holly. Even if he wanted to, the company is cutting all the fat. All of it. Louie sold the jet."

Rolling my eyes at the door I mouth, *I hate you!* Declan could never understand what it feels like to want something, something deep down you know you'll never get. He's just sad they lost the jet.

"You can't even be nice to me when I'm getting fired." I am not *fat*. I've held almost every position in this store, trained every position in this store—I'm valuable to this company.

"I'm always nice to you."

A snotty laugh bursts from my chest. "No—remember Coachella?" I'm not sure why this is the first of his many offenses that comes to mind.

"You mean when we had to pull George out of a mosh pit?"

The company jet came in handy that day. I was told to drop everything, pack light, and accompany Declan on a rescue mission to save George from himself. That had been a very, very tense flight if I remember right. "You were really mean then."

"I was pissed I had to go rescue my older brother from embarrassing the family name on the company dollar. He was supposed to be courting the Free People reps and working out a deal for that year's summer-sale special buy."

"What about that time when you were working in shoes?" Declan has worked just about every sales job there is at Lorden's, but of course never administrative, which is beneath him, I'm sure.

His feet shift and I swear, he stops himself from angrily tapping a toe. "You mean when you returned twenty pairs in Customer Service, then plopped them on our cash wrap in the middle of a Friday afternoon rush?"

I can't believe I'm doing this with him while sobbing on a toilet, but he always knows exactly where to poke, exactly how to get me fired up. "It took me three trips up and down the escalator with boxes stacked above my head! What was I supposed to do with them?"

"Holly, *shoe-dogs* work their asses off. Do you have any idea how hard it is to schlep boxes of shoes for people to try on all day? You've been back in the stacks. It's hot as hell and tight as tick's ass in those aisles of boxes. They have their own returns to run, they don't need some priss support person adding to their workload. Put them back yourself, I said it then, and I stand by it now."

God, he enjoys being domineering.

"Come out here so I can say all this to your face."

"I can't."

"Bad attitude or not, we'll find a place for you, Holly." He keeps saying my name and, on his tongue, it sounds like an insult. "I've been brainstorming where to put you for weeks."

Bad attitude? Where to put me? Like I'm a liability?

"We wouldn't leave you out in the cold," he continues. As if he's got a moral code about it.

I work my ass off for this store. I've worked my ass off for this family for years! "I can't." But I'm defeated. If support is cut, there's nowhere for them to put me. Maybe as extra holiday sales help, but the holidays just ended, and I couldn't sell a ball of yarn to a kitten.

"You can, we'll help—"

"I can't come out! And I would not come out for you if you begged with your knees on the floor of the women's bathroom!"

"You know, I'm redoing them to be unisex—"

"I would rather pee on the street, get arrested, and have indecent exposure on my record for life than ever be stuck in another bathroom with you." How's that for a bad attitude? Even though Declan doesn't command attention like George, charm crowds like Lenny, or instill fear like Louie, I'd still bet there aren't many people in this store who'd refuse him. His directness is hard to evade.

"Come out of there and insult me to my face, Stewart."

"No."

"Why not?" His tone is exasperated as he throws his hands in the air; the sound of a caveman, one who wears cashmere, and glasses, and worships his free weights.

"I-I need a tampon, okay!" The words pop out of my mouth, the hackles in me rising and wanting to shock him into listening to me and getting the hell out.

I only wish I didn't actually need one.

"Oh. Well. Shit." Through the crack in my door I watch him square his shoulders and give himself some sort of pep talk look in the mirror. "Okay, um, I'll go get Alice?"

"Alice will not have what I need, Declan."

"Oh."

"Just get out. I'm fine—"

"No, no. I can handle this." The pacing commences as if on cue. "Just sit tight."

He did not just say that. But he did, and the Jordans disappear from view, the door to the bathroom swinging shut.

There are options here: one, I can use toilet paper and make a dash for my purse, which is stowed in my desk in George's office. Or two, I can actually wait to see if he comes back with a tampon.

Declan has never helped me, not once. Well, until this morning. Odd.

As kids, he went above and beyond to make trouble for me. When I was working in Visual, the department in charge of decorating store windows and keeping mannequins dressed, he was there to poke me in the ribs and make me drop a head. When I was just back from college, before George was the store manager, I worked in the espresso bar lovingly nicknamed the E-bar. I was shit at making lattes. And guess who showed up every morning before I'd even finished filling the register with cash to order the most complicated custom macchiato?

But the door opens moments later and he says, "You still in here?"

"Yes," I groan. He doesn't shy away from a challenge, I'll give him that.

"Here, you were wrong. Alice did have what you need. I, uh, didn't know who else to ask."

Good old Alice, she must keep them behind the register for anyone who might find themselves in my exact predicament. The internet can't do that for their customers, now can it?

A tampon appears under the door, long lean fingers, unexplained calluses for such a pretty boy, handing me my pride on a platter in the form of feminine products.

My face heats and I lean over to snatch it. "Okay, you can go now."

"You mean, thank you, Dec. You're the best, Dec. What would I do without you, Dec?"

"Get out, *Dec*." I parrot him with sticky disdain in my voice and I hope it lands.

"Fine."

I do my thing and wash my hands—mortified all the while—and when I head for the door I spot him sitting in the small side room meant for mothers or women who just need a damn minute, an ankle resting on his knee.

Decorating the sitting area are lush sofas covered in jewel-tone velvets, sturdy commercial side tables with dimly lit lamps, and a large watercolor of trees on the wall behind him.

"This is borderline criminal," I seethe. I need to freak out in peace.

"Waiting for you in the restroom?"

"Exactly."

"The last thing I want to do is track your bathroom habits, though it is natural and we all do it. I need to talk to you."

Oh dear, he seems to be feeling sorry for me as he sits there smug in his smarty-pants glasses. It's written all over his perfectly shaped head, in the way he runs a hand through the loose waves with closely cropped sides. He's got these insanely plump lips that are protruding into a pout. He's pouting. What the hell has he got to pout at *me* about? He's gotten his way; conned his brother into taking the position no one wanted in Hawaii. And he's always wanted to get rid of me. Why else would he have been such a thorn in my side all these years? He's been wishing for me to get fired since we were kids!

"I'm not doing the let's-be-friends-after-years-of-hating-each-other, then witty banter, then you pretending to help me while secretly throwing a party the second I walk out the door on my last day thing.

All so you can look like the good guy in a farewell pic on social media."

"Wow, that was a lot." He stands and I think I've truly offended him.

It came out as a joke, as *banter*, but I think I may have squeezed a wound. Declan doesn't have many friends in the store, though the college girls preen like peacocks when he's around. He's too prickly to make friends, but I usually steer clear of that topic because I'm not a monster.

He pushes a hand through his hair in exasperation. "I'm not doing that either."

"Then what are you doing? You've never tried this hard to be nice to me."

"I'm trying to save my store and I need your help." This is slightly surprising. Not the part about needing my help, the part about him caring so much. I didn't know he cared at all.

"Nothing's going to happen to the flagship. Even if you don't have the slightest clue how to run the office and, as of today, no support staff to do it for you. Now, excuse me while I go file for unemployment and apply for any Corporate jobs Lorden's has posted. I don't suppose you've heard of any?" Like he'd tell me. "Do you think I can use your mom as a reference?"

"Corporate doesn't exist anymore. I mean, it's not what it used to be. It's basically the board of directors, a couple of tech people, and then it all trickles down. I know you've always wanted to work your way up to the Seattle office but…marketing, the catalog, special buys, and textile design?"

"You don't think I'm up to it?" My hands are on my hips now and I give him my best glare. I'm not sure why I care. He's never supported me, why would I expect him to now?

Those damn lips meet my glare and raise me a twitching jaw. "It's all gone, Holly. The marketing department consists of influencers we pay to post about us. The catalog is dead—no one does mailers anymore—we were the last holdouts."

"What about design? You still do special buys with brands. That's always where I was headed, in my heart…" I hadn't realized that until

I just said it, but that would be the perfect fit for me. A little design, a little marketing, the best of both worlds.

"That's all done under the brands umbrella. The days of us collaborating with designers are long gone—that's what I'm trying to tell you." He crosses his arms and waits patiently for me to digest what he's said. When he realizes I'm holding my ground, chin in the air, he adds, "The parties are literally over. No one's sadder then Len."

"You get what you want then, I'm out. I've spent years here building creditability." I'm going to have to start all over in Seattle—fight creative, driven, high school graduates and fresh-from-college go-getters for entry positions. Not to mention kids with silver spoons.

"That's not what I want at all—"

"I thought Corporate was the natural next step—" I thought I was finally going to fall in love with the man of my dreams. I've been wrong about so many things it's making me spin.

"Just listen." He takes one of those deep breaths, exhaling through his nose, chews that lip, and continues, "I'm offering you a job in sales."

Sales. The only job I've never done. The only job I'm completely unqualified for and terrified of. "No, thank you." It's a joke. It must be, because he knows I could never make rent selling sweaters. I have zero sales experience.

But he stands just slightly in my way when I try to reach for the door.

"When are you going to open your eyes and see what's actually in front of you?" His eyes hold mine for a beat until he continues. "You would shine on the floor, you'd be a guaranteed top seller—"

"No way, I know nothing about pushing product. And not getting paid *at all* unless I sell enough to make rent via commission? Again, no thank you."

"Holly, come on. You've put out so many fires over the years, I swear, selling stuff you love would be *fun* compared to what you've done here in the past."

But his words hit all wrong. Shaking my head, I say, "You're just trying to trick me. Watch me fall flat on my face. You don't want me to succeed, you never have—"

"You think you have a pretty good read on me, don't you? But are you sure you know me so well? You think you know George, but do you? Do you truly know the man you've been pining after for years? Perhaps I'm trying to help *everyone*."

It's as if he's dumped a bucket of hot water on me, I flush and startle at the same time.

He doesn't move to stop me as I pull the brass handle of the heavy bathroom door. Just stands there, calm, cool, annoyingly collected while my life goes through a food processor.

"I would rather pack raw chicken into those gross vacuum-sealed bags for the rest of my life. I would rather go without a sip of caffeine for all of eternity than work for you. I would rather have hours of oral surgery." The list goes on, and I pretend to believe myself as the door glides closed behind me.

He's offering me a lifeline. I really, really try not to wonder if I've been misplacing my severe dislike for this man all along.

"You wouldn't be working for me. Sales isn't my department!" he shouts from the other side.

All of the halogen lights are on and the store is in full swing. I missed opening announcements but George basically said everything in the meeting. The escalators have been repaired and I head up to the third floor, letting my gaze roam. This may be the last time I see this store. If I'm truly fired, if George is leaving, this is it for me.

I wave to a few glum-looking salespeople as I curve down the hallway to the support offices. George's office door is closed and usually I'd find something else to do until it was open, but today I plow through.

Lenny is there, sitting in my chair. "How are you?"

I don't respond to Len, instead I glare at George.

He shifts in his plush leather swivel. "Can you give us a minute, Len?"

Lenny stands. "Thanks again, man," he says, and George nods.

Before closing the door, in an unusual show of authority, Lenny adds, "Holly, as the new head of store functions and sales, I'll expect you in my office first thing Monday morning—you're taking the job. We'll give you the weekend, but then it's back to business. And you'll have to go through training."

I can't even think about Monday right now—training! Am I supposed to train myself on the registers? How to scan a barcode, add a discount, and ring a return? I wrote that manual too!

Lenny shakes his head, as if he knows exactly where my priorities lie at the moment. "I'll leave you to it."

The door clicks closed and silence stretches.

George has always been everything to me, but now I'm seeing him in a new light. It's not bad—it's just not the usual golden halo filter I normally apply to him.

"You have to say something. You owe me that," I mumble, taking the chair opposite his desk. It's as if I've called my own meeting to get properly fired.

"You're right. I just don't know where to start. There's so much—"

"How about sorry I let you lose your job on the spot with no warning? Sorry I'm leaving and didn't have the decency to tell you before a storewide meeting." I let my eyes survey his desk, already half-boxed. "I actually thought you'd take me with you—"

"Is this about the Christmas party?"

"You're Jewish! It's a holiday party!"

"I know, but we always have the trees, you know what I mean. Damn it, Holly. I know you think there's something between us, but—"

I'm not letting him off that easy. I've got nothing to lose now. "Not just me. There was something between us. I didn't make that up. Maybe I've been the lovestruck dummy in this office for the past three years, and maybe I did make the first move a bit prematurely... without a lot of consent. Sorry about that," I stutter, thinking of my embarrassing attempt at a holiday seduction. "But I haven't been flirting with myself either."

"Please, let me explain."

I blow at a chunk of hair that's gotten stuck in my eyelashes. "Fine, explain." It's freeing not to care what he thinks about me right now. It's downright liberating to have finally told him how I feel.

"I wanted it to be you."

My heart cracks at his words.

"Did you know, I mean, I thought you knew...I'm bi?"

"Yeah, I mean we never talked about it..." And we hadn't, we'd always kept our conversations neatly focused on work or our families, but of course I noticed. "I'm fine with that."

"What if I'm not?"

Oh.

He drags both hands through thick dark hair and today, it moves. Upon second inspection, rose-colored glasses firmly in the garbage, I see him. He's struggling in a wrinkled suit, stubble, and zero hair gel. Muscles in his chest flex through the light blue button-down he's wearing as he leans his elbows on his desk. He's taken his tie off and rolled up his sleeves. About as undone as I've ever seen him.

"What are you trying to say?"

"I've got some work, some real exploration, to do with myself."

I push into my chair and wish this conversation wasn't headed in the direction it is, for his sake. George is under a heavy weight, I see that now. I feel it as I sink into my own thoughts and feelings for him.

How well do I really know him? Not as personally as I thought, I guess. All my feelings and fantasies that I've been playing in my head like my own personal Netflix feel a bit tainted now. Like a scam. Like a cop-out for the real thing.

"Vohs Academy is an all-boys school, where my dad and Lenny went, where Dec and I went. I was captain of lacrosse, then went on to an Ivy League college, big brother to the most inherently *mannish* little brother you could find. Being bisexual was enough, but...hell, I don't know." He leans back and drops large, heavy hands into his lap, his face ashen. "I was trying to fix something in myself. Or slide down the spectrum to a place my parents, my future as a businessman, could afford—"

"What do you mean, trying to fix yourself?" In this moment, my heart breaks fully for this big man. This clearly struggling friend in front of me. How have I been so blind? "George, you haven't been able to slide on the spectrum and fix yourself because there's nothing wrong with you, whatever the parameters." But if I know Louie Lorden, and I know him enough, he's probably not been the best father for a bisexual son. "And forget everyone else. Lenny's a great businessman, and he looks fabulous in a dress. You have to do *you*, you know."

"You're amazing. I don't deserve you, I know that."

"I'm still pissed at you," I say, shifting in my chair and trying to let all of this settle. To let it be about him and not about me.

"I should have said something sooner. But you should know, there's so much more to come for you, Holly. You're so talented, but I recognize some of the same fear in you that I'm fighting in myself. I don't know what you're scared of, but it's time to face whatever it is. It's time to live, for both of us to really *live*."

"You almost broke my heart, George Lorden." My voice cracks on a half laugh, part of me struggling to rein in my emotions, part of me laughing at myself for falling in love with a complete fantasy.

"Almost?" he smiles sadly. "I have to admit, I did like the attention."

"You let me swoon daily—"

"Holly, it wasn't intentional. I think the world of you, and I *wanted* it to be you. My life would be so much easier if I could—"

My heart stings for him and for me. "You don't need a woman by your side to make your family proud. You know that, right? Lenny will probably never marry, even though I think he'd be the best husband a man could ask for."

"Lenny has his own story. He's been clear from day one about who he is. At least I have Dec. He's been the most solid friend and brother I could ask for, especially the way we grew up."

"I'm happy for you, that you're getting a fresh start. A new life, if that's what you want—what you need."

"This is a fresh start for you too, if you'll let it be."

I know he's getting at something, he said I'm *scared*. But whatever he's hedging at, my subconscious is not ready to go there. I need to figure out where my next paycheck is coming from before I dive head-first into emotional excavation.

"Declan's living on his boat, did you know? That's my biggest regret with this whole thing. He has to stay here while I run away."

"Has to?"

"I think he wanted to go, truth be told. He just didn't want to give Dad the satisfaction of knowing."

I shrug. "I didn't know he lived on that boat. I guess that would fit for him in Hawaii. But Declan always finds a way to be the odd man out. He prefers it that way."

"Well, he's got Len and you, which helps me worry about him a little less." A snort escapes me, but George goes on unfazed, "And Len has a new man, I hear. Maybe he'll get along with Dec? He needs to live a little, he definitely needs to branch out from his childhood gaming crew."

"Someone serious?" Lenny is never serious with the men he dates. The second they want more, he bolts. Something rooted deep inside keeps him from committing, but I'm also hoping he just hasn't met Mr. Right.

"I think it's new, but I've never heard him talk about anyone like this before. He's really helped walk me through this. It was a lot worse for him coming up."

"I know. I mean, he's shared some of that with me. I think he puts all that out there when he performs."

"Yeah. You know my dad's never been to see him?"

"I know. But I also know Lenny's never outright invited him."

"Hmph."

"I'll miss you," I say, standing awkwardly. "Can I help? Packing?"

"Nah, I got it. Not a lot in this desk that I need to take with me." The small smile that crosses his face confirms this is a good change for him. "I'll miss you too, Holly dolly. More than you know. But I'm excited, as an almost middle-aged man, to finally leave the nest and live my life. Take my advice, don't lean into your comfort zone too long. You don't get that time back."

CHAPTER
Six

TOAST, honey, thoughts. Breakfast in bed isn't nearly as glamorous as it sounds, but the morning after being fired it's all I can manage.

With sticky fingers, I fumble around my bed trying to find my phone while mentally replaying my conversation with George. I frantically texted Lenny last night to get his opinion. Of course, he'd known what George was going to say to me, had been coaching George through it, but his hands were tied with loyalty to his nephew in regard to clueing me in. He'd been in a difficult situation the past few months, knowing that George was exploring his sexual identity and listening to me yammer on about loving him at the same time. Knowing this didn't make it any easier for me to swallow.

To make matters even more confusing, Lenny lamented, *you have to take the sales job if only to continue paying your rent. You owe that much to your gran.* Only one problem—it's not just a sales job. As the details of the offer came through hours later via email, I realized it's a sales job on the Personal Stylist team. The only department showing any growth, therefore meriting new hires.

Can I work for the legend that is Jenny Yoo, the manager, day in and day out? She's currently very pregnant, which means I'd get some time off from the Snake (her personal nickname) when she takes maternity leave. But she eats people like me for protein. She's venomous and her reactions when her team doesn't meet their sales goals are downright poisonous to even the most upbeat personalities. They don't call her the Snake for nothing.

I don't share Declan's delusion that I'd be a natural in Sales, I'd most definitely be the team gofer. And not just for Jenny but for her sidekicks Molly and Angel as well. The three of them are the stylists for store one, and they are ferocious. All three of them can do that thing where they wear a slinky nineties-style dress with cowboy boots and it somehow looks chic as hell. Everyone calls them *the chosen ones* because of all the special treatment and gratis gifts they get from department managers for making big sales.

But if I do take the job, I pay my rent. Even when you don't sell enough to make commission, you get a draw. That kind of grace doesn't last long though, three strikes and you're out. At the least, I'd embarrass myself and buy some time to figure out what I really want to do. *What do I really want to do?* I know what the General would say. Speaking of which, I owe her a Zoom.

Stop wallowing!

I lick sweet honey from my fingertips before finally finding my phone under my pillow. First, I type a quick message to Lenny.

ME

Still thinking. I'll let you know by 5:00.

There, that gives me the day. Then I'll have Sunday to deal with whatever choice I've made, maybe visit Gran, and put together a plan for Monday. Which sounds like I'm clearly going to accept. But I have serious reservations.

My phone pings.

LENNY

I'll pretend that you're not saying yes for the day if it makes you feel better. Send me outfit options if you need help deciding what to wear. Don't take this the wrong way, but you'll need to up your game a little for Jenny.

As if I'd need a ball gown to run back and forth from the E-bar with her coffee. To stand in the aisle of the quietest department's sales floor —Hosiery—and pray for a customer. There's no way anyone is actually going to expect me to have appointments and fully dress people when my store experience is solely with printers, registers, upset customers, George's emails, and the list goes on, but it does not include telling people what to wear.

Now, for Mom. I open a chat on my computer and let it ring. The General answers right on time for our regularly scheduled Saturday morning programming.

"Good morning, honey," she says briskly into her screen. She's always seated at her desk with approachable nude lipstick miraculously in place while sipping an Americano, shuffling papers and the multiple cell phones she uses.

"Hey, Mom. How's the capital on this fine Saturday?"

"Good, good. Go ahead, debrief."

"I got fired."

"What?"

A spike of adolescent adrenaline runs through me. It's not every day I get to throw her for a loop.

"Yup."

Her face twists into a pucker of disappointment. "Holly! You *insisted* on putting in the time at that company. I've told you on numerous occasions you needed to demand a promotion to the corporate offices or move on, or something like this would happen."

"Well, you were right." I roll onto my back, tucking my knees into my chest and awkwardly holding my screen over my head. She hates when I do this.

"Honey, when are you going to realize I don't say these things to hurt you? I'm trying to toughen you up. If you don't go out there and take what you want, no one's going to hand it to you."

"What does almost ten years at a company look like, Mom, if not me trying to get what I want? I've done everything they've asked. I probably know more about store functions then all of them put together—"

"Then why have they fired you? If you're so valuable?"

Tell me how you really feel, *Mom*.

"The company is struggling like everyone else in this economy trying to keep up with rapid change."

She stiffens—she takes the economy personally. "Well, brick-and-mortar's had issues for over a decade now. We're struggling to grow jobs in the U.S. and—"

"It's not just about buying overseas, Mom." I know where she's going and I put on my debate face. "It's our own competition. We can't compete with Amazon, and that's how a lot of mom-and-pops are taking a piece of our pie, by selling through them. We can't, and—"

"There. That."

"What?"

"No one wants a defeatist attitude around when they're trying to save a sinking ship, Holly."

Her words cause my body to freeze and my mind to melt. Does she want me to move on? Or save the ship? Somehow I get the feeling she expects both. "I'm just saying, people are up shopping at midnight in their pj's with a bottle of rosé. They want packages on their doorstep by the time they wake up at noon with a hangover."

She's finished signing a stack of papers, hands them to someone off-screen while mouthing the word *immediately*, then looks back to me. "Then do something about it. If you've identified your opponent, that's half the battle. You find another angle."

"But—" *I will not cry, I will not cry, I will not cry because she's treating me like a job.*

"Yes, but. We both know why you've been idling, Holly. Diverting from the five-year post-college plan."

I readjust the screen above my head, this could take a while. "Enlighten me."

"George Lorden." I drop the computer, *oww!* And hear her sigh dramatically while I peel it off my face.

How? How did she know? "He has nothing to do with this—"

"Holly, I've got two more minutes before I've got to be in another debriefing, one involving the president of the United States. So forgive me as I lay this out—you let yourself become stagnant. You stopped looking out for number one. You love him and, whether he knows it or not, the fact remains that he doesn't love you. And what's worse, he's held you back. Knowingly. I've met the Lorden boys enough times to know George knew exactly what he was doing when he kept you as his personal assistant for three years. He knew."

I bring the computer with me on my way to the bathroom. It's time to get moving, so I don't dissolve into a puddle of *I told you so*. The General will hate watching me brush my teeth. "They've offered me another position, they're not just casting me out."

"Good. Take it. Whatever it is, even if it's going back to that coffee bar, the E-bar. But hear me when I say, you'd better be looking for another job. One that is worthy, and one that will be there for your future. Not a boy you can drool over while you ghostwrite his emails."

The rest of Saturday flies by in a storm of binge-watching decluttering shows, and then half-ass attempting to organize the house. I wander from room to room moving things from one spot to another. I let my fingers graze fabrics in Gran's sewing room and even indulge in a few sketches for a dress with lots of sequin detail at the cuffs and the neckline until it's dinnertime. I fall asleep on the couch. By Sunday morning, I'm feeling more deflated than ever, but I roll out of bed, make myself more honey toast and loose leaf tea, and dress for a visit to Gran's. If anyone can pep talk a shit show into a diamond, it's Gran.

Before I leave the house, I dip into her stash of needlepoint.

Gran keeps a yellow plastic bag that I know holds a lifetime's worth of half-finished works in progress on the floor under her sewing machine. A tiny rose on eighteen-inch mesh that I'd like to add to a bag or the lapel of a jacket is near the top of the pile. She probably has a project she's working on so I shove the bag back under the sewing machine and head out.

Thorn Briar retirement community is a nice place, if not a bit sterile. Built before developers thought such places should have any sort of architectural aspirations, it resembles a washed-out limestone grade school but gets more inviting as I walk through the sliding front doors.

I'm given a visitor badge to pin on the red silk blouse I'm wearing tucked into dark denim, and try my best to ignore the smell of old people permeating the halls. My bangs are straight as sticks, tickling my eyelashes from time to time, and the rest of my dark hair is tamed into waves held back with my favorite bejeweled headband. Gran is sitting in a sunroom surrounded by green plants in clay pots when I'm dropped off by the receptionist.

"Holly!" Her wrinkles stretch into an assortment of pure joy with sparkling eyes. She's rested and looks years younger than her age. Retirement is treating her well.

"How are you, Gran?" I hug her around her petite but sturdy shoulders and hold on to her as she settles back into a tufted chair.

"Just fine. Thorn Briar is taking good care of me." She pats a matching cushioned seat next to her, and I sit.

"Glad to hear you don't miss me at all." Morning sun pours through three walls of windows.

"Oh hush, you need someone your own age to spend your nights with, preferably a man. And not Lenny. Which reminds me, Bernie's going to stop by at half past ten to meet you. He's a peach." She says it so sweetly, but she waggles her eyebrows like a teenager with raging hormones. "What time is it?"

I check the watch I've had since high school. It was the last thing Dad gave me for my eighth-grade graduation. It's held up pretty good, but the leather band is finally giving in, now hanging by a thread. "Just past ten."

"Oh good, did you bring something to work on?" She's got a quilt in her hand. I can't believe she can still manage the tiny stitches. They take her a long time to complete, and she uses a sewing machine for big passes, but her effort on the details always show up in the final product.

"Do you mind if I work on this?" I pull the canvas of the rose out of my bag and hold it up for her as I fish out the threads and floss I grabbed to go with it; clarets, magentas, and hunter greens with a hint of mint for shadowing the leaves.

"Of course, it's yours. How are you enjoying the house to yourself? It's yours now too."

My heart skips a beat, but I give her a solid smile; it's mine if I can keep up with the payments. "I love it, but I miss you in it."

We sit and stitch together. She tells me about Bernie, resident Thorn Briar heartbreaker, but she means to tame him. Just days ago, I'd thought to do the same with George, but that's obviously not going to happen. Good luck, Gran. There's no hint of the fiery side of her personality today—she must be really smitten.

Another woman comes in to offer us coffee and we both accept. I have to give it to this place, they go the extra mile with china cups and saucers.

"So, how's work?" she asks.

"Oh, that. I got fired Friday."

She takes the news in stride. "Surely, Declan's just messing with you. Remember the time he photocopied your employee of the month picture and added devil horns and a mustache? Pasted it up and down the halls, in the tailor shop, the break room! He likes to get your goat."

"No, this is nothing like that. But Declan is a cretin, I'd forgotten about that one."

"George would never let that happen. Shoot, Mira wouldn't let that happen. What happened?"

Her sputtering makes me laugh. If only this was another one of Declan's pranks. He's grown up a tad since those days, I guess. Now, instead of pranks he just chases me off proverbial cliffs. "They're cutting support, companywide. Can't afford it. I should have seen it coming really, they kept downsizing all the departments. And the Hawaii store is about to go under, so George is transferring indefinitely to try to save it."

"So, who will manage your store?"

"Who do you think?"

Timeworn wrinkles in her cheeks stretch into a Cheshire grin. "This is better than *The Bachelorette*. Your nemesis is your new boss? Wouldn't that make you his assistant?"

"I'd rather cut off my own arm," I say, "using this needle." I hold up the shiny metal in my hand as proof that I'll do it. *Don't test me, woman!*

"Holly, you two need to bury the hatchet. Whatever got under your skin as kids can't be that bad."

"You were there! When we first met he looked at me like I was gum stuck on his shoe. George was the nice one, always has been."

"That was years ago, dear. The tension that's built up between you two over a grumpy sixteen-year-old experience is unreal." She fans herself, as if the tension she's talking about is something other than pure loathing.

"It doesn't matter, my job's gone." I put my needle in my teeth and manage *"Poof,"* while my hands mimic a small atomic bomb. "I don't know how they plan to run the store, but they seem adamant about it," I finish, switching threads and beginning a new section on my canvas. "Makes me think things are worse than they're letting on."

"I heard rumblings before I left, but nothing like this," she agrees. "Still, there has to be something for you—"

"There is." I arch an eyebrow in her direction.

She slaps my knee with more pep than I realized she still had in her. "See? I knew they wouldn't let you go."

"Declan or Len? I'm not sure who, but they're offering me a spot on the stylist team, it's the only department that's growing."

"Declan is a dog with a bone, he's always wanted you in Sales."

"You're right. Maybe this is his idea of a twisted joke—"

She sips her coffee and looks at me over the rim of her cup, then slowly puts it back down. "No. He sees your potential. He knows you enjoy the artistry, the imagery of fashion, the creativity in dressing. You have your own personal style and at such a young age that says a lot. He knows you'd be good at it, even if you don't."

I look down at my plain-Jane outfit and wonder what I'm missing. I don't think I could sell a K-pop fan a pleather skirt. "I'm sure they want me to ring sales, schedule appointments, and handle gift wrap. Mom thinks I should take it and be looking for something else. Something more permanent, preferably with a title."

"Holly."

"Hmm?"

"Do you really want a desk job?" Her tone is so firm, you wouldn't think she was being supportive right now. But this is her way. She says all the sweet stuff with a dash of anger because she wants the best for me so fiercely. "Do you want to go into some corporate position wearing a suit every day and taking meetings? There's no wrong answer, but I'll be damned if I sit and watch you blindly make the wrong choice!"

"I can't imagine not working there, on the floor with all the hustle and bustle. Popping into the café for lunch, down to Cosmo to have my eyebrows waxed on my lunch break, and getting to see what the new season's lines have to offer first." And I do love watching the rest of the store express their own personal styles, it's like a visual pu pu platter of cropped jackets, flowing dresses, body-con, oversize, prep, emo, punk, and everything in between.

She leans in as if she's going to share a secret, but her voice is still gruff, "You're a hard worker, your mother did that. I'd like to think I'm responsible for the creative parts of you, the artist you hide inside. Your dad deserves credit there too. He was a master of his own craft. What do all the fine traits you have look like when you put them together? That's what you need to figure out. And do that."

"It doesn't look like being at the beck and call of *the chosen ones*." But that would be the smart choice, the choice with a paycheck. And then making a smarter choice for my future, a serious job. A desk job with a future.

"Oh, them. Spoiled, that's all. You can win them over and maybe even teach them something. I sure couldn't have worked a nine-to-five desk my whole life, I know that."

"Mom wants me to do something serious. A career in *fashion* is a silly goal—"

"Your mother is scared, she wants the best for you. And *the chosen ones*, as you like to call them, are just scared too. All of us operate from a place of fear from time to time. Their job is hard, especially if, as you say, they're carrying the company."

"What happened to the Granny O. who would lecture them on filling out the alteration tickets correctly? You didn't let them slide just because they're the money makers!"

"I'm not telling you to let them slide. That's the worst thing you could do. If you take the position, you'll have to take the horse by the bit. They will walk all over you if you let them. But if you respect them, understand what it is they're doing and why, then you'll be able to earn their respect in return. Power has to be an even trade, no one can have it all. Same goes for respect."

"So, you think I should do it. Join the personal stylist team?" I motion down at myself. "What will I wear? I can't compete with them." My heart starts to race just thinking about welcoming strangers into a department and trying to sell them things!

"And why should you? If you try to look like Jenny with her chignons, accordion-pleat skirts, and designer platforms, or Molly with her bracelets stacked to her elbow, or Angel and the way she almost always looks like some version of a Disney princess—that girl likes tulle—you'll only be a fuzzy copy of the butterflies they are. But if you dress in a way that tells them who *you* are? What *you're* about? All the vintage touches you add, the classic styles you let stand on their own without tarnishing them with too much trendy crap. That red you're wearing, with the matching lip and those new bangs? That's personal style, and that's respectable."

Chills run the length of my body. I feel like I just got hit with a Coco Chanel wisdom stick.

A grandpa shuffles into the sunroom wearing a windowpane tweed jacket with a baby blue pocket square that's seen better days stuffed haphazardly at the breast.

Gran's face turns absolutely gooey. "Bernie! This is my grand-daughter, Holly."

I stand and stuff my needlepoint back in my bag. "I've heard lots about you but not that you were such a sharp dresser. I see why she likes you."

"Thank you, dear. I've got reason to try to clean up nice. Are you ready, Ms. O'Hare? Luncheon is being served and Doris has some records she wants to play for us after in the living room." He turns to me with a warm smile and the biggest, fluffy, salt-and-pepper eyebrows. I can see why the ladies love him. "Will you be joining us for luncheon?"

"Oh no, it's time for me to go. I've got some errands to run—" I adjust my headband self-consciously, still affected by Gran's words, but she chimes in before I can finish.

"And decisions to make. If you need inspiration, or a little ammo, check the attic. What's mine is yours."

"Yes. Decisions, decisions. Thanks, Gran," I say, waving to them both.

"Oh, and Holly." I turn to see Bernie pulling Gran from her chair, handing her a vintage wicker handbag that's so kitschy, it's chic. She's dressed for the day in a sheer floral overcoat, underneath is a light pink shift that falls to midcalf, and smart one-inch wedge heels are on her feet. "Don't let *the chosen ones* walk all over you, and don't let Declan Lorden fool you either."

At home I take a hot shower and throw on my favorite Topshop sweats. Being engulfed in the cozy Sherpa lining is like being eaten by a teddy bear.

It's mac and cheese again tonight, and finally I'm going to get around to finishing that fantasy show about the fairy and the prince who is supposed to kill her to save the kingdom but is falling in love with her in a creepy forest instead. It's scrumptious.

After the two fools finally get to a first kiss that took almost eight episodes to work up to but was so freaking worth it, my phone buzzes. That'll be Len, looking for my official answer to the job offer.

But it's not Lenny. It's Declan. I don't even know how he got this number or how I have his. We must have swapped ages ago.

Past me had a sense of humor and nicknamed him. I also put his name in all caps, probably so I'd never accidentally text him. It makes his text look like he's shouting at me. And I hate that he'd love it.

LORD DECLAN

Hello, this is Declan. I need to speak with you.
Are you available now?

Could he get more robotic? It's as if we've never met.

ME

Now?

LORD DECLAN

I'm only asking if this is a good time. Are you free, like to text, for a moment?

ME

Yes.

LORD DECLAN

We didn't get to finish our conversation the other day.

ME

Because you were stalking me in the women's restroom.

LORD DECLAN

I'm actively pushing the board to make all our restrooms unisex.

ME

(bubbles)

LORD DECLAN

I was trying to make sure you were okay and I had something I needed to say, in private, so I waited.

ME

?

LORD DECLAN

I hoped you'd WANT the stylist position, it seems you don't...but I need you to take it anyway.

ME

Why? You can't stand me.

LORD DECLAN

Why do you think that?????

ME

Because you've given me shit in every position I've held...

ME

Oh, and Gran reminded me today about when you defaced my employee of the month photo!!!!

LORD DECLAN

I forgot about that. Were we seventeen? Eighteen?

ME

Does it matter?

LORD DECLAN

Considering I'm twenty-four now and you're twenty-five?

ME

I'm twenty-four, you're twenty-five. Get to the point, please.

LORD DECLAN

How is your gran? I miss her being in the store.

ME

She's fine.

LORD DECLAN

I need you to train me in the office.

ME

Find someone else.

LORD DECLAN

> There's no one else. This is all on me and I
> need you.

I don't know what to say to that. This doesn't sound like the Declan I know. But when I think about it, I've never had many exchanges with him other than tossing spiteful word bombs at each other. We've never talked about anything serious.

ME

> I'll think about it.

LORD DECLAN

> I'm asking for a favor. This is hard for me.

ME

> Don't push me!

LORD DECLAN

> What's your concern?

What's my concern? My thumbs can't move fast enough to peck out the list.

ME

> I don't relish being a sad little girl in khakis next
> to the fashion plates that are Jenny, Molly, and
> Angel. I don't know the first thing about being
> a personal stylist. SALES IS SCARY. You know
> employees call Jenny Yoo the Snake. Would
> you want to work for that?

LORD DECLAN

> You in khakis is like vintage Meg Ryan and
> Audrey Hepburn had a baby and she was
> oblivious to her easy perfection. So stylish.

ME

> You're making me blush.

LORD DECLAN

(bubbles)

There are bubbles for a very long time. They start, they stop, and it begs the question... What is he debating writing?

LORD DECLAN

I won't allow them to treat you poorly. You'll be trained to sell. It's a skill like everything else and I know you'll kill it.

The compliment is surprising and makes my chest heat up. All teenage practical jokes aside, all pecking and *constructively* critiquing me aside, he's never treated me *poorly*. I hate him, but I'll admit it's always been in jest, all the jabbing between us. And now...

LORD DECLAN

As the store manager, that's my job. And as head of Sales, it'll be Len's job to make sure you're competent.

Right, of course. It's not like he'd be defending my honor. Just upholding company policy.

ME

I'm thinking about it...

ME

I need a week.

It's not my proudest moment, but the truth is I don't want to be there to watch it all fall apart. I don't want to say goodbyes. It's why I don't have many close friends—it hurts too much to lose someone and I'd rather, just, *not*.

LORD DECLAN

I don't have that kind of time.

ME

> I'll work remote, do all the closeout paperwork and field employee questions via email.

LORD DECLAN

> Fine. But know this—I'm not really asking. I'm begging. I hope I see you next Monday morning.

LORD DECLAN

> Honestly Holly, I'm not sure I can do it.

His face conjures unbidden in my mind. He's taking one of those trademark deep breaths, exhaling through his nose. Biting his bottom lip…

I don't know what it is about this last text. Of all the years I've spent disliking Declan Lorden, for the second time I'm a little torn.

It's a lesson universally learned in childhood, and for me it was pretty early when the General and I came to a mutual understanding about our expectations of each other, that our parents are not perfect.

But it occurs to me now that neither are the other people in our lives. Our friends who are loyal to us but also have loyalties elsewhere, or secret loves that we put on a pedestal only for them to inevitably fall, and maybe even our enemies are flawed, and layered, and ultimately, human.

CHAPTER
Seven

A WEEK LATER, it's my first Monday as a stylist. Not only am I as scared as the first time I wore a homemade dress I'd designed to school (complete with iron-on nautical sequin patches) but I'm here two hours early to help Declan Lorden. Of all people.

Walking down the office hallway is like walking through a torn city in ashes. Phones are ringing, somewhere a printer is beeping, but there's not one employee in sight. I'm glad I opted for a sensible black outfit with Mom's loafers. During my week off while working from my couch—and not because of Declan's comment—I watched old movies with style icons to brush up just in case I actually had to help a customer. Today, I'm Audrey in *Funny Face*, my bangs swooped low and to the side with a bit of gel.

The Administrative and Customer Service departments are gone. They've gone so far as to construct a blank wall where Customer Service opened to the public, and they did not go gently into the night. There's wreckage—leftover buckets of paint from the wall, boxes of paperwork, half-used office supplies, old furniture, and debris line the halls. George gave everyone clearance to take what they'd like, and the staff took that literally. Sporadically placed paintings that had been sprinkled throughout the long hall are now nothing but naked bolts in the wall.

George is gone, though his office door is cracked while most other office doors are firmly closed. I'm glad I didn't have to watch the dismantling in real time. This is the end of an era and it's a miserable sight.

Declan appears, a lone soldier, with frantic energy in his eyes. "You're here."

"As promised," I acknowledge, moving down the hall toward my old desk in George's old office. I'm sure it's not my desk anymore, but no one's being hired as Declan's assistant, so I'll keep it until he tells me I can't.

"Where are the reports that get posted at the end of the hall?" he asks.

"Didn't the operator post them this morning?" That explains the beeping.

"Daisy called in sick. But I did figure out voicemail." He looks proud of himself in a red sweater that somehow doesn't clash with his burgundy glasses and only accentuates his dark denim.

Great, the one person who's not expendable chose today to not come in.

For a guy who knows everything about the mechanics on the floor, he truly knows zilch about Admin. How the hell is this store going to keep from descending into utter chaos? Floor employees have no idea how much work goes on behind the scenes.

"Help, please?" He takes his glasses off and slips a Lucite arm down the collar of his sweater causing it to form a slight V. No button-down today, and my gaze snags on the triangle of tan skin just below his clavicle. He's like his mother, one lick of sun and the boy looks like he's been lounging poolside all winter. He must pick it up while working on his boat, that's why all those muscles in his forearms are tensing now, as we speak, as he pushes the sleeves up, and... *Wait, what?*

"Help. Please," he says again.

Hands on hips, I ask, "What's in it for me? I'm paid on commission now. My time is valuable." I'm brazen today. It's the fear of the sales floor talking and the fact I know today might be my one and only day as a personal stylist.

"Okay, I've been thinking about this because I knew you would ask that. If you help me in the office so I can learn everything while managing the rest of the store, I'll never speak to you again."

My face drops into an open-mouth, gobsmacked expression I can't quite force myself to hide. "Excuse me?"

"Don't act surprised on my account. I thought it over, all night. Tossed and turned and then *boom*! I know you hate me hovering, asking you questions all day. I'll stop. Cold turkey after you teach me how to run the office, no more talking to Holly."

"Even if I miss filling a whole department with gift cards?"

"That's not your job anymore."

"Whose job is it?"

He quirks his head like an inquisitive golden retriever, that strawberry-golden hair a mass of unruly waves on his head. "I guess it's mine." It sinks in a little exactly how much he has riding on his shoulders. "I'm begging," he adds in a low voice.

"Say it again." The beeping fax machine is like a ticking time bomb, *beep...beep...beep...* But I've waited a long time to put him in his place.

That tension Gran was talking about fills the hallway, but it's got a new edge to it. We've warred with each other before, sure, but we've never negotiated.

"Holly..." he swallows.

"Again, Declan Lorden." Yes, I could tend to the paperwork and get most of the office sorted in less than ten minutes—I used to do all that *before* I started in on George's task list—but I want to see him sweat.

Just as I'm feeling nice and satisfied about us swapping hero and villain roles, to my horror, he reverently drops to a knee and bows his head. "Please, from the bottom of my guts, which my dragon-father *will* rip from my body and eat for dinner, help me put this fire out. You will never have to hear one word from my lips again. I will not hover, I will not question—"

He grabs my hand and I let him take it. "No texting," I add.

A slow smile widens as he peeks up at me through long lashes. "If that's what you want."

A tiny knot of guilt sticks in my throat for making him work so hard for help, even though he seems to be enjoying it. Clearly, he's at a precipice if he's unabashedly begging me like this. "Okay, okay, get up."

I pull my hand from his, ignoring the shot of heat between our palms. I'm doing it for the family. They've always been good to me and Gran.

Wide shoulders rise slowly so that he towers over me once again. Silently, he follows me to the operator's booth to watch as I grab a headset, sit in the swivel chair, and start punching buttons to take the phones off perma-hold. "Thank you for calling Lorden's Pine Street, this is Holly, how can I help you?"

I pull off my coat and shove it at him. "Take this to my desk," I say, as I punch buttons and pass the caller through.

"You're letting this little moment of power go to your head." He scoops up my bag that I'd dropped haphazardly at the door. "It's hot."

I simultaneously hush and glare at him while answering another call. He zips his lips with his finger and mimes throwing away the key before disappearing with my things.

The headset stretches quite far and with a swivel chair, I'm able to get the printer going behind me. It starts to spit out copies of yesterday's numbers and I'm satisfied with myself for saving the day. As if he's heard a dog whistle in the form of no more beeping, Declan returns and grabs them.

My watch tells me I'm going to be late meeting Lenny in the stylist office, but I can't leave the phones unmanned. Declan has disappeared with the store reports and obviously doesn't care about where I need to be or how he's going to answer the phones all day with no operator.

I buzz the Activewear department and right on cue, Alice answers, "Women's Active, this is Alice, how can I help you?"

"Alice, we're not even open yet," I say, pulling a long strip of tape from the dispenser on the desk, unbuckling my watch, and wrapping it around the piece of leather band that decided to snap in this moment. It's probably poetic, or some sort of allegory, maybe? I don't know, that's never really been my thing.

"Sometimes Daisy puts calls through when she knows I'm here. We got a huge shipment in and I had an early call with our regional."

"Where's your manager?"

"The Bahamas. Where's Daisy? Are you in the booth today?"

"Out sick, and no, I've got training with Len."

"I'm glad they didn't can you, honey. What department this time?"

"Stylist. I'm the one in training." News of my new position clearly hasn't circulated.

Silence echoes in my headset along with some static. Alice is as shocked as I am that Declan and Lenny would think I could hold my own with *the chosen ones*.

"Listen, can you come man the booth until we find someone who can take it for the day? Have you ever answered the phones?"

"Not here, but a million years ago I worked the phones at a Macy's, my first summer out of college. Bet I can pick it up."

"Lifesaver. Just holler at whoever's on your floor to cover when we open. And when you need a break, call another manager on the floor. If Daisy never shows, we're going to have to take turns for the day."

This is a true imposition, because Alice makes money by making sales and she can't do that from the operator's booth. But she rallies like the team player I know she is. "Okay. Be right there. And Holly?"

"Yeah?"

"If you're going to sell, remember one thing: take no prisoners. I mean it, no one gets ahead on the floor being a doormat." Wow. That bit of after-school advice coming from the nicest mother hen who works here.

Oh. God. This day... About five minutes of phone calls later, my savior, Alice, arrives.

"Sorry, I stopped to use the bathroom so I can make it chained to this desk for a while. My bladder's not what it was in my twenties— enjoy it while it lasts."

I hand off the headset and she plops in the swivel chair in a cerulean sweater dress with timeless cream boots.

"Thanks again, Alice. Holler at Declan if you need anything. Worst-case, just page me."

She winks and I make my way down the hall, worried being late for training is going to start me out on the wrong foot with an already volatile woman.

It's quiet now, other than a few salespeople trickling in and heading down to their respective departments with half-asleep smiles or faces in phones. Declan's posted the numbers along one wall where all employees can check sales stats on their way to the floor; everything from the top seller in the store yesterday to the top ten stores in the country and what they did as a whole. For the first time, I let my finger scroll to the top of the seller's page. I've never had the need to track sales this closely; now I do. Yesterday, Jim Love (a name made for sales) sold almost fifteen thousand dollars in men's suiting.

Holy shit, that's my competition now. I realize, especially after Alice's comment, how unprepared for this job I truly am. How the hell am I going to sell fifteen grand worth of dresses and shoes and belts and bras? But the General raised a winner, a girl who only knows how to do things 100 percent, a girl who feels almost physically ill when she tries to half-ass something as trivial as teeth brushing. I still boast a cavity-free mouth.

Even though I know I'll be the gofer for the stylist team, I'll need to make sales on the floor to pay my rent. It's time to get excited about tights and tube socks.

CHAPTER
Eight

JENNY YOO IS GOING to crush me under the toe of her designer shoe, that's a given. The woman is a Pine Street legend in sales, much like Jim Love. She often competes with him for annual top seller. Every February, the winner is shipped to an all-inclusive luxury vacation on Lorden's dime with fellow top sellers from around the country, but it's not just that. It's the way she carries herself; it's her style, of course, and the success she's amassed with the personal stylist team in such a short amount of time.

I stand at her office door and look down like a hesitant fifth grader on the first day of school. There was no time last night to dig into Gran's attic for the treasure she'd alluded to, but what I thought was a perfectly respectable look for a stylist assistant now looks as drab as a dark lampshade. I know I'll be working on the floor of a department most of the time, selling to foot traffic. It'll be months before I'm trained to take appointments, and until then I'm sure I'll be at her beck and call. Comfort was a realistic concern.

A lion's head on my statement ring, the one piece I added to my *no-frills* Audrey look before heading out this morning looks back at me as I grasp the doorknob, emerald green eyes winking, daring me to walk in.

I am a lion, I am a lion.

I'm a cub at best but here goes nothing.

The scene in the office when I open the door is ripped from an episode of *Emily in Paris*. Sketches of next season's buys are pinned to the walls and three beautiful women in unique and equally beautiful outfits are typing at computers and pecking into phones. I tiptoe across the threshold trying not to make a sound. *The chosen ones* turn in unison from a round lacquered table to see who dared disturb their slumber. The Snake remains unmoving at her desk, so I hover and look anywhere that's not directly at her.

"Ah. There you are. Len said this was happening today. I thought he was kidding." Jenny has readers perched on her nose and what I'll assume are sales numbers in her hand.

Angel sits in a floor-length tulle skirt, with an oversize leather jacket perched on her shoulders.

She motions to a folding chair in the farthest corner of the room. *"Bienvenida, Bienvenue, Benvenuto,"* she chirps. I've always been jealous of the bilingual.

When I don't budge, she adds, "Relax, we won't bite. Even though you're the reason my calves are still sore. " Her flawless complexion glows while perfectly arched eyebrows rise. "I had to drag everything for my appointments up flights of stairs for days because of you."

I hold my head high. "The escalator was down for one day."

"I felt so bad for you!" Molly laughs. She's wearing a sleeveless butterscotch silk dress, with black cowboy boots that are becoming her new personal statement, and has goose bumps on her delicate fore-arms that are strategically stacked with an assortment of woven and colorful beaded bracelets. The apples of her cheeks are tinted deep red and pop on her black skin.

"Lenny was supposed to meet me for training." I am a deer in a spotlight on a runway I am sorely underdressed for. My all-black, chic neutrals mock me in the presence of greatness.

Jenny stands in platform heels, molded, round, and covered in snakeskin—it's a feat of balance. I take in her very pregnant, very posh belly. "We're finished here. The two of you can go." She nods to *the chosen ones* while I freeze because I sorely wanted to be part of the dismissal. "But I want to see all of you back here tomorrow morning. We'll see who hit their goals. Including you, Holly."

"Tomorrow?" I croak. Surely, I'll get more than a day to find my feet.

"You'll be clocking in on my team today, training or no. No sale wasted. Gucci gratis is up for grabs for the biggest sales number by 5:00 p.m. this Friday."

The two stylists gather their things into handbags that cost more than my car. If I were a bird, I'd fly far, far away right now. There is no part of me that wants numbers under my name publicly posted for the Snake and the world to see.

"I want that studded Gucci belt," Angel says, pushing bright blonde hair over her shoulder. She checks her cell, scrolling with one manicured finger faster than she can possibly read. "It's sold out everywhere."

"You're literally going to have to fight me for it," Molly replies. "I have Stacy Taylor today, she's an easy five grand in less than two hours. I've got another regular after that, and I took an M.O.B. that put in a request for an appointment through the website last night."

They stop in the doorway and I watch the friendly but competitive looks in their eyes as they size each other up, wishing I had a bag of greasy popcorn.

Angel pulls on Molly's elbow. "You took a mother of the bride *virtual request*? Are you crazy? You've got no idea what's going to show up this afternoon. Probably a tourist getting *ideas* in the big city!"

"That's part of your job, need I remind you?" Jenny chimes in. "What do I always say?"

"The sale is what you make it," they reply in unison.

Angel whispers to me under her breath, "They go home and order knockoffs every time." She turns to Molly who's checking her lipgloss in a studded compact. "Now I know I'll win but I'll let you borrow the belt," she finishes, dropping her cell into her handbag.

M.O.B., mother of the bride. That's what they call the moms who spend hours upon hours shopping for a dress and heels and usually end up in the same champagne number that we've been selling for years. And they're not happy about handing over their credit cards.

Who would be for a drab brown dress that you hate but have no better options?

"You never know what a mother of the bride appointment will turn into. I've gotten some good clients that way."

"Pick your poison, I guess. Every M.O.B. I've had has been hours of scouring the floor for dresses with sleeves, heels with arch support, and jewelry that elevates the look but they don't want to buy because they know they'll never wear it again."

Molly's smug look falters, but before I can find out what happens next, Jenny moves around me more fluidly than should be humanly possible for a woman in her condition and closes the door. "Have a good day, ladies. I'll check your numbers at noon."

"Sit." She motions to a chair in the corner opposite her desk as she gingerly lowers herself behind her computer and begins typing.

"What are your goals for today?" she asks without looking up.

"Umm..."

"You're training with Len on the floor, but you will be expected to sell, Holly. You can't drag our department numbers down. Don't look at me like that."

I pull my face out of whatever form of shock it was in.

"You know how this store works."

"Ugh..."

"This is a long shot, but I've known Len for a long time and he asked for a favor. And his name is on the door, isn't it? But no coasting, you're going to have to work hard, Holly. We don't play dress up in this office for living, we sell. Goal for the week, then?"

I look at her, I'm guessing doe-eyed and full of fear. Unfortunately, my show of fear only angers the Snake.

"Okaaaay. Why don't you run down to the E-bar for me while you have a moment to think on it? Come back with an answer." I'm wasting her very valuable time. "I'll have my regular."

This I can do. This is what I figured I'd be doing anyway. "Sure."

"After you train with Len, you'll clock into Hosiery."

Also what I figured I'd be doing.

She hands me a binder with a label that says Hosiery Department on the front. I take it, resist the urge to bow, and back out the door.

At the E-bar, with the binder tucked under my arm, I wait behind a few employees chattering and smiling because they're not currently stuck at the beginning of the worst day of their lives.

"Coffee for Jenny Yoo. Her regular, please," I order. My mind is a million miles away. Conjuring scenarios of selling the cottage and telling the General I can't make rent.

But Zak, who's been here almost a year—I know because I trained him, but thankfully he came from Starbucks so he pretty much took the reins from the start—looks at me blankly. "I don't know her regular." He's got double French braids and they hang over his shoulders in dirty blond ropes.

A tremor of terror rattles through me that might end with turning tail and running for the hills.

"She takes an Americano, iced, with one pump caramel syrup and one pump sugar-free vanilla. Extra ice. Then you top it with about a cup of cream."

"Where have you been?" I demand, turning to find Lenny behind me dressed as the epitome of preppy today in a polka-dot blazer with brass buttons that say Dior. "*The chosen ones* basically declared my existence null and void, and the Snake—"

He shakes his head and laughs, "You can't call them that. They're nice enough once you get to know them. Sorry, I thought I said to meet me down here."

I let out a long yawn—*this day.* "You did, didn't you? How do you know her order?" I ask, when Zak nods acknowledgement and we move off to the side of the line.

"I'm a nice guy, I do coffee runs for employees all the time. I could tell you how almost everyone takes their coffee in this store, it's a gift."

"Well, that much sugar is probably what makes her so bitchy. Must be a hell of a crash."

He shrugs and guffaws, as if my working girl antics are pure entertainment.

"When did you get here? When I walked in this morning it was like a bomb went off. Declan was sweating through his cashmere trying to answer the phones and print reports. It threw me off, so I guess I forgot about meeting you downstairs. Things can't go on like this, Len. Declan said something about closing…"

My words hang in the air and I freeze wondering if I shouldn't have brought it up.

"I know," he says, face turning grim, clashing with his cheery outfit. "I'm trying to talk to Louie. It's tight, Holly. Our business is in real danger. There's a rumor going around the board about Louie selling his shares."

Jenny's coffee, along with an identical one with my name on it, appears at the end of the counter.

"I heard it's your first day on the floor." Zak winks. Then he's off in a flurry of grinding and order-taking.

After shoving my department binder at Lenny, I swoop them up, nod my thanks to Zak, and skirt around a long line that's formed. I do not miss my coffee-slinging days.

"Mira would never sell, would she?"

I doctor both cups with a heavy dose of cream—*when in Rome*—and watch the white swirl mix with the dark roast.

"No. But if there are rumors, it means there's blood in the water. I'm glad you decided to go for it as a stylist."

Sipping delicately, not even realizing it because I'm chewing on a thought just out of reach, I'm smacked in the mouth with pleasure. "Ohmygod," I gush. "This is so good."

Before we exit the E-bar I holler over the line of customers to Zak, "Remember this one: The Jenny!" He gives me a quick thumbs-up and then goes back to making foam. "I'm going to need more caffeine-laced sugar rushes like this one if I'm going to contend with *the chosen ones*."

We walk down the center aisle on the first floor. There are two mirror-image light installations that cover all of women's shoes on one side of the store, little orbs of light on chrome that look like constellations in the sky. This is the only modern update the store has gotten, I'm pretty sure Declan pushed for it a few years ago. The other side of the store is half men's wear and half cosmetics.

"You'll be surprised at how naturally it'll come to you." Lenny pats my back.

I snort and motion to myself with my elbows; I look like a goose flapping its wings because both my hands are full of precious cargo. "She was not impressed."

"Well, I mean, old loafers?" he chides.

"I thought I was going to be gofering most of the time, running dump from fitting rooms. I didn't seriously expect to be a stylist—with clients," I whine. "She put me in Hosiery." I motion with my nose to the binder now tucked under his lean bicep.

"Yeah, you're not doing that, and I've never known you to back away from a challenge. Why is this one any different from learning every other position in the store? Make an effort."

He has a point. I could have tried harder. A little research and maybe a trip to Gran's attic for whatever magic wand she was alluding to the other day.

"*Please*, come up with me." I nod toward the escalator. "I'll drop Jenny's coffee and we'll go train on the floor. Have a movie montage makeover scene where you give me gobs of pretty clothes to satisfy the Snake's taste. And then poof, next scene I'm a top seller."

"I'm afraid it doesn't work that way, darling. You've got to face the music yourself starting today and every morning from now on when you report to your new manager. But lucky for you she doesn't have time to train and that part falls to me. I'll meet you in Designer—"

"Designer?"

"Did you think I'd let her put you in Hosiery? You at least get the advantage of selling clothes you already love."

"Come with *meeeeee*." My loafers dance as I run in place on tiptoes full of anxiety. Jenny may hate them, but they're perfectly padded for a day of hoofing it on the floor.

He's nodding in the negative when something catches his eye. "What's that?" He points to my right hand, the lion.

"Found it in a stash of Gran's. Hear me roar." I roll my eyes because it's something Gran would say, or maybe even the General? I'm not sure, but I'm beginning to realize I'm a product of both in a twentysomething body. "She said there's more stuff in the attic..."

"I like it, fits you." His phone pings. "This might be Louie." He holds up a finger and reads a text. "Shit, it's David," his voice falters.

"David...?"

"The photographer I told you about."

"The biscuit?"

"Yeah, he's…he's special."

Oh. So, this *is* why Len didn't want to go to Hawaii. I've never heard him refer to someone as special.

But his face is more stricken than full of moony love-beams. "Everything okay?"

"No. Come on," he says, and we both head up the escalator not waiting but taking the steps two at a time.

Lenny does come back up to the Stylist office with me. On the way he explains that he and David have been seeing each other a little over a month, since David first scoped his apartment for the AD shoot. But he's sick. Lenny doesn't give me any more details than that.

"Good morning, Jenny," Lenny says, walking into the room. "She's not here to get your coffee, by the way."

We speak in unison. "I'm not?"

"She's not?"

Lenny ignores us. "Something's come up and I need to go. Now. For the day, most likely."

I hand Jenny her coffee. She mouths *thank you*, while we both watch Lenny, worried.

"Who's going to train her?" Jenny finally asks.

"Can you? You are her department manager and I'm sure she could learn a lot from you—*in Designer*. It's not clear when I'll be back."

"Len, is it something serious? Are you okay?" I follow him around the room as he roams circles going nowhere.

"He means a lot," he whispers under his breath. "It's happened quickly, but I need to go to him."

"Of course. I don't need anyone babysitting me, just go. I'll go downstairs and sell some socks or something."

"She doesn't know how to sell, Jenny. And I want her in Designer, she's got a good eye. Can she shadow Angel or Molly?"

"I don't think that's a good idea. They're top sellers. I've got them competing for Love's spot in the Maldives this year and a Gucci belt this week. If she's weighing them down it could cost the store big numbers…"

"Why can't you—"

Jenny stands and angles her shoulders toward Lenny; it's a feminine power pose at its finest. I should know, I've seen the General invoke the same stance hundreds of times. "Do I look like I need one more thing on my plate right now? My team is carrying this store, I'm eight and a half months pregnant, and I have Mrs. Smith today—"

"You do?" He grimaces as if that does it, I'm untrainable.

"Yes, I do. And then I'll be, you know"—she gestures around her at the less than glamorous piles of papers and Post-its littering her desk—"managing a department!"

"Fine." Lenny goes to another desk that looks like Angel and Molly might share, picks up the phone, and dials. "Declan Lorden, please."

From the hall I faintly hear Alice's voice come through speakers, *Declan Lorden, five-six. Declan Lorden, five-six.*

"Dec, it's Lenny. *She's fine, relax.* Yes, I know but…I need you to train her. An emergency. Yes, it's an *emergency.* Meet her in Designer in ten." He hangs up.

"I'm not training with Declan." I just got him to promise never to bug me again, and training him in the office every morning is more than enough to pay for it.

"Can you go have your crisis of the heart somewhere that's not my office," Jenny says sitting again at her desk very pregnant, a little sweaty, and covered in mint green silk pleats that have stretched wide as an accordion on a long note.

There's enough venom in her voice to push us both out into the hall.

"She's right, you know." Lenny scuffs a toe into nondescript commercial carpet.

"Have I officially fallen down the rabbit hole? What is she right about? And who is going to take me seriously on the floor in Designer? I absolutely would have worn something different," I say. "And by the way, I'm not about to train with the man who has enjoyed watching me squirm my entire professional career."

"Yes, yes, you hate each other, we all know. But I'm asking you to deal, and bury it, because I have to go."

"But, Len—"

"Do me a favor and ask yourself why he might be so hard on you, okay? Love you." He kisses me on the forehead.

And that's all I get from him. My friend who I've talked through countless uncomfortable situations in life, danced and drank with in drag, snickered and plotted with in the back row of rallies and meetings, even looked up to as a kind of father figure, just upped and bounced on me in my time of need. This new guy must be really important to him, so I squish my jealousy and abandonment issues into a box and lock it tight. I need to support my friend.

My phone buzzes in my back pocket.

Lenny: *Sorry I had to dash. This should be said over a few bottles of wine, or a joint, but this thing with you and Declan needs to stop. George is gone, and you know he wasn't right for you. Declan is the store manager now and you need to be able to work with him. It's up to you to figure this out.*

More tough love. I already get this from my mother. It's a bit hard to swallow from Lenny too.

I head down to Designer with the full intention of telling everyone to piss off, like I'm an editor at *British Vogue*. I'll train myself.

"'Bout time, Stewart." Declan fits in perfectly on the floor, leaning against the cash wrap with a sequin dress on a hanger dangling off two fingers. He's recovered from his previous flirtation with madness this morning and has returned full circle to riding his high horse. Probably he has a lot of experience with women's clothing—taking it off, that is.

I hate myself for even having the thought. His large hands surely know exactly how to pop buttons on blouses, shred zippers, disintegrate a lacy...*abort, abort!*

Now I have a visual of Declan undressing a woman on his romantic boat, as if he's popped Mary Poppins-style from an unusually spicy Vineyard Vines ad. *What is wrong with me today?* It's as if seeing him all crumbled and helpless this morning has opened some sort of portal to fantasies I didn't know I had.

"We both know I don't need you to train me. I can ring a sale just fine on my own. Shouldn't you be spending your time saving the empire?"

He pulls his glasses off and slides them into the neck of his sweater, casting aside something he was pretending to read. "But can you *sell*?"

After making a face at the dress in his hands, he pops it back on a rack. "I don't think sequins are very *you*."

My feet stutter and I startle like a pony. Why is he even thinking about what's *me*? "I *love* sequins, you cretin."

He smirks knowingly as if confirming a secret. "It's not going to help my bottom line if you're taking up space on the floor and you can't sell, Stewart." Crossing his Jordans at his ankles, he lazily resumes leaning against the cash wrap with arms folded; he certainly has nailed his *signature style*. Maybe that's what I need, to find a signature style so I don't have to overthink it every day.

"It can't be that hard." This is a lie. I have no idea how the salespeople at this store, the successful ones, rack up the numbers they do with shoes and swimsuits.

"If I'm going to train you in the one position you haven't held in this store, it will only add to the payoff of our bargain."

I look at him confused, not following.

He rubs the bridge of his nose and puts his glasses back on. Pushing off the counter slowly, he takes two steps, and taps me lightly on the shoulder. "Remember? I never speak to you again after you teach me how to run the office? I'll teach you how to sell in return." The expression on his face is pained, as if he doesn't like the deal he's making. Probably because he's making a deal with me in the first place, and neither of us is used to conspiring with the enemy.

He takes a deep breath, exhales through his nose, and chews his plump bottom lip before clearly forcing himself to finish, "Then blissful sounds of silence. Do we have a deal?"

"Lenny will be back."

"But I have the most experience in sales of anyone in this company. I can teach you how to sell like Jim Love, like Jenny, better even. You wanna give *the chosen ones* a run for their paychecks?" He wiggles his eyebrows at me, and it's playful, suggestive, and challenging all at the same time.

Customers casually walk through our department. We both smile and say *good morning*.

Yes, I do want to try to sell, I realize. If I'm going to do this, I want to do it well. I want my paycheck to afford more than just mac and cheese. But instead I say, "You've always been so cocky."

My words fall flat between us. We both know there's something different in the air, there's something different about this conversation. Heat vibrates between us. A challenge has been set. One he might usually want to watch me face-plant on, and vice versa, but there's something in it for both of us if we succeed.

"Confident," he corrects with a half smile, lowering his voice and taking one step toward me.

I think this is the first time we've not shouted at each other if you don't count the kneeling and the begging this morning. Just thinking about him on his knees in front of me makes odd things happen in my stomach as I look into his eyes now.

"Just give me a chance. People *like* you, Holly. You've got a well-rounded sense of style. I've watched it evolve over the years. You know this store better than you know *Buffy* canon. Yes, I remember what a stellar *Slayer* fan you were your senior year of college."

I snort-laugh at this because it's true. I still comfort-watch *Buffy* at bedtime.

"You've got a background in tailoring via your grandmother, and an in-depth knowledge of textiles via that degree you don't use. That knowledge is sales *ammo*. You're going to take to it naturally," he says on an exhale. It's almost as if he's proud of me? Admires me? Has faith in me? One of those...odd. "You're literally the perfect stylist. Let me coach you just a little, I'll give you the last set of tools you need—"

How many deals am I supposed to strike with the devil? He's always been in my business—down to my binging preferences, apparently. He loves to micromanage, but he's really being a dog with a bone today.

"If I have to spend even more time with you, letting you teach me things—don't make that face—" He rearranges a dirty look that crept across his brow. "I need more."

"I'll get you transferred to Hawaii," he responds, stepping back abruptly. Leaning against that counter like it's his job.

That catches me off guard. I've made peace with George leaving. I know he's not the one for me, even though Declan seems to think I'm still pining for him. That's the only reason he'd offer me Hawaii.

Still it might be a nice change of pace. I could travel, and try the local coffee. The cottage would be an issue, but I could rent it out for a year... A fire kindles inside me, warming to the thought of a whole new life.

Even though he hasn't initiated a shake, I stick out my hand and say, "Deal."

There's a moment I think he won't take my hand. "Deal," he says, reluctantly reaching out.

I eye him head to toe—shouldn't he be more excited than this? We both get what we want, and we get to never speak to, nag, bother, humiliate, or torment each other again.

He drops my hand after the briefest and firmest of holds and his mouth settles into an "all business" line. "Now, what's your goal?"

As if it took years off his life to touch me, he turns away and gives his head a shake.

Clearly, I've given him cooties. It makes me smile.

"Why does everyone keep asking me for a goal?"

He checks an expensive watch on his wrist. "You've got four hours on the floor today. This is your new department, Designer, which means you've got high price points. So, what's your goal? When Jenny asks you this, when I ask you this, we want a number."

I hate not knowing the answer. How much should I be able to sell in an hour on my first day? I can't do math quickly enough, so I blurt, "I want to sell as much as I possibly can. That's the goal."

Declan's entire face splits into a wide grin. "Spoken like a true salesperson."

CHAPTER
Nine

BY FRIDAY MORNING, Declan and I have settled into a shocking new normal. I come in an hour early every day before my morning meeting with the Stylist team to instruct him in office ways: how to stock copy paper (he growls), how to accept the money drop from Dunbar and count it safely into the safe (balancing that monster to zero is a job in itself), and most enjoyably, I time how quickly he can answer and connect calls in the booth in case we have another operator dilemma. He compares the booth to being in a medieval torture chamber; he's not totally wrong.

If I do end up packing my bags for Hawaii, he's going to have to take care of the administrative tasks on his own because Lorden's is showing no signs of bringing back support. It's a good thing he knows the rest of the store functions like the back of his own calloused hand. Rumors about the company being in trouble swirl around the store as if another Seattle snowstorm were brewing, instead of the early spring that's popping outside. We've had three sunny days in a row, though I've spent most of them chained to the Designer cash wrap picking up foot traffic.

Meanwhile, he's taught me nothing, but there's been a lot of metaphors about sharks. We've walked the store together as he's pointed out the different departments and their respective commission rates. I've even watched him work with customers himself. Although his cold manner comes off a bit rude, he gets the job done by meeting customer needs and building out the sale with additional suggestions. He wants me to be strong, effective, a shark like him.

Today, I'm thrilled to be at the end of another week full of *Alice in Wonderland* moments; helping chic society women with gowns, then turning around and helping elderly women into undergarments.

"I ordered everyone *The Jenny*," I say, breezing into the stylist office as if I belong there, taking my seat for our morning meeting. My now catch-phrased coffees are accepted greedily, and Jenny's cheeks brighten; she loves having a drink named after her that half the store is ordering now on the reg. I wouldn't say I feel accepted, but I'm learning their ways.

Jenny's sitting and ticking off tasks and goals for the day finger by finger, backed by a whiteboard covered with astronomical sales targets for the month. She's wearing her husband's button-down shirt open to a deep V with traces of a lace camisole and an ever-growing chest over stretchy velvet leggings. A smart solution to the lack of stylish maternity wear that's *still* unavailable to the evolved working mom. Those leggings could stretch to Mars and back. I know because I've helped customers with them this week. They're a man-made miracle. *Ladies, don't pay attention to the number on the label of a garment, everything is negotiable!*

True to form, she's stuffed her feet into pre-spring raffia platforms covered in pearls.

After giving us our morning marching orders, she stands slowly and with great effort. "Cool?" she asks, as way of adjournment.

Angel won the Gucci belt for hitting last week's numbers and immediately wraps it around the puff-sleeved baby doll dress she's wearing.

Before I can follow them into the hall where I know Declan will be waiting for me—because I've begged him *not* to—Jenny says, "Holly, your cup."

"Oh, sorry."

"I'm not your mother, here to clean up after you all day," she says, and lets a hand rest on her belly.

It's the first time I've heard her speak about motherhood. I pick up my coffee cup. It's left a sweaty ring on the white lacquered table.

"Cleaning products are in that cabinet." She points to a wall mount.

I huff, put my stuff down, and press to open. There's a smorgasbord of products to choose from, like the vanity cabinet of a woman obsessed with antiaging but in this case, cleaning. I've got options, and for condensation no less. But I don't want to poke the Snake.

A light knock on the door frame sounds behind me and sure enough, Declan appears. "I'm waiting."

"Sounds like a personal problem," I sing, then look back to Jenny with an inquisitive smile that says, *how can such an attractive man be so annoying? Am I right?*

She rolls her eyes at me as Declan waits, doing something on his phone.

"This is a lot of product. Alphabetized, and it seems you've stacked them exactly one inch apart. Did you measure?" I can't help my blurt as I choose a cleaner. I'm a little in awe, if she ever leaves Lorden's she could definitely get a job on one of those home editing shows, though her disposition would not fit with the happy hosts.

A pregnant cat caught with a canary, she cracks a smile and nods. "It's a tic. I'm afraid I'm going to struggle a bit when this bundle of joy gets here. But we don't have to lose ourselves to procreate, you know?"

My mom would certainly agree with that.

"So says my therapist," she continues. "There's no task so mundane that you can't make it chic, or at least aesthetically pleasing. You should see her closet"—she nods down to her tummy—"I've merched the whole thing. My husband warned me it won't stay that way long, but I don't think I need to change who I am to have a baby. My goal was always to have both: a career and a kid but make it fashion."

"My parents certainly did, and look how well that turned out." Declan's acid-laced comment from the doorway startles both of us.

"We all have to learn from our parents' mistakes," Jenny says evenly.

"Funny, that's what *my* therapist says," he retorts.

This woman could be a glimpse into my future. Or maybe, my past. Is this how the General felt, balancing career and kid? Young, working her way up in Washington as a female with a family?

"Do you plan to have more?" I ask, filling a gap in conversation before one forms. If Declan feels pushed aside or second to the company in his parents' eyes, that answers a lot of questions.

"Hell no!" Jenny drops with a grateful groan into her desk chair. "I plan to take this one to Korea to see extended family, all over Europe, and NYC fashion week. One and done."

I spritz with an organic option—worried that bleach fumes might hurt the baby—toss my paper towel in the bin, and head out the door. If I'm not mistaken, Jenny Yoo is smiling. And like it or not, I feel like I understand the General just a little bit better.

"What's with that look?" Declan falls into step with me as I move down the hall.

"Good morning, shadow."

"We already said that to each other, hours ago. Why are you sunshine and rainbows all of a sudden? You were sunshiny for the Dunbar guy this morning too..."

"Tony?"

"Are you interested in him?"

I pause to give him a look. "He's gotta be pushing seventy."

"Ageist."

"I'm not interested in Tony."

"So why am I the only one today getting grumpy Holly? Everyone else gets shiny, bright Holly. That's the way it's always been, you know."

Could the reason he doesn't like me simply be because he thinks I don't like him? I don't but still. "Maybe because my entire life you've been a demanding grump. Things don't turn on a dime because you need something from someone."

He follows me into what's now our office and watches as I switch my computer on as if we've been doing this for years.

He perches on the edge of George's desk and my heart tugs a bit but for what? I'm not sure. I haven't thought much about George since he left, almost as if his leaving was a weight off my shoulders. He did lean on me more than he should have for an assistant, and it's nice to focus more on myself and my new role. I was so scared of Sales but now that I've been selling for a week on the floor, it feels less terrifying and a lot more like a challenge.

How much can I sell? Can I make the Snake proud? Lenny? Even Declan?

But more importantly, once I prove to myself I can hack it as a stylist, I can move on to the next challenge. I've still got ladders to climb. Possibly Hawaiian ladders that have tiny drinks with umbrellas in them at the top of a coffee bean mountain. That's if I can rent out the cottage of course. I don't ever want to give up Gran's cottage, but I can't imagine a better scenario right now than a shiny new bikini, dark roast, and cocktails on the ocean. Spending some time away with new experiences then eventually coming home to Seattle to nab a title for the General. Could I have both? A life and a career?

While checking my phone, I apply some lip gloss without looking, and toss it back in my bag. "Ready to hit the floor?" If only George could see me now. Would he be shocked? Me, a stylist? And it hasn't been horrible. In fact, I'm good at it.

Hold your horses, you positive pony. You haven't had any appointments yet.

"You need that. Your phone."

"Oh, yeah." It's hard to remember that stylists are supposed to have their phones at all times for client 911s about things like broken heels, sensors that have been left on clothing only to be noticed minutes before they're leaving for an event, or realizing in horror they have nothing new to wear to the yacht club on a Saturday night—*gasp!*

I need options messengered over from my personal stylist, STAT!

"You didn't answer my question," he pushes while standing in front of the doorway. "What's with the servings of sugar for everyone but me? You're doing well on the floor, taking to Sales like a fish to water. Just like I knew you would." The way he says it makes my cheeks heat.

That damn boat he slaves away on has made him lean and burly at the same time—muscle stacked upon muscle with a tall frame that can carry it well. At least, that's what I felt the day he caught me on the escalator. I wonder if he has hair on his chest? A lot? A little?

I hate that I'm now thinking of him shirtless while he's inches from me, but it's hard to stop. A heat, a needy energy is building between us. I lick my lips, then cover my mouth to stop the insanity. This is *Declan*.

"I'm just bonding with my coworkers," I finally manage. "You catch more flies with honey, right? Gran always says that, but I don't really get why you'd want to catch flies—"

"To get them out of the house."

"What?"

He chuckles. "It's an old-fashioned saying, back when people worried about flies in the house. This isn't about making friends, Stewart. You've got to look out for yourself or someone will take adavantage. What did I tell you?"

My mind shifts to Declan, and what could have put this massive crater on his shoulder. He's always been full of so much grit and attitude, as if he's got something to prove to the world; constantly on the defensive. So why is he picking at me because I'm *happy*? "Why are you so determined to run this store like a tyrant? Making friends is a good thing."

"Just because I'm not a cuddly bear like George doesn't mean I'm a tyrant. This is my job, Holly. This is three generations of our family. Our business is on the line. I'm not here to play nice, I'm here to save the bottom line."

"It's not all on you though. You'll never make it if you don't let people help. You want me to be *nice* to you? Then *you* be nice. No one's going to help if you're always growling at them."

"There are other ways to get what you want, Holly. I asked for your help," he says, his voice getting softer. "And I had to barter for it with my silence. With you eventually leaving me altogether."

Me *leaving him*? Why is it that my gut just plummeted and my heart is all jumpy? This is what he does to me, gets me all riled up. And confused. And angry for reasons I don't understand when only moments ago, I was blissfully content without him.

"Your silence is something I'm *not* getting, by the way."

"Because someone's gotta train you while Len's off."

True. Lenny is still out of the office, a mysterious "family emergency" blanket response attached to his auto-reply email. I can't remember the last time Len went this MIA. We've only exchanged a few nondescript "checking in" texts.

"You know your dad has put you in a horrible situation, right? With no support staff? And now Lenny's out."

Declan runs a hand through his hair. "Ah, but we all know George could have done it on a shoestring. Have you seen Hawaii's numbers? Already up. They'll be adding a Customer Service department in no time. He'll swoop up your application for management."

"So why'd you let him go? If this was the harder job to take?" Which it is. All the full-line stores require a lot to run, but the flagship has extra bells and whistles. Hawaii is newer, smaller, and more streamlined. It would be much easier to manage.

"You know George. You saw how he *altered* himself to make my parents happy. To be what he thought they wanted. He needed a way out—and I don't do that."

"Don't do what?"

"Alter myself—for anyone."

I shift on my feet. He's still blocking the doorway. I would leave, but I can't. I'm not sure he wants to have this conversation, but he's not shying away from it either. "I'm glad he's figuring himself out, but that doesn't mean you should bear the brunt of a losing battle."

His face brightens, but there's a question in the quirk of his mouth. "You're not pissed you're stuck here with me? I thought it was the end of your world when George left. That was only a few weeks ago, Holly." His soft brown eyes bore into mine.

Suddenly, he's looking at me as if we've never met. As if I'm dinner. This little doorway convo has taken a serious, steamy turn, and I hate my racing heart. I am not attracted to Declan Lorden. I have never been attracted to Declan Lorden. I'm going to write it on a sticky note and put it on my bathroom mirror when I get home, just in case I need reminding.

"I'm glad George got to go." Because he needed an escape, and Declan clearly knew that too.

His cheeks are tinging pink and it makes me shiver when he says, "Is that not why you want to go to Hawaii now? Not for George?"

"Maybe I just need a change of scenery. A leap of faith? I don't know... Everything in my life changed at the start of this year. I was scared, but now I think I'm starting to figure out what I really want."

When his only response is heavy breathing and searching eyes, I change tack. "What do you mean when you say you don't alter yourself? Everyone has to bend in life, don't you think?" He takes one thoughtful step back. I move forward, ready to walk down the hall and get on with my day. But he reaches up to grasp the frame of the door and I barely manage to stop myself from barreling into him.

We're less than an inch apart now and I know I should step back, or tell him to move, but I don't.

Add thickly veined, muscled forearms to the list of things that make my knees weak. I beg his sweater to ride up and expose an inch of torso. I'd settle for half an inch, but it stays put. I'm going to need Post-its all over my house.

"I live on a boat instead of a glass house of their choosing. My dad still hates that I don't wear suits to work. I run the company—what falls under my jurisdiction—the way I want. I keep my head down. I get the work done. I've got my own set of rules and my own goals."

The way he says it makes me wonder how much these rules apply to his personal life. He doesn't socialize with anyone in the store, and I understand that as a future owner. But I've seen him a few times with B-list celebrities, local gossip blogs... He doesn't keep girlfriends long. How lonely he must be.

"Maybe that's why the employees..." I was going to say *don't like you*, but I lose the nerve.

He guesses anyway and leans into me, letting his arms pull and stretch against the doorway. "Say it."

It's a mystery why I don't just back the hell up. Instead, I welcome him into my personal space, give him my full consent, and dare him closer, all the while his hands remain secured to the door frame, nowhere near touching me. It's a game of cat and mouse that neither of us is going to admit we're playing.

Audibly, I gulp into the thin air between us.

"I'm not here to make friends, Holly." His breath is warm and minty on my face—the rest of him smells like water and wind. "I'm here to work. This company will be my legacy, and while George runs off to find himself and pinch-hit for Hawaii, I'm here. Left holding up the corporate umbrella and trying to keep it from blowing out in the shitstorm we're in."

He pushes away, into the hall until his back is against the wall, his arms crossed defensively. "I don't have time to play games."

He's mad. Did I push? Is that breaking a rule? It's all I can do not to follow him, not to take steps into his personal space when I find myself suddenly and unbearably cold.

"I'll see you downstairs." I start past him instead, unsure of what just happened, what's going on between us, or what's going on inside me. I'll admit I'm out of my depth when it comes to the emotional turmoil I can read in his eyes.

But I stop short and turn to face him one last time. "You're supposed to be training me in Sales, but the past week I've seen you struggle in the art of Customer Service, which is a big part of Sales. I think I've had enough of your guidance." Maybe this little game we're playing needs to end. We've both got a lot to learn, but I'm not so sure we're meant to teach each other.

"I've built Sales on the floor. Added items from other departments that the customer needed and would have had to find on their own. I save them time, which is a commodity harder to come by than money."

"Yeah, but bullying someone into buying something—"

"I'm not a bully."

"You're right, you're not. But you never have a smile, and you never say what the customer wants to hear. Icing someone into buying a pair of shoes, making it clear that you don't have more than five minutes for them is not my way. People respect your taste and quick work, but you're"—I'm just going to say it, and he knows I'm going to say it, he *wants* me to say it as he follows me down the hall—"kinda mean."

He falters and hits the wall just before we round a corner that will dump us onto the third floor near Lingerie. Clutching his heart, pulling his glasses from his face, and wiping nonexistent tears from his eyes he mock-wails, "They think I'm mean?"

A burst of laughter pops out of me as his emotional range runs full circle back around to playful. The tension between us simmering. "Were you a theater kid?" I ask. I don't know why I'm so happy to see a smile back on his face.

"How did you know? They hounded me every year to play lacrosse but I got the lead in *Fiddler* and was like, let me entertain you, boys!"

"Figures. All I'm saying is, you could try to be a little nicer. *Act*, if you have to." It's hard to get the words out with a straight face. Unfortunately, I'm getting to know Declan and he's not who I thought he was going to be.

I'm starting to suspect his rough exterior is all a ruse, hiding a truly nerdy and sensitive human with a quirky sense of humor.

"Okay, I'll try to be *nice*." His eyes hold mine and I'm surprised he's taking me seriously. "But you think you don't need my training? No mountain this girl can't climb! No dragon she can't slay!" Gone is the moment of softness and clarity. He's lost his mind again, he thinks he's still onstage. "You know a lot about the store, Holly, but—"

"I've picked up enough." For the life of me, I don't know why I'm laughing with him. "Consider me a fully trained saleswoman," I say, motioning to myself and giving him my Customer Service smile.

He gives me a large puppy grin in return, full of white teeth. "True, you're good. But I could make you better."

There's heat in his eyes that makes me uncomfortable but kinda in a good way. I don't know what to do with the feeling in the pit of my stomach so I half-heartedly slap him in the chest, letting my hand linger about three seconds too long as I say, "You're supposed to say I'm amazing. No one is better than me."

We are grade schoolers right now, how long and how many times can I get away with touching him? How many innuendo-heavy statements is he going to make? How many ways will we equally crowd each other's space.

This is so weird.

He doesn't hesitate. "You are fucking amazing. I've always known that."

Zing! That one hit me right in my center.

"That's why you've plagued me for years in this store?" I narrow my eyes at him, "Because you think I'm so *great*?"

We've just come to the end of the hallway when he spins toward me, takes one determined step, and backs me into a wall covered in company rhetoric posters.

We freeze, our breaths catching at the same time. He comes so close I think he's going to touch his nose to mine.

Where has all this hating gotten us? I've forgotten who I thought he was. When did sparring turn to tension-filled canoodling? When did I start thinking of him as tough on the outside but with a nerdy gooey center on the inside?

"That's exactly why."

"You think I'm great?"

"Amazing," he breathes. "Brilliant. Strong. Fascinating." His gaze holds mine and I try to ask him *why? How?*

How does he feel this way, after all this time? Why did he let me believe he thought the exact opposite for so many years?

"But you still think I need you?" is all I can manage to get out.

"One can hope…"

I gulp as his fingers start to reach for mine. Our knuckles brush and I wonder, if someone walked down the hall and discovered us all pressed against each other like this, what would we say? What would it mean?

I don't know what to do, where to put the unspoken words moving between us as his gaze holds mine, so I say, "You're so weird," and slip past him, pushing myself down the hall on weak knees.

"None of my friends would argue with that," he calls after me.

CHAPTER
Ten

ON THE FLOOR OF DESIGNER, I key my employee number into sales mode with sweaty palms, ready to start my Friday and praying I can ring enough sales to help the stylist team hit our weekly goal. Declan's words in the hallway, the brush of his skin, and all his pheromones weigh heavily on me.

And I told him I didn't need any more training! Not because it's true but because I had to get out of his vicinity. How am I supposed to set up an actual appointment? I forgot that little detail, didn't I?

Focus, Stewart!

I'll figure it out, but it's daunting to have only two weeks to sell enough to pay my bills via commission. Sometimes, one employee is helping three customers at a time and it's an intricate show of smoke and mirrors as they make each customer feel special, but that's how you set sales records. If you're not multitasking and moving quickly, losing one sale for the day could be catastrophic for your numbers and your paycheck.

From the corner of my eye, I catch Declan coming down the escalator to the second floor just as I'm digging my dressing room key from my pocket. These things are surprisingly hard to hold on to and I've added mine to a silver bangle bracelet so I can slide it on my wrist and hopefully not lose it. It takes only once to be stuck at a locked door with twenty pounds of clothing in one hand and the other digging in your pockets for the key needed to open the door as an executive shopping on her lunch break glares at you and checks her watch.

He sidles up to me as if we're buddies, as if nothing happened between us moments ago in the hall. As if he didn't just tell me I was *amazing, brilliant, strong, and fascinating.*

Maybe he was just taking what I said about being nicer to heart.

"Last day of training, and you can be rid of me. Deal?" he says.

I try to read his body language. No longer challenging and secretive, now open and bright. "Then I get my silence, bought and paid for? You're trained in the office. I've walked you through most the procedures."

His face falls as he inhales deeply, breathing through his nose. His jaw ticks.

"And a spot in Hawaii," I add. I haven't decided if I really want it. Do I want to be so far from Gran? But I want the option on the table. "If I can rent out Gran's place?"

"It hurts that you're so desperate to be rid of me," he mocks. He looks away as he says, "Deal."

"Look at you putting others before yourself."

"Look at you noticing," he fires back. Something in the slight mist in his eyes causes me to pause.

We shake, our new custom, but this time he holds my hand. His rough skin grasps mine until I pull away. I can't let this dissolve into another hallway moment, whatever that was.

"Stop posturing, you can barely stand one week with me, either," I say awkwardly, shaking off the feeling that he wanted to hold my hand longer.

"Not true, but I've learned all I can about toner and how to stock the stockroom. You must let me wage the war of the back office on my own now."

"You're letting me off the hook easy." It's surprising—so much so that I wonder if I wanted him to.

"I want you down here selling your little heart out every spare moment of the day. It's where I need you."

"Not sure you're ready to take on balancing that safe every morning but"—I pat him lightly on a rock-solid shoulder—"remember, honey, make good decisions. Don't lose your temper."

"I assure you, darling, the best decisions look like bad ones at first. And you can trust me with the money bags."

"Spoken like true, high-born male privilege."

He shifts uncomfortably and looks out toward the store that's barely showing any foot traffic. "Believe me, I'm not the golden son at any of my family gatherings, and I don't reap the rewards either. You ever see me take off on the company jet? I care more about my carbon footprint than that." He pauses. "Got any appointments yet?"

"No." I know I'm supposed to turn the customers I help into future appointments, that way Lorden's has them on the hook to return again before they even walk out the door, but it's hard. It's like being single at a bar and dropping pathetic pickup lines. *Would you like to schedule an appointment to see me again? Why? Oh, because I can make your shopping experience more streamlined and save you time, I'm very helpful, lots of experience. No time to talk now? You don't use the calendar in your phone? Running late for a meeting? Okay, I understand...*

You're just not that into me.

"Come on, Stewart, you're going to have to put yourself out there and seal the deal sooner or later. It's easy, you just—"

"I know how to seal the deal."

"Is that so?"

"Yes, you may be surprised to know I've had my fair share of people fall in love with me. I can schmooze when I want to."

He stills. "Who's talking about falling in love?"

Horror rolls through me from my toes up. I was bantering, we were bantering, *right*?

I shrug and pray he lets it drop.

"This is different. Your nice-girl attitude is not going to cut it on the floor. You've got to be tough." He pushes on when I open my mouth to protest. "Don't take it as a criticism. That's not how I mean it, you're not a pushover. I'm well aware, Stewart. But I watched Lauren steal a sale right out from under you yesterday. I'll speak to Dorian—"

"Don't you dare. The last thing I need is for the store manager to come to my rescue." But he's right, I did lose that sale. And I know exactly what it means to my paycheck.

Dorian is the manager of the designer department and he has one employee under him, Lauren. They are best friends, they go out together every night, and rehash drunken stories within earshot every morning just to rub it in. *You aren't one of us!* Got it.

But if Declan starts complaining about Lauren stealing sales, it's like stamping *Lauren's reason for living is to make Holly miserable* on my forehead.

"Excuse me, I'm your mentor," he mocks. "I've taught you everything you know. And I'm one of *them,* I'm not George the *boss.* I'm Dec the employee. They'll listen to me without getting put out—"

"Is that what you think?" I laugh while sorting through a drawer of pens and tags. He hands me the tagging gun I was looking for and then I tidy up the cash wrap in case we have a rush later this afternoon.

"Yeah. I thought about what you said." He holds the seam of a t-shirt taut so I can easily pop the tag in place. We move in unison, making our way through the pile. "Employees don't think I'm *mean.* They just consider me one of them, on their level. That's why they don't pretend to like me, I'm—"

"Stop." I turn and quite literally without thinking, press the palm of my hand into his very hard pectoral.

We make eye contact. *This is the second time you've touched me in under an hour,* his gaze says.

I know, don't make it weird.

"Don't talk yourself into believing that for one more minute," I sputter. "You're a Lorden. You're Harry Styles in a Ralph Lauren ad. You're a prince. And we all know it."

His gaze softens and I don't like it. Not one little bit. "I've got a hunch—" I say, before I can stop myself.

"Oh geez," he mocks, as if we're two kids embarking on a fantastical quest. "Alright, I'll bite. Out with it." He looks down at my hand, still firmly planted on his chest.

What has gotten into me? Where is this boldness with him coming from? "Maybe you were pretending this whole time not to like me." *Amazing, brilliant, strong, fascinating.*

"Maybe," he says, stoic and still. He's no longer kidding around and it catches me off guard.

Hastily, I remove my hand. I have to remember I'm not talking to Lenny, even though it kinda feels that way. As if I'm talking to a good friend. Len's been gone all week—I miss him, that's all. That doesn't make Declan and me friends.

"You should go lie down, you're sick. Delusional. You must have a fever," I say, finding a stack of denim and pulling the trigger on the tagging gun, *pop!*

Am I right? Could I be right? There's no way...

"I've got a hunch too, Stewart," he says, voice gravelly. "Maybe you were in love with the wrong brother all along. Ever think of—"

"What?" I drop the gun and it clatters on the faux marble countertop.

"I have."

My heart stops when I manage to look at him. We don't speak. We just stare until he breaks the silence and releases the tension I was about to choke on. "I'm not George, Holly. He's the prince, and for a long time that's what you wanted."

Those words hang heavily between us as I go back to tagging. There's no way I can unpack everything he's saying on the sales floor. Did someone slip him a truth serum in his coffee this morning? What the hell?

He must notice my reluctance, my shutting down and focusing on the task in front of me because I *cannot* look at him. His tone shifts to a mock humor that sounds all wrong, like a lie. "But I'm an everyman." He waves his arm all Shakespearian.

He's making a joke again. Was it all a joke? Or is that what he wants me to believe? Does he already regret what he said? "My head is spinning." I didn't mean to say that out loud.

"Relax, Stewart. I'm messing with you. I'm just another employee. Don't mind me," he goes on, but there's no feeling behind his words. They're hollow and hurt.

Have I hurt his feelings? Declan Lorden? I only just realized he *had* feelings.

It's so confusing, this back-and-forth he's playing at. Saying one thing then switching to another—I can't keep up. There are still parts of my body I can't feel. Why would he say I was in love with the wrong brother? Declan and I hate each other. To insinuate anything different is downright distressing.

Amazing, brilliant, strong, fascinating.

I shake my head at him and play along. "An everyman who didn't know where the buzzer was to open the door for deliveries on the dock? You thought you knew it all. Admit it, you were *wrong.*" He was a chicken with his head cut off when he realized merchandise didn't *disaparate* into the store. He thought he knew everything about how this place functioned, was so smug for all those years.

"That buzzer is hidden as if it's a trick door in a spy novel. Who could guess it's under the operator's desk!"

Something in the air crackles. I think a vent just kicked on overhead because I suddenly have goose bumps. "All I'm saying is, you're trying to make me a shark. I'm not a shark, Declan."

"And all I'm saying is, you have to go after what you want, Holly."

"Fine, but I'm going to do it my way. Deal?" I stick out my hand—*yes, I'm using it as an excuse to touch him again!* It's as if I'm seeing him in a new light, all those years he poked at me, was he actually trying to help? But at that moment, the most terrifying thing happens. Mrs. Smith walks into our department.

"Deal. Go get 'em, and do it your way." He nods his head ever so slightly toward Mrs. Smith.

"I can't take her. You can't be serious. You're the shark, you take her!" I grab his forearm, all hard and muscled with a dusting of soft hair.

He grabs both my arms, pulling me close and so we're holding each other in some sort of trust hold he probably learned at an Ivy League leaders retreat. It's so much worse than when I felt him up a moment ago. His grip on me is making me tremble. The buzz from his fingertips on the backs of my arms causes an unexpected jolt to run through me, all hot liquid and shivers.

He nods again toward the woman who shall not be named. Truly, I don't actually know her real name. Everyone has taken to calling her Mrs. Smith, in part because there's a rumor that the first employee she worked with couldn't pronounce her last name correctly so she demanded he stop dribbling and just call her Mrs. Smith. Second, because she is just that damn rich. She can assume an alias and Lorden's is happy to bill whatever name she likes.

"You can do this," he whispers fervently. So she doesn't hear? Or because this is the most heartening moment of my life, someone who believes in me cheering me on for only my ears to hear? "If you need me, I'll be right here."

Is he shaking? Nervous for me?

Watching their favorite new reality show unfold, Dorian and Lauren space hangers in the back corner of the department.

They both snicker and take steps back as if to say, *the floor is yours—go hang yourself and let this Hunger Games trial be done with.*

No salesperson worth their salt on commission would walk away from the kind of sales this woman racks up—except this woman is that petrifying. Money can't compare to the force of her glare if you get something wrong. I've seen it myself.

But fine, I can do this. I've been around her before, like a fly on the wall bagging, or ringing, or bringing coffee while she shopped. Who knows why she's alone now, without Jenny or another salesperson chained to her hip, but I don't need a crystal ball to know she wants something.

The General's words ring loudly in my ear with an accompanying image of little ballerina Holly, coming home from not snagging Clara in *The Nutcracker*. *Pull yourself up by the bootstraps, use what you've learned, and try harder next time.*

"She's going to eat her alive." It's a barely repressed giggle from Dorian, diamond studs twinkling in his ears—and he's the nice one in this department.

Lauren fakes shielding her eyes, her shaggy blond hair shining, but peeks through the cracks as if to watch a slow-motion car crash.

Declan cranes his neck, glaring at both of them. They snap to attention for all of two seconds, then fall into sputters again.

After rolling my eyes at all of them, I march up to Mrs. Smith with my first day of school smile, and say all too brightly, "Good morning!"

She's startled from looking at a camo anorak covered in patches and studs, cut roughly at the waist leaving shreds of fabric dangling. It's a little tacky—even designers can take wrong turns while trying to please the masses. I'm surprised to see her holding it with a fifteen-hundred-dollar tag dangling from the cuff.

Generally, she has impeccable taste. But when she holds it up to me with a question in her eyes I can't help myself, I can't lie to her no matter how much I want to shove a huge sale in everyone's face. I crinkle my nose as if I've smelled food that's turned, she gets the message, and, while I'm afraid I've pissed her off, she replaces the hanger with a clink.

The woman is a vision in cream, bright silver hair styled away from her face contrasting sharply with black skin. "Who are you?"

"Holly Stewart, Mrs. Smith. Can I call Jenny for you?"

"I'd like Lenny Lorden."

"I'm sorry, he's not in. I can page Jenny, or maybe Dorian can pull some things? What brings you in today?"

She doesn't deign to respond, just begins perusing the department, so I hover-follow.

There has to be a reason she's here with no appointment. Once Lorden's realized when she worked with someone she was familiar with, someone who could suss out her needs before she could and sold her everything from her husband's underwear to squishy neon dinosaur toys for her grandsons' Easter baskets, her spend in the store increased by 35 percent—in layman's terms, a shit ton to an extreme shit ton. Thus, *the chosen ones* were assembled and are out to get into every Lorden's customer's wallet and do the same.

The stylist program was born and went nationwide just in time to keep up with the blogger boom and the influencer age that came soon after. They want to sell you kitchen gadgets, baby gifts, a diamond ring for your engagement (they'll stealthily get ahold of your intended to sell the rock while sipping a glass of scotch on the rocks just as the store is closing so it feels personal and the only customer Lorden's has) and when *your* baby comes along don't worry! They sell top-of-the-line strollers as well.

I turn and watch Declan, Dorian, and Lauren shrink from the floor. They fall into the back room leaving me alone in the jungle to fend for myself.

Traitors!

"Would you like me to page Jenny?" I try again. "Can I take your purse so you've got two hands to peruse?"

"No, no. She's not expecting me today and, in her condition, I'd hate to send her into early labor. That girl is wound tighter than my granny used to tie my braids." This is surprisingly thoughtful for a woman who once called Louie Lorden to open Pine Street at 3:00 a.m. because she was *desperate for a cup of corn chowder, darling.*

"Oh, my gran too. She'd pull my hair into a ponytail so tight I could feel my eyes pull around to the back of my head."

"Yes, that's exactly the feeling." She looks me over more closely now, working through a clearly scant list of reasons to give me a chance. Her glance moves up and down my clothing, less than impressed.

"I need something for next Thursday night. Cocktails and an auction for the boys' school."

I'm not positive, but I think she's talking about her grandsons who go to Vohs Academy where the Lorden kids went. High-end, top-notch, preppy, preppy, preppy little prepsters in blue blazers with brass buttons.

"We have new pieces in from Akris Punto, and St. John—"

"St.-St. John?" she gasps.

I put the hanger I was about to pull from a dark wood armoire, meant to look like it was in a French boudoir instead of a department store, back.

"No St. John for you?"

She arches one steely gray eyebrow though the rest of her face is still supple and youthful, beautiful. "It's Holly, right?"

"Yes, ma'am."

"Go dig my file out from under the nest Jenny's sitting on. I will call you and let you know when I'm coming back. And, Holly—"

"Yes, ma'am?"

"I want you, not Mrs. Yoo. You'd better pull a good room. None of that power clashing, Jenna Lyons J. Crew crap circa 2010. She got the ax for that, you know."

I've never pulled a room. I've never had an actual appointment. I've heard of Jenna Lyons, and I know J. Crew had a solid moment in the early aughts that eventually got so knocked off by generic bloggers and poorly executed celebrity brands it became boring, but...I'm *so* swimming in the deep end with no floaties right now.

"I don't actually have any customers yet, maybe you should—"

She holds a diamond-encrusted hand up to stop me, cream nails and sparkles pop bright against her rich skin. "Yes, I see your training has been negligible. What is happening to this store? First, I am not a customer, I'm a client. Second, this is not a purse, it's a handbag crafted in Italy." She holds the handbag up so I can have an optimal look. "Third, I don't care what you have or haven't done for anyone other than myself. Give me your card." She snaps. Not her words, she snaps her fingers. She hasn't got all day, *darling*.

"My—"

Declan appears at my side. So close his bicep presses into my shoulder. I demand myself not to lean into him for literal support in this moment. "Ms. Stewart's stylist cards came in just this morning," he says, proudly handing a business card with gold-embossed writing to Mrs. Smith who snatches it quick like one of those frogs with sticky slap-tongues.

"Ah, Mr. Lorden. Nice seeing you. I heard you're taking the helm for your brother, who escaped to finer shores?"

"*Please.*" He uses all the syrupy sweet emphasis he can and forces the widest smile I've seen his mouth produce to date, and I know, *I know*, it's for me and not for her. "Let us know how we can accommodate you further. Anything for you, Mrs. Smith, as always. We may have had a change in management on Pine Street, but nothing will change in regard to our service."

"I hope not." She eyes my card and pulls a patent leather Chanel bifold from her hunter green Birkin bag. I know my designers, from working here but also because I've seen every episode of *Sex and the*

City. "First run, first edition. I'm honored." It's snark, it's a challenge, and she's picked the right day to throw down that gauntlet.

Maybe I haven't learned to pull for an appointment yet, but when someone immediately assumes I'll fail there's nothing I like better than proving them wrong.

"When you're ready to schedule—"

"I will let you know when I'm coming—*answer my call.*" She snaps her purse—handbag, I stand corrected, it does sound nicer—closed.

Once she's gone, I turn to Declan and punch him on the shoulder. "Look at you, Mr. Charming, Mr. Customer Service. *Anything* for you, Mrs. Smith, *Anything…*" Seems to me Declan Lorden can be damn nice when he wants to be. What a turn of events. He'll alter, he'll bend, he just doesn't want anyone to know for some reason.

"Shuddup."

Despite myself and my impending doom, I smile.

"But we could have used that sale," he adds, walking toward the back room. "I saw her eyeing the camo."

From somewhere behind a rack of clothing I hear Dorian, "He's right—our department is down 50 percent for the quarter."

I hear him, I should care too, but I can't seem to take my eyes off the broad back of Declan Lorden.

CHAPTER
Eleven

I DID my best and sold over two thousand dollars for the afternoon in Designer. I'll call that a win, and Dorian seemed happy. Not a bad way to kick off the weekend, but before leaving the office, I text my long-lost buddy, Len. I haven't seen him and he hasn't been in the store since Monday, when he left to help David.

> **ME**
>
> I'm about to teleport back in time

Declan's sitting at George's desk opposite mine, banging away angrily at his keyboard.

> **LENNY**
>
> Jenny's that bad?

> **ME**
>
> Actually, not at all. Heading home for the night and going to hunt in the attic at Gran's. Supposedly there's fashion treasure hidden up there.

LENNY

> Angel and Molly give you shit about dress
> code?

ME

Nah. I need to find a signature style. I think I
have an appointment with Mrs. Smith, but I
don't know when.

LENNY

> WHY ARE YOU TAKING MRS SMITH??? I
> should be back tomorrow. Do you know the
> Star Trek wave?

ME

Long story. Thanks for the vote of confidence.
Wave?????

LENNY

> There should be an emoji. Live long and
> prosper.

ME

Everything okay with you? How's David?

LENNY

> Recovering, but it got pretty bad for a second.
> We're okay. Home for a shower now, then
> we've got an exit meeting with his doctor.
> There's a lot to do for home recovery. Cancer
> is a bitch.

Cancer. The pain that sparks in my chest with the mere word is one
I haven't let myself feel in a very long time.

There are bubbles, but then he doesn't say more. He wants to say
sorry but doesn't know how. Lung cancer ended my father's life. I dig
the palm of my hand into the bone over my heart and glance at Declan
who's still scowling at his computer screen. He looks up abruptly,
reads my face, and I watch *horrified* as concern washes over him.

How can he read me so quickly? Hastily, I look back at my desk
and fumble papers like a broadcaster posturing for the credits.

"Everything OK?"

"Fine." It's hard to shake off the pain that I've done my best to work through over the years. It makes me worry for my friend, if he might have to go through the same anguish I did. I've never heard Lenny talk this way about someone. It happened so fast—last I knew David was just a biscuit Lenny wanted to bite.

> ME
> I want to meet him.

> LENNY
> I'd like that. Love you, Holly dolly.

I roll my eyes at George's nickname for me and glance again at Declan. My, how quickly things change. Now, Lenny's the one obviously madly in love, and I'm...I'm sitting across from an entirely different Lorden brother, one I thought I hated but turns out I'm not sure. I don't even know him. I thought I knew George, but I didn't really know him either. And for some reason, it's as if Declan cracked right open for me the second his brother left; for better or worse, showing all his bruises and oddities—sweet ones I never knew were in him.

My phone buzzes, a distraction from wherever my mind was going.

> LENNY
> HELLO!!!!!

> ME
> (Eye roll emoji) Love you too.

My tote bag is sitting like an open-mouthed fish at my feet. I absently toss in my phone and keys, and take a last look at Declan, willing him to look back at me. He doesn't, just chews that fat bottom lip, breathing steadily through his nose, then moving on to an equally plump upper lip with a well-defined Cupid's bow. The cosmetics department would die to line those lips.

"Night, then," I say, all too chipper.

"You sure you're alright?" he asks without glancing up.

"Oh yeah, tired. Wild day."

"You'll let me know if you need anything?"

"Sure." My voice wobbles because I'm not used to this kind of treatment from him.

"OK, night," he mumbles. Half the time I can't shake the kid, but when I want his attention…zero. Figures.

Bundled in a vintage double-breasted camel coat, which will be chic until the end of time, with bag over shoulder, I push out the door, barely able to talk myself out of looking back like a brand-new junkie.

On the way home I stop for takeout, my favorite chicken parm from Spinasse is calling my name. I've worked up a serious appetite after running around the store all week and the way my sales are going I think I can afford the splurge.

My couch is a cloud I sink into with a plate of parm that could feed a family of five. There is zero shame in my game as I shovel, chew, shovel, chew until I'm in a happy little cocoon of carbs. I've finished the first season of the fantasy series I love and I Google around a bit on my laptop after opening a bottle of wine to see how long I have to wait for more.

When my eyes start to cross from reading online, the worry of how I'm going to handle Mrs. Smith starts to creep in. Why does she want me? It's certainly not my personal style that's made her want me like Beyoncé wants J.

And it's time I fix that. Even Declan has a look.

I wander around the house, stemless glass of red in hand, and look up at the ceilings. The attic has to be in the ceiling somewhere, right? Gran's little cottage is a two-bedroom, one hers, one mine, and I've never seen an attic door or cubbyhole in either. I've scoured her closet already just to double-check. It's full of muumuus and mothballs but no hidey-hole or trapdoor in a wardrobe to Narnia.

Finally, I try my bathroom in the hall. And there it is, a square in the ceiling that looks like if I push hard enough, it'll open like the vortex to fashion-land I'm hoping for. Gran has always been a clotheshorse, and even the General has a shopping habit that involves every white blouse on the planet. I'm hoping there's pure gold up there.

After hauling a small stepladder in from the kitchen, I wobble on pink tile floors, climb, brace my arms, and push hard on a square of plywood. It pops easily, and I hoist myself with a grunt—earning scrapes on both elbows—through the looking glass.

Dark, stinky air greets me. *There's a dead something up here for sure.* I find a light bulb string and pull.

Now, I can't blame Gran because she's basically a hundred and who knows the last time she was up here, but it is pigpen-disgusting. The dust is so thick it's become sticky. I wish I'd thought to cover my mouth with something, I can barely breathe. There's not much of a floor, just rafters and pink cotton-candy insulation. Thankfully, the attic elves have smiled upon me and there's a box within reach labeled *Vintage Treasures.* God bless the women in my family and our orderly tendencies.

I pull it down, refill my glass, and prepare myself for moth-eaten disappointments. Isn't that why people pay to preserve wedding gowns? Clothes don't keep in cardboard. Maybe I'll find some more good jewelry.

But I'm shocked as I pull dress after dress (handmade from patterns probably by Gran herself when she was my age). One looks like it may have been for a high school formal, all baby blue tulle and soft sweetheart neckline with stitches you just don't find in ready-to-wear anymore. Then it turns into T-shirts packed in yellowed tissue—not just any T-shirts, badass band T-shirts with graphics and appliques. Then, pause for every designer-loving fashion addict to squeal like a piglet, labels.

Vintage DVF wrap dresses wink at me, Marc Jacobs jeans that must have been part of his first line say, *hello there!* This stuff is my moms, I realize. Perry Ellis sweaters, Prada prints, Veronica Beard blazers from the early 2000s…a Chanel scarf. A boatload of Calvin Klein workwear. Before I know it, my little girl bedroom is covered with decades of fashion; a tour of both my grandmother's and my mother's coming-of-age styles. My heart swells.

This will be the bedrock of my signature style. Old stuff. Mom's stuff. Gran's stuff. And with a twist or two and a boatload of Febreze, I'll make it mine.

Just like that I know I'm going to make it through the next few months.

I'm not a shark, I think trying on blouses, blazers, and dress after dress and adding my lion ring for effect. *I am a lion!*

Watch out, Mrs. Smith, I will show you what service with a smile is. Don't worry about your numbers, Dorian, I got you. Jenny Yoo, go have that beautiful baby, I'll sell enough to make the team quota one-handed. Oh, and Declan, dear, grumpy, hard-shelled with the gooey center of a nasty Cadbury Egg, Declan, I will save your company before I find a job with a title that the General would be proud of. And maybe before that, I'll treat myself to a year in Hawaii.

Damn. When they say dress for success, they're not kidding. I got all that inspiration from a wrap dress and a lion ring! I resist the urge to call the General and demand she put me through to the presidential stylist to share my epiphany.

The euphoric adrenaline is short-lived though, which is probably what keeps everyone coming back day after day to Lordens for retail therapy. I dig through my bag for my stylist phone. If I want to save the day like a modern female badass in Ganni boots, I should probably start with answering when my one and only mega-client calls.

Nothing.

I know I threw it in my bag. I dig again.

Still, nothing.

I run outside and search my car, thinking it probably fell out.

Nada.

Oh. My. God. It must be at work. When am I going to learn not to dump my bag on the floor like a hobo and instead rest it gently on the back of my chair like any self-respecting professional?

Normally, I wouldn't sweat it. I can literally get it in—I check my watch and the Scotch tape is starting to brown—ten hours when LP opens the employee doors at eight.

But in my gut, I know if I miss Mrs. Smith, I'm dead in the water. There will be nothing Lenny, Declan, George, or even Mira can do to save me. I can kiss a rec to Hawaii from *anyone* named Lorden goodbye. If I mess up with her, my goose is cooked. And so is Declan's.

I scramble to my laptop and silence the rom-com I had put on as background noise. I need to think.

I'll email Declan and pray he's checking his work email on a Friday night. He's kinda nerdy, so he might be.

DeclanLorden@lordens.com

I can't find my phone and if Mrs. Smith calls, I'm toast. Can you meet me at the office?

Sorry, Holly.

I refresh ten seconds after I hit Send, as if it's humanly possible for him to receive, read, and respond that quickly.

For another ten minutes, I pace, refresh, and pace. I can't even drink the tension away because I'm going to have to drive, aren't I? Damn it, Holly. The General's voice demanding, *Screw your head on straight,* rings in my ears. All the childhood mistakes I've made seem to wash over me in one large debilitating tidal wave of emotion.

CHAPTER
Twelve

LENNY IS MY FIRST THOUGHT, but he's in the hospital getting doctors' orders on how to care for his sick boyfriend. I cannot bother him with this, I will not.

That leaves… I could drive to Declan's house and beg his mercy. But I can't do that. He'll think I'm insane, and he's probably out on a Friday night with some billionaire's daughter anyway.

But I'm going to chance it and try because there's no other choice, is there? Why did I have to be so know-it-all today about him learning Customer Service and how to be nice?

Let's see if he thinks I'm so great when I crash his Friday-night.

In a tizzy, and still in an emerald green peacock-print wrap dress, I jump into a pair of Uggs. This is not a well-thought-out plan because it's still cold out, but there's just no time for pants.

I try desperately to drive while my lips chatter. My heart is pounding like one of those giant drums in a marching band. I'm so screwed if she's already called or texted and I've failed to reply.

Whipping through the gates of the mansion I drive around the Trevi Fountain and slam on my breaks. My tires slide in the gravel.

Hundreds of motion sensors spotlight my run around the side of the house. No way I'm ringing the bell at eleven at night to risk waking Louie or Mira. Thankfully, Declan lives on a boat.

I scamper down their lawn, past the bocce ball court, the putting green, and down another set of stone steps until I'm at the edge of the lake where the dock begins. It's colder on the water and I hug my arms against my middle to block a breeze.

It smells like him here, all water and outdoors.

The soles of my Uggs slap on the wooden planks of the dock and echo across the water until I'm standing in front of his sleek sailboat.

It's even bigger up close and has a shine in the moonlight.

"Declan," I whisper. "It's me, Holly."

The boat rocks in its slip. Water slaps the hull. There's no trace of Declan.

Living in Seattle, I've had my fair share of boating encounters. A few kids from my high school had parents who enjoyed the lifestyle and belonged to the marina in Lakewood. Unfortunately, this doesn't mean I know how to board one without being led by the hand.

I walk the length of the boat a few times, rubbing my hands together for warmth. I'll be happy when spring finally sprungs already.

"Declan Lorden!" I whisper-yell. But still nothing.

Taking my life in my own hands, I get a running start and leap like an untrained ballerina. My wrap dress splits up my thighs as I vault to the back deck, land with a loud thump, and scramble over a perfectly polished chrome railing to an interior deck made of spotless teak. There's not a whole lot of room on the sailboat, even though this is a big one. I follow naked masts with my eyes all the way up to the starlit sky as I try to assimilate to the gentle rocking of the hull. What would it be like to live out here? My gaze drifts to the mansion. How bad must it be for him in there?

Double doors directly in front of me burst open, making me scream, "Ahhh!"

Declan appears, in gray sweatpants, a backward cap, and a tank top with a picture of Baby Yoda. A baseball bat is poised overhead.

"What the... What the *hell*, Holly?" His chest moves rapidly up and down as he pants and thick collarbones pop against cords straining in his neck. His eyes dart around the boat. His biceps flex as he grips the bat.

"I'm sorry, I'm sorry!" I hold my hands up like the intruder I am. "I left my phone at the office. I emailed you!" His gaze moves down my body as he registers there's no ski mask and he knows me. Fiery eyes snag on my bare legs.

The wrap dress is slit almost to my hip. I tug it quickly together and tighten the belt.

"You're going to catch your death of cold. I don't usually check my work email on Friday nights at 11:00 p.m.," he grumbles. "Are you drunk?"

"No! Sorry. I didn't know what to do."

"Wait ten hours and get your phone in the morning."

"Mrs. Smith might call or text," I plead, willing him to understand why my interrupting him is absolutely necessary. "She's done it before to ask the store to be opened early. I didn't want to risk pissing off your biggest client."

"Oh."

Despite the closed doors behind him, I hear voices on the inside of the boat. He takes a step back. "Can't lose Mrs. Smith when the chips are down, can we?"

My chest burns with anxiety as I take a step closer. It's as if I'm mad he's got people over and didn't invite me. Didn't I know he'd be on a date or something? As if I'd needed to prepare myself for the letdown... *Ridiculous.* My feelings cannot be hurt right now, it must be my nerves. "No, actually, we can't. You're not alone, are you?"

"Uh..."

More voices, a wild bunch judging by the sounds of it, probably the world's tiniest game of beer pong in the galley. He must see my face twist into some form of emotion I refuse to name. "Holly, wait—"

"I'll go. I just—can I have your code? To the office? I've got my employee code to open the employee door, but I know it won't let me in before eight."

"Hold on, I'll come with you. Let me grab a coat." He sets the bat to the side and tosses his hat on a nearby bench. He's going to try to squeeze through the doors without opening them wide enough for me to see in.

What is he hiding in there? A girlfriend? Probably a socialite with privacy issues... "No, you've got guests—"

"They'll be fine without me," he says through the crack.

"The hell we will!" A man, short with red hair and *actual elf ears* pushes the doors wide open. "You can't leave us now! Hullo there..." He's wearing a long brown robe and some sort of wood medallion hangs off his neck.

"Damn it, Jeff. I told you to wait for me," Declan says, pulling a fleece over his head.

Elf Ears replies, "But I just rolled a natural twenty!"

"Get your magical warlock ass back to the table and let him be," a girl wearing a white wig says from inside. There are about four other people crammed inside the hull. I crane my neck to take them in, all surrounding a table where they seem to be playing a game but it's not beer pong.

"You're busy, I'll go," I say, eyeing the railing of the boat and wondering if I've got the guts to jump.

Declan's pulled the doors almost closed again, leaving a crack to speak through as he rustles around. "Don't move, Stewart."

"You're busy." I cross my arms. Am I pouting? "I'll figure it out."

"It's just a game, they can wait," he says through the opening before disappearing into the back of the hull.

From the table inside, he gets a load of four-letter words slung at him in return.

"Really, you don't have to come. If you don't trust me with your number, I can—" Now, I'm speaking through a crack, trying to get a peek at anything on the table or see more of his friends.

Declan appears back in the doorway, breathing hard with pink cheeks.

"Let her in," the elf man says.

"Is that the gift card girl?" the wig asks.

"This is a closed group," he huffs at me, squeezing through the doors, keys in hand. I get another eyeful and give everyone a little wave.

"Nice meeting you! Come back, we'll let you in the game!" White Wig shouts.

Declan winces as if embarrassed. "No, you won't." He takes my hand in his. "You should have yelled for me."

"I did." Why won't he introduce me to a room full of people when I was only feet away? So much for blue-blood manners.

"Something could have happened, Holly." He tugs me across the teak and I register the slide and pull of our palms together. He tightens his grip. "What if you'd slipped and smacked your pretty little head and sank to the bottom of the lake? Hmm?"

"Pretty?" I can't help it, the question pops from my mouth as he jumps to the dock and turns back reaching for my hand again.

I give it to him and let him wrap an arm around my waist, lifting me up and over the rail of the boat. I seem to have gone numb all over. My mind simply won't register that Declan Lorden is *holding* me in the moonlight as waves slap against the dock.

But then I make the mistake of looking into his eyes, and I feel everything. All over.

He speaks slowly, his voice just a touch gruff as I slide down his front. "Stubborn. I meant to say stubborn thick little head of yours."

My feet hit solid ground and I'm jolted back to reality. "Okay, but what if—"

"I don't need to hear any more excuses from the mouth of a micro-risk-taker."

"Micro-risk-taker? What does that even mean?" The nerve! If anyone is a risk-taker, it's him. *Hello, living on water!*

"It means you take calculated, informed, thoughtful risks. But risk, nonetheless." He's dragging me back across the dock, up the stairs two at a time, and toward the driveway. "That's what I..." he hesitates, as if catching himself from revealing some deep dark secret, "know about you. We're taking my car."

"I can meet you there."

"Doesn't make sense. Your car is closer to your house here. Don't you live in Capitol Hill?"

"How do you know where I live?"

He shrugs and continues around the side of the house toward a large separate garage, like where Sabrina should be living in an apartment above with her chauffer father.

"I'll be closer to home from Lorden's, so I should just drive."

"It's late, it's dark, and you'd have to backtrack. This way, you just drive straight home after we get back."

It makes no sense that I drive with him, even though yes, in total, I'll be driving fewer miles this way. I'm not going to question him now. He's willing to help me—help himself from losing the largest customer Pine Street has but same difference.

One of six garage doors begins groaning open. A black sporty something that Batman would be proud to parade around town is what I'm ushered toward.

"I don't need you to open my door," I say awkwardly when he walks around to my side.

But he's already behind me and I have a choice to make: turn into him and stand firm on my point that my female hands function or let him reach around me for the handle.

"Thank you," I murmur, unsure why letting him do this small thing for me makes me feel so cared-for, so protected.

In the car we chat, or rather, I chat to avoid uncomfortable silence and my mind wandering toward Mrs. Smith.

"So, how's business?" I wince. The company is struggling, I know that, but I want to know exactly how bad things are because we've got to figure out a way for him to stop chewing those pillow lips.

"Things are tight, that's common knowledge. Have you read the business section lately?" His hand flexes on the steering wheel and he shifts gears between us with the other. The motor grumbles and it's pure personification. What else can this silly, sad, angry boy do with his hands?

Oh. My. God. Holly, stop. I need to download a dating app ASAP, or this is going to be a problem.

"What do your parents say?"

"Dad says if I can't pull Pine Street out of its slump, we have to sell. We won't last the slow hot months of summer to make it to the next holiday rush. Why do you care so much?"

Though I'm used to him being short, his question cuts me a bit more than I expected. "I've put in a lot of time at Lorden's. People don't stay with companies anymore, you know? I was hoping it would pay off."

"Exactly." He eyes me like I'm an alien. "In the time of every man for himself, selling direct online, and four-day work weeks from home. Your hoping isn't going to be enough. This is what I've been tryin got tell you, you've got to look out for yourself. Someone needs to."

"I want to stay loyal to your family. They've done a lot for me and for Gran. She talks about her years at Lorden's like glory days. It may be old fashioned, but that means something." I shrug.

"You talk about loyalty, to what end? Were you going to be George's assistant forever? Or just until he popped the question?"

"No." I bristle. "My goal has always been Corporate."

"For what? You want to sit at a desk all day? That doesn't seem like you."

"Everyone keeps saying that. It's just the obvious goal. My mom said if I was going to stay with Lorden's I should climb the ladder. Corporate, COO or something."

"There are other ways to be successful, Holly. A title isn't everything."

He pulls right up to the curb. When we're at the back doors, he punches his employee number into a keypad and pushes the door open with sweeping arms, as if to say, *after you, princess.*

I take the stairs two by two. At the top, I flick on the halogens in the hallway and race to the office where I dive to the floor of my desk and search on my hands and knees for my phone.

"Victory!" I shout, popping up like a prairie dog. It must have bounced out of my bag, or I'm a really lousy shot, which makes sense because I've never been a sporty spice.

It's still dark in the office, the only light spilling in through the doorway. He's staring at me, leaning against his desk with ankles crossed, arms crossed, and looking like he wants to make a tut-tut sound.

"It must have fallen out of my bag." I check it twice, no email, no text. I'm in the clear. Crisis averted.

"Because you sling it around like it's spelled closed but really it's just a gaping hole doing its best to contain your most valuable possessions."

I stand and come around my desk but at the same moment he decides to march toward me.

The result is me pinned against the piece of commercial furniture. Cold metal bites into my hands as I brace myself.

"You really do need someone looking out for you," he murmurs.

"We can go now," I breathe. But I'm not sure if I want to go, not at all. I'm human, I have desk fantasies like everyone else.

He takes a breath, holds it, and lets it out slowly as I accidentally become mesmerized by his mouth.

"Why did you stay?" he asks lightly. "I-I need to know, Holly." He leans in and everything goes hazy. His nose brushes mine ever so slightly and I barely hold back a whimper. "I thought you'd leave after my brother. It was gutsy, what you did at the holiday party—"

"You saw?" My eyes pull up to meet his.

He nods, a strong determined look on his face. "Did you love him? *Do* you love him?"

This moment has taken an unexpected turn, but he's asking so honestly. There's a tinge of desperation in his voice that makes my heart skip a beat. He's never spoken to me like this, so open and almost needy. "I *thought* I did, yes."

Undeterred, he continues to lean in until I'm almost sitting on my desk, my back arching away from him so our fronts don't touch. Trying to put some distance between us so I can think clearly. "Declan—"

"He was so close to you for so long. Got to sit in this room with you every day. You know, he couldn't let you go. We all told him he needed to promote you, but he… I hated him for it. I love my brother, but I hated that he was holding you back."

"It wasn't like that. I-I think I was holding myself back, if you want me to be honest."

"I can't tell if you're being nobel or just very well adjusted." He takes a step back, then another leaving me instantly cold. "But that makes sense. And I always want you to be honest. You have no idea how important that is to me."

Before I can respond he retreats like a puff of smoke. From the hallway I hear his voice, "Come on, Stewart, we're going to have one quick lesson before we leave."

I balk, ready to tell him we've already completed our bargain, but he adds, "You want to impress Mrs. Smith, right?"

It's hard to recover from his closeness. I'm beginning to crave these odd little moments between us, but I tell myself to pull it together and march down the hall with him. If he can handle whatever this awkward heat is, so can I.

On the second floor, in the last and largest fitting room the designer department has, he teaches me how to pull a room for Mrs. Smith.

"How do you know what she likes?"

"Haven't you realized yet that I pay attention to everything that goes on in this store."

"Need I remind you, All Knowing One, you had no idea how to work the—"

"Yeah, yeah. Okay, you got me—my one weakness is Admin. I don't give a shit about paperwork, so sue me. Thank goodness I have you." He mocks a bow as if I'm a queen on a throne.

I shake off a little shiver that runs through me. "So, what now?"

We've pulled the newest designer shoes in size eight and a half. I had no idea her size was reserved for her when shipments came in on a shelf actually labeled "Mrs. Smith" in the shoe stacks. *Noted.*

"Now, you pull for her cocktail party. Vohs alums are mostly elite Seattle society, so make it tasteful, elegant. I'll give you"—he grabs my wrist and looks at my tragic watch. "Holly, why are you wearing this?"

"So I know what time it is and when I need to administer your meds."

He admonishes me with a half grin. "But... What can it possibly be doing for you other than giving you a rash? Is this Scotch tape?"

I wrench my arm back. I would be embarrassed, but this is Declan, and I don't care what he thinks of me. "My dad gave it to me."

He reaches out, slowly, and inspects the watch when I let him take my arm again. "I'm sorry, it's a great piece. You just need another band. Or it might be time for an upgrade?" His thumb nudges the wad of tape holding my watch together.

"Declan…" He drags the pad of his thumb slowly across my pulse then drops my hand. "Anyway, I'm giving you twenty minutes. Pull three *ensembles*." He employs a horrific French accent that lightens my mood. "And I'll come back and check. And don't forget the surprise and delight."

"Surprise and delight?"

"Didn't Jenny cover that? It's what makes the room special. Think of it like…adding a little piece of yourself. Something that no one else but you would think to do."

"Something special?"

"Don't look at me like that, Stewart," he says. I realize my face must be painted with fear. "I know you're special, you know you're special. All you need to do is be yourself and Mrs. Smith will know you're special too…in a heartbeat."

CHAPTER
Thirteen

Mrs. Smith texts at 6:00 a.m. I've had exactly four hours of sleep when I jolt awake. The tiny jingle bell of my phone signaling I've had communication from the devil herself.

No time to dig through, try on, and de-stink everything from the attic, she wants to see me at eight sharp. I pull on a pair of wide-leg denim trousers, Dolce Vita neon wedges that are *sooooooo* comfortable, and one of Mom's vintage blazers that I Febreze to the point of damp. I sleep-eat breakfast, grab my keys, and head out the door in record time.

The trouble with regulars or VIP customers is they know daily procedure and how to find the loopholes; they know all the cheats. Mrs. Smith knows the store doesn't open until ten. She also knows most of us will be there around eight to stock, steam, tag, fold, and attend department meetings. If she's left standing in front of the entrance, regardless of the time, and no one opens the door for her? Well, then Louie Lorden gets a call and nobody wants that.

I'm greeted in the stylist office by the sound of Jenny's heavy breathing before I see her lightly rubbing her belly and reading reports. Angel and Molly are at their shared desk flipping through planners, simultaneously texting and working on laptops.

Both girls have shiny new manicures, hair that looks photo-shoot ready, and jewelry placed anywhere the body can hold it in the form of gold, silver, rhinestones, and pearls. Maybe my natural lean toward quirky minimalist does help me stand out in my own interesting way. But where do they find the time to make themselves so damn *shiny*? I could never keep up with nails and hair appointments on the regular, clearly, because I chopped my own bangs just a few weeks ago. They're growing out nicely though.

"Good mor—"

"Why do you have an appointment with Mrs. Smith?"

The girls' ears perk up and then all three of them shoot laser beam eyes with heaps of mascara in my direction and, shit... I completely forgot to do my makeup. Mentally, I smack my forehead. I am sorely lacking a flawless foundation, a cat-eye, and a lip—those things I will not live without.

"She came into Designer and she asked for me, Jenny, I swear."

"I know, I know. Declan told me. He said you two set up the fitting room in Designer last night? It looks good, you're a natural at layering and making a room look appealing to the eye. Truth is, I needed to unload her before my leave."

"Declan helped me with some of the details," I confess, "but I'm confident I can take good care of her." I'm so not.

"Let's hope so. When the hell is Lenny getting back? Everything is turning crazy. This is going to put me into early labor!" She is a pregnant terrier with a short attention span, moving this way and that across the small office.

"When's your due date again?" Angel pipes up.

This earns her a glare from our boss. "I've got less than a week, don't remind me. There's too much to button up."

"Good luck, Holly. I wouldn't want Mrs. Smith as a client for all the Hermès bangles in Seattle." Molly wrinkles her nose, the assortment of bracelets she always wears clink as she takes a drink of her coffee.

"Don't play—you'd take her and gobble up the weekly sales like the rest of us would," Angel says under her breath before getting back to her phone.

"At least I'm wishing her luck. You're betting with employees on how long she'll last—"

"Good luck!" Angel says quickly. "If she starts shopping online we're all done for. Her sales carry our department."

All I can do is shake my head and give them a military salute. If this is war, I aim to win.

At the E-bar, I order Mrs. Smith *The Jenny* since everyone seems to love it, then I jet up the escalator and tweak the room Declan and I worked on last night. I place the coffee on a little gold table I pulled from the back room, a castoff from the Visual team. In the center of the trifold dressing room mirrors, I've put a mannequin and dressed her head to toe; this is my idea of surprise and delight. I hope she likes it; mannequins are heavy and I smashed a toe dragging it in.

My phone pings with a text. Mrs. Smith is running ten minutes behind. She'll meet me in Designer at exactly 8:15.

Nerves wash over me making me feel light-headed so I sit on the padded bench and bounce a knee, surveying the room and making sure everything is just right.

Unlike her vicious reputation, it was thoughtful of her to let me know she was behind. Now, I have time to sit here and think of all the ways this could go horribly wrong; of all the ways I'm very unqualified for the job I'm about to do.

Instead, I bolt to Cosmetics to distract myself. One of the artists will take pity on me. If I go down in flames today, I'm going to do it with a pretty face of makeup.

Of course, Declan makes an appearance halfway through my mini makeover with Tamisha, the manager of the department who always helps me if she can. He looks crisp as a spring leaf in a light green button-down tucked into jeans with a pair of Jordans. The swoosh is green and despite his grumpy countenance, he looks even more adorable today in his signature style.

"Isn't Mrs. Smith supposed to be in that chair? Or is she letting herself into her own fitting room and managing her own gift wrap?"

"What happened to my promised silence?" And all the hand-holding and doorway canoodling?

He lowers his lashes. "Apologies, gut reaction."

Tamisha eyes us both, shaking her head. The entire store knows we hate each other, there's been no hiding that from the employees who've been here for years, but this new heat between us is readable. Clearly, as Tamisha is now smirking at me.

"Is everything ready upstairs?" he asks, scuffing his feet in an attempt to look like he's going to leave me alone without actually *leaving*.

"I have a few minutes and I didn't get much sleep last night. I needed to do something with my face. How did you know she's coming now?" I ask, trying to move my head to meet his eyes, but Tamisha swiftly pulls my face back to her and begins applying blush to the apples of my cheeks.

"Saw you running around the second floor pulling more options. Did I see you hauling a mannequin around by the neck? Do I even want to know?"

"Nope."

"Hmm." He pauses. He's got something to say and can't decide if he should say it. "You never wear makeup."

"She doesn't need it!" Tamisha pipes up, her ample chest jiggling as she laughs and works on my eyes. "Just a baby cat-eye. And this skin…" She tilts my face from left to right and makes a deep sound of approval like an auntie.

"As long as you look like you," he murmurs, under his breath while he shoves his large hands into his pockets. "I mean, look like you want, of course…"

Now it's my turn to roll my eyes at him.

Tamisha stifles a laugh.

"I'm just saying," he continues, off-balance like I've never seen him, "I like the way you look. You always look nice."

"Nice," Tamisha hums under her breath with a knowing smile. *Are we liking the attempt at flattery that's happening right now?* she asks with an arched brow only I can see.

I shrug and pucker for lipstick she applies with a disposable doe foot wand. "Go to town, Tamisha. I want to look like I'm going to dinner on Valentine's Day in a dark room."

He stops, turns, and looks at me as if to say, *what the hell, Holly?*

She chuckles and tuts, "You're like two alley cats, always have been."

I revel in my win, but I can't ignore the fact it's not as sweet as it usually is when I best Declan Lorden.

"Have a great appointment, Holly," he says, very professional and all business. A real show for Tamisha.

"See ya, *Mr. Lorden*."

He's walking away, but I don't miss the hitch my sarcasm puts in his step. It really is fun messing with him.

"Blot," Tamisha says. The tissue comes away with a pink heart print from my lips.

"You're the best, T."

"I know, that's why I'm management. Does Mrs. Smith need any replenishments today? La Mer? I can have the spa room booked for her."

"Not sure, but I'll do my best." Man, *everyone* is trying to make numbers.

Back in Designer, Mrs. Smith arrives in all her glory just as I've placed myself at the cash wrap, looking as if I've been patiently waiting for Her Majesty the whole time.

"Holly, good morning." She kisses each of my cheeks. For as demanding and scary as she can be, she's really quite pleasant.

I lead her to her room, unlock the door with the key on my silver bangle, and wait for her reaction.

"I'm not wearing stripes. Why would you choose that for me?" she blurts, blunt and taciturn.

Oh no, she doesn't like it. I've worked so hard on this room. There are rows of shoes placed atop boxes so she doesn't have to hassle, jewelry options on little trays on the cushioned bench, and loads of outfit options carefully arranged on hangers and hooks around the room.

But all she sees are stripes, and she's pissed.

She gestures at her ample chest. "Stripes aren't flattering and a striped sweater is not cocktail." She wanders the room touching garments as if they might bite, shaking her head. "This is not what I asked for."

Everything gets hot. My armpits sweat and I'm suddenly light-headed. This is not going well and I'm prideful enough that I don't want to admit to Declan, or the General for that matter, that I couldn't hack it as a stylist.

The room is filled with cocktail dresses and pantsuit options, but of course she's focusing on the one chance I took by suggesting a few casual pieces we've just gotten in for spring.

This is it—my time to stand up and fight or cower. She's eaten so many salespeople and stylists like a hungry wolf cutting her teeth, but I think maybe it's not because she's a mean woman. Maybe it's just because she knows what she wants, and needs someone to be firm with her while helping her get it.

Gran says respect goes both ways; time for Mrs. Smith to show some.

"Everything else is cocktail," I say, sidestepping my way into the room with her. She seems a little affronted. Maybe stylists don't normally come in the room?

Well, this one does.

"These three dresses are the best options in the store. If we'd had more time, of course, we could have ordered. I've pulled shoes for each, and proper hosiery and support garments. The pantsuits are if you want to do something a bit different, either you're tired of dresses, or want to stand out when most of the other women will be wearing ankle-length gowns. The sweater"—a chunky but slightly open-weave knit—"is lightweight enough to be worn on its own without getting too hot. It'll breathe."

I know this is of the utmost importance because I've worked around all manner of women for years now. Many times, a group of ladies lunching and shopping would rest, bags at their ankles, in the quiet seating area in Customer Service, fanning themselves while complaining about heat no matter the season.

Refusing to be deterred by her power stance, I keep going. And while she might be giving me bored, resting bitch face, she's listening. "And I've pulled multiple pairs of white denim." I pull the door almost closed to show a hook on the back stacked with every new delivery of white denim for spring. "Different cuts come and go, but I suggest a straight leg ankle, that will always be in style. Slim white on bottom will highlight your long lean legs, and I promise it will be flattering. If you hate it, well, you win and I lose."

She seems to like this little challenge and plays with the cuff of the offending sweater again. "Fine. Check on me in five minutes."

"I will."

The rest of the appointment is just as choppy, but I think I've won her over in the end. At the cash wrap I ring quickly but competently. She's chewing delicately on a piece of minty gum when she finally says, "You were right. I can't believe it, I love that sweater. It just hangs in a flattering way. How does it do that?"

"It's the material and the weave. Horizontal stripes get a bad rap, but I saw a few women try it yesterday afternoon and realized the exaggerated weave makes all the difference. I pulled your size back immediately."

"Thoughtful, and appreciated. Oh, and those white jeans by Mother? Who would have thought, a *grandmother* wearing Mother? I've seen them on many girls but never thought they'd be for me."

It may be the high of success going to my head, but I think she almost giggles. I've experienced this around cash wraps at Lorden's for years, but it's still shocking to see how the right clothing can change someone's attitude instantly. Even I've felt a little more commanding today in the General's blazer.

"I'll have these bags delivered to your car. Anything else I can do for you today? Would you like to schedule your next appointment?"

"Yes, keep me for Monday mornings at eight. And let's take a walk through Louis Vuitton—my luggage is looking a bit ragged these days. I've got a trip coming up with the boys for spring break, but we have to order—"

"ASAP to have them monogrammed in time."

"Exactly."

The operator pages for help (LP since we have no Customer Service) and they load her purchases on a cart to be delivered to her driver. We walk through the store, a little more relaxed with each other, toward a whimsical spiraling back staircase that will take us from Men's suiting directly to the Louis Vuitton in-store boutique. There are pockets of ambiance like this hidden around the store, a moment to feel like you're in the Lordens' home instead of a department store. There are also a handful of designer boutiques, encased by glass and shining like the diamonds of retail they are; we have Chanel, Chloé, Gucci, and Louis Vuitton at Pine Street.

"Tell me about yourself," Mrs. Smith says, offering quiet hellos and nods to employees we pass. She uses Mr. Love for all her husband's suiting needs. No stylist has been able to penetrate that bond.

"Well, I went to high school and college right here in Seattle. I moved around a lot before, when I was little. Army brat."

"Really?"

I shrug. "My mom's a two-star general. She lives in D.C. now, travels a lot. Gran was here and worked for Lorden's for almost twenty-five years. She got me started sweeping in the tailor shop when I was a kid—"

"Who is your grandmother?"

"Colleen O'Hare."

"Colleen's your grandmother?"

"Yes, I think you've worked with her a lot." I smile up at her, she's a bit taller than me even in my wedges. If only she knew the stories that circulate the store about her. Does she know she's as much a legend here as Gran? As the corn chowder? "She just retired."

"Of course, I see the resemblance now. I was devastated. Tom tries, but he's just not the same. Your grandmother should get a medal for her service. She remade most of my dresses over the past fifteen years. I'd always want a shorter hem, and take off the sleeve, or longer hem and add some sleeves!" She laughs at herself, light dancing in her eyes; a woman who knows what she wants and is not afraid to ask for it.

"She just moved into a retirement community, Thorn Briar."

"Yes, I know it. Nice place."

"I think she's met a man."

"You're kidding? Good for her!" She stops short at the staircase we've been meandering toward and grips my arm just as I'm taking a step down the stairs. Unfortunately, these green wedges are higher than I'm used to and I lose my balance quickly.

Mrs. Smith holds on to the railing and bless her, she tries to hold on to me too, but I'm going down fast and she rightly choses to save herself.

I'm tripping over my own feet again.

Oh. My. God. This cannot be happening!

Unlike my close call on the escalator, this time I go all the way down. My knee takes the brunt of my weight as I try unsuccessfully to grasp the side of the railing to stop myself. Somehow, my mind clings to the thought, *Thank goodness for carpet!*

Just as I'm on what I hope is my last roll—grateful I'm wearing pants—my face smacks the last wooden tread with a *crack!*

Perhaps I passed out for a moment because when I open my eyes Mrs. Smith's face is all I can see. Like a fairy godmother hovering above me, the whites of her eyes wide and terrified. "Are you okay, honey?"

The operator's voice cuts through music and *Kelly Bear, five-five, Kelly Bear, five-five,* trumpets overhead.

Oh, no. I'm another Kelly Bear. I push myself up to my elbows and look around. Everything is foggy and awash in a rainbow of colors that aren't right. Who even had time to call the operator? How long have I been down? As I try to sit up and rub the pain that's spider-webbing along my jaw, I groan.

A crowd forms around me and I duck my head into my knees.

"Again?" I hear Declan's voice before I glance up to see him push through my audience.

"It's my fault. I grabbed her arm and she wasn't ready. She managed to be graceful about it, but hit her head on that last stair. I tried—"

"We'll take it from here, Mrs. Smith." He turns and gives me a view of my manager, coming in hot right behind him in all her pregnant designer glory. "Jenny, can you—Oh. Shit."

Kneeling swiftly, his hands go to each side of my face, pulling my gaze to his for a good look. He turns me by the chin with his thumbs, carefully assessing. "Jenny, can you please help Mrs. Smith with whatever she needs," he says, without looking away. "And comp a lunch for her in the café."

Heat streaks across my chest as embarrassment cloaks me. It feels like the entire store has stopped and surrounded me.

Jenny takes Mrs. Smith by the elbow with a polite smile.

"I'll just go home now. I was finished anyway. I'll see you Monday, Holly," she says over her shoulder while Jenny leads her through the crowd. "The Louie order can wait till then." God bless this woman, she knows how to make a quick exit.

"What's wrong with my face?" I look down at my hand that's just come away from my mouth bloody.

"We need a dentist."

"What?" Am I toothless?

"Up you go." He hoists me up by the waist and wraps an arm around my lower back, supporting most of my weight as we limp back up the staircase.

"Why are we going up?" I slur through blood that's pooling in my mouth.

"My keys are in my office. This is also the most inconspicuous way. We can catch the back elevator to the third floor, grab your things and mine, and go."

My words aren't forming the way they should, but I push more out anyway. "Where are we going?"

"To see my dentist. You've chipped a tooth." So, not toothless. I smile wide and he makes a face. I must look like a comic book criminal all satisfied and bloody-mouthed.

"What if I have my own dentist?" Arguing with him takes my mind off my throbbing face for a moment.

"Do you? I'll drive you anywhere."

I expected him to fight with me. "Well, I haven't been in a few... years. Bet he's still there," I grumble and swallow without thinking.

His eyes light up with a chuckle. "While that is a rave review, I'll take you where I go. He's the best. And you really should be staying on top of your oral hygiene, you know."

Yes, I've been lax with appointments, but my oral hygiene is top priority, I want him to know! But I don't even care about the lecture, because my tongue has found a sharp spot.

"Is it my front tooth?" I look up at him once we've gotten into the elevator. He hasn't let go of me. Mortification blooms in the form of butterflies in my stomach.

He doesn't answer.

"Declan, is it?" The lisp in my speech tells me everything I need to know; it's a front tooth for sure. My words aren't coming out right because I'm a kid on Christmas who really needs a new front tooth.

The elevator dings and the doors slide open. He pulls me tighter. "You're going to be fine."

CHAPTER

Fourteen

HE BEGS me not to get blood all over the Batmobile, so I hold the wadded-up shirt he pulled from a gym bag to my face. It's clean and smells like him, fresh deodorant with wind and lake water. It doesn't quite match him. When you look at Declan, you see a posh, polished, twentysomething from a yacht club—all starched shirts and hair cropped closely at the sides with flirty waves on top. You expect him to be tying off sailboats like the one he lives on, fat wallet in his back pocket, calling his buddies, *brah*.

Except that's not the guy currently driving me to the dentist. The man next to me doesn't care that his expensive mint green button-down is covered in my blood. He looks flustered as if someone important to him has just taken a crack to the face.

I pull the shirt away and flip down the visor to survey myself in the mirror. My two front teeth are chipped, each on the inside corners, a little triangle gap looks back at me.

When I think about it, it makes sense that his dentist is on speed dial, his teeth are perfect. I think I've always hated him a little more because he has perfect teeth. Teeth are kinda my thing.

After swiftly parking and a quick chat with the receptionist about an emergency appointment with Dr. Thompson, who I learn is an old school buddy from Vohs Academy, I'm ushered through an office and deposited in a chair with a corner view.

Declan is low-key laughing at me as I sit and fidget.

"What?" I ask, petulantly.

"Nothing."

"I hate the dentist, okay. Are you enjoying this? I take very good care of my mouth so I *don't* have to come. You probably come here weekly. Is that why your teeth are so military straight and white?" My lisp is fully pronounced now that I'm aware and my words come out much less threatening than I'd like.

He holds back a chuckle, wrapping both arms across his chest as he leans against a wall, trying not to let his broad shoulders jiggle with laughter.

"Dec! What's up, brah?" Ah, there it is. Dr. Thompson breezes into the office with a hand already raised and waiting for a high five. Declan slaps it nonchalantly.

The good doctor looks like a slightly round JFK with skin so orange it cannot be natural. Together, they do the manly half hug. It's like watching a polished all-American runway model embracing a carrot.

"Your girlfriend took a nasty fall, I hear?" he asks, sitting and gliding toward me easily on a stool with wheels.

Latex-gloved hands are already in my mouth. "No gilfrensh—" I try to say.

"She fell down a flight of stairs at work."

"Ouch." The doc offers a rueful smile that's probably reserved for kids who end up here after playground squabbles. Shouldn't he be wearing a mask?

"NOAH flighstrsh!" I garble.

"Okay, not the full flight, just half. She was adamant. I wasn't there, but when I found her she was bleeding from the mouth and clearly needed your assistance." Declan winces and pushes off the wall to move toward me.

"Ah hvmuh drnist."

"She has her own dentist, she wants you to know. But I told her you're the best, we have the same insurance, and you owe me a favor."

Wow, Declan Lorden has a kind bone in his body. For a moment I black out and remember my dad taking me to my first dental cleaning as a kid. With a mouth full of silver fillings himself, he was always extremely worried about my teeth.

"Well…Miss…"

"Holly," Declan supplies.

"Well, Holly, we can take care of this—anything for Dec. And now we're even," Dr. Thompson says, looking up at Declan who just nods. "Give me a few minutes to get a room set up." He pushes his stool across a shiny white floor and says through an open door, "Josie, prepare room nine."

"He's not my boyfriend." Now that my mouth is my own, I try my best to speak without the lisp, but it's obvious I'm doing everything I physically can to avoid it.

Dr. Thompson smiles at me and shrugs before winking at Declan and disappearing, most likely to prepare a torture chamber.

"I don't want surgery!"

"Oh, calm down, it's not open heart. He'll just build up and bond those tiny chips and you'll be good as new. Half of my mouth, and George's, are full of bonds and veneers. You don't grow up with an almost five-year age gap like us and not have monumentally unbalanced wrestling matches. At least you finished with Mrs. Smith. Seems she's taken a shine to you."

"I know, I can't believe it," I breath, hearing a faint whistle through my teeth. To Declan's credit, he keeps a straight face.

"I can."

Before I can respond and tell him to stop patronizing me, I hear two people whispering in the hall. I turn in my chair, trying to see them better and catch what they're saying. It's probably details on my impending torture. I'm torn between wanting to know and wanting to stay oblivious.

A woman I presume is Josie has her hands all over the good doctor, saying some really interesting things about their evening plans—graphic things. Then he plants a swift kiss at the base of her neck and pushes her into the room with a pat on the rear.

"Follow me," she says sweetly.

Another chair, a bib, and goggles greet me in a room much more sterile than the last.

"Just sit back and relax, please." She's in front of me with a high bun, large hoop earrings, and a blinding smile that stretches a mile. "Time to fix those choppers!"

"This is just a little gas so you don't feel any pain. It'll relax you— your shoulders are pushed up around your ears." Dr. Thompson is all business now. Mask on and ready to *operate*.

"My dad used to take me to the dentist," I blurt, looking up at Declan. My heart is racing.

"He must have been a really good dad," he replies softly.

Does he know I'm terrified right now? It feels like he knows. That soft, low cadence in his voice instantly bringing my anxiety level down a few notches. "I don't think my dad knew of my existence till I was old enough to refuse to swing a golf club."

I inhale the gas, grateful and deep. Dr. Thompson puts two plastic contraptions in my mouth that spread my cheeks so wide I think they'll tear like tissue paper.

My chest is warm and tingly and my eyes search the room, landing back on the large face hovering inches from mine. Dr. Thompson pulls his mask down and smiles reassuringly before popping it back into place.

My eyes dart back to Declan. As if I asked him, he sits in a low chair near me just as the good doctor adjusts my recline. I'm not ready and my hands shoot out as if to stop myself from falling. Declan catches them and presses them firmly back in my lap.

"Whoa, Nelly! She's a jumpy one," Dr. Thompson says.

"She's fine," Declan murmurs. He pokes me playfully in the side and looks deep into my eyes. "You do look like a horse getting its teeth checked."

A laugh bursts from my throat. With no way to close my mouth it comes out like, GHAAA!

"Not helping, Dec," Dr. Thompson says as he gets to work. "First, I'll clean for bacteria, then dry with polish so the adhesive will bond to the tooth. You shouldn't be able to tell you've had a chip. It'll last five, ten years maybe."

"How's Claire?" Declan asks, still leaning close.

Wait, who's Claire?

I must really be high because I take his hand and place it on my belly. It's refrigerator cold in here. I need a warm blanket, but instead my brain has decided that his large palm will do.

His shocked gaze cuts to mine, but he leaves his hand right where it is. The weight, the heat, it's all I can think about now, and it *is* comforting.

"Great. Vacation we just took to Bora-Bora could have lasted longer but duty calls." He smiles down at me. I'm the duty he speaks of. Saving clumsy people from lisps one mouth at a time.

He has a girlfriend? Vacation to Bora-Bora? What about tonight's plans with Miss High Bun and Hoops?

He puts the straw-sucker gadget in my mouth to clean out the acidic rinse I was about to choke on. "Are you going to the thing Thursday for Vohs?"

"My mom emailed me this morning about that. I'm supposed to, now that George is in Hawaii. Guess I have to start showing up for stuff."

"It's charity."

"For a school that doesn't need a dollar."

Dr. Thompson presses the bond firmly into my front teeth as my eyes ping-pong between them having a casual chat during my trauma. "It'll be a nice night out for you and Holly."

The gas must be kicking in because I look up at Declan and make a sound like a teenager excited for prom, *Eeeee!*

"You want to go to a party with me?" Both his eyebrows raise in surprise. I've caught him off guard and it's delicious.

"Yoooo nu eee?" Doesn't he want to take me?

"I wouldn't mind taking you," he says, with a lopsided smile, answering my gibberish question like a parent interpreting toddler-speak. The hand that was on my belly reaches and squeezes my hip. His fingers graze my side where my shirt has ridden up, and I gasp at the warmth. Unfortunately, with my mouth pried open it comes out like a rather erotic moan— *Ahhhh.*

After the bond dries and the doctor buffs and shapes, he hollers,

"Josie, check please." This is clearly part of the Dr. Thompson show. He motions as if he's at a table and wants a waiter, writing on his palm with an imaginary pen. His own laughter bounces around the bare white walls. "All done. It just needs a few minutes to set and I'll let you out of the ortho-mussel."

High bun and hoops Josie appears again. She stands very, very close to Dr. Thompson, who admittedly, is the youngest and most handsome dentist I've ever seen. She leans over to inspect his handi-work, letting her chest almost rest on his shoulder. If I were Claire, I'd be pissed. "Looks good, Dr. T!"

They high-five. A growl emits from the back of my throat.

"Thanks again for helping on such short notice," Declan says easily.

"Anytime."

"Give my love to Claire—"

"Meeeeee oooooh."

Maybe they're not exclusive. Maybe I've jumped to drug-induced conclu-sions about a stranger whose life I have no business judging.

Declan eyes me curiously then continues, "How long has it been?"

"Almost three years, and yes, I'm thinking of popping the question. That's all you women want, right? A ring, am I right?" He stands, looking down at me still helplessly reclined, and chuckles.

I hold back vomit. "Errrrrr." This is a full-on guttural growl and I'm hoping it scares the doctor shitless, but instead he just looks at me confused.

"Not all, I can guarantee that," Declan responds, reaching for my hands as if he's going to haul me up himself.

"Don't tell her I said that," Dr. Thompson says, finally buzzing my chair to a sitting position. "Careful on those stairs, now, Holly. I heard about the escalator."

He pulls out the plastic spreaders and my cheeks deflate sorely. My tongue checks his handiwork, and things feel normal enough though my head is still spinning from the gas.

"I'll keep my eye on her." Declan hoists me up but I'm liquid, my body is totally zenned-out.

"I'm gonna make it hard for you!" I say in a singsong voice.

"Nothing new there, love." After propping me on my feet easily —*showoff*—he nods at Dr. Thompson. "We'll see you Thursday."

I am mush in the Batmobile while Declan smiles ear to ear on the way home. Something tells me I'm saying things I shouldn't.

"We're going to a paaaaar-tay!"

"You're still high? It's not really that kind of party."

"But it's at your old school, with all your old buddies. *I'm gonna get to know you!*" I sing. I am Lenny doing a show, right now. I am another persona altogether and I think I'm covered in glitter.

"Didn't realize that was something you wanted." His glance cuts hard from the road to me and back again.

Oh no, did I say something I shouldn't have? Something outside our general enemies of the state script? But we've been friendly recently too. I'm confused. "I don't want anything from you," I pout. I'm mad at him and I have no idea why—other than the usual reasons.

"So, she wants to get to know me." His words are weighted, bemused, and delivered as if he's playing to an audience.

"Who?"

"You don't actually hate me, do you?" He cuts another glance my way, chewing on his bottom lip.

"I don't think I hate you. Maybe we can be friends who do yoga and go putt-putt golfing, because I know your swing needs work," I cackle. "You don't hate me, either." I point peace sign fingers at my own eyes and then at his. "You see me. Like on the inside."

He shifts in his seat. "I think we need to change the subject."

"Nope. I'm on to something. What's this?" Suddenly, my attention snaps from his cut jaw and catches on the slowing scenery outside my window. "Hey, this isn't my house! I don't have a fountain at my house!" I wail with laughter, cracking myself up. Dr. Thompson and I could start an improv team. His jokes are bad, but the pervy crowd might like them, and I'll carry the rest of the act.

"I can't leave you home alone like this. I'll set you up in Lenny's room and have the maid check—"

"Noooooooooooo."

"What?" He says it like, *geesh,* as he smiles all his big teeth at me.

"I don't want to go in the big house! Too big. All by myself. I've been all by myself my whooooole liiiiiife."

"But—" His face softens.

"And your dad is scary."

"I can't argue with that." He pulls me out of the passenger seat as if he's extracting a blackhead.

"Ew."

"What did I do?"

More insane laughter. "Nothing, that was just in my head."

If a stranger saw us right now, they'd think I'd been heavily day drinking. I skip, I twirl, I bounce around the side of the house. I introduce myself to statues. I bow.

I kick bocce balls, run over to the putting green where Mr. Lorden so rudely treated his sons, and take a crack. I am going to pretend this ball is his head and send it all the way to Hawaii.

I whiff so badly!

"Oh, no you don't," he says, after I chuck the club into some bushes and start to stumble downstairs toward the dock.

He wraps an arm around my waist and pulls me in tight. "A staircase would do you in right now."

"How much gas did he give me? Is it too cold for a swim?" When I turn my head, my cheek grazes his. And I don't pull away horrified.

Interesting.

"You're a lightweight. Yes. Don't you dare."

Gingerly, he helps me onto his boat and unlocks the double doors leading into the cabin. The rocking water is doing nothing for my balance and he promptly deposits me on a small couch as if I weigh no more than an air-filled bag of potato chips.

"Those potato chip people have no moral code!"

He rolls his eyes at me as he putters around, putting things away.

I absorb his surroundings as if I'm drugged, which I am, and let every detail of his home sink into me with unnatural clarity. A cave on the water in which to hibernate and ignore the rest of the world. The cabin is small but lived-in. Very clean. Some sci-fi novels are stacked in the corner of a small window. The smell of him is *everywhere*. I breath deeply.

"I like your boat." It's not what you'd expect from the interior of a sailboat, instead of bland cream and dark wood, it's all blue and white with cozy nautical pillows. "Did you have a decorator?" It sounds like a joke except it's clearly not. This cabin is a snug little fantasy, totally staged but beautifully lived in.

"Mira insisted, you know her. I bought it after saving for three years and rehabbed a lot of it on my own, but she wanted it to be *nice*." He reads the back of a packet of tea and points at me. "No caffeine for you."

Watching him read the packet has made me fixate on his glasses. He gets to work, and I immediately reach for them and plop them on my own face.

He squints at me, laughs almost tenderly.

"I love your mom. You had to save? Didn't—"

"Didn't Daddy buy it for me?"

My face falls and I remove the glasses. *Sorry.* I place them slowly back on his face as a peace offering, taking time to secure them behind his ears, and letting my fingers gently trail the length of his neck before pulling away.

He shivers but doesn't stop what he's doing. "I worked hard for this Sun Odyssey. She's my baby and she's all mine. This boat is the only thing I've ever had that my family didn't have a hand in, minus the throw pillows and paint, but I consider that a housewarming gift and couldn't expect less from Mom. Tea?"

"Yes, please."

I take the steaming cup he's offered and peel myself from his side to continue touching everything he owns. There are pieces of him everywhere. A vintage *Jurassic Park* movie poster somehow fits on a door that probably leads to a tiny room with his bed. His laptop is on the little table where his friends sat last night. There's a neatly stacked deck of cards, but not just any playing cards—these are covered with odd symbols. Underneath them is a board, with a forest and skulls looking up at me. I finger the edge of a large three-ring notebook with the letters *DM* on the cover.

Declan is still fiddling with the tea things, rinsing, putting away. How does a man over six feet with an exceptionally cut physique manage in this tiny space? He does, and he's distracted, so I pop open the tin next to the cards. Toys. It's filled with little figurines of elves, wizards, trolls holding pitchforks, and oddly shaped dice.

"Hey!" he says, suddenly behind me, scooping everything out of my hands. He opens a small storage hatch and dumps it inside.

I'm snapping my fingers, trying to come up with the words I need. I know what this game is, that monster game that people play in their basements and coffee shops. I've seen a documentary about some famous celebrities starting groups and building out fancy game rooms. Something about campaigns…

"What's this game called? Is that what you were doing last night with Elf Ears?"

"That was Zoron, and he'd love you to call him Elf Ears. It's D&D."

"Dungeons & Dragons!" I clap my hands together. "That's it. Oh. My. God. Declan Lorden—"

"What?" He turns with kettle in hand, his arms flexing, tense under a still blood-spattered shirt. His hair is all mussed and disheveled from having to haul my bag of bones all over the place.

"You *are* a nerd but, like, a preppy, *man*-nerd!" The tea, knowing the inner workings of an escalator, loner type in smarty-pants, closet theater kid, *D&D*! The pieces of the Declan Lorden puzzle slide into place.

"It's cooler than it sounds. Campaigns take a lot of planning and organization. It's strategic, immersive storytelling. A lot of famous people play—"

"Wait—is this why they called you master?"

He puts clean mugs away in a hatch on the wall, then leans against the stove, crosses his arms, and just looks at me.

"Yes. I am the dungeon master. Funny you picked up on that, specifically."

"Oh. My. God. Say it again. That you are," I lower my voice and attempt to sound like a blockbuster movie trailer, "*the master*." My fingers wiggle as if I'm shooting him with magic.

"Are you serious, Stewart? Yes, I am the master—"

"Again," I giggle, but it's a throaty giggle. What is wrong with me?

"I think you need sleep."

I'm faintly aware I'm trying and failing spectacularly at innuendo.

"I'm not sure what kind of twisted fantasy you have playing in your pretty head—" he says, reading my thoughts exactly.

"I don't have fantasies about you, Declan." Of course, I say this louder than necessary.

He points to the *Jurassic Park* poster. "Okay then, that's the bathroom." Then he opens another set of skinny double doors. "This is the bedroom. Can I trust you to take a nap?"

The boat rocks gently from side to side. "I think I should go home." For a moment, a stunning sense of clarity washes over me. There should be a fight. I should say, *Oh no, I couldn't sleep in your bed, Declan!*

"We're already here. And you being alone right now is not an option. I'll make you a deal—"

I look up at him, standing in the threshold to his bedroom. "Are we gonna shake on it?"

"Sure," he says, moving closer and placing one hand on my waist to steady me as the boat rocks. "I'll stay here and work from my laptop if you get some rest. Nap off the drugs. I need you sober." His eyes turn predatory and I blink.

All the clarity vanishes in an instant. Why would I ever fight with this man? He's taking care of me.

"You'd do that for me?"

"I'd do just about anything for you, if you want to know the truth. And it'll make me feel better. I won't worry."

I should say more. I feel like we're having an additional conversation between the words we're actually saying, but I don't. I don't want to ruin this moment where the drugs are making everything rosy, and warm, and safe.

Somehow, my feet carry me into the room and he sets my cup of tea on a tiny floating table built into the wall beside his bed.

"Come on, love, I can't skip out on work. I'll check on you in a bit and drive you home." He ushers me toward the bed—again I'm wrapped up in his smell and instead of questioning him, I sink into all of it. I play make-believe.

"I need a shirt." Suddenly, I'm sad and I don't know why. I need to feel arms around me and if I can't have that, wrapping myself in his smell will have to do.

"Oh, sure." He pulls a large T-shirt from a tiny drawer in the wall, hands it to me, and turns around.

I shimmy quickly out of my blazer and blouse into a hunter green Vohs Academy T-shirt, one tiny hole at the neckline. A tear falls down my cheek that I hastily wipe away.

Outside, the sky has turned overcast. He pulls curtains and flips on a reading lamp hovering just over my head while I snuggle myself into his bed. The warm light casts a glow about the room, *so cozy*.

My eyes lock with his but I can't hold his gaze because I know he'll read me like a book. So I take a moment to size up Declan Lorden in his tiny boat bedroom. This big, nerdy, man somehow fits comfortably in this bed, which is no more than a full-size mattress at best. I wonder how he fits with another person.

Our eyes snag again. "You've got to stop looking at me like that," he says.

"Can't," I reply.

He takes two steps toward me and kneels at the bedside, raising a brow as if he can hear the questions rolling through my mind like pinballs in a machine. "You okay?"

"I don't know what's wrong with me." I sniff, pulling the comforter up to my chin.

"It's the gas—it's making you emotional. You're okay. I've got you." He chews on his lip, takes a deep breath, and hesitates with what he's about to say.

I can read all of this play across his face, just as well as he can read mine.

"If you need anything, you can ask me." When I open my mouth to protest he stops me. "I want to take care you you."

"Why? We're not even friends."

"I asked you to help me—first time I've ever asked anyone for help in my life. Not sure I'll do it again, considering you don't even think of me as a friend. That hurts."

"That hurts," I repeat, something sad about the way the words come out.

He shakes his head. "Why don't you have someone to take care of you?"

"I'm not sure I've ever had someone to take care of me, not really." I look up. I can't believe I said that aloud but he takes it in stride. Doesn't fuss or feel sorry for me, so I go on. "I miss my dad. And I'm never going to make my family happy." Gran because I don't have the nerve to do what I love, and the General because I don't have the stamina to follow her dream.

"You and I both." He brushes the pad of his thumb across my lips. It's so unexpected, the rough skin, the gentle touch.

"It's funny," I say, as his hand continues to wander the perimeter of my face, but neither of us laugh. "I thought a relationship, your brother actually, would fix things."

He stills. "I'm sorry you didn't get what you wanted."

"That's just it. I think I'm getting what I needed instead." I offer a small smile, he gives me one right back. "Say something to make me happy again."

"It was easier getting you into bed than I thought it would be." He laughs at his own joke, the sound falling flat when I reach up and let my hand wander down the curve of his cheek.

My gut reaction was to tell him he'd never get me in bed, but he's right, I'm already here. And he didn't have to ask twice. My temples begin to throb and my head feels like a weighted balloon. "I'm weird," I say, letting my hand drop. The pillow is so soft.

He braces his hands on either side of me and leans in close. "You're just realizing that now?"

"We're two peas in a pod, you and me."

He brushes my bangs off my forehead while I let my head sink into the pillow and begin to drift off. "You are way weirder than me."

"You play with dragons and dice." Slightly aware that I'm inviting certain imagery into my mind, I willfully conjure a vision of Declan as an elf, no, a prince with a sword in a forest. It looks just like the show I just finished except the hero has his face. The heroine mine. There's a lake, I hear the water. And then there's me, a maiden, a supersmart, competent maiden who's just having a quick nap, lying in a bed of soft green grass.

Laughing gas is potent stuff but it doesn't last forever. Mental clarity is threatening to come back but instead of letting it, I happily dip deeper into the active dream.

The knight leans over me, his strong fingertips reverently gliding across my face from temple to chin. His breathing is strong and rhythmic.

As his lips graze the top of my hand, the inside of my wrist, he whispers, "Sleep well, Holly." The sound tickles my elf ears, but I'm too tired to respond.

CHAPTER
Fifteen

ANGEL AND MOLLY are excited about the spring shipments, chatting and gesturing wildly in a corner. The stylist's office feels too small today. It makes it hard to concentrate. I need to keep my thoughts clear of Declan and his tiny boat, his huge muscles that practically carried me to and from the dentist just days ago, and his distinct, lakey, man-smell. And his bed, which I crawled into all on my own.

The week has flown by. It's almost five o'clock Thursday, and yes, I have a date with Declan Lorden. But it's OK because I shamelessly invited myself—or did he invite me?—while under the influence.

When Declan's mother heard he'd accepted the invitation to the Vohs Academy charity auction, she took the liberty of offering a dona-tion from the store—an after-hours VIP appointment with a personal stylist. In a shocking turn of events, now I'm the chosen one.

The girls continue gushing around the computer scrolling through prints and sculpted shoes, while Jenny begins preparing me for the charity event. She's mortified I'm the one representing them but I volunteered when Angel and Molly refused. Neither of them thinks one VIP appointment is worth working late on a Saturday night.

"When you speak about our program, make sure you highlight the experience. A five-star luxury vacation—*but make it fashion.* They receive complimentary drinks, an after-hours appointment with the entire store open only to them, and chef-prepared food with take-home jars of our signature corn chowder. Above all, highlight that you are there to serve them. Make the experience sound as fairy-tale as possible. Sell it. Cool?"

"Cool," I say, using my military salute.

"How has my life come to this?" Jenny rubs her belly as she sits at her desk and kicks off platform heels—today they're all white, very mod. "By the way, I won't be in tomorrow."

All three of our heads pop up. Jenny hasn't taken a Friday off, ever.

"I'm being induced. The doctor said it's time."

"Oh my—"

"Really—"

"Yay!"

The three of us are sorority sisters cheering on our mentor.

"None of that, and I'll still be checking your numbers at five."

"From the hospital?" Molly asks.

"Yes." She narrows her eyes, daring us to question her judgement. "We need to hit our goal for the month. Declan's made that perfectly clear in manager meetings. February will be slow, March too. We've got to make it through spring break, through resort, and into the summer collections."

Angel and Molly log off computers and I begin to pack up my things. Our meeting went well, we're all on track, and I feel like I've contributed even though I'm the newbie. My appointments this week with walk-ins and call-ins were well over my projected sales numbers. Everyone's calling me a natural and I'll be able to pay rent this month as well as put a little in savings.

We're saying good-night, and I think this might be the first time *the chosen ones* invite me to the E-bar, but Jenny stops me. Maybe next time. "Holly, before you go," she says, "I want to give you your gratis for the week."

"Oh? I didn't win any competitions."

"I know, I just didn't want the girls to think you're getting special treatment, which of course, you are. You've always been the boss's pet, haven't you? No matter who the boss is."

Ouch.

"I'm sorry, that's the hormones talking," she sighs. "Ignore me. But you do need to be careful, Holly. You've always been a bit of an idol in this store and now you're doing well in sales out of the gate and—"

"An idol? Hardly, I—"

She cuts me off with an impatient hand wave. "You're connected with the family, but you still manage to play nice with all the employees. It's a balance, you know what I mean. And you've got confidence which you're just figuring out how to use. But don't think people haven't noticed the shift between you and Declan. You two used to be like water and oil, now we see you side by side more often than not… Anyway, here." She hands me a Lorden's box, then gathers her own things, wrapping a quilted trench coat around herself that doesn't come close to closing. "Declan pulled a lot of strings, but I can't even be jealous." She pats her bump lovingly. "I've got nothing but my husband's shirts and leggings in my immediate future."

"Thanks, Jenny," I say, setting the large box on the round table in the center of the office.

"You're welcome. You're a fast learner. Keep the girls on track while I'm gone. I can't believe I'm saying this, but I know you've got a head for business and I need them on task, okay?"

"You got it. Go have that baby, and don't worry about a thing here."

She nods and pads out the door.

"And Jenny?"

"Yes?" She turns as I poke my head into the quiet hall.

"Congratulations."

A warm, genuine, terrified smile explodes across her face, and I wish everyone in the store could see it. This is the real Jenny Yoo. She's not a snake, she's a mama bear. "Thanks."

Back in the office, the box winks at me. It's shiny, white, and heavy. The top pops off easily and tissue flutters to the floor. Inside is a red dress with short, slightly puffed sleeves, a deep plunging V neckline in the front and mirror plunge at the back, a band at the rib cage, and long accordion pleats that will most likely hit me at the ankle. A box of Chanel heels, four inches of petal-pink suede that are going to kill my feet but be so worth it. And one tinier box tucked in the corner.

The shoes are begging me to try them on, but I pull the small box out instead.

It's a box inside a box, and when I get to the center, I find a watch. It's silver with a mother-of-pearl face and tiny diamond markers in the dial.

I have to sit. This is too much. I've seen these watches in velvet-lined cases in Fine Jewelry. No wonder Jenny warned me. She knew what was in this box—way more than gratis. This is nothing like a Gucci belt. This is like getting a car with a bow on it.

A *knock-knock* on the door frame makes me suck in a breath. "Thought I might catch you before you left. I'll pick you up at seven?"

"Declan, this is too much." My words come out in a rush. The store manager has to approve gratis before it's allotted to employees. This is from him, his doing.

He waves it off. "It's gratis. The store had it to give, you've been doing a great job, and I know you need it. So, see you at seven?"

"But—"

"I know the watch your dad gave you must mean a lot, I thought maybe—" He steps into the room, takes my hand, and begins delicately removing the peeling tape that's barely holding the band together. He uses the gentlest touch. "I thought you could wear this"— he nods at the box in my hand—"while I have this one refurbished. Do you trust me with it?" His eyes are full of so many questions. I've learned to read his face well, but I can't quite tell what he's asking me in this moment.

A lump forms in my throat, tears that I've been holding back for years threaten to fall. "Okay, thanks," I manage.

"Yup."

"I'll text you my address."

"Great. Hey, chin up. This is a good thing." Two fingers gently lift my chin and when our eyes meet, all I can do is nod.

The red silk dress slips over my body like liquid, and I have to twist to zip the low back. I don't need any kind of bra because this dress fits me like a glove, the empire band so tight it holds me in place. The deep V in the front is equal to the mirror image in back. Almost instantly, I'm ready to take on the tall order of representing Lorden's this evening.

How did I get here? Five-year plan to Corporate derailed, fantasy love life shot dead before it ever took a breath, and I thought everything was a mess. But is it a mess, really? As I look into the same bathroom mirror in Gran's house, I realize my bangs have settled in nicely. I have settled in nicely to this new chapter of my life. Do I want out?

In the past few weeks I've somehow almost seamlessly transitioned to selling and working as a stylist, as if this is what I was supposed to be doing all along. I love working with customers, and I love the fashion, the fabric, the craftsmanship, and the details.

Do I want more? Or does the General want more? I still want to travel, maybe Hawaii, maybe as a stylist. *Maybe* Corporate, but sitting at a desk all day is never what *I* really wanted.

Before I left, I popped down to Cosmetics and had Tamisha do my makeup again. The nude lip she used this time is a perfect complement to a bright blush on my cheeks and dark smoky eyes. I happily bought all the products with the generous amount of my paycheck I had leftover for the month.

What should I do with my hair? Lenny would know, but I don't text him. Instead, I go with my gut and twist it up off my neck, securing it with a few bobby pins. I let my bangs hang fringy, drawing attention to my eyes.

The doorbell rings, right on time, as I'm clasping the watch from Declan on my wrist. The weight and opulence of it makes me feel ridiculously special. I try to shake the feeling of missing my dad. He never got to see me go to a school dance, never saw me dressed up for prom. I hope, in whatever mystical or spiritual way possible, that he sees me now.

The bell rings again just as I'm opening the door. "Patience is a virtue, Mr. Lorden."

My breath nearly gives me away as I choke on a cough. Declan is in a navy blue tuxedo with a black lapel and a paper-crisp white button-down with tiny black buttons. I take him in from head to toe, every inch. The pants to the tux are cut so slim I can see the definition in his strong legs.

A fat watch sparkles on his wrist. It's the same as mine, just a bigger version. "I was wrong," he says.

"About tonight? Are you worried about the auction?" I clutch a small velvet bag of Gran's filled only with necessities.

"About makeup. You're stunning without it, but you're stunning in a completely different way with it. Either way, you're—"

"Declan Lorden, you're making me blush," I laugh lightly, pushing past him as my cheeks heat, stopping only to lock the door behind me before beelining for his car. "I only just figured out you wouldn't chuck me off the top of a building, but compliments are a bit much."

An unbidden memory of sleeping in his bed washes over me, making bumps pop on my skin. He hasn't said a word about it; it was just a nap, anyway. He drove me to my car like he promised, and that was it. But he's been this new *smitten* version of himself ever since.

He's by my side in an instant, reaching around me, and opening my door while shooing my hand away. "I can open my own door—this isn't a date."

"I know you can." He double-checks that all my appendages are inside before he pushes the door closed, then rounds the car, and slips into the driver's seat with the greatest of ease.

I glimpse plaid socks when his pants hike up at the ankle and he starts the car. After a beat of weighted silence, he pulls out of my driveway and we cruise to the event, but I can tell his mind is working something over.

"You think I'd push you off a building?" he says at last.

I pause before answering. "You covered for me with the escalator disaster, and you did fix my teeth, and take care of me after I fell down the stairs, so let's just say, the verdict's out."

He checks his rearview mirror before glancing at me quickly, then looks away. "I don't know how to make you believe me. All those years, I never disliked you—not even close."

"You can't exactly blame me," I say, laughing to keep things light-hearted. His face is veering dangerously serious and it's making me sweat. "Examples of your hatred for me run all the way back to childhood."

"So that's what you think we were doing when we were kids at the store? Hating each other?"

"Uh, yeah. Clearly you had it out for me. Don't feel bad, I wished you dead daily."

A muscle in his jaw ticks as though I've hit a nerve. "It felt like that at first, I guess, but then I grew up and realized what it really was."

"What it really was?" My pulse is racing and I rub my wrists to try to slow it. "Are you going to share with the class, Mr. Lorden?"

He lazily steers the car with one hand, and drops the other between us. For a moment I think he's going to touch me, grab my thigh or pat my knee, but it lands solidly on the gear shift.

He finally answers, "Sexual tension."

That's not what I was expecting. I sputter and gasp, but my brain simply can't form a reply. I press my hand against the cold glass of the window and look away to steady myself. "I don't think that's what this is," I finally manage.

"What it *is*, or what it *was?* You were talking about some wild D&D role-play in the bedroom the other day. Something about a prince, with a big sword?"

"Oh my God! I was on drugs!" Except I remember every minute of it; his deep voice uttering the word *master* over and over at my command, snuggling into his bed and letting the *smell* of him press on me like a weighted blanket.

He briefly looks at me, takes a breath, and exhales slowly through his nose. Takes his glasses off, puts them back on.

His glasses. They are sexy. So sexy. Have they always been? I soul-search. Yes, yes they have. *Damn it.*

"What should I expect tonight?" Shifting in my seat, I change the topic to work and crack the window. "It's hot. Are you hot?"

One corner of his mouth lifts humorously at my discomfort, and I try not to notice. "Vohs is an all-boys school, so the testosterone will be raging even though most of my friends are married now, or have partners."

"And the auction? How does that work?"

"Honestly, I'm not sure. I haven't been to nearly as many of these as George or my parents. PR is usually their thing."

"Don't you like the social stuff?"

"I don't express myself well. You of all people should know that." A little nerd, wrapped in wolf's clothing.

"So, that's why you lashed out with practical jokes on poor unassuming girls just trying to work in their grandmother's tailor shop? Did you lash out at school too?"

"There were no girls like you to pester, so I pretty much kept to myself." The way he says it is introspective, his face working through the emotions. "But I was a nerd at heart, you're right about that. King of the dorks, that's what George used to call me when I'd squirrel away in our basement with the same D&D crew I play with today. He was there my freshman year, so any of the guys bigger or meaner than me left me alone."

I nod and watch the sun finish setting out my window. The way he's speaking now, so candid, makes me feel like I'm seeing a side of himself he rarely shows.

Declan makes a slow turn into a parking lot lined with fir trees draped in little twinkle lights guiding the way to a covered valet drop. "What were *you* like in school?" he asks. "I know at the store you were all, *nice girl gets the worm*, but I always wondered—"

"A cappella-choir-singing, art-loving, craft-obsessed—that was me. Found YA paranormal romance and did nothing but read for an entire year."

"I remember that."

"Went through a very real preppy phase."

"I remember that too. You went from goth girl to *Gossip Girl* overnight."

"I was trying to find myself, just like everyone else in high school, I guess. Trying on personalities, keeping the bits I liked…"

"What made you pick textiles?"

"That, I did for myself. Gran was a big part of it, but my mom hated the idea. She didn't want me to end up a lowly seamstress. The General only allowed me to continue working at Lorden's if I promised to go for a corporate position after graduation. She liked the idea of me moving up at a big company, being a part of Seattle's royal family, but only if my goal was COO. I've disappointed her on that point, quite a bit."

"All the more reason to make our numbers and save the store," Declan says with slightly less enthusiasm than I think he'd hoped for. "Then you can bail for Hawaii. You're a great stylist already, think of what you could do in a few years with a client list under your belt. Or go be a designer—you're talented enough. You could crowdfund."

"It sounds nice, but I can't imagine what the General would say." My words are barely a whisper.

The car pulls to a stop and Declan jumps out, handing the keys to an attendant. He gives the valet a sizable bill and waves him off, appearing at my door moments later.

As I find my bearings on these heels and the car pulls away, he grasps my elbows. "I'm sorry," he says quietly.

Guests continue to drop their cars, some walking around us arm in arm to enter a stately reception hall.

I look up into crystal clear blue eyes. "Sorry for what?"

"For being a dick to you when we were younger. I didn't know how to handle my emotions—still working that out," he adds with a huff. "But I think you're worth it, putting things right between us is worth every minute of the self-help, personal growth podcasts I've been listening to."

"You are not," I sputter, going so far as to punch him in the arm. He's joking, right?

Silence. So I try again, "Why would you be doing any sort of self-help? Your life is…. " But it's not. His life isn't what I always thought it was, what I was about to say. Perfect. Still, "You can't be serious, Lorden."

"I'm more serious about *knowing* you, having a— " he pauses to take a breath, "solid relationship with you then I have been about anything in my life for a very long time."

I offer him a small, shy smile but no reply. Around us heels are clacking and doors are slamming. All the while, we stand there as if frozen in our own bubble of startling revelations. There's confusion swirling like a coming storm in my head and I'm desperately trying to drop an anchor to steady my heart.

CHAPTER
Sixteen

DECLAN LEADS me inside where a highbrow cocktail party is gaining steam. Low light, dark wood halls, and a grand ballroom that has at least sixty round tables set with gold cutlery welcome me to a world I'm wholly unprepared for.

We get drinks from a long curving cherry wood bar— a cabernet in a long-stemmed glass for me, a cut crystal glass of whiskey for him. Mrs. Smith is across the room wearing the pantsuit I sold her, velvet bustier underneath, tailored to perfection; Tom's getting better. She raises a glass in my direction and knowingly smiles. I nod back, raise my glass.

"I'm glad you're here. These things kinda make me nervous," he grumbles.

I shrug. I'm not surprised. Everyone is staring at us. "Mrs. Smith is wondering why I'm here, I can tell."

"She's wondering how the second son, the spare, will differ from the golden boy. They all are, they're sharks—"

"Listen, you've got a weird obsession with sharks," I say. "I'm thinking the self-help isn't such a bad idea. I went to therapy as a kid, after my dad. It helped."

"It's been surprisingly enlightening and cathartic, thank you. And that's not what I mean when I'm telling you to be a shark. When I tell you that, it's because I want you to be as strong as I know you are, to not let people walk all over you because your personality leans toward kindness first and survival second. *These* people are circling like sharks because they smell blood in the water. They know my family is struggling, they know our stores are failing to compete online, and they won't hesitate to take advantage if it can better their own bottom line." He knocks back the dregs of his drink.

"Thirsty?"

"I needed it."

"You just stick with me," I say. "I'm not afraid of these people. Besides, I'm the one who has to stand onstage and be auctioned to the highest bidder—"

"Don't make it sound like that." His voice is tight as he grasps his empty glass.

"Like what?"

"Like I'm willingly giving you away, because I'm not."

There it is again, those unexpected words he flings at me out of nowhere that cause my whole body to shiver.

Dr. Thompson makes his entrance at the worst possible moment because all I want to do is chew on what Declan just said. "Dec, Holly, how's it going? How's the mouth?"

I put on a happy face and show off my smile. "Great! How are you, Dr. Thompson?"

"Please, it's Chuck. This is Claire." He motions to a tall blonde who instantly reminds me of an elegant racehorse.

"I've heard so much about you, Holly," she says, dripping in sapphire sequins from head to toe. "I think we're seated together at table twelve. I already put my things down. Would you like to? We can check out the band."

Grateful to have someone who clearly knows their way around functions such as these, I say, "Sure, thanks." Then I focus on Declan, "See you guys shortly?" I want him to know he's still got me to lean on tonight, but I'm assuming he's okay with an old friend.

He reads my thoughts and gives a small, tense nod.

I gather my things but just as I'm turning to follow Claire, Dr.

Thompson lets his hand graze down the center of my back as he pretends to usher me toward the tables. "We'll join you ladies momentarily," he says.

"Chuck." Declan clasps him by the elbow and removes the hand that's still on my back. "Let me buy you a drink."

Claire and I put my things at our table and stand idly chatting while a band tunes up in the center of the room. The guys join us after as a bell chimes, the overhead announcement telling us to take our seats for dinner.

Relaxed, easy-listening elevator music plays in the background while Claire and I chitchat about fashion, her job in marketing for a not-for-profit children's literacy center, and how long she's been dating Chuck. I wonder if she knows about his assistant?

"You know, they call him the lone wolf?" She motions to a waiter passing by with wine and asks him to leave the bottle after he caps off both our drinks.

"Declan?"

"Yes, everyone thought he'd ditch the family business and take off for Alaska or something. Get picked up by one of those outdoorsy, reality survival shows," she says. "He sure is handsome enough."

It feels intimate, this knowledge she has that I don't. "How do you know that?"

"Chuck talks about him a lot. I think they used to be rivals, but they buried the hatchet. Something like that."

"I think he's a bit more of a pirate," I counter, "but I know what you mean. I always thought he'd leave too. Never thought he'd take his brother's place."

"How is George?" she asks, sipping from her glass. "He was a good one too. I went to the all-girls school here in town. We had a lot of events with Vohs boys."

Tables are filling quickly and the swell of conversation fills the cavernous room. "He's great, as far as I know. I think he's settling into the position in Hawaii, but we all miss him," I say.

"That would've been a much better fit for Declan, Hawaii. I wonder why he wasn't the one to go." Her eyebrows are trying really hard to rise in question, but I think the Botox is fresh.

I smile back and sip my wine. I'm not about to spill the beans that George wanted out.

Our dinner is pure choreography. Waiters come at us from every angle and place salads on chargers. Then they give us soup, and when the bowls are cleared, we're presented with tiny medallions of steak and roasted carrots with mushrooms drizzled in béarnaise. I soak up the sauce with bread from a basket until I notice Claire's crinkled nose. I stop.

A podium is brought out by two burly servers just as dinner is wrapping up with dessert and coffee. An older gentleman wearing an actual cravat, like a seventeenth-century paramour, adjusts the microphone. "Good evening, Vohs Academy alums!"

There's a rowdy cheer from many male voices around the room and a smattering of golf claps from dates accompanying them.

"Tonight is about raising funds for our school. We've got a scholarship for the education of a chosen student who merits Vohs Academy fundamentals. And a renovation of our main gym is on the docket this year!"

More resounding applause. A few shouts about the gym being overdue for a facelift.

"It's my pleasure to introduce our auctioneer for the evening, and if all presenters could please form a line at the stairs, we'll call you up."

That's my cue. I jump from my seat as if a fire's been lit beneath me.

Declan grabs my hand, pulling me back before I can take off like a racehorse to line up at the stairs. It's not that I'm eager to do this, it's the exact opposite, I'm eager to get it over with.

"Hey—"

"What?"

"Um…" He shifts in his tight navy pants, looking for something to say.

I avert my eyes and ignore the heat blooming in my chest and settling in my belly. "Declan, what is it?" I ask, dancing on spider legs.

"Good luck up there, and thanks for doing this."

"Sure, no problem. It's not like Jenny could in her state. I wonder if she's had the baby yet? I'll be right back and we can call the store to check in, maybe someone's heard from her."

"I've already sent flowers to her hospital room." He doesn't let go of my hand when I pull. "Maybe this was a bad idea, I'll go talk to them—"

We're both blubbering, buying time as if we're being separated for life. *What's wrong with us?*

"I can't back out now. *You* can't back out now." People around us are beginning to stare as I finally pull my hand from his. "What's the big deal? Some guy will buy me for an appointment for his wife, and it'll be a good thing for the store. Jenny will be thrilled there's another customer on the books, no biggie. I might snag a big fish and help us with numbers to keep the store alive. Win, win, win. Okay?"

He braces his elbows on the table then pushes back, shoving his hands through his hair. "Yeah, you're right. I'm being weird."

Well, that makes two of us, now, doesn't it? "I'm nervous enough without you balking."

Reluctantly, I leave him in his state of anxiety and find a place in line next to people holding boxes of jewelry, basketballs with signatures, and envelopes probably filled with time-share vacations.

What has gotten into him? It's surprising he's not more worried about the store's numbers. Now that I think of it, he hasn't mentioned it much. But an appointment with someone from this crowd could really make a difference in our month. And every little bit helps.

As the minutes tick by, my toes start to ache crammed into the unnatural points of my gorgeous shoes. I check my watch, counting the tiny little diamonds. I've been standing here for thirty minutes.

Turns out, these yuppie auction things are boring as hell. The woman who's taken the mic is milking the crowd for every dollar in their pocket. First, she goes through a few of the items, which means my line gets shorter, but then she stops to play a video about the school and boldly *asks* for more donations. The increments range from car payment to house payment to close to what I make in a year. Declan holds up his paddle, number fifty-one, and donates on the last increment. I can't decide if he's doing an insanely good deed for his alma mater or if he's trying to make a statement: *don't come for me and mine, we're just fine, everything is under control, we're still the Lordens with a shit ton of money to spare despite what you read in the business section!!!*

Finally, it's my turn and by the time I'm taking the stage, all my nervous energy has burned off into sweaty armpits and adrenaline.

Declan is not the only former theater kid.

I smile when I'm announced as Lorden's newest personal stylist. I do a twirl and curtsy. Clearly, the crowd has been bored almost to tears because I'm met with a resounding cheer and a few whistles.

"Okay, looks like we don't need to wait one minute longer. Let's start the bidding on Ms. Holly Stewart!"

Declan's eyes go unnaturally wide, easy to spot in a sea of tipsy guests. He never had another drink after his first. I grin, showing off my teeth again in thanks to Dr. Thompson. Claire gives me two thumbs-up, Chuck winks and adjusts himself in his seat next to her.

Suddenly, Declan looks downright pissed off as he tugs at his crisp collar and I wonder if I've done something wrong. I squint at him through the low lighting, and yes, for unfathomable reasons, his face is now beet red.

"Do I have five hundred?"

Multiple paddles pop into the air like popcorn.

"Okay, do I have one thousand?" The emcee has lipstick on her teeth but probably no one in the audience can see.

More paddles pop in a sea of black candlelight and wealth.

"Well, Holly, it looks like we've got quite a few alumni in need of a new look. Gotta keep those profile pics fresh, am I right? Tell me, are you available for both women's and men's appointments?" There's a gleam in her eye. This gal should write soap operas—she knows how to up the tension. There's absolutely nothing sexual about what she's said, but somehow, that vibe permeates the room.

I dip my head toward the microphone, committed to catching a big fish for Lorden's. "Of course, I can dress *anyone*." My eyebrows wiggle because I've yet to explore the world of Botox. "I will dress anyone, anytime. As dressy or as casual as needed."

The crowd laughs good-naturedly. *We're all adults, a little sexual innuendo is funny, right?*

My head swivels to Declan, and I give him a wink. More applause lights up the room. Dr. Thompson pats Declan on the shoulder, but he shrugs him off, stands, and walks to the back where it's so dark I can't track him with stage lights in my face. Who knows if he's pissed about something I said or just needs a bathroom break after all the sitting.

There's no time to ponder because Miss Emcee is chugging right along. "Do I have five thousand for the woman who can dress anyone? Anytime?"

Paddles fly into the air. Why is this so exciting? It's glorified shopping. Who would pay five grand for that?

Someone shouts, "Ten thousand!"

The emcee makes a visor out of her note cards and peers into the crowd as the rest of the audience turns this way and that in their seats, trying to spy the high roller. "I can't quite see—"

Another voice shouts, "You could use a new wardrobe, Chuck!"

It's Dr. Thompson, right smack in the middle of our table.

"Twelve." The heads in the room swivel again, following the new bidder's voice.

It's Declan. He's somehow made his way around the back of the room and is now at the side of the stage near the stairs.

Invisible daggers are exchanged between Dr. Thompson and Declan, so much so that Claire wraps her arms protectively around herself. Looks like the rivalry she spoke of is alive and well.

"Mr. Lorden, bidding on your own donation?" The emcee tsks.

"Play by the rules, Lorden! But I'll bite, fifteen thousand. Apparently, I need a new look." Dr. Thompson leans across the aisle to fist-bump another man and smiles wide.

Declan's face is covered in a sheen of fine sweat. He takes his glasses off, huffs, and puts them back on.

"Fifteen thousand, going once, going twice, sold to number?"

Claire hoists his arm high into the air as he exchanges high fives and clinks glasses.

"Sold to number ninety-five for fifteen thousand dollars."

My ears are ringing. I give the crowd another curtsy and they roar. I'm blinded by footlights and shining diamond jewelry, and before I know it, I'm descending the stairs batting my eyes so I can see clearly.

What a rush.

"What the hell was that?" Declan is there, pulling me by the elbow to the side of the ballroom.

He pushes us through double doors and we're instantly in the hustle and bustle of a massive kitchen. Pots and pans clang around us as the staff hurriedly cooks and cleans.

"What's wrong with you?" I stammer, pulling *him* by the arm into a semiprivate corner. Even through his tux jacket I can feel his arms are flexing on high alert. I follow the veins popping in his neck up to his face only to realize he's not *mad*, it's something else.

"I-I just—" He stops to think, biting his bottom lip, deep breath in, long breath out. He looks pitiful, but also...

"Declan, what's wrong? Are you okay?" My hands come to rest on either side of his face. He's worrying me. The look in his eyes is so intense.

"Holly—" He cuts himself off by crushing his lips to mine.

I think I'll push him away, but I don't. His hands slide down my front, over the thin silk of the dress that's between us. A little groan escapes my mouth as I suck his bottom lip. My body is on autopilot, reacting without my consent. All my nerve endings are instantly on edge at the electricity in his touch.

His hands are everywhere.

I have a split second to question: What the hell is happening? Declan Lorden is kissing me deeper and better than I've ever been kissed in my life.

There's no choice but to let him, not only let him, but participate, encourage, and reciprocate. I want him to kiss me harder, longer. *Again. Again. Again.* We're like two magnets who've been warring and pushing away from each other until, *flip!*

"Oh. My—" I gasp, cutting myself off to kiss him again. Whether it's my oral admission of pleasure, or my corroborative reaction to his touch, he responds by pressing me farther into our little corner of unexpected heaven until my back is against a wall.

It's as if neither one of us wants to stop for a moment to think about what we're doing. Instead, we act in flashes of fast hands and even faster kisses.

One hand grasps my rib cage while the other slides down my waist. He bends slightly to reach behind my thigh and hikes my knee to his hip, pressing himself into me.

I can feel exactly how turned on he is and as his hips rock into me making tiny figure eights—*Where did he get these moves?*—my body responds instantly.

So good, can't stop, won't stop runs through my mind on a loop.

I arch my back, moaning into his mouth, wondering if I can actually get off this way. He's turning my body into a live wire and it feels absolutely possible.

I've almost forgotten we're in a commercial kitchen and press my nose against his neck to inhale the scent of him instead of the stale food smells I noticed when we barreled through the doors. I could take a bath in his pheromones.

"Can I freeze this moment?" he rasps, letting his mouth fall to my neck. "I want to live this exact moment in time forever. Will you please make the clock stand still?" he begs.

That is by far the most poetic thing anyone has ever said to me—drunk, turned on, sober, or otherwise. Declan Lorden is begging me for more, and what's worse, I'd give him anything right now. Anything without thinking twice. It feels so right. Like everything we've done, everything we've said before this moment was backwards and *this* is what we've always needed from each other.

I pull his lips back to mine and kiss him harder to say thank you. Most likely, we'll go back to dancing around our feelings the second this is over—the thought makes me shudder—but we'll always have the banquet hall kitchen and my half orgasm from grinding against him in a spectacularly cut tuxedo.

Until then we act as if we've found a slice of paradise all our own. We're sneaky kids on a couch, arrogant twenty-one-year-olds in a seedy bar daring anyone to stop us from fornicating right here under the halogens. On some level, I know I'm standing in a fully staffed corporate kitchen. But God help me, I would let him push this as far as he wanted right now.

"*Mmm, Dec...*" I meant to only think it but the moan escapes.

His sharp-witted response is "Fuck," as his arms wrap fully around me and slide up the bare skin of my back.

Rough fingers trace the nape of my neck and a shiver rolls the length of my body in response. I push my hands into his tux jacket wanting more of him and find a rock-hard abdominal wall, a nerd with abs. I am converted. From now on, I'm only dating bookish, fantasy gaming men who live like pirates. I pull at the hem of his shirt and continue to arch into him. So greedy. So close.

"Wait—" He pulls back, cheeks flushed, mouth red from kissing, and swallows hard.

That one little word breaks the spell. *Yes, wait!*

What the hell am I doing kissing the man I loathed only weeks ago, the man who has plagued me half my life? Sure, we've come to a sort of truce, haven't we? But that doesn't equate to kissing!

"I'm sorry," I say softly, my fingertips lifting to my lips. My knee retracts and my foot plants firmly on the floor. "I don't know what that was. It's been a while—"

He clears his throat and tucks his shirt back into his pants. Looks over his shoulder concerned as if he's only just realized there are people around. He's still pressed against me, our chests touching, his hips refusing to detach from mine. The spell may be broken, but our bodies didn't get the memo. "For me too. Definitely, don't apologize. It's just, this is a... Anyone could walk in."

Mortification hits me as I realize, yes, he may have initiated the kiss, but I'm the one who started undressing him in public. Glancing around while patting my hair back into place, I take in a staff of penguin waiters who decide at that moment a round of applause is necessary.

I smack my forehead. *Well done, Holly.*

Declan, to my surprise, laughs and gives them all an embarrassed wave. We both find our feet, take a breath, and make zero eye contact as we walk back out to a party that's now in full bloom.

I think we've communicated without words. I think we're both on the same page. I think I'm going home right now with Declan Lorden.

The dance floor is rocking like an eighth-grade mixer with alcohol, people gyrating as if they've never cut loose in their life. This highfalutin charity gala has gone from black-tie decorum to raunchy post-porno, real quick. And I'm on board.

Declan has my hand in his and weaves through the crowd. There's an intensity in his grasp, the way he moves quickly around tables and chairs. He is a man on a mission.

When we find our table, he grabs my bag and pulls me toward the back doors. The music changes and the band plows full steam ahead into a cover of "Single Ladies." Grown women scream and run to the square of hardwood blocked off for dancing as if they're performing in the Super Bowl halftime show.

"Holly! Single ladies!" The room has darkened quite a bit and Claire materializes inches from my face, seriously feeling her buzz. She points to her ring finger, then the dance floor, singing along.

One glance at Declan, and I know there'll be zero dancing for him tonight.

No matter. I'd rather go home and fall down whatever rabbit hole this thing between us is. "Sorry," I shout back to her and shrug. I point to Declan like, *the old ball and chain wants to go home early, what can ya do?*

But then, in my peripheral vision, Mrs. Smith cuts quickly from a conversation with a bunch of men in tuxedos and heads straight for me.

No, no, no. Not now, don't pull a power play now, when I need to go finish what I started with this man.

She's removed her jacket, showing off a claret-colored velvet bustier and billowy cream pants that flow behind her as she moves. "Holly, a word."

"Hello, Mrs. Smith," Declan's smooth voice is almost in my ear. He's pulled me to him, arm around me. He is not going to let her derail us. My heart swells and I tell it to stop. I don't even know what this is, so I can't go getting emotional about him showing affection in front of others.

"Nice to see you, Mr. Lorden. Your family is well, I hope?"

"Doing great." His smile is all business as he takes a casual step toward the door, moving me with him.

"I've heard your flagship may not be fairing so well, I'd like to speak to your father—"

"I'll tell him to reach out. Now, if you'll please excuse us—"

"Not so fast. Holly and I have business to tend to." She turns to me.

"I'd like to go over my Louie order now, since we weren't able to the other day." She's kind enough to move on quickly and not make me relive my trip to the dentist. "I want the order in first thing in the morning, and I need to introduce you to a dear friend who is in serious need of your services as well."

"Oh—"

Declan interjects with a tight smile, "That's not possible this evening—"

"Of course, it is," she scoffs. "Correct, Ms. Stewart?"

I look up at him with apologetic eyes and say to Mrs. Smith, "Let's find you a fresh drink. I'll take notes on my phone."

"Perfect. I see you're on your way out, Mr. Lorden. My driver and I will see that Holly gets home."

Declan looks at me, I look at him, and again we're saying something to each other, but we've just started this noncommunication-communication thing.

This time, I'm not exactly sure what his half-pained, half-guilty expression means. "Okay, then," he manages, "I'll see you at the office in the morning, *Ms. Stewart.*"

CHAPTER
Seventeen

"See you tomorrow, Dorian," I call toward the back of the department. After working a fourteen-hour day post evening of cocktails, I gratefully clock out and mumble g'night to the rest of the closers heading up the escalator to turn in money bags and mobile registers.

Declan's driving me home. We haven't seen each other much today during the whirlwind that is a busy Friday in retail sales. A kid puked in a dressing room (that happens at least bimonthly), someone was trying to return a sweater purchased in the nineties and I was called in to help since there's no Customer Service, and Declan spent the majority of his day filling in where staff is thin. He insisted he give me a ride so we could talk.

"Good work today," Dorian says, walking out of the back room and shrugging on a thick leather biker jacket. "Your appointment helped our department make a 10 percent increase for the month over last year. And thanks for covering the floor, I know you've been here way overtime."

I smile, grateful I've helped and still a little shocked that Sales isn't nearly as scary as I thought it was. Physically exhausting to the point of pain, yes, but not scary. "You got it, glad I could help. I get to pay my rent this month too." I give him a thumbs-up after shrugging on my coat and laugh at myself. But I am proud.

"You headed out?"

"Yeah." I cannot wait to get out of this wrap dress and I grab my bag. We head up the escalator in easy conversation. Who knew?

"I had doubts about you." He flashes a rueful smile. "No offense, but nobody starts out as a stylist with no sales experience. You're a natural. Want to grab a beer? Some of us are headed across the street to Fredy's."

"Thanks, but I've got someone waiting on me."

"Ah, I see. You know, I always had a hunch he wasn't such a bad guy. Must be true if he's snagged you." That's all he says, leaving me with my mouth wide in shock, before heading down the hall.

The first thing Declan says as we pull away from the store that evening is, "I fucking hate Chuckie."

My seat belt clicks. "What am I going to do about my car?"

"I'll pick you up for work in the morning. I just needed to talk," he glances at me to confirm before he finishes, "you know?"

Talk about *what*, exactly, is the question. There seems to be so much to talk about.

He wasn't wrong about people smelling blood in the water. After Mrs. Smith placed her Louie order via my notes app at the bar, she had a lot of questions about the company—its numbers, history, Louie and Mira, where I saw the future of retail going in an ever-present Amazon world. And it wasn't just her—Dr. Thompson corralled a group at one point and proceeded to publicly question me about the Lordens: What I knew about the family, my thoughts on how the company's doing, and if they'd weather the internet storm. I ended up bailing to dance with Claire until Mrs. Smith's driver pulled me away, ushered me to the car, and deposited me on my doorstep like a character with an escort in a Victorian novel.

For me, the kiss is creating a ball of confused nerves, a Molotov cocktail of anxiety, shock, and raging *need*. All I know for sure is this is the brother I should have been kissing from the start. And that scares the hell out of me.

Someone's got to slice through the tension we're both choking on. I decide to play it safe. "That auction was pretty crazy." I'm hedging, pushing him to tell me how he feels about what happened between us.

He glares at the road, shifts his eyes to me as he comes to a full stop at a light, and softens his demeanor with obvious effort. "I'm so sorry, Holly. That was some real male Neanderthal bullshit I pulled last night."

Which part, exactly, is he sorry about? "It's okay. Claire said you and Dr. Thompson used to have, um, a beef?"

He chuckles and I watch his muscles relax. "Yeah. He was always a dick about my uncle. A lot of the kids hung out underage at the drag bar. Some are big fans but some... Chuckie comes from a long line of privilidged, unaccepting assholes."

"That's awful."

"Yeah. And, well, George didn't exactly fit the mold of Vohs at the time. It's different now, better I think, but—"

"*Chuckie* had a group hanging on his every word last night after you left, speculating about business, your business..."

"Asshole."

"So, why'd you take me to him, after the stairs?"

"He's good at what he does, and I wanted the best for you."

"Well, now I hate Chuckie. Even though he does good work." I suck on my front teeth to give me something to do with my mouth. It makes things worse.

But he smiles. "Thanks, that does make me feel better."

The topic of conversation and how upset he is makes me focus and push thoughts of the *O.M.G.* kiss into a black box that maybe shouldn't be unearthed. Maybe now's not the time for either of us to start something. Maybe it wasn't even that hot, maybe it's just that it's been—I quickly count on my fingers—six months since my last boyfriend. Wow. I really did take pining for George to an artistic, pent-up, sexually frustrated level.

We're halfway to my house, both of us silently brooding, when our phones ping; first his, then mine. I fish mine out of my bag as he taps at the screen in his console. When I think he's going to put his hand back on the gear shift again, he lets it fall to my thigh instead. So, we're not totally forgetting about the kiss, are we?

Electricity rockets through me with only my thin dress between us, but just as I'm trying to figure out what to say, the car begins to ring and goes automatically to speaker when someone answers.

"Hullo?"

"Hey, Len," we say in unison, grinning at each other. His hand is warm, heavy, and grips my thigh.

"Just saw your text," Declan continues.

Lenny's voice is projected through the car's sound system, "Are you with Holly?"

I remember the phone in my hand and sure enough, I've got a missed text from Lenny too. "I'm here. What's up?"

Declan gives me sideways glance, a closed-mouth smile playing on his lips.

I eye him back. *Yes, I like being in your car. I like you driving me home and I don't care who knows it!*

"We just got home from the hospital, routine checkup post-discharge last week. David's resting. I just...I just wanted to catch up." I hear the exhaustion in his words. He's been struggling—I really should have tried harder to check on him.

Declan voices the thought on the tip of my tongue, "What can we do?"

"Sushi?" he says it with a laugh, and I hear some fight return to my dear friend's voice. He's coming out of a hard time, but he's determined to emerge. Fear and anxiety can take anyone to task, but I've seen how specifically it can eat at Lenny.

"You got it—we'll be there in twenty," I say, winking at my nemesis across the dark interior of the Batmobile.

He gives my thigh a squeeze, and I melt.

Twenty minutes and ninetyish dollars later, we blow through the mansion, past the maid who scuttles to procure a silver tray for our bags of sushi. *No need! No time to spare, this is a BFF emergency on a chick flick level!*

Both of us push into Lenny's suite, knocking each other over while trying to hug him first. Declan wins and slaps Len on the back.

I deposit spicy tuna, spider, and dynamite rolls onto plates and pour little pots of soy sauce.

Everyone stands around his kitchenette munching with chopsticks. Declan and I stand on opposite sides of an island, nonverbally claiming amnesia and eating our feelings instead.

Lenny pulls beers from a fancy wood-faced refrigerator you'd never know was there and passes them out. "So...you two were together?" He eyes us both with an overexaggerated shocked expression. "After work?" He stuffs a large piece of sashimi into his mouth with expertly clutched chopsticks. "What's up with that?" He dabs his mouth with a napkin. "Thanks for the eats by the way."

"How's David?" Declan asks, ignoring his digging.

"He's okay. Did he thank you for the flowers?"

I eye Declan, confused. "Yeah, he texted the other day. Hope you guys brought them home. That was a shit ton of flowers and a huge waste if—"

"Are you kidding? He insisted. Loaded them right on top of him in the car. I think he has a crush on you and I'm pissed about it." He looks directly at me. Is he saying I'm the one with a crush on him? Do I have a crush? No, I don't think I have a crush...do I? The man does seem to send a lot of flowers to hospitals. I spoke briefly to Jenny and it sounds like he filled her room the moment the baby arrived.

Declan laughs as if he's reading every thought in my head via whatever look I have on my face and takes a drink from a bottle of Stella.

"How'd you know?" My voice is too high as I look first at Declan and then at Len.

"While you were playing *The Devil Wears Prada*, Dec visited the hospital a few times," he says.

Guilt pools in my stomach. "Len, I'm so sorry, I—"

"It's okay." He pats my hand and I know he means it. "I'm proud of you. I hear you're killing it. David took a shine to my nephew, against my wishes, but it brightened his days so I allowed it. You know how cancer is." He pulls at the hem of a Nirvana concert T-shirt. His feet are bare and his jeans are torn—this is Emo Len coming at us full force. "But he's on an upswing. Lucky." He pats my hand again. "They caught it early a few years ago. He's done multiple rounds of chemo, but it keeps cropping up. This little bit hit especially hard in the lungs."

Now I know why he wasn't texting and oversharing like normal—David has the same type of cancer as my dad. "I'm sorry."

"They still think he'll beat it and go on to live a long life—if only they all could. *I'm* sorry, Holly. I didn't want to drag you through old trauma."

Declan's gaze ping-pongs back and forth between us as Lenny continues to speak elegantly between bites. He's putting the pieces together. He knows my dad died young and he knows I've grown up most my life with Gran because I had only a general as a parent. He just didn't know it was cancer. Now he does.

"I'm sorry." Declan leans down a little to murmur in my ear and lets a hand fall down my back. In all this seriousness, his touch still elicits shivers.

"It was a long time ago," I say, because what else is there to do in these situations? "It was fast for him. They caught it late, even though he was a surgeon. He ignored the signs, focused on his own patients..." I drift, leaving out the part where I was angry at him for years for not caring enough about me to care about himself. The part where I felt completely abandoned by both my parents in the span of a month: Dad buried, Mom at work, me shipped off to Seattle to live with Gran. "Is David asleep? I can't believe I've never even met him. He went from decorator extraordinaire that you were lusting after to major person in your life." Again, the words unspoken are *you hurt me, I thought I'd lost you for a second.*

Lenny's expression answers back before he does. *I found someone that makes me happy, but I still love you.* "You know me, I move fast. I... that's not fair though." He wipes his mouth with a napkin as if he's wiping off bravado. "Holly, you and I, we go so far back. I should have at least called and filled you in, but you were so consumed"—he glances at Declan but plows on—"you were so consumed with George, and I knew what was coming. Not him leaving—but I knew he knew —how things were going to go between you two. *And* that you were going to lose your job... I didn't want to drop another bomb. I think, you know, I may have leaned a little too much on you in the past. And

I'm sorry for that—" he breaks off because, what else can he say? He's found someone, he's moving on. He doesn't need our codependent friendship quite so much anymore and yes, that's a good thing. But where does that leave me?

"I shouldn't have put all that on you. Lovesick is one thing, obsessed because you don't have the guts to deal with the truth is another. I'm sure I was like talking to a brick wall. All the signs were there with George, I just didn't see them." I glance at Declan to see how he's digesting my words and what I say next. "I don't even think I was in love with him as much as I was in love with the idea of being in love, you know? Wanting desperately for someone to care about me... Not to be alone."

Declan coughs, takes a swig of his beer, and looks away. Is it bad that he won't meet my eyes after what I just said? Maybe that was too much too soon. I've never been good with parsing out my emotions. I'm kinda all or nothing, and I think I just freaked him out.

"Well, I've been a wine-soaked brick wall myself from time to time, so we're even. But I feel different now." The way he lights up makes it clear how he feels about David; a Valentine, candy hearts kind of love; help you to the bathroom when you can't make it there yourself because you're so pumped full of poisonous meds to pee kind of love. "I'll go see if he's awake. If he's up to it, I'd love you to meet him. He's been wanting to meet the woman in my life."

My cheeks flush at that. We're good, Len and me.

When we're alone in the room, Declan turns toward me. I want to reach out to him but the look on his face stops me.

"George should have told you sooner." It seems like he wants to say more but doesn't.

"Was I just the dumb girl pining after a guy who would never, could never want her? What a laugh I must have been for everyone in the store. Why didn't I see it?" I wanted so badly for it to be George. And now that I'm chewing on it, I missed a lot of potential happiness because I was pining over him—the man standing next to me, potentially included. It's not a good feeling.

"I don't think he knew himself, or he wasn't ready to accept it for whatever reason. No one laughed at you," he says lightly.

I shrug and sip my beer. "It's a two-way street though, isn't it? He's just not that into you, and all that. I feel like an idiot."

"I hate that you got hurt. I knew you liked him the second we met—the three of us, remember?" He sips his own beer, licks his lips as his eyes drop to my mouth when I take another drink. He's watching me like a hawk and not hiding it.

"Yeah," I say on an exhale. "Gran paged you both on my first day in the store, introduced me in the tailor shop while I struggled to use the steamer. I burned myself—"

"You burned yourself while staring at George, I remember. Fucking love at first sight."

"I can't believe you remember that."

For a second, I think he's going to make fun of me, but crinkles line his forehead with concern instead when he says, "I knew you picked him, in that moment, and I knew you were going to get your heart broken. None of it is your fault, none of it makes you less than."

I look deep into his eyes, considering what he's just said, and put a big piece of sushi in my mouth because I have no idea how to respond. His words are the polar opposite of what I would have thought Declan Lorden would say to me a month ago.

He smiles a crooked smile and watches me chew. I'm totally conscious of my own tongue licking my bottom lip, and his eyes following it like a cat watching a canary.

We continue our staring contest until I pick up another roll and hold it up to him.

He opens his mouth and I feed him. Before I can pull my hand away, he gently grabs my wrist, chews, swallows, and then delicately licks each one of my fingertips for dessert.

My insides combust and I know I'll be thinking about him in bed tonight. Each fingertip tingles and the sensation runs straight through my core until Lenny pokes his head into the room, effectively dousing me with cold water.

He eyes us and says, "He's feeling up to it, if you want to say hi for a—" but stops short, reading the electricity in the air as only someone so wholly in touch with their emotions, like Lenny, could.

"I'd love that," I manage, unwilling to look away from Declan's mouth. Trying desperately to calm the pounding in my heart. It's in my ears; the *thump, thump, thump* is so loud.

When I sense Lenny's presence, it's difficult to turn away. But I do, and after a beat he whispers, "Go on in."

As I do, I hear him say firmly toward Declan in the kitchen, his voice so low I almost miss it—and maybe my ears do, maybe I'm making it up.

"You hurt her, and I'll never forgive you."

On the way home, something between Declan and me has changed.

His hand is back on the gear shift, so I reach across and give him a taste of his own medicine. His thigh is hard under my palm. This man must eat nothing with sugar and scrub his boat day and night for this body.

But despite my attempts at flirting, he's still awkward and folded into himself when we reach my front door. Where is the guy who pulled me off a stage so he could make out with me? The guy who only an hour ago licked the pads of my fingers with his tongue?

"So, about last night—" I try again. My attempt at intimacy and communication feels wrong all of a sudden. It feels like I would have assumed it would feel before Declan kissed me, before I knew how much my body would react to him. Something has caused things to turn stale and off-putting between us. I've no idea what it might be.

It's dark outside, no stars overhead because of a thick layer of fog. "Yeah." He's working something over in his mind. "How old were you again, when your dad passed?"

Oh. That was not the direction I was hoping this specific conversation would go. "Ten."

"That's...that's young."

"Mmm-hmm." I nod.

"I'm sorry that happened to you." He stuffs his hands in his pockets and scuffs his feet on my welcome mat. "You really do deserve a win, Holly Stewart. Like a big badass job in a high-rise with a view of the Puget. That's what you want. I could get you an interview with Amazon—"

But I want so much more…

"Your enemy? They're more than half the reason Lorden's is struggling. You want me to work for them?"

"I want…"

"What *do* you want, Declan?" I've always wondered. What does this stubborn, prideful man—born with a silver spoon in his mouth and a chip on his shoulder—actually want?

"I want what's best for you, I guess."

Which is suddenly a job at Amazon?

"*Thanks?*" It comes out as a question, the arc of my voice rising at the end because I'm so damn confused right now. Meanwhile, he's literally taking steps back. He's put about ten feet between us and I'm actively wishing we were still in the car, pressed into the same small space where he was within reach.

"Thanks again for doing the auction, and staying last night to work with Mrs. Smith. It means a lot for the store. Amazon, Hawaii, I'll do whatever I can to help you get what you want when the flagship is flush again."

Okay, so we're back to business completely? He regrets getting personal? It was the whiskey kissing me? I guess that makes sense. We are in this to save his store and for me to get out from under his thumb. Kissing seems to be going in the wrong direction, which is a shame, because I wanted another before we went back to hating each other.

"So, this is it, between us?" I wave in front of me, into the nothingness and night air. "Last night was a mistake?" I have to confirm it, I can't go to bed tonight wondering.

It makes him uncomfortable, but I don't care until he says, "Emotions and I…I don't do well showing up for someone. For anyone."

Ridiculous. Insane, that I ever thought he could be more than a dick in Prince Charming's clothing. "Understood! Buddy. Pal. Amigo." Trying to make a joke, I fire two finger guns at him and then nervously laugh at myself.

He doesn't laugh.

Abruptly, I stop, letting my hands fall to my sides. This isn't funny. What he's doing to me right now—bailing—isn't funny at all.

Much as I'd like to, I can't ignore it. Whatever spark there was between us is dead and gone now. He just killed it. On purpose.

"I'll order myself a ride tomorrow morning. Don't pick me up."

"Okay."

CHAPTER
Eighteen

THE MONTH of February flies by. Lenny and David move into Lenny's freshly painted apartment. Just after they cross the threshold, Lenny gets down on one knee and asks David to marry him. The wedding is set for next winter, a little less than a year from now. They want a lavish ceremony, which came as a surprise to no one. It's all we've been talking about, which has been a very welcome distraction from whatever happened between Declan and me.

Very welcome.

Because the kiss that made me suddenly hungry for him, that lit a raging forest fire of longing in me I didn't know was possible, is a thing of the past. Sometimes I wonder if it even happened. Maybe it was a figment of my imagination, a plot line from a TV show that I self-inserted into.

A dream.

Because...what has Declan been doing? Working, yes. Talking to me in any terms greater than grunts, nods, and pained half smiles, no.

During the downtime and the *not* thinking about Declan, I've finally found my signature style. Today I'm wearing one of the General's vintage DVF wraps with a seventies print and shiny new patent leather combat boots, a splurge after my fourth stylist paycheck sort of blew my mind.

It's a solid, feminine style with a side of *I don't give an F*, and a sprinkle of unexpected that I personally love. The boots are also just plain comfortable and won't send me careening down stairs anytime soon.

The store is atwitter with Saturday shoppers and I'm on my way to fetch coffee for myself and Mrs. Smith. I take both escalators down to the first floor where I hope there's no line at the E-bar. Glass counters sparkle, mannequins are dressed in fresh trends, and there's enough traffic to give the store a happy shopping buzz. We are definitely on our way to meeting our numbers and saving the store, but we still need spring break sales to increase over last year.

Outside it's rainy and cold, a typical kickoff to March in Seattle, but everyone in the industry knows rainy days are the best shopping days. I grab two *Jennys* from Zak. It's been added to the menu after getting so popular that customers started asking for it. Its namesake is still out on maternity leave with a happy, healthy baby girl. Jenny texts me regularly now for updates on our department numbers, and lately, store numbers too. Word is spreading that everyone's job, and the store itself, is on the line.

It's going to take a boatload of sugar and caffeine to keep me going today. I've picked up an additional three clients that I plan to schedule for seasonal wardrobe appointments moving forward, and last week no one would pick up the stylist page for a M.O.B. It turned out she wanted to buy Louis Vuitton pens for every place setting at her daughter's one-hundred-fifty-person wedding. That sale put me on the map, and now I'm working with her on resort style.

I've researched a few corporate positions around the city. Declan was right—there's nothing open at Lorden's. He's still pushing the Amazon interview, threatening to call a friend to set it up, but I've put him off so far. Hawaii is calling my name more and more. Getting to stay with Lorden's, but not seeing Declan's face every day, not even being in the same state as him, seems like my best course forward. Funny that I want to avoid him for entirely different reasons these days.

Mrs. Smith's text said I should have her coffee and alterations waiting at the Designer cash wrap, and to be ready to *meet my future*—as cryptic as an old, rich titan can be.

She should be here—I check the watch Declan gave me and beg my heart not to ache—in five minutes.

Later tonight, I'll be fulfilling my duties from the auction. After Mrs. Smith's alterations appointment, I'll pull outfit options and accessories for my appointment with Dr. Thompson (I can't bring myself to call him Chuck) and Claire. I'm a little shocked they're still together, to tell the truth, but since I've met them both and Claire is akin to a runway model, I think this appointment will be a slam dunk.

My stomach drops a bit when I think of the last time I saw them. I remember Declan's clear dislike for his old school buddy, the auction, that kiss.

Lucky for me, Mrs. Smith saves me from having to stew about it and breezes into Designer where I've got her garment bag hanging on a hook at the cash wrap.

She's got two tiny people in tow. "Holly, so good to see you. This is Jordan and Jameson, my grandsons."

"It's nice to meet you both." I smile at two well dressed and completely identical twin boys. "Are you out for a nice day with your, er…" Something stops me from calling Mrs. Smith a grandma.

She pushes them both gently on the shoulder. "Go on, give her your pitch."

Their pitch?

"We want to do a pop-up this Saturday," Jameson says. A red bow tie with tiny blue skulls makes me take him seriously.

"A pop-up?"

"At this store," Jordan tags on in a matching bow tie and plaid button-down.

Both boys stand firm in red Converse, waiting for my reply.

"Oh," Jordan says with a palm up for emphasis, "and we promise we'll bring it. Our goal is to increase store sales for the day by at least 8 percent. We've got everyone from our school and our cousins' school coming. And a bunch of influencer moms have been sharing posts of our shirts online."

"You have shirts?"

"We make shirts. It's called Kind Klub, and we've already sold over a thousand on Etsy."

"This isn't exactly the pitch we worked on, but I took the liberty of emailing a packet to you, your store manager, and Louie Lorden. I expect you can make this happen, can't you, Holly?"

"It's gonna be OOTW," Jameson chimes.

"I'm sorry?" I shrug, old enough to know I'm not down with teen-speak anymore, if I ever was while holed up in my room trolling vintage needlepoint canvases I couldn't afford on Etsy.

"Out of this world," Mrs. Smith supplies as she takes her alterations in hand.

"Well, I'll look at that email and get right back to you."

"See that you do. We'd like a prompt reply."

"Absolutely. Did you want to try these on?" I ask, motioning toward the fitting rooms.

"No, no. Tom is getting better every day. I'll try them at home."

I nod and start to wave as the twins walk away, heading for the escalator with mischievous twinkles in their eyes. "Who needs *Shark Tank* when you got Grandma?" Jordan says. They high-five.

"And Holly?" Mrs. Smith says, stopping to glance at me over her shoulder. Today, she's dressed down in stiff denim and a striped button-down.

"Hmm?"

"If we are successful, I may have an offer for you. You've mentioned looking for a new job though I'll hate to lose you here."

I have, I'm shameless. Even though I enjoy being a stylist, and I'd actually enjoy staying on and making more money than I ever did in Admin, I just can't stay here and work with Declan. Whether we hate each other, or something else, I can't.

"I'm taking the twins' company national. I'll act as CFO, of course, but I'll need a chief operating officer."

"Wow, I—" A job with twelve-year-old twins as my bosses?

"Don't say you couldn't leave Lorden's, Holly. This is your life. Corporate loyalty does not exist. Do you think the bottom line would be loyal to you?"

"It's something I would definitely consider, Mrs. Smith, thank you," I sputter, wondering if I'm lying to this woman's face or not. I'm not sure.

"This will be a national brand. Our business plan is to hit YouTube, eBay, and Etsy hard in the first year. Do more pop-ups with chains, like we're doing here. Then we'll go for a big dog: Walmart, CVS is an option, their margins are phenomenal, but preferably Target."

"We're going to be like the girl on Disney with the bows, only with shirts!" Jameson shouts from the escalator.

"And then we want a TV show!" Jordan adds.

"Think about it. Give my love to your grandmother!"

They step on the escalator, and then they're gone.

My head is spinning as I pull outfit options for Dr. Thompson and Claire. It's been a long day, and I might be dehydrated, but Mrs. Smith and her grandsons could be my ticket to the kind of job that allows me to use my degree and my new found knack for sales. *And in an industry I've always been interested in.*

A waiter from the café delivers appetizers and goodie bags as promised for my VIP appointment just as the store's closing. I check my watch and realize I have enough time to jet to the office and check a few emails.

"Aren't you supposed to be down there already? The store's been closed for thirty minutes." Declan walks into our office and eyes my watch. "Is it working?"

"It's working fine. I'm catching up on email." Mrs. Smith's Kind Klub pitch is spot-on. I think they're really on to something. It's easy to fire off a reply that yes, we'd love to have them as a pop-up on the first floor next Saturday. I may not have the authority, but who's going to stop me? There's no one to police this sort of thing in the store anymore.

I apply fresh lip gloss and pop a mint in my mouth as he strides toward my desk with palpable determination.

"Let me see." Gently, he pulls my wrist to him just as I'm standing up from my chair. The air goes still between us and I'm acutely aware of my rapid breathing along with every single one of his fingertips.

I implore my body to ignore him. I have to. He's made it clear nothing's going to happen between us. That our kiss at the gala meant nothing. That it's easily forgettable.

His eyes are saying so much, but I refuse to look into them. "I think I should check it," he finally murmurs.

"But it's working fine," I say hesitantly, as if even exchanging words is going to light that spark again. *Who am I kidding*? It's still here. It may always be here now, but if he can ignore it so can I.

"Sometimes they need maintenance." He slips the watch off my wrist and pulls another from his back pocket. It's my dad's watch, but it's got a new chestnut croc band and the face has been shined to look brand-new.

"This is the best present anyone has ever given me," I gush in shock.

He has the boyish confidence to smirk and pockets the watch he gave me. Sure, that one has diamonds, but this one is from my father. I can't believe he did this for me. "I'll have the other tuned up. You'll always have it as a backup."

"Okay, I'll see you tomorrow, then," I breathe, still looking at Dad's watch on my wrist. "And, thank you, really." I hold up my arm, hoping he understands how much he just gave me.

Maybe we're not friends, definitely not friends who will ever kiss again, but we're not enemies anymore.

"Have a good night," I say, as a way of dismissing him. The sooner he leaves the office the sooner I can get back to focusing on my appointment tonight.

"I'm not leaving yet."

"Have you moved in? You've spent every waking minute here the past few weeks. Don't you have any hobbies? Something to do?"

He huffs before forcing a smile. "Someday, I'm going sail around the world. But today, I'm going to sit at my desk until you're finished with your appointment. You think I'm leaving you alone with

Chuckie? After the way he ogled you? He spent fifteen thousand dollars on you—"

"You're making me feel dir-ty," I say in a singsong voice, but I smile at him anyway. For whatever reason, he's just as tense as he was the night we drove to Len's, as if no time has passed since his hand rested on my thigh as if it belonged there.

"Sorry. I'm sure it's fine. It was a charitable donation. But I know Chuckie, and I know he'd love to take what I want."

What did he just say?

As I turn to question it, Declan pushes past. "So, I'm staying, till I know it's over. You better go or you'll be late."

I've set up the largest fitting room in Designer, the one I usually reserve for Mrs. Smith, and welcome Dr. Thompson and Claire when our LP manager, Antonio, drops them off. Antonio hands me a walkie-talkie for paging him when we're finished so the couple can be walked safely to their car and the doors can be locked. After hours, the operator sends the phones to voice mail and if you tried to page someone from the office or the floor, the phone will only ding, hence a horror movie dream scenario and walkie-talkie time.

Dr. Thompson is clearly in a mood. The man seems to get uglier every time I see him. Perhaps now that I know who he really is, I'm not blinded by the white coat.

Claire greets me cheerily; this girl has really put on the rose-colored glasses.

"Holly, this is fabulous," she says, as she walks into the fitting room. "I hated waiting so long to book the appointment, I just knew you'd be good. You always look so cool but classic, ya know?"

I've dropped rose petals that I'll have to pick up on my hands and knees when they leave, set a tiny bistro table and chairs in a corner with a chef's spread of sweet and savory aperitifs, and have a jug of margaritas—at the guests' request—bookended by salt-rimmed glasses.

"I'm your clay," Dr. Thompson says as he pours himself a syrupy drink. *This is nothing special*, his body language says, *I'm accustomed to VIP treatment*. "Mold me, Holly."

Claire looks away, pretending not to hear his tone and begins toeing on a pair of red-soled Louboutins.

"Well, as you can see, I pulled looks for both of you. Casual per your request Dr. Th—" He gives me a look and clucks his tongue in disapproval. "Chuck," I manage to get out.

"And for you, Claire, we've got some options for dressing up and dressing down. Add heels of your choice to dress up denim, or"—I pull a pair of sequined pants from the options on the wall—"these would be great paired back to the Gucci sneakers with a chunky sweater for a fun day out. Spring is almost here."

"Thank God, right? I can't take another drab, cold day."

"You live in Seattle, honey." Dr. Thompson is making like he's going to pull off his polo shirt right here, right now. I angle my body away from him discreetly.

"But I'm from California, I'm wilting," she pouts with puffed lips.

"That's why I'm taking you on spring break. Didn't I promise you I'd give you a vacation good enough for a princess?"

I laugh lightly at their banter though it sounds more pointed than it should. "Well, I'll leave you to it. Let me know if you need anything," I finish, trying to close the door behind me, but Dr. Thompson swiftly stops me.

"Leave it cracked, I want you to hear if I call on you." He winks.

About ten minutes later, while I'm wiping down all the four-way chrome fixtures with wax paper so the hangers won't stick, I'm beckoned.

Down the hallway I go; it's a bit sinister-feeling with all the other fitting room doors in the hall vacant and locked. Their door is still cracked and I stop a few feet before I catch a glimpse of something I'd rather not see. "Do you guys need anything? Another size? How are the shoes fitting, Claire? European sizes can differ—"

Dr. Thompson answers, "The heels you picked out for her are perfect, even though you seem out to bankrupt me," he laughs. I can hear the tequila in his lame joke. "Why don't you come in here and check the size yourself?"

I roll my eyes at the door.

Wait till he sees the forty-thousand-dollar Rolex I put on a side table with a few fun pieces of costume jewelry for Claire. Let's see if he'll drop the big bucks on himself. Something tells me he will and it'll make a huge difference in the store's chances of ending the month with profit over last year's numbers.

If he wants the royal treatment, I can do that for Declan. If it gets him to buy that watch to prove what a big shot he is, I can do some ass-kissing.

But as I gently push the door open, I do not see two clothed humans trying on shoes and watches. Instead, I see two nearly naked bodies—one covered in dark hair, another almost hairless like one of those creepy cats—sprawled on the cushioned bench in the corner just opposite the trifold mirrors.

His chunky thighs, Santa belly, and shit-eating grin are multiplied in the mirrors—everywhere I look, *there's no place to hide! Take cover, man!*

"Oh! Excuse me," I sputter, backing away quickly.

"Don't leave!" he blusters.

I take a few steps down the hall and face the opposite direction, hands on my knees trying to reconcile what I just saw. I left the door ajar and just ran, which is more than he deserves. And poor Claire, on her knees in nothing but heels, she didn't even look up.

"We better wrap this up, okay, guys?" I speak into the wall and hope the acoustics bounce back clear as a bell. "Bring whatever you'd like to purchase up front—"

"But we thought you might want to help us a little more? You are a *personal* assistant, correct?" His voice carries down the hall and I gulp down bile.

It is a miracle I'm able to hold back profanities. "Personal *Stylist*, and I don't think so, Chuckie!" I yell, high-pitched. This guy has got to get a clue.

As I take off down the hall I hear, "We're sorry, Holly."

Poor Claire.

Every alarm bell in my head is sounding. Frantically, I pick up the phone and dial the operator. It takes a few overhead pings for me to realize I'm on autopilot and the phones are off, but before I can pull myself out of my stupor, he answers.

"What's wrong?"

"Declan?" My voice is breathless.

"I ran down the hall to the operator booth. What's wrong?"

"Uh, well, they went rogue."

"What the hell does that mean?"

All I can think of is the General, describing different tactics and scenarios to combat unexpected maneuvers to me as a kid over a bowl of Cheerios.

"I think I was just propositioned for a threesome?" My voice ticks up in a question because I don't know what the heck that was! I've never been asked to join another couple before. Maybe it's a compliment, but even if I wasn't on the clock, I would have to humbly decline. Claire is gorgeous, but Chuckie just does not do it for me. At. All.

The phone clicks dead—Declan's hung up.

My walkie-talkie garbles something and sounds like an ex-smoker growling like a bear. Still, I can tell it's his voice. "LP, Antonio, you copy? I'm headed down to Designer. The appointment is over, effective now. Please meet me to escort the customers out and prevent me from throwing down with this piece of shit."

Oh no.

When I look up, Declan's taking the escalator steps in twos on the way down because it's been shut off for the night. Only half the lights in the store remain on, except for my department where we're still lit up like an operating room. You can't miss him coming at me like Jason Bourne but with better hair.

He slides to a stop in the semidarkness of the store and demands, "Tell me you're okay. Where are they?"

"I'm okay. Still in the—"

"Declan, my man!" Dr. Thompson walks out fully clothed as if nothing's wrong. He holds his hand up waiting for Declan to return a high five that never comes.

Claire slinks behind him holding the box of Louboutins.

"You're out of here, Chuckie," Declan says, coming to stand shoulder to shoulder with me.

"Wait a minute, has someone gotten the wrong idea?"

I hesitate for a millisecond, but no, I most definitely did not get it wrong. And I am most definitely not at fault. The General's chin up, straight back, and fend-for-yourself attitude permeates my stance. I even employ a little Mrs. Smith air of authority and Jenny Yoo disdain as I stand taller in my combat boots, grateful I look ready to kick ass if needed. This is absolutely my personal style.

Dr. Thompson plucks the shoebox from Claire, and I notice he's got the fat, square Rolex box in his other hand.

Declan has tight fists at his sides, breathes in through his nose and out through his mouth, and is actively working to bring his temper down from a boil to a simmer. "Your money's no good here. Claire, I'll send you the shoes myself."

Antonio arrives about a half minute later while Dr. Thompson is still standing there, gap-mouthed.

"Antonio, would you please escort Dr. Thompson and his date out. They're finished here."

"I want to buy that watch and those goddamned shoes, Lorden. You deny me, and you'll never hear the end of it. And neither will your father. I'm sure he wouldn't like to hear his sinking flagship is turning away forty-thousand-dollar sales."

More than forty thousand dollars in sales including the shoes. This could take us to the goal. This sale could save Pine Street, at least this month.

"Tell my father if it makes you feel better, Chuck." He shakes his head as if he feels bad for the dentist. I absolutely feel bad for his date. "Just makes me feel all the better about kicking your ass out."

"Claire, you alright?" I ask.

"Um, can you call me a cab?"

"Claire?" Dr. Thompson sputters in half rage, half shock.

Bravo, Claire, bravo.

"My pleasure. Antonio?" Declan doesn't take his eyes off his enemy, not once. He pushes his glasses up his nose, seething.

"I'm on it," Antonio responds, pulling his phone out of his back pocket and tapping a few times.

"You can't be serious, Declan. You're going to end it with me over this? We've been friends for fifteen years." He completely ignores

Claire. If she needed closure, she just got it. This guy clearly only cares about himself.

"It'll be here in five, on me," Antonio says sweetly to Claire. "This way, please."

Dr. Thompson's barrel chest puffs up and his face goes red. "You are dead in this town, Lorden," he spits, pointing a finger in Declan's face. "I'll make it my personal mission to take this store down, to end your company once and for all." Then, he bolts, stomping down the escalator to the first floor toward the door they entered. All full of bark but clearly afraid of Declan's bite.

CHAPTER

Nineteen

"I STILL CAN'T BELIEVE that happened. Is this why you were so edgy about him bidding on the appointment?" I ask while we put away the last of the shoes. Declan helped me clean up the entire appointment; he ran all the menswear dump while I ran the women's, then we met on the first floor to put the shoes away.

Slowly, he looks at me after sliding the last shoebox into its spot on a dusty stack shelf. We're in a tight aisle of women's pumps, surrounded by boxes and labels and I feel a strong sense of déjà vu, as if I've been here with him before. I have, but not like this. Even if we're not going to act on the tension between us, things are just different. There's no going back.

"I didn't think he'd go that far. Yes, I know what an entitled sleazebag he is and I didn't want to chance it with you, but we really needed a big sale to round out this month—"

"Then why didn't you let me ring him up?"

He winces and pushes his sleeves up. "That was a big loss for you too, your paycheck took a hit."

"My paychecks fine, but I care about the store. We needed that sale to hit our numbers."

"Come on." He takes my hand in his, so much more intimate than he's been the past few weeks, and my heart soars even though I've been trying for a while to tie it down. Truth is, I've been missing him madly.

We walk silently to the freight elevator in the back of the shoe stacks and ride all the way up to the third floor. My body gravitates toward him and I lean into his shoulder while he wraps and arm around me.

I list reasons in my head why I shouldn't ignore all the hot, spicy ways he makes me feel even when I know it's not going anywhere: it's not healthy to repress emotions; it is healthy to orgasm; it's not healthy to—

I'm interrupted when the doors open and he keeps hold of my hand, leading me past our offices across the quiet and dimly lit third floor to the café. "Hungry? I figured you would be after working late."

"The chef's gone home and isn't Antonio waiting for us? To lock up?"

"I sent him home to his wife. I'm the store manager, at least for a little longer. I can use my power for good. To try to impress a girl instead of torment her, right?"

He pulls me inside the café before I can question this change of heart, since the night he dropped me off and said he couldn't get emotional. Maybe I don't need his emotions? *Nope, not possible.* I've been raised on all kinds of romantic content from eighties movies to fantasy romance fanfic. I'm a solid relationship girl if there ever was one—bonus points for defending me with your *life.*

"Declan, what's changed?" I ask.

I'm met with a table in the center of the room, all the others have upturned chairs, but this one has a white tablecloth and two candles flickering. "I tried to turn it off, Holly. I really did. I can't."

Wait, what? "What is all this?"

"I meant what I said, the other night after Len's?"

Like I could forget. "I remember."

"I'm not great at relationships, hence the recent therapy. I'm worse at acting on my emotions. And it worries me, especially with you."

"Why especially with me?"

"Because I know the trauma you went through losing your dad. I don't want to hurt you and I know myself enough to know I might."

"That was a long time ago. Yes, it still hurts, I think it always will. But it doesn't stop me from wanting, someone… "

"My family is messed up, Holly. My father's not really the *man in a loving relationship* anyone would want to model."

"Who's life is perfect? Mines not. So much so that, yes, I think I've been scared to try with someone for real. Your brother was — "

"I know how much you cared about him."

"I did, but it was also easy to care about him from afar. Without actually having to take any chances. I had a long time to dream about it but now, I'm not sure if that wasn't the part I loved most. The dreaming. The doing is a little harder."

He looks away and takes a long, measured breath. "I don't want to be something else that fails you," he says, then cuts a glance my way, "but I want to try."

The soda machines are covered and the kitchen is dark, but on the table there are two plates with those silver domes you see in movies.

So many responses sit on the tip of my tongue. I can't believe how much he's thought this through, dissecting feelings I was wearing on my sleeve but that I'm just beginning to acknowledge myself. "Declan, I—"

"May I?" He pulls out a chair.

I sit and wish my heart would stop hammering in my chest. Why is it physically impossible to ignore these feelings welling up inside me when it used to be so easy to hate him with so much self-assurance? It's like that kiss we had at the gala unlocked something, started a gush inside both of us and now neither of us, apparently, can turn it off.

He sits, pulls the dome from my plate, and then from his. Spaghetti. I am Lady, he is the Tramp, and we are officially on a freaking adorable date. At least, that's what I tell myself, and I don't even care anymore if I'm wrong. Somehow him caring about not hurting me makes me feel fearless.

"While you were downstairs, I was making this. It's the only thing I can do. On the boat, I have a tiny oven and a burner." He nods toward the darkened kitchen doors. "I don't understand half the gadgets in there."

"I'm sure it's not the only thing you can do." My cheeks burn hot when I say it, but I force myself to look him in the eye. Is he thinking of the last kitchen we were in, like I am?

"No, I meant the only food I can make. Holly, I promise you, there are so many other things I can do."

A man has never spoken to me with such pointed innuendo.

"What?" he asks, but he knows damn well *what*. We're about to pick up where we should have left off the night we kissed.

"Is this because I was just propositioned? Like a I-don't-know-if-I-want-it-but-I-know-*he*-can't-have-it kinda thing?" I have to make absolutely sure, I want to trust him.

"I've had this dinner going for hours. I don't have any delusions that you're very, very wantable. I just—"

"What?"

"What..." he repeats on a sigh, pouring wine in each of our glasses. "You're not a decision to be made lightly, Holly. Never in a million years did I think I'd actually get a chance... You're making a face."

"I'm not!" I scrub my face with my hands hoping to wipe off whatever he sees that's giving my hand away. He doesn't need to know how badly I want to figure this out, whatever this is between us.

We both place our napkins in our lap.

"You're learning something new. Figuring out a puzzle. Something you want to be good at. I've seen this face." He motions to me with his fork after he takes a bite. I take a bite too, following his lead because my mind is elsewhere—definitely not on food, but I haven't stopped to eat since breakfast. "It's the face of determination. When Holly Stewart sets her sights on something, she figures out a way to get it. You *are* a risk-taker, but you also like to have all the facts straight."

"Where did you study psychology again? Dr. Lorden?"

"Ha," he deadpans. "I've studied you long enough to have a master's in 'Stewart.'"

"You could have had a career, reading people," I counter.

"Yeah, but then I wouldn't have the discount." He pulls at his cashmere sweater and then pushes his glasses up his nose thoughtfully.

"And who could live without cashmere?" I ask wistfully.

"Or merino wool?"

"Sequins?"

"Houndstooth?"

"Artfully placed basting stitches—"

"Now you've gone a bit out of my depth."

I wipe my mouth, not wanting to have sauce on my face. "How do you know me so well, again?"

"Because I know what I like and when I find it, I don't divert."

My cheeks heat. We both know we're talking about him, about me, about all the years fighting that may have been a total miscommunication and leading to this exact moment—*flip!*

"Fine, I'll bite. Then, why'd you run from my door the night you brought me home from Len's? And you haven't been able to stomach being within ten feet of me since?"

He takes another bite, chews, and puts his fork down. I put my fork down too.

"Have you had enough?" he asks, standing and walking around the small table.

"I was starving—this was exactly what I needed." I stand too, meeting him toe-to-toe.

Swiftly, he pulls me close and I gasp. "Pasta coma?"

My stomach is not in a veg-on-the-couch-and-comfort-eat mood. There's just too much going on for my senses to keep up with tonight. "No, I'm too wound up from earlier with Chuckie to eat any more."

Declan's back stiffens and he doesn't reply right away. We stand in the dark of the café, in a store his family opened a hundred years ago, and I wonder what he's thinking.

His face softens and he pierces me with his gaze. "Please, don't say his name. I hate the way he treats people. I would never let him touch you, if that's not what you wanted..." He stumbles, warring with himself while he wars with his words.

"Definitely not what I want." And to prove it, I lean up to my tiptoes and kiss him, softly, on his deliciously full lips.

I meant for it to be a gesture, to be sweet. But the internal pull for more is almost instant.

He kisses me back, teasing me by biting at my bottom lip before he says on a long exhale, "Do you know how long I've wanted you?"

"Do you?" I counter, because I don't believe what he's getting at.

But he responds with a solid, "Yes."

"You have a funny way of showing it," I say, even though his words, along with his hands that are roughly gripping my waist, push heat straight to my core.

Briskly and before I can register the movement, he picks me up by the backs of my thighs. My traitorous legs wrap around him like a spider would a fly and my eyes squeeze shut. My forehead nuzzles into the nook of his neck and I drink in the scent of his skin; always water, fresh and crisp, as if he's been outside every minute of his life that he's not been in this store.

And then we're kissing again and he's walking. His mouth opens and accepts my deepened kiss, communicates his own want with needy strokes of his tongue until we're in an even darker corner of the café.

A row of booths line the wall behind me and I'm dropped unceremoniously into one, but the feeling of falling is only momentary before his body is over mine, pressing me into vinyl cushions. A deep, gravelly hum rolls through him.

I'm half reclined in the booth, only my ankles hanging off the edge.

He stops to inspect my boots. "I like these," he says, then pushes the table as far to the side as it will go, wedging his thigh between my legs.

"Is this okay?" His hands pause at the V of my dress.

"Yes," I breathe, the words barely off my lips before his hand plunges underneath to palm my breast.

Electricity rockets between us, one of us is Earth the other the sun. Everything inside me clenches under his touch, just one little touch and I'm already panting.

"Have you thought about doing this since the gala, then?" I ask, trying to hide how much I want him with cheekiness. But I want his answer to be the same as mine: *yes*. It's all I've thought of. Day and night. I never knew I could want something so badly.

"It goes much, much further back for me." His thigh presses harder between my legs as if using punctuation. Period. End of story.

Oh.

He goes on with a low, gravelly voice as if he's holding himself back enough to try to get the words out, "I told myself the gala was a fluke. I made myself sick believing it. But I couldn't not try, I had to know. I don't want to hold you back like my brother did. And I don't want Lenny to have to murder me in my sleep if I fuck up, but I know now it won't be my fault if someone here gets hurt."

He leans in closer, nuzzling my neck, my collarbone, dragging his mouth down the center of the V of my dress, slowly kissing while his thumb roughly strokes the peak of my breast.

"No one's going to get hurt," I sigh, pulling his hair lightly and getting a satisfied groan in return.

Declan's lips trail across my clavicle. *"Amazing, brilliant, strong, fascinating, and sexy as fuck,"* he whispers the words reverently into my chest until he pulls up, taking the sides of my face in his hands and looking at me as if I'm suddenly all he needs in the world. I've never in my life seen him so emotional.

Those words. "Declan," I murmur.

When you've only shot daggers at an opponent, you take note when the tide turns, when you realize you're now playing for the same team. It's as if I've given a kid who's never had candy the keys to Wonka's factory, just by uttering his name. He wraps an arm around my waist, pulling me so tight I almost can't breathe.

"Did you mean it? Are you really over him? Are you sure, because if we go much further there's going to be no turning back for me."

"Yes." I put as much emotion as I can into the one little word. "I meant it, I swear."

He thanks me with kisses, showing no mercy in lavishing my neck with nips and the velvet smoothness of his tongue. His hands alternate exploring down my shirt, then up my dress, then back again in an excruciating circle. It's exactly what I want. He is everything that I need. He's the missing piece to my puzzle and he's been right in front of me this whole time. At least, that's what it feels like as he grinds gently into me with his thigh and I press back fully with my hips.

"There's a bed in Home Goods," I breathe into his ear.

"Hell yes."

The Home Goods department is located conveniently just outside the café. Surprisingly, Lorden's does a line of mattresses in conjunction with a major hotel in Seattle. I don't think they sell more than two a year. It's a waste of retail space, an archaic sales model that needs a revamp. I'll be sure to talk to him about a better use for the space. We could bring in a new product to help our margins, but right now I'm *thrilled* they stock beds no one buys.

He carries me all the way, and when I'm dropped on a bare mattress, his hips sink into my spread thighs. He hovers above me, bracing on forearms.

"Come here," I whine, reaching out and making grabby hands at him.

"I just want to save a mental image. You in this bed, in my store. How did I get this lucky?"

It all seems so normal, so real, that a gurgle of giggles spills from my mouth. "Then don't push your luck and get down here," I say.

"You got it."

His elbows press gently on either side of my head until he reaches back to grab my knee, hitching my leg around his waist so he can press deeper between my thighs. We've been down this road before, and I'm ready for more. I moan gratefully when he adds more pressure, I'm not proud. The way his tongue moves, the way his lips suck and tug, it's as if he wants to know every part of me. I kiss him back just as completely. I push my hands under his shirt and drag my nails down his back, getting a guttural growl in return.

He wraps an arm around my waist, pulling tight, but this time he flips us over so that I'm on top.

"What about the cameras?" I pant.

"I'll wipe them."

"I'm not sure you can do that, but okay," I laugh. *Holly the rule breaker forever!*

"Of course, I can. And if these are the final days of this store, at least they'll be ones I'll want to remember. Maybe I'll make a copy." He gives me an evil grin. "If you say I can."

The split in my wrap dress is spread wide open. He toys with the top of the black silk thong I'm wearing that's fully exposed, dipping his thumb beneath.

"What do you mean, last days?" His shirt's already untucked, thanks to me, and I slide my hands up and under. I'm feeling him up as if it's my first time and I'm rewarded with mounds and mounds of abs. Rebuilding his boat has turned his muscles into rocks and they are divine.

"Let's not talk about it now." His hands push up my thighs, higher and higher they go, pushing my dress back and gripping me hard.

It's difficult to get the words out, not to fall into the sensation of his hands and my need, but I know when a secret's been spilled. "No, tell me. We've hardly spoken, I thought you regretted—"

"Holly, no." He grabs my wrists to still my hands. I've gotten his shirt completely unbuttoned and I don't protest at taking a moment to stop and admire him fully. Broad shoulders, narrow hips, and abs that fade in a deep V into his jeans."If I regret anything, it's wasting time I could have spent with you."

Rising on my knees, I begin to unknot the belt of my dress.

"Fuck, Holly," he rasps.

Then I stop. "Oh, did you want me to tie it back up?" I ask sweetly, pulling the dress back together slowly.

"No," he grunts, eyes thinning. He doesn't like my little game.

But I'm enjoying being on top, straddling him, way too much. "Then tell me." I tease.

"Please, don't make me—"

I give him a look that says I'm serious, then very slowly start to unknot the belt again, waiting for him to spill the beans.

Without further hesitation, he says, "The store's closing." He drops his head back on the bed and sighs a resigned groan when instantly I freeze.

"No. It can't be. We can make our numbers, even without Chuckie's Rolex. We still have time—"

He pushes up onto his elbows and gently pulls me closer by the backs of my knees. "My dad told me a few days ago, he's pulling the plug because we're too far behind to make a profit for the year and we're bleeding cash. My mom doesn't even know yet. I've been toying with some last-minute Hail Marys to convince Louie otherwise but nothing's come through, and maybe...maybe it's for the best. I'm not as good at managing the store as George was, but he's only one guy, he can't be the manager of every store we have."

"That's not fair. You're great at what you do. We just need to fight harder. Maybe we can reinvent the Lorden name with a new product, like these mattresses but something fresh. Scalable, with high margins."

"You sound like a business grad, and you're not wrong, but we can't beat Amazon, that's clear—"

"No one can." I roll off him and lay beside the man I feel, in this moment, I would do anything for if only I could wipe the look of pain off his sweet face.

"I don't want this to stop." He wraps one large hand around my thigh while lying next to me, defeated, but doesn't make any other moves. I'm confident enough in what just happened between us to believe him, but he's also got a shit sandwich on his plate right now that he's been keeping entirely to himself.

"We have to do something. You can't lose Pine Street. The twins are having their pop-up Saturday—maybe that will help? How bad is it? How much more do we have to earn to make a profit? To convince your father to hold on?"

"The company is hemorrhaging. We need more than a kids' pop-up to save us."

"Buy time with Louie. Do whatever you have to do. Tell Mira. She won't let this happen, will she? Call George, get his take."

"I'm not going crying to my big brother for help."

"Declan, it's not a weakness to ask for help. This place is an institution in Seattle, it's history. We just need everyone to rally around you." I think better when I'm moving, and I swing my legs to the side to stand.

"Don't get up, I'm not done with you, Stewart."

But I'm already pacing in front of him, pulling my dress back together and tying the belt in a double knot, counting the square footage of the Home Goods department and trying to think of how we could use it more effectively. "And I'm not done with you either, Lorden," I say, "but right now, we're on pause while I think."

"Pause? But we just—"

"That's on you that we *just*. You froze outside my door the other night. You bailed on me before even asking how I felt. What I want."

He pulls up to sitting, scrubs his hands over his face. "Not going to let that one slide, huh?"

"Nope. But we'll pick up right here, well, maybe not right here, because I have thoughts on this wasted space but you know what I mean. We do the work first, then we get the cookie."

He stands, meets me toe-to-toe, and sweeps my bangs from my eyes. "And in this case," he drops his voice to a whisper, "you're my cookie."

"I'm your cookie."

"Not sure how this feels, you being in charge. But I've made up my mind, I know what I want. So okay." He sticks his hand out, laughter in his eyes when I take it and we shake.

"Is this new for you? Listening to someone else's ideas? *Waiting*?"

Somewhere in my mind I realize waiting is not such a bad thing. If I'm honest, I'm already falling for this man, and I want to make sure it's going to stick before I get even more attached to him.

"Maybe, at least I'm working on it. And your cookie's totally gonna be worth it."

My cheeks burn as his mere words and the sound of his voice turns me on. "Maybe it'll do you some good."

As if he can't believe I'm sticking to my guns but is challenged at same time, he says, "You really were raised by a general, weren't you? So tough." The pad of his thumb rubs across my lips in promise of what will come.

"A general and a self-made woman. I think I'm a bit of both of them."

He takes a step back, resolved, and rakes his hair from his face, deep breath in, slow breath out. He really has been shouldering a lot on his own. "While we're on the subject of you being in charge, and being a team, can you stand in for me as store manager tomorrow?"

"Look at you, asking me for help, again."

"I always seem to find myself in the same position these days, ask you for help or let you go. Anything is better than the alternative." My head falls to his shoulder as I soak in his words.

This isn't an abnormal request. When the store manager is out, another manager will fill the spot for the day—take the pages, put out fires, greet the customers, things like that. But it's still a compliment that he's asking me.

I can't make fun of or poke at him for this anymore. He feels comfortable asking me for help, above anyone else. "You got it. What's up?"

He tugs gently on the belt of my dress. "There's something I have to do, make an appointment. If I'm really going to change my dad's mind, or maybe make a move on my own, I've got some decisions to make."

CHAPTER

Twenty

IN A PAIR of Gran's insanely tailored trousers with low-profile sneakers and an oversize I'm-the-manager Anine Bing blazer, I bend at the waist to speak to two tweens. "Okay, boys, hit me," I say. "What have we got here, and how can I help?"

The twins have set up on the first floor of Lorden's. They've got a long table with a screen-printing machine at the end. It's a pretty clean setup. The press is four sided so they can quickly work through shirts —press and spin, press and spin. I'm just not sure what it is they're making.

"Drum roll," Jordan says. His brother rolls his tongue while miming drumsticks on the table. "We are the Kind Klub. Every shirt you buy gets a number. Every shirt and number gets you into the Kind Klub of Seattle, but we plan to have clubs all over the U.S."

"And," adds Jameson, "once you have your number by signing up and buying your T-shirt, you can log on to our website and put your number on almost anything. Dog tags, coffee mugs, hats, beach towels, whatever."

"Supercool, boys." I'm showing them my millennial spots. "But what exactly is the point of the club? Why do I want to be a member and have a number?"

"Kindness." Jameson leaves off the *duh* because Mrs. Smith is staring him down watching her boys' pitch.

"Watch this, your number's on us." He walks me from the beginning of the table, where he signs me in quickly on a tablet and issues my number. Then, with a flourish, he whips out his own debit card and slides it through the reader to pay the twenty bucks that will be charged to each customer that walks through their line today. I select a medium white T-shirt and we move down the line to the screen-printing machine.

The boys have premade plates of plastic for over a thousand numbers that fit neatly into their four-way press. He uses what he explains is special paint, wipes the plastic with a window-washing squeegee, pulls the top plate down to press, and *voilà!* The front of my shirt proudly states in approachable black script: *Kind Klub of Seattle Number 142*.

They've just placed the shirt under quick dry lights when I give them a little round of applause. "Wow, that's amazing. So, if I'm 142—"

"We've already sold the previous numbers. The next customer will be 143, 144, and so on. And the deal is, you have to be kind. Lift others up. Every day. When you wear this shirt, everyone knows you're part of the Kind Klub."

He hands me a clipboard. "What's this?"

"The contract. If you wear our shirt, if you rep kindness, you have to sign the contract."

I get a little teary. These two kids have come up with a club, an inclusive club that has a twenty-dollar entry fee but with the goal of being kind to others. "How did you come up with this?" I ask, scrawling my signature across the bottom of my contract.

Jordan takes the contract and places it in a large accordion file—they're really going to hold us to it.

He looks at his grandma as if asking for permission, and she grants it with a tip of her chin.

"A bunch of kids were being shitty to us at school. Saying we're bussed in from outside the boundary to fill a diversity quota." He stubs his toe into the tiled floor but catches himself, lifts his chin, and looks up to make eye contact with me.

"My boys are going to change that school," Mrs. Smith says, her eyes watering slightly. "And it's about time, wouldn't you say?"

"I think your solution to fight cruelty with kindness is the most inspiring thing I've ever heard. I'm so glad we decided to do this. You boys sell the hell out of these shirts today. And I'm going to try to find you a permanent spot in this store. Not only is this a great idea, but I have a feeling you're really going to help our bottom line."

"Spoken like a true COO," Mrs. Smith says.

Hours later, I peer over the edge of the second-floor railing and watch the boys in the heat of a rush-crowd. The shirts have taken off—I had no doubt. Even employees stand in line over breaks to get a number and sign the Kind Klub contract. The premise of Kind Klub seems to be infectious and is rolling through the store today like a tidal wave, washing over everyone. Faces are brighter and smiles decorate every department. Customers are more patient at cash wraps, employees that I know normally wouldn't care are going the extra mile walking bags around counters so customers don't have to reach, holding fitting room doors so they don't slam, and patiently walking through aisles behind slower patrons.

But like Declan said, we're not going to keep Pine Street open with twenty-dollar T-shirts and happy thoughts, are we?

I push off the cold metal railing and head toward the escalator, catching a glimpse of Angel darting through a department with an armload of clothing in one hand and balancing a shoebox in another; she must be in the middle of an appointment. Our stylist team is still going strong, selling and putting up numbers every day. But we need to do more. I've got an appointment with a friend of Lenny's in an hour and I'm looking forward to adding to today's numbers.

Upstairs in the office, I inhale corn chowder from the café while I find the notes for my appointment via email exchange on my desk. Her name is Amanda. From her lifestyle questionnaire, I know she's a

curvaceous, athletic, and very tall woman that designers are just beginning to account for in American fashion; her sizes are going to be hard
to fit, especially size thirteen feet. I'll need to get creative when I pull
options from around the store.

On my way out, I let my hand brush the top of Declan's desk, the
one that used to be his brother's. Now I can't imagine not seeing
Declan sitting across from me every day. I hope whatever he's doing
today is fighting and not giving up. He's too damn proud to ask his
brother for help, and he definitely won't ask his dad. But he needs
someone to lean on nonetheless. Maybe I can be that someone.
Maybe I can be his rock, and he can be mine. Gran has moved to
Thorn Briar; I know she loves me, but she's starting something new
for herself. Len has David, and I love that for him. The General
would be there for me in a pinch if I need her, but especially now
that I'm an adult, the country and the president are her focus and her
passion.

And maybe I wasn't okay with that before, if I'm being honest.
Maybe I wasn't strong enough. But I am now. I can stand on my own
two feet, pay for and live in the cottage, and find my own dreams
without needing others' opinions. And maybe...maybe I'm learning
that I'm strong enough to lean on someone too, if it's the right someone, without the fear of losing them.

Back downstairs I pull every size I can find that will accommodate
Amanda. She said via the questionnaire that she wants casual,
comfortable options for the weekends, but that her job has a very strict
business professional dress code. People rarely dress for the office
these days but she's an attorney and needs to look polished. She was a
little less forthcoming when asked about hobbies and what she does on
the weekends, so I pull feminine athleisure that centers around the
always flattering combinations of black and white, with pops of color
in sneakers and tanks.

It's become my trademark move to add support undergarments on
the back of the fitting room door before the customer has to ask for
them because A: I have learned that everyone will eventually ask for
them and this saves me from sprinting to Lingerie on the third floor in
the middle of my appointment, and B: whether you're a size two or

twenty, every woman (and man—they are making serious headway in men's support garments) can benefit from smoothing spandex.

Back down on the first floor I get four thumbs-up from the twins as I pass their table, making my way to the E-bar where I'll meet Amanda. They've still got a line, and their stack of T-shirts is dwindling. A few kids have even put their shirts on over their clothes, already proud to be part of the Kind Klub. I spy number 198 and confirm my hunch that these twins are a success story in the making. They'll probably be on all the late-night talk shows by the end of the year.

Hovering around the E-bar, I wait patiently for Amanda, and then I know her when she's coming toward me.

She's about six feet, broad-shouldered, and wearing flowy linen pants with a Chanel bag hanging off a chain across her body. Immediately, I know I'll try to find her a chic tote instead of a crossbody—it'll be much more flattering. Amanda is clearly comfortable in her skin, though unsure of how to dress. I register that she's a beautiful part of the LGBTQ+ community, proudly sporting a rainbow pin on her lapel, but the girl needs a mini makeover STAT.

"Amanda, nice to meet you," I say, crossing the gap between us. "Let's get you a coffee? A tea?"

"Oh." She's caught off guard, but it almost seems to jostle her out of her obvious nerves. This was not the question she was expecting. "Tea, mint. Thank you. Holly, right?"

"That's me. Lenny said you're a good friend of his. I'm looking forward to shopping with you today."

"Yes, he said you'd be good."

She fidgets, still uncomfortable but warming up to me by the minute.

We head up the escalator and I try to put her at ease, sometimes the beginnings of these appointments feel like you're walking into a gynecologist's office.

"Oh, oh, Holly," she says when I use my key to open the fitting room door. "I can't believe there's so much! So many options!"

"This is what I do. Didn't you expect this, after your stylist questionnaire?"

"This isn't my first rodeo, honey. I've tried appointments like this before. I'm a professional woman, with specific needs," she says the words as if she's talking in code.

"Did other stylists not understand your requirements?"

"They never had things in my size, and most didn't want to find creative workarounds. But I see that's not going to be a problem for you."

She sits on the gray velvet-covered bench in the corner and pulls off her shoes as she continues, sounding world-weary. "They see my sizes, they hear my voice if we speak over the phone, they see me when I walk in the door and they rarely know what to do."

"I'm sorry to hear it. Your sizes aren't a problem. Creativity and impeccable tailoring, that's all it takes."

She beams. "That means a lot. This is going to be fun."

Flying high after my success and a bear hug from *Ms. Amanda*, I race my dump back to respective departments and dash to the third floor. I want to pull sales numbers and see how Kind Klub affected our Saturday.

When I breeze through the office door, I'm shocked to see the Lorden men here: Declan, Lenny, and Louie. A preppy mafia has taken up residence in my office. Declan is sitting at his desk with his head in his hands. He's definitely not supposed to be here. I'm the store manager on duty because he was taking the day off to cryptically *"do something important."*

When he doesn't look up, and no one says a word, I slink back toward the doorway, but Lenny reaches out a hand to stop me. He's pacing in Gucci mules, khaki pants, and a lemon-colored blazer. "I think you should be here for this," he mutters.

Louie is making himself comfortable in my desk chair and doesn't bother with eye contact.

I hug the wall and try not to gag on all the glum in the room.

"How did things wrap up with Amanda?" Lenny asks loudly for everyone's benefit, his way of slicing through the silence.

"She's great. Maybe the best appointment I've had. It didn't even feel like work—"

"Maybe that's the problem." Louie's got the nerve to speak to me from behind the financial pages, not bothering to lower his newspaper. "Building a sale is work. Convincing the customer to buy add-ons is *work.*"

"In two months she's grossed what our average salesperson does in a year, Dad. Holly has turned this store around more times than I can tell you."

Pride swells in my heart and I stand firm, then look to Lenny. In the week since Declan told me Louie was pulling the plug and closing immediately, we've all put our heads together to come up with ways to save the store.

"He's all but called it," Len says under his breath. "Declan wants to wait till five when our day officially cuts off to pull the store reports. He's hoping the Kind Klub put us so far in the green for today vs today last year, that Louie might reconsider."

I check my watch, the hand ticks to five on the dot.

Declan jumps from his chair and it continues its swivel even after he's left the room. The familiar hum of the copy machine next door lets us know he's printing reports. He's back before I can think of something to say that might sway Louie to give us another chance.

I hadn't realized it'd come down to this, to today's numbers. I wouldn't have taken a break, I would have come in earlier, I would have somehow found a way to sell a year's worth of product in an hour if that's what it was going to take to keep these doors open. We haven't even had a chance to fight.

Declan sits at his desk, sorting various reports and finding cover pages that will have all the forecasted numbers, per department, and per store companywide. He so desperately wants to prove he can do this, it's written all over his handsome face.

When he finds what he wants, an audible sigh escapes him as he rises in slow motion. He walks it over to my desk. Louie is still behind the newspaper hiding his face. It's hard to read the body language of hands and a torso.

Declan slams the page on the desk and his father jumps, folds the news in half, and deigns to look at what his son has presented.

He squints through spectacles pulled from his pocket, and Declan clearly can't take it. "We doubled our day compared to last year. That should tell you we're making effective changes. If we can just hold on—"

Louie looks up, a hint of something that appears like remorse on his face. "It's not enough, son. Truth? You would have had to move heaven and earth to change my mind today. I wanted to give you the meeting, as a courtesy." He stands and shrugs into a bomber jacket that makes his argyle sweater look even more dated. "Pine Street will close. Liquidate the fixtures, relocate them if it's cost-effective. Though, if she falls"—he looks around the room—"all the stores will follow."

Louie Lorden has given up. The ship has gone down. The captain is saving himself.

"Just like that? Our family business means that little to you?" Declan asks, his voice breaking. "Generations of our family have walked these halls."

"Mira and I are due to retire. The writing's been on the wall for a while, Declan. If something had been done sooner, if someone would have stepped up...maybe." No one has to wonder what he's saying.

Declan's shoulders fall. "What about us? George and me? Lenny? The board wants a Lorden as president—they support our family."

His father moves toward him, until he's very close. "All those years I asked you to make something of yourself, to show me some initiative. All you did was play games in your room. Wouldn't come to the club, refused to learn to golf, begged to go to those damn fantasy camps. Your brother has carried the family name long enough. And now even he's gone off to, to—"

"Say it, Louie," Lenny prompts from the corner of the room.

"To live a life I'll never understand."

Lenny turns toward me, toward the wall, shielding himself as best he can.

Louie walks out the door without another word. Then he pops his head back in, startling all of us. "I want it on the record that I love my sons, both of you. And I love my brother, but this is what I think is best."

There are tears in his eyes and I know, in that moment, that Louie Lorden is not a bad man. He's just very, very scared of things he can't control and things he doesn't understand.

"Damn it." Lenny walks out after him and I don't expect to see either one of them return.

"Dec…" I hesitate.

He just sits in his chair, head in his hands again.

When I go to him, kneel down so that I'm wedged between his knees, and force his face up to look into mine, he has tears rolling down his cheeks. Oh sweet, sweet boy. "We'll figure something out."

The tears move like a tiny river all the way to his square jaw, stubbled with a beard that he either hasn't had the time or the care to shave away. I wipe them from his chin, missing one as it hits the floor between us.

He sniff-laughs and wipes at his face as if he's appalled at what he's done. "I was in the middle of something when Len texted and said Dad was here. I raced over, but I've got to finish—" When I try to speak he raises a hand and lets it brush hair out of my eyes. He cups both sides of my face with rough palms. "Can I stop by later? I know you wanted to focus on the store but—" He forces a laugh I don't believe. "Clearly, it's over."

I nod at him and turn my face in his hands to kiss his palm before his thumb glides over my cheekbone.

"I'll text when I'm close to your place?"

"Okay." He pulls me to my feet.

We both gather our things in silence and walk down the long hallway toward the employee doors. I let Daisy know I'm off the clock as store manager and I watch her ring the night manager on duty. The store is still in full Saturday night swing out on the floor, with no idea that its Saturday nights are numbered.

I think of Alice, of Dorian, of Jenny on maternity leave with no job to return to. I don't think she needs the money, but she needs the job—it's part of who she is and she can't lose that now. And Angel and Molly, who are so good at what they do. What will they all have to fall back on? Retail is different at Lorden's. It's not just slopping a sweater into a bag, it's finding the perfect costume jewelry to complement a well-cut T-shirt and heels; the prom dress of your dreams; your son's first suit.

He walks me to my car and opens the driver door. I toss my things inside so I have both hands to hug him with.

"Don't do anything serious or stupid," I say, looking up into deep blue eyes that, if I had to bet, are going to shed a lot more tears once they're alone.

He guffaws, "What am I going to do, Holly? There's nothing left to do, my dad made that clear. I ran the store into the ground—"

"You didn't."

"It's closing under my management. Under my watch. There's no getting around it, I just wasn't good enough. My dad knew it, I knew it..." He trails off and I don't know what to say. There's nothing left to say.

He checks the time on his phone. "I'm late. I'll text you."

And then he's gone.

CHAPTER
Twenty-One

WHILE I'M DRIVING my phone pings three times with text messages and I worry about Declan. I do everything I can to ignore them, a promise I made my dad way back when I was still years from having a license, never to text and drive. Heart surgeons see a lot of trauma cases from car accidents.

Once home, my bag hits the kitchen counter with a *thunk*. I've learned my lesson about tossing it willy-nilly on the floor. I read my texts with one hand while the other pulls a box of mac n cheese from the cabinet.

Not from Declan. Maybe that's a good sign, but maybe not.

THE GENERAL

> I'll be in town Monday, want to see you. I'll stay in Gran's old room. Let's take her to dinner— make sure she's available. She has more social events at Thorn Briar than the First Lady has at the White House. Also, want job search update ASAP.

Pushing a lazy Susan until I see the pot I like, I begin to prepare my gourmet dinner for one. While the water boils, I pad back to my room for sweatpants and my trusty Wonder Woman slippers. My phone pings two more times and I run back to the kitchen.

THE GENERAL

> It's time to get serious about your future, young lady.

My last text is from a new number with Google contact information.

MRS. CORRINE WOOLWRIGHT

> Today was a success, much more than anticipated. The boys are over the moon and starting a YouTube channel. We want you on our team, Holly. There will be benefits, travel, and every perk you deserve. Say YES.

There it is. Mrs. Smith has just given me her real name and her personal contact. She's offering me a job. I know I won't be able to keep *Corrine* waiting long. And maybe I don't want to. A bloom of heat that I think is pride and a racing heartbeat that might be nervous excitement flows through me. She thinks I'm good at my job. She thinks I'm smart. She thinks I can run a company.

My hands shake as I stir orange noodles and contemplate my future. If I took this job it'd be the best of both worlds: fashion and business, a corporate title *and* textile design. Even dipping into creative marketing. This is everything I want. "This calls for wine," I announce to no one.

I uncork a bottle like a speedy server at a nice restaurant. This could be huge for me, but I'd have to leave the only company I've ever known. I wouldn't see Declan every day, which was my goal all along but now, not so much. The thought of *not seeing* him is suddenly loathsome. But the store is closing anyway, and the plan was for me to find a new job. Wasn't it? Somewhere along the way that part seemed to fade, and my wanting to help Declan and save Lorden's took on a whole new meaning. Watching those tears roll down his cheeks today gutted me. I'd have to trust that my leaving Lorden's wouldn't come between my friendship with Len and whatever it is that I have with Declan.

What about cocktails with Hawaiian umbrellas and taking a *fun* chance for once? I blow bangs out of my eyes and transfer dinner to a deep soup bowl.

Corrine has lifted me up since day one. Taking a liking to me and requesting me as her stylist when I had no real training or background. I want to be loyal to people like that. Not people like Louie Lorden who so easily toss their kid's efforts out like today's trash—no matter how many times he says he loves them. I want to be on the side of the people who don't only say it but show it. Like her grandsons. I like what they stand for and would be thrilled to make something like *kindness* cool.

My phone pings, yet again. Not Declan, and I groan at my glass of wine.

CORRINE WOOLWRIGHT

I'll text with details soon. We'll have a meeting and sign papers. Welcome to the family.

My lack of response isn't going to stop her—she should lead a sales retreat. Sell time-shares. This is going to be a hard press.

My dinner isn't as comforting as it normally is—it tastes like paste. I probably need to stop eating like a toddler and cook myself some real food. When I've finished and washed up so the tiny kitchen is spotless, I move to my room and continue to stress-clean. Declan Lorden is coming over, who would've thought. I really hope he's okay.

He texts shortly after I'm done which gives my anxiety some relief, so I light a candle in the living room and put on a Netflix original about witches that I think we'll both like.

The doorbell rings and my stomach drops to my knees. My heart kicks up to a speed that seems lethal, and I wish my dad was still around so I could ask him what's normal and when I should seek professional help. The effect Declan has on me feels every bit as deadly as a heart attack.

His words come to memory, *Chill, Holly.*

But I can't, not when I'm finally admitting to myself how much I like him. Despite being in the midst of life-changing decisions. And definitely not when he's spiraling after his dad's big announcement.

When the door opens it's worse; much worse than liking someone. Seeing him makes my chest pinch with pain and I can't find my breath. If I work up the guts to take the leap and accept the job offer with Corrine, if I'm going to have the guts to leave the company I've worked for my whole life, I would really like someone like Declan behind me. *Yes, I want it all.* I don't want to lose him being a part of my life, that's clear in this moment via a galloping heart and lack of oxygen.

"Hey, sorry it's late." He's still sullen and I wonder who he's talked to and where he's been?

I look at my watch. "It's nine thirty."

"It's been a big day. Feels later." He walks in and heads straight toward the couch. "Cute place."

He takes his jacket off and I'm not surprised to see him wearing a Kind Klub shirt instead of his usual crisp button-down and sweater combo. "Declan, are you okay? I've been worried."

"I need a minute, can't talk about it yet."

Okay, I can give him time. I like that he's making himself at home in my little cottage. "Nice shirt."

"Those kids are sitting on a gold mine. And their message is one I can get behind." He kicks off his Nikes and falls into a recline on the old couch that's really more Gran's size. "Come lay with me," he says, his denim clad legs hanging off the edge.

Oh. I wander toward him and sink into the couch between his legs. But I can't keep from asking, "How are you? After everything? I'm worried."

"Fine. Devastated. Not ready to talk about it yet...but I know I should. Being here with you is already making it better."

I lay next to him, half on him because there's just no room. It would be a pleasure to curl up right here, my cheek on his chest, for a nap.

Should I tell him now about Corrine's text? Her offer? Is this going to hurt him when he's already reeling? Make things worse?

My head moves slightly up and down with his breathing, his heart pounding in my ear. A low, heavy something kindles in my center.

"Speaking of the twins' company," I say, snuggling into him, "Corrine texted me to say how happy she was with their pop-up today."

He hums and the vibrations tickle my cheek. "Who?" Leisurely, he plays with my hair, brushing my bangs away from my face.

"Mrs. Smith, her real name is Corrine Woolwright—"

"I think I knew that?"

"She's interested in me," I hedge, speaking slowly and trying to feel him out. It's not that I need him to approve of my choice—if I accept— but I really don't want to add to his plate of problems either. "I think as more than a stylist. Kind Klub could be an opportunity..." I'm excited to tell him, I realize. This is a big deal for me and I want to share it with him.

He goes still, absolutely still.

I sit up, pushing my palms into his firm chest. "What?"

"There was something I was going to ask you tonight. But now..." He runs his hands through his hair, sits up, and pushes me gently to the side so he can brace his elbows on his knees. "I'm not sure I should..."

"Ask me." I want him to talk and get everything out.

"I want to sail around the world and I want you to come with me."

"What?" I stumble, caught totally off guard. "What about your business? Your family, your future?" Is he giving up on the store? Regardless of what Louie announced today, he's still got options. He can plead with Mira. He can implore Lenny to make a move with his stock. He can do something; fight for his dream!

"I don't have any of that anymore. But I have a boat that I love, and a girl that..."

I shake my head no. "Declan, you're not making any sense."

"Come away with me," he says all at once in an exhale. His blue eyes imploring me to jump off a cliff with him, that's what this is, what he's saying.

Four words, and I'm speechless.

But as much as I want this to be a fairy-tale moment, it's not. He wants to run away from his problems, instead of standing up and fighting. How can he bail so easily?

He sits up tall, grabbing me by the shoulders. His face is pale, but his cheeks suddenly flush, his chest moving fast with his breath. "Holly, answer me, I'm dying here—"

"I couldn't, I mean, what about rent? Food? Who would take care of the cottage?"

His hands find mine, pulling me closer. "I'll figure that out."

"You? But I spent the last few months turning my life upside down so that I could take care of my own responsibilities. What about the store? What about the life you've always wanted, your family's legacy?"

"Never mind what I want. What do you want, Holly?"

Can I be honest? Should I tell him about the career I want? The life I've only just begun to imagine—with him in it? Instead, I chicken out and say, "I want to stand on my own two feet." True, but not the whole truth.

"You are. You've done it, you've proven it. What else do you need to do?"

"Declan, you can't be serious right now. This is too fast—"

"This is not what I expected you to say." He looks away.

"What did you expect?"

"At the very least, I thought you'd jump at the chance to go away together! You were ready to leave for Hawaii with George the day I found you crying in the women's bathroom—"

"Declan, look at me." I turn his face in my hands. "That was different."

"But was it? Is it, really? You were ready to pull up roots and leave. Now you won't even consider it."

Things are changing so fast I can't keep up. I've never seen him act like a billionaire playboy until this moment. It doesn't suit him. "You're upset. You're not thinking this through. You'll want to fight for the company tomorrow and you'll realize I'm right not to drop my life to follow you."

"Is that a no?" A deep rumble in his voice makes me want to cry. "This is more than a *pause*, Holly," he says, referring to the night he told me his dad was selling the store. "This is a flat-out stop sign."

"That's not true. We can't just run away. You wouldn't be happy." I look him square in the eyes. "I wouldn't be happy."

As much as his offer is thrilling, I'd eventually wonder what I was doing with my life, following a boy around like a poodle. It's one thing to accept some gratis from his store, but I can't let him pay my way through life, until when? Unto what end?

Declan sits even taller. "I could take care of you."

It's a stab to the heart as he says it, everything I've ever wanted, just under all the wrong circumstances and in all the wrong ways. "Declan, I don't need you to *take care of me*."

Support me, yes. Encourage me, yes. Love me...maybe, yes. But I can take care of myself. I know that, I've always known that. I've just been floundering a bit trying to decide what that *looked like*. What it meant. What I wanted, not what my mother wanted or even what my gran wanted. This is about me. And I want Declan, but not like this.

"You know, I had another deal on the table, but I thought no—I'm going sailing. I've always said I'd do it one day. Maybe today is that day. I thought your feelings had changed... Stupid, huh." His voice is full of accusations and I'm not sure where it's all coming from.

"Declan, they have changed—"

"Are you sure? Because right now you're saying no to me, and you always said yes to him."

If there ever was a moment to flat out tell him about Corrine's offer it would be now. Telling him I can't leave because I'm taking a new job might make him see reason, but he's gone so off the rails I don't think it would make a difference. He can't possibly think I'd drop everything and let him support me, after everything I've worked for. "This has nothing to do with George. I'd love to go sailing with you but—"

And I would. Those cocktails with umbrellas I've been dreaming about? I could share them with him.

"I don't want to make this harder on you than it should be. I misunderstood what was"—he motions between us weakly—"going on. I just...I can't be anyone's second choice, Holly."

"You're not listening to me. You're not fighting fair—"

He pulls a box from his jacket on the floor, opens it, and pulls out my watch. The one he gave me. "None of this is fair." He fixes the watch around my wrist, right next to my dad's. "Spit and polished. It's perfect, and so are you."

He gets to his feet, shrugs on his coat, and is at my door in a matter of seconds. He's going to bolt. "It doesn't define who you are, Holly. Where you are, what you wear, who you're with. It's about the choices you make."

I follow him through the doorway, dancing on the cold pavement in bare feet, and halfway down the walk littered with spring's first blooms trying to push their way up in Gran's old garden. The air still smells like pure winter.

"Wait."

He shrugs, his lips in a sad line of acceptance. "I gotta go, Holly."

He walks to his car, slams the door, and pulls out. The red of his tail lights get smaller and smaller until they're nothing.

This cannot be the end.

ME

> I'll see you in the office tomorrow. Cool down, and we can talk about everything. We can find a way to make it all work. For both of us.

No reply.

No reply.

No reply. Not even bubbles. He doesn't even think about replying.

After I brush my teeth and hold back tears, I take both watches off and set them in a porcelain dish on my sink, put on my Pjs, and slip into bed.

But sleep doesn't come. I think of our first kiss, all passion and fire and confusion and pheromones when he said, *Can I freeze this moment in time? Will you please make the clock stand still?*

I think of the slew of words he continuously uses to describe me, *amazing, brilliant, strong, fascinating*. We could have been everything together. It was right there for the taking. I felt it and I know he felt it. But now, it's as if we're even less than enemies. We're nothing to each other at all.

CHAPTER
Twenty~Two

WHEN I WAKE, I have an emotional headache. Okay, maybe it was the bottle of wine I finished in bed while scrolling through social media and creeping on Declan Lorden before I actually dozed off. It never occurred to me to look him up, and what I found was a world of personal secrets and details. His account is private, he's got a handful of followers, and is following even fewer. I must have followed him a long time ago, when we were kids, I don't remember. But thank God I have access to him, even in this small way.

His feed is all about his boat. When he bought it, a picture of him shaking hands with the previous owner; posts about him learning to tie all the sailing knots; shirtless pictures anyone would drool over, and pictures of him scrubbing the deck that made me ache for him. Then he's patching the hull and polishing the wheel. This man never stops working on his boat. Mira and her decorator forcing white paint and stripes make an appearance; he liked their ideas on blue. A few of his friends make cameos, all D&D players with alter egos and names. Lots of inside jokes I can't begin to understand and wish I could.

Cold water on my face helps me wake up as I push my bangs aside and give myself a good hard look in the mirror. He said he had to go. But I'm not going to give up on him.

Determination rises in my throat along with a little nervous bile as I dress. The plan I'm hatching just might work. It could get us both what we want, and despite him acting like a jackass last night I can't wait to tell him.

At my desk, I frantically compile a list from social media: a woman who makes glitter hair bows, another who embroiders denim jackets— I've already placed a personal order—and a dad whose side hustle is hand-painted skateboards. My email swooshes as I fire off proposals to all three of them. The turnaround has to be fast, no time to lose. I hope these hustlers can hustle.

Dec breezes through the office in wrinkled khakis and a white button-down that's seen better days, plopping a paper cup of coffee from the chef's kitchen on my desk, then sitting down and getting right to it. Through the strong coffee I can still smell him, all fresh and natural, and I tell myself to focus. We've got business to tend to.

"Hey."

"Hey," he grumbles, face already buried in his computer screen.

"Hey, again." I snap my fingers until he begrudgingly looks up. "Last night, you leaving upset...I want you to know that really freaked me out. If you need time, just tell me so I know what's going on... But I'm not giving up on you, Lorden. I've got some ideas on how to salvage this before your dad sells. Make numbers so profit-heavy at Pine Street, he'll rethink pulling the trigger."

A muscle in his jaw tics, but his smile is soft. "I truly believe you could save Pine Street all on your own. I'm not so sure about me though. You might not be that good."

"If you're sailing around the world, I will be saving this store on my own." I shift in today's outfit of jeans, heels, and a new blush-pink blazer. Challenging him to tell me outright he's giving up on his company, on his dream.

No response. So I press harder, "Last night when you said, and I quote, 'gotta go.' Did you mean for the night? To blow off some steam and think? Or did you mean you're leaving on a boat in a matter of days?"

I need him to fight and I'm prepared to fight with him. Corrine assumes I'll accept the job with Kind Klub, and I've done nothing to correct her, but he doesn't need to know that. Not yet. Not until we save Pine Street.

"That ship, pun intended, has sailed." Around us the bland office sighs with regret.

"Dec, I've known you for a billion years. You can pull out of this. We can still convince your dad—"

"I sold my boat this morning." His eyes meet mine and they're layered with shadows of pain, regret, and wisps of last night's anger.

Why would he do this? "But…you love that boat."

"I did."

"Where are you going to live?"

He takes a deep breath and braces his elbows on the desk. "It was my plan all along. I was going to sell to help with Pine Street's debt. Why I took Saturday to meet with a potential buyer. But then Dad pulled the plug. And I thought, maybe this is meant to be? Maybe I'm meant to do something else, like sail around the world on my dream boat with my dream girl. Anyway"—he leans back as if settling into a good story—"when I left the office last night, I went back to the buyer and backed out of the sale. Drove to your house thinking I'd help you pack and *boom*. No dice. So I called him up and went through with the sale this morning."

I roll my eyes at the overambitious assumption that'd I say yes and bail on everything I've worked for. Maybe he had a point. The day I realized George was going to Hawaii and I was jobless, I *was* ready to bail. Not anymore, I have too much here to fight for.

"But that was your house!" I say loudly picking the easier of the problems at hand.

"Yeah, it was. It was everything to me. And I thought"—he looks directly at me, meaningful fire burning in his eyes. "But turns out you can't have it all. Hard decisions must be made—"

"Can't you have it all? Professional goals and…" We both know I can't say *us*. Sailing around the world, maybe not today, but someday.

"My parents couldn't make both work." He winces as he says it.

"We're not your parents, Dec. We were just getting started—"

"I'm crashing with Len and David. I promised David I'd be out before the wedding. Honeymoon couple and all that. I don't want to shit on anyone's Valentine."

"But why?"

A faint flicker of a smile appears on his handsome face. "Because I'm going to save Pine Street on my own. The money I got from the boat is going to keep the lights on until I can figure out how."

Thank God! He's still going to try, he's stewing and acting like an idiot, but he's going to try. I jump from my chair. "Then I'm helping."

"On my own, Stewart. You need to focus on—"

Oh, no. No way. "You're not giving up without a fight, and I'm not either. Not just for you," the big dummy looks up at me with puppy eyes, "but for Lenny, for George. I want to see this place continue on for another hundred years, run by little control-freak Lorden heirs."

I come to stand beside him, resting my hands on his strong shoulders, but he doesn't look up, he doesn't even turn in his chair. "My father's been waiting for me to trip over my own feet for years. I could lose everything."

"You won't. Especially if you let the people who care about you help."

"I'm listening." That's a start, I'll work with it, but something is still bothering him and I make a mental note to press him more about it later. For now, we need to get down to work.

Deciding to take a professional stance, I sit in the chair opposite his desk and dive in to telling him what kept me up all night—just not the part about him shirtless on the deck of his old boat. "Okay, so, Kind Klub was a raging success, right?"

"Yes, but we can't bank on them every Saturday."

"Exactly, we need more of them."

"I don't follow."

"I'm reaching out to entrepreneurs all over Seattle, like smaller types but those who have already garnered sales and proof of concept."

"Creatives who need that one big break."

"Exactly."

"Okay, I see what you're saying. You're thinking like a shark," he says, unable to hide his pride while leaning back in his chair, stretching his arms, and tucking his hands behind his head. "I like it."

"Thanks. I should be hearing back from them soon, and then I'll set them up for pop-up events just like Kind Klub. That should increase sales monthly by a nice percentage; not only with their sales but by increasing foot traffic in general. But I think you need a product too. Get rid of the beds and the home department upstairs. It's wasted, valuable space. Find something like the soup to license, those are big margins, right?"

A rolling boil takes up residence between us, over the desktop we meet gazes and know we're both thinking of what happened on the bed in the home department.

"Way to think outside the box. Nice work, Stewart." His words, generic and professional as a business card, hit me hard. He's closed himself up again. He's back to the Declan I grew up with, prickly on the outside, no idea what's really going on inside.

Standing slowly, I place both hands on his desk and lean in. "Is that how it is? Back to square one between us?"

He must be able to read the hurt on my face. "Holly, it's about what you want. And it's about what I need. I told you, if we went any further and you hadn't fully moved on from your feelings for my brother, I wouldn't recover. I meant it."

"If you think this is about me, you're dead wrong. Dig deeper, Dec. Please."

He moves swiftly, standing and rounding the desk until he's grasping me by the waist, looking deeply into my eyes. "Holly." We breath in tandem, fast, chests pumping, wondering who's going to break—and what that will mean—until he says, "It's so," he gulps, "scary. But I'm sure as hell going to try."

Declan Lorden wanted to sail around the world with me. And I wanted to go with him. Instead, here we are, moving in opposite directions but still working toward the same goal.

And soon, I'll be leaving this store entirely. Whether it's saved or not. Whether we hate each other, like each other, or mean nothing to each other at all.

Every Saturday in March is filled with me running around the store like a chicken with my head cut off hosting local pop-up artists and entrepreneurs. A few of the originals bailed, but the dad with the skateboards showed up and the store was flooded with an onslaught of teenagers ready to spend their allowances. The week after that was custom dog collars, the week after that organic shampoos and cute bucket hats with SPF—we put them next to the Goop counter, sent a few to local Mom-fluencers, and sales rang all day.

"How's it going, Alice?" I ask, passing the activewear department. Alice has about fifty swimsuits in her arms and is struggling to get them all on a four-by-four rack.

"Ready for spring!" she says, more enthusiastic than I would have guessed. "Shipping is a nightmare, but we finally got more swim stock in, and it's flying for spring break."

I wink at her and keep moving. I've got a big appointment today and I cannot be late. Just as I'm breezing into the office to grab my things, I halt, skidding on my heels. Declan is in the doorway, and we collide in a tangle of uncertain emotions and hot bodies.

His arm wraps around me before I pitch forward while the other braces both of us against the doorjamb.

He doesn't let go. Instead he breathes, ragged and rushed, in my ear. My own breath catches and I gasp, *oh!* into the starched neck of his collared shirt.

His arm around me tightens and we both decide on a truce via body language for exactly thirty seconds while clinging to each other in the doorway. I press every part of myself I can into him. He responds by leaning harder into me, moving his arm so it takes the brunt of our weight against the door.

We are cocooned, and it's bliss, until I open my mouth. "I've got an appointment."

"When?" he asks roughly.

He thinks it's here, a stylist appointment, and I feel a terrible pang of guilt when I don't correct him. "Pretty much, now."

These little moments have been all we've allowed ourselves over the past few weeks. We don't speak about George or Corrine, or what's going on with his family.

We do talk about daily tasks, numbers, and department sales. But when we talk about these mundane things, in the office or in the middle of meetings, his eyes are always searching mine. It's as if he's looking for the answer to a secret, and I know what it is. He thinks I'm still in love with his brother. I'm not. He thinks he's a second choice. He's so not. But right now, I don't know how to make him believe me.

We're basically existing in a little pocket of reality, fully embracing our pause, and from what I can tell, mutually pining for each other on an Austen level.

"I miss you," he says, low and needy, his lips grazing my neck.

Sharply, I suck in a breath, hold it, and look into his eyes. *Why are we doing this? It doesn't have to be this way. We could have it all if we just got out of our own way... I'm sure of it.*

He releases me and says genuinely, "Good luck." He turns, then turns back to plant a kiss on the top of my head, then stomps off.

I shrug into a vintage Burberry raincoat of Gran's, grab a black leather backpack that I've been using lately so I don't have to worry about things like phones going missing when I forget to be gentle with my bag, and head out the door.

Thoughts of Declan need to wait. I've got a meeting with Corrine at the original Starbucks on Pike Street, not a stylist appointment. I'm determined to show up and prove that I believe in myself. I believe I can turn Kind Klub into a fully functioning, successful business. Building a brand, one involving fashion and creative use of textiles no less, sounds terrifying but also exhilarating.

It's an overcast ten-minute walk from the office. Sometimes, I feel like Lorden's is the only entity in this great city; I eat there, work there, shop there. What else do you need? But as I take a deep breath and watch a whole world matriculate that has nothing to do with the department store, I feel a little weight lift off my shoulders. Turns out, there is more to life than pining after a Lorden brother.

As I step over cracks in the sidewalk and listen to traffic, I try to mentally prepare for what's coming after my meeting with Corrine. The timing couldn't be more inconvenient.

The General arrives in town tonight. She's not going to understand a move to a fledging upstart that can only offer me a title and prayer. No matter how much money Corinne has to sink into her grandsons, if this business doesn't work, I won't have a job at the end of the day.

The Pike Place Market is lit up just in time for dusk to descend, the first wisps of spring in the air mingling with the unavoidable fishy smells.

I have a little extra time so I let myself wander through vendors, enjoying the colorful fruits and veggies on display. People are packed as tight as the sardines another vendor is selling, while across the street on the corner men throw fish and tourists record videos.

Before long, I wind my way back around to the coffee shop and step into the distinct smell that comes with the iconic mermaid.

I check my watches—I've taken to wearing both Dad's and Declan's with a mishmash of bracelets. Maybe it's an odd look, maybe it's charming and unique, either way it's my style and very *personal*.

Thoughts roll from happy old memories of Dad, to memories of Declan. I don't even try to banish him, rather, I swim in a fantasy for a moment where he and I are together, madly in love, and working furiously to pursue our goals in life. It'd be nice to have someone hold my hand through dinner tonight too. I'd really like some backup when I explain to my mom I'm leaving a hundred-year-old company for twelve-year-old twin bosses. At least Gran will be there, but you never know which side she'll land on. In this version of reality, Dec holds my hand and I'm strong while telling the General exactly what *I* want and how *I'm* going to achieve my dreams.

Someone bumps me while trying to get through the entry I'm blocking.

Fantasy over; my watches say I'm on time for my appointment with Corrine.

Her silver bob shines in a corner near the back with two cups in front of her. More tourists wait at the counter as baristas shout names for pick up.

"Holly!" she greets me warmly, motioning to the chair across from her. "I got you mint tea. Everyone likes mint tea."

"Thanks. How are you?" I start, I've never began a business meeting and don't know if I should approach her as a friend or with a handshake and a résumé. Probably somewhere in between.

"I'm glad to be getting this done," she says, all business. "I need a break after spring break."

"Did the twins have a good time? You were in Hawaii, right?" I sold her outfits for all three of them to last a few months of island hopping.

"We worked half and played half. They had a ball doing both and are obsessed with surfing now. I stopped into Lorden's on the big island and said hello to George. But it was raining nonstop, almost three days, so we took a puddle jumper to Oahu. Talk about an amazing cup of coffee." She eyes me, waiting for a reaction, but I don't have one. "Let's get down to it, shall we? I have a date with my husband tonight."

She produces a folder from a briefcase I've never seen her carry and notices me appraising it, only because it's far from her usual style.

"Hideous, I know," she says. "I used to practice law and old habits die hard. I just can't bring myself to upgrade. I really trudged through the mud with this thing, you know?"

I nod, though I'm not exactly sure what she means. "Corrine, I'm grateful for the opportunity but—" I stumble.

"But you're nervous about leaving Lorden's?"

I shrug, trying to ignore the chill in the coffee shop. "Yes, I guess I am." And so much more.

"Even though rumor has it that Pine Street is closing and the company as a whole may fold in less than a year?"

"Where did you hear that?" I rub my arms, trying to warm up.

"The retail world is smaller than one might think."

"It's complicated."

"Hmm. Does this have anything to do with one of the heirs to the throne?" Now she sounds like Lenny. Even this, the thought of Len and Dec and our office, makes my heart hurt for all I stand to lose. I can't believe I won't see them every day. They're like family, though I no longer think of Declan as the antagonizing, evil brother. Much to my dismay, I want him in a wholly un-sibling-like way.

It must show on my face because she says, "I see."

I take a sip of tea and try to let the heat and mint warm me while I flip idly through the stack of papers she's set in front of me. Tiny yellow flags signal everywhere that I'll need to sign my old life away. Up until this point, I've done everything in my power to keep my job at Lorden's. I've worked every position, I've come in early and stayed late, I've even taught myself how to dress others and how to sell...and now I'm walking away. And no one knows but me.

"Do you know why I chose to meet in this specific coffee shop?"

"It's close to Lorden's?" Magically, a pen has appeared in my hand. It feels right, the weight of it and the weight of my decision, as if the story of my life is unfolding exactly as it should. As if I'm at the very beginning.

"No." Her eyes dial into mine good and slow as if to say, *Do you really think your commute and comfort are at the forefront of my thoughts?* "It's a symbol of all the possibilities in life. What we control and what we do not. The difference a left turn can make, versus right, to your future."

I will her words to make sense but they don't.

She smiles kindly and elaborates, "The men who started this coffee shop weren't out to achieve one of the greatest consumer products—or experiences—of our generation. They just wanted to make good coffee. Two well-born white guys who were products of the sixties, out to establish a *counterculture* product. Can you imagine?" She lets her gaze travel the store, the hustle and bustle of aggressive commerce. "The irony is that it backfired. Another man ended up buying this little coffee shop, toned down the logo, and made the cup a *status symbol*."

She holds up her cup and I'm once again struck by how beautiful she is, wearing a signature cream sweater with simple diamond studs the size of my thumbnail.

"Status. Money. Privilege. That's what this cup says to people. A long time ago, I was proud of myself that I could lunch here with my laptop and my six-dollar coffee. I thought that meant I'd made it. The American dream."

Now, I'm hearing her, I truly am. Is that what I'm doing at Lorden's? Settling? "I'm grateful for this opportunity, Corrine. The fact you believe in me..."

"I'm grateful I didn't stop after the first sign of success. If you keep going, Holly, I think you'll feel the same. If Lorden's is all you want, that's fine. It's more than fine, but... It's scary having the guts to go after a dream, especially for women and minorities. But the benefits of conquering that fear can outlast even our lifetime."

"You mean the twins."

"Yes. I wasn't able to get through to their mother. I still try. But I've taught those boys that they have every right to buy six-dollar cups of coffee if they work for it, and what's more, to sell twenty-dollar T-shirts. To scale and make moguls of themselves. It's my intention, and the boys too, to lift others up as we go. The sky's the limit, for anyone who wants to join ranks, dream big, and work hard."

"That's something I'd like to be a part of."

"Sign the contract, Holly." She taps a finger on the last signature line in the contract. "You already are."

CHAPTER
Twenty~Three

"YOU'RE EARLY!" The electricity from signing Corrine's contract is still coursing through my body when I burst through my door. I'm sparking with energy.

The General's plane landed early and she beat me home. She has the garage code, so she's dressed for dinner and waiting at the kitchen table.

"And you live like a pig," she offers, tapping a well-manicured nail. She may be in the United States military, but she's always believed in the art of dressing well. Tonight, she has on a maroon pencil skirt with a gray snow-leopard-print blouse.

What a warm greeting, Mom, you've outdone yourself.

"I was going to come home and clean," I say through gritted teeth, *"you're early."*

"I tidied what I could. You've rearranged parts of the kitchen in ways that make no sense. Why are your tea towels in a cabinet instead of a drawer by the sink?"

Why do we pick at each other like this? Will we ever be the sort of mother/daughter who hug, and kiss, and say *Oh, I've missed you, tell me everything!*

In my room, I quickly change into one of her wrap dresses. "Is Gran waiting for us?" I yell down the hallway.

"Yes, she's looking forward to Spinasse. She's bringing a man named Bernie?"

"Oh my God! Is she still dating him?"

"You knew about this?"

I run down the hall in ankle boots and shrug into a leather jacket that I got as gratis, earned by selling the most in the month of February.

"Nice coat," she says.

It's unclear whether her comment is a compliment or not. "Sales has its perks."

"I recognize the dress." She reaches out to grasp the tie of the belt and I freeze.

"Thought you might," I say. The story goes that Mom and Gran used to sew clothes together when she was younger, but then she grew up and went into politics. Mentally, I will her to remember when she loved something other than the president of the United States.

"I can't believe you're still working retail." She drops the tie and my shoulders fall. "Have you been looking for another job? Something more respectful and promising than *sweater slinger*?"

Her easy judgment makes my skin crawl, but it's just the way she is. She doesn't understand what I do at Lorden's. She never did and that's not going to change. "As a matter of fact, I signed a contract with a new company today." Nothing like ripping off a Band-Aid.

"A contract?" She's still staring at me in her old dress.

The moment is here, it's inevitable, so I drop bombs. "It's a start-up. A fashion label by two twelve-year-olds, and I've already signed a bunch of noncompetes."

It's a little too fun to shock her. I've shocked the General into silence.

When she still doesn't say a word or make a move to leave, I change tack. "Gran told me I could go through the old things in the attic. Some of her stuff was in there and some of yours. I actually thought you might like to see it."

Finally, emotion washes over her face. It's something I see so rarely,

I feel the need to sit down. "It's just...that dress has so many memories."

Oh. Not what I expected. "Of?"

"Your father. I wore that on a date with him, not our first, but one of the firsts." She swipes at her eyeliner though the small amount of mist there is no real threat to her makeup. "I still miss him."

More unprecedented territory. I've never seen my mother cry, except at Dad's funeral and I had to look away. Seeing her emotional throws my world off-balance in ways I don't yet understand. "I do too."

"It's why I push you so hard, Holly. Life is short. So, so short. And I worry..."

It dawns on me that my mom, a general at that, is just scared like the rest of us. But I don't know what to say. There's a lump in my throat the size of Texas. "Come on, let's get Gran and her geriatric date. Pasta always helps."

"That is a universal truth I cannot argue with." She follows me out the front door and gets into the passenger seat of my car.

She doesn't speak, doesn't update me with cryptic half information about her job, she doesn't question me further till I'm about to burst with annoyance about mine. The General's silence is a much bigger concern than if she were laying into me right now. It's a testament to how much they loved each other, and to her strength, that she still misses my father this much. She's dated over the years, but in her own way, without words, she's made it pretty clear she's married to her job for life.

Halfway to Gran's I break the silence. "Are you going to say anything?"

"About what?"

"About the job? I know it's not what you want for me but—"

"A start-up?"

"We have a very serious backer, and I believe in the concept. I will eventually be everything you wanted me to be, just on my terms, in my own way."

She turns a bit in her seat to speak to me. I keep my eyes locked on the road, hands at ten and two. "You're right, it's not what I would choose for you. But I'll tell you what, I'm proud of you for making a choice. For moving on. I know some people make a great living selling in that store, they make an art of it and I'm not taking that away from anyone. I couldn't do it," she huffs, as if it's so hard to admit she's not perfect. "But you weren't flourishing there. You haven't been happy there for a long time. You're so smart and capable. All you need to do is figure out what it is you want to do with your life, and go after it. If you believe this is a chance you should take, I support you."

So, there it is. Mrs. Smith and the General think anything is better than staying stagnant, and I agree. And she supports me.

I bite my lip hard, unable to cry in front of her. Unable to show her how those words affect me. How much I needed to hear them.

When I cut a glance her way, she's got tears in her own eyes. Fighting them just like me. She knows.

Gran and Bernie are ready and waiting while Mom and I sign them out of Thorn Briar. The receptionist gushes to Gran about having a decorated military daughter, and we all pack into my car to head to Spinasse.

The restaurant is old-world Italian, cozy with red vinyl booths along the walls and warm wood tables in the center. Mom requests a booth and we all slide in, Bernie and Gran in the center like middle schoolers on a date. The waiters come and go, responding to Mom's air of authority with grace and speed, and before we know it, plates full of creamy pastas and spicy Diavolos appear.

Halfway through our meal, Lenny texts, and I discreetly read under the table. Bernie's third story about how he owned an automobile repair shop works nicely as a buffer. He's saying something about a carburetor and Mom's eyes are glazing over while Gran's bug out into the shapes of cartoon hearts.

LENNY

Contract signed? You're officially working for Mrs. Smith?

ME

Corrine. Yes. I signed. Haven't told Dec yet.

Bubbles. While Lenny types my stomach churns.

LENNY

Congrats, doll. I won't say anything. He hasn't
been himself. Said you got in a fight?
Something about a pause?

ME

We had a tiff. He asked me to go away with
him, I said I couldn't leave. Long story.

LENNY

He seems sorry. I think your nemesis is on the
brink of a tear :(He's asking if I know where
you are.

ME

Tell him I'm at dinner. I'll text him later.

LENNY

You two, Meow.

At the table, Mom is trying to drive the conversation to climate change and why our president is such a forward thinker and going to save our planet if she gets another term. This has caused Bernie and Gran to strike up their own side conversation about their last bingo party and whether Mary Ann Higgins cheated. All around me there's chatter, and smells of oregano and red wine, but all I can think of is a man who smells like water and wood and how much I don't want to leave him behind when I embark on my new adventure in industry.

Tears spring to my eyes and threaten to outright gush. I don't know where this babbling brook of emotion is coming from, and I try to sniffle and dab without drawing attention to myself. Lenny is happy for me, maybe even proud. Mom is here and apparently supportive of my new job. And even if she wasn't, I'm done being *scared* of her. And Gran, well, she's clearly in love and that just makes me happy.

I'm happy for my ninety-year-old grandmother because she has something I desperately want. Mom had it with Dad, Gran had it with my grandpa, so I'm told though I never met him, and now she's got a second chance at love with Bernie. My fingers toy with a loose thread on the checkered tablecloth while I watch them all continue to banter.

It's humanly impossible to hold it all back and a tear sneaks down my cheek, plopping onto my phone balancing in my lap. I want him to be here. I want Declan here, smushed between me and my family, eating pasta and leaving smelling like garlic and herbs. To take me back to his boat and kiss me like crazy while the hull rocks gently in the water.

But his boat is gone. The store is as good as gone. And I'm about to be gone from his life too. That's too much *gone* for anyone to handle and I wish I could tell him so. That I understand why he reacts so passionately because he's had the short end of a golden stick handed to him his whole life.

Thankfully, Bernie is now talking about spark plugs and why changing oil regularly really is the dental floss of motor vehicle care. No one notices my sniveling; I hold the brunt of my tears back.

A centipede of waiters carrying sparklers approaches our table. I harrumph a laugh. Someone's probably being proposed to at the next table while I'm left here to watch and wish.

"Miss Holly Stewart?"

"Yes?" I sniff and smile, willing my face to look normal. "That's me, but it's not my birthday." I try to wave them away. *Not today, no signing for me, just holding on to my sanity and making big life decisions over here! Alone. Did I mention that part? I don't have anyone to arrange sparklers for me!*

"Compliments of Declan Lorden." He pulls a small card from the front pocket of his jacket and reads, "For the woman who has single-handedly taught me how to be nice, and how to keep trying when I want to give up. I'm sorry. Love, Dec."

"What's all this?" Gran asks.

Like a lunatic I push back from the table, bumping it as I go, forcing everyone to grab their wineglasses. Could he be here? I see a bald man and a curvy woman with pink cheeks toasting at one table. At the front door, two men walk in and make my heart jump from my chest, but it's not Lenny and Dec.

"Who are you looking for, dear?" Bernie asks with concern.

I settle back into my seat. "No one," I cough-cry-cackle at myself.

"This is an odd reaction to handing in your two weeks," my mom huffs.

A champagne bottle pops. With a flourish, the waiter begins filling fluted glasses. The staff behind him pile our table with cheese boards, fruit bouquets, soufflés, and slices of pie until there's no room to spare.

"He doesn't even know yet. This isn't about that," I laugh-cry, sniffing into my napkin.

"I think they're going to miss you," Bernie laughs, pulling a cheese board toward him.

"I think that's an understatement, dear," Gran says, smiling wide at me.

"Well, it was about time they recognized your worth." And to my shock, the General kicks back her champs in one satisfied glug.

CHAPTER
Twenty~Four

I'M at Lenny's door with a buzzy, fuzzy brain; not drunk on actual liquor, I stopped after one glass of champagne, but more so on the prospect of seeing him. Something stops me from knocking.

How am I going to tell him I signed with Corrine?

What do I want? Do I want Declan in my life permanently? Would I have sailed away with him? I know I would have. If I could have sorted things with Corrine, and if he hadn't gone and sold his boat, I definitely would have if he'd given me the chance to have both.

Nerves rattle in my belly because I have a big problem: I have no idea what Declan wants. He's been distant. But he did make the grand dessert-sparkler gesture. He's trying to be *nice*…to not give up, on us? Or the store?

Just as I'm chewing on my cheek and thinking I should turn around, the door opens and I make shocked eye contact with Lenny over the heads of two short men in business suits.

"Holly, what are you doing here?" he asks.

"I-I—" I will add stammering to my résumé tomorrow, just in case I'm a flaming failure with Kind Klub.

"Excuse us," the suits say, awkwardly moving around me and out the door.

"Thanks, Dick, Oscar. We'll speak soon."

One suit waves as they make their way down the walk to a big black SUV I hadn't noticed parked on the street.

"Who were they?" I ask. It's an odd time for a meeting.

"My lawyers." Lenny pulls at his face, looking as haggard as I've ever seen him allow. "You're not the only one making deals, Holly dolly. Congrats, by the way. Did you tell him?"

David appears at his side. "Holly!" he says, as if he'd been expecting me. "Come in, it's chilly out."

"You look great!" I hug him in the doorway then whisper discreetly to Len, "Not yet."

"Feel great." David smiles wide and the handsome cleft in his chin deepens.

Inside, I take in the remnants of a meeting. Glasses filled with untouched water sitting on square linen napkins, sweating and forming rings.

"You got anything else?" Dec walks into the room holding up a Lady Gaga concert T-shirt with a pained expression.

He's shirtless, I assume debating donning the one in hand, and clearly wearing a pair of sweatpants that belong to Lenny; they're camo, about three sizes too small and have silver grommets along the sides of each leg, studs at the cuffs. They ride so low on his hips that I think I should look away but I don't.

"Holly stopped by," David says as a way to give him a moment to recover from the pure shock on his face.

Declan tosses the offending T-shirt on a couch covered in Hermès pillows. "Hey."

"Hey." He looks delicious with nothing but a bare chest and chartreuse walls behind him. My mouth dries, but I can't get ahead of myself. I don't know where we stand. He doesn't know I'm leaving. There's a stampede of mustangs galloping in my chest and I think I'll die of missing him if I lose him again without ever actually *having* him.

"Did you sell all your clothes too?" I blurt.

"Huh? Oh." He looks down as if shocked by his own state of dress, but simply says, "No." He leaves it at that, no further explanation.

We might as well be standing outside a high school trying to hash out our first fight and whether or not we're still going to prom.

Lenny and David exchange glances and begin to slowly back away toward a tapestry-covered hall that leads to the primary bedroom. "You two make yourselves at home. Food's in the fridge if you're hungry. Let me know—"

"Shh. Sweetie, come on," David says, taking Lenny by the hand. They both disappear like concerned parents who will listen at the door.

"I wanted to say thank you for the champagne and all the desserts. There were sparklers in brownies. No one's ever given me sparklers."

My eyes lock on his while I think of what I want to say next.

"You deserve so much more than sparklers." He heaves a breath. "You're welcome."

We stand there, at opposite ends of a beautifully decorated living room. Me, twisting my hands, him shuffling his feet.

"How's it going here?" I ask, my heart breaking for him even though it's his fault he's been going through all this alone.

"Fine. It's…it is what it is. I hope it's enough."

"Enough for what, exactly? What are you two planning?"

"Dick and Oscar put together a proposal for my parents. Lenny and I are going to try to buy them out. It looks like Louie's going to play ball," he says, shrugging one golden shoulder.

"That cannot be the real names of your lawyers."

His laugh is strained but it's there, guiding the way to a conversation neither of us seems ready to have. "Hate to break it to you, they are brothers. Dick and Oscar Siegler, of Siegler's Law Firm, Seattle. Anyway, Len's got savings we can put down as earnest money. I've already paid some outstanding bills with what I made off my boat, which puts my name on Pine Street paperwork. I don't know, they say that's good. Shows the bank I can carry weight. Then we'll make payments over the next lifetime with a percentage of company profit. We'll both be living like college kids eating ramen, but David's a good guy. He's up for it. And in the end, we'll own the company. Zero risk for my dad, all potential reward for Lenny, George, and myself. The company keeps its name and stays in business. Everyone wins."

"I'm happy for you."

We both know there's an elephant in the room. One dripping in diamonds named Corrine Woolwright. I had told him she was interested in me as more than a stylist, but has he put it all together?

Slowly, he closes the distance between us. He doesn't even make me come partway, he comes all the way to me. "The plan is great. I'm happy for me too. But I really hope I still have a chance with you. *I don't want to do this alone*, Holly."

"Stop," I say, holding a hand up.

"Stop? But I've been rereading all of my personal growth books, I'm ready for *the talk!*" His face falls and the false bravado in his voice goes with it. It's only then I see the shadows under his eyes. He's been hurting. The past few months are going to leave a mark.

My heart twists in my chest. I'm so proud of him for uttering those words. For coming so far but… "I need to say something."

A hand rakes through his hair and then he folds his arms. "Okay." He moves into Lenny's dark moody kitchen, all navy cabinets and splattered gray marble. "Should we sit?" He motions to barstools. I follow him but neither of us sit.

"Dec, I learned something about myself tonight…"

He stops whatever he was going to say and quietly whispers, "What's that?"

"When those sparklers came out, I thought they were for someone else. I thought someone was getting engaged." I laugh, still embarrassed by how happy I felt when I realized they were for me. "But even as happy as they made me, something was missing."

"I told them to send out two of everything on the dessert menu, an extravagance I promise I won't be able to afford in the near future," he deadpans, knowing good and well that was not my meaning. "If you're wondering if I was trying to impress the General and your gran just as much as you, the answer is yes."

In the future...

"The food was beautiful. But when those sparklers burned out, I was still sitting there. Without you."

Slowly, I step into him. My hands shake as I press them into his chest. His skin is warm, all those muscles from boat building and hull scrubbing, tense at my touch. My voice shakes as I push myself to continue, "I like you, Declan Lorden, former bane of my existence. A lot, I think. I don't know how we've come to this point, after everything, but the second I was starting to trust you, you pushed me away. Twice."

"I'm sorry, I am. It doesn't change the way I feel. Holly, you say you like me? A lot, you think?" He wraps a hand around both my wrists, pulls them up to his neck. "Can you imagine how I feel hearing that? That I still have a shot when I have," he gulps down air as if it's fueling his words, "I have loved you my whole life. I just needed you to pick me. And then, I think you did, and I almost blew it by walking away. Because I'm no good at this, no," he shakes his head and lifts his chin, "because I was scared. *Twice.*"

He's loved me his whole life? But how? "You bailed," I say, because I need to be clear. I need everything on the table if I'm going to believe what he's just said. If I'm going to allow myself to feel that way too. "The first time outside my door after Lenny's. And the second when I couldn't put my entire life on hold and run away with you—"

"You know me well enough not to be surprised by self-sabotage, love."

Love? "How can you say that?" I'm asking him how can he call me his *love?* Does he mean it? Is this how he feels, under all the armor and spiky edges?

He drags his hand roughly through five-o'clock shadow. "I think I was shocked, when you finally looked my way. And then the rest of my world started falling apart, and I couldn't figure out what to do. It felt like you were saying no to me. To being with me. And it obliterated me. When I had been longing for you for so long…"

That's not really what I was asking at all, but answers my question nonetheless.

"I've been alone my whole life. I can't take having someone disappear on me, I think, because of my dad. Because things have never been… My mom and I are just different. I don't know how to explain it, but we've come to an understanding I think we can both live with. Gran won't be here forever, and I just can't take it from *you*—the walking away. I mean, I can. I did, because I'm tough." I square my shoulders and laugh a little, because it's both sad and empowering to say out loud. "But I don't want to."

His eyes squeeze shut. "That's why I froze after the gala and after sushi with Len, and why I pulled away and sold my boat. I was in shock at what was happening between us, that you seemed to reciprocate. *And I was afraid* of losing you before I had you. Of messing it up, or you moving on without me. I know it's been rough for you growing up, and it's not been a walk in the park for me, though it may appear that way. You and I," he takes a breath and considers what he's about to say, plows on, "We should have put down our weapons and called a truce a long time ago."

"I don't disagree," I say, giving him a tentative smile. We're walking a tightrope right now and we both know it.

"Lenny is going to kill me if I hurt you—"

"You're afraid of your uncle?" I laugh.

"When it comes to the ones he loves, he can be vicious, you know that." He curls a hand around my waist, gripping me as if I might slip away.

"Are you going to hurt me?"

"Can't you see, love? It's you who's in the position to hurt me."

"That's not the way it felt watching you walk away. Don't do it again."

"Never," he whispers into my ear, his lips brushing soft and featherlight.

"Okay." I let my forehead fall to his chest.

"Never, Holly, I swear it," he states, this time the rumble of his voice is like thunder over a lake, so firm, so serious.

Tell him, tell him now. This moment feels like a fresh start, a new beginning on level ground. I want to tell him about Corrine and the offer, but I hesitate, "Declan…"

He hugs me tight and I shiver at the feeling of being all wrapped up in him. Protected. "My family isn't exactly warm and snuggly. I could do with some of you in my life."

"Mine either," I say to his clavicle, letting him hold me. This was the missing piece, this feeling like a lost puzzle piece that finally fits with another. We've come through something together, fighting for the store and fighting for each other, finally on the same page.

Curling into him feels so good. I want to be even closer and drag my hands down his sides to wrap around his bare waist. But something scratches me; I've been scraped by a spike. "Why are you wearing Len's sweatpants?"

"How do you know they're not mine?"

I whine in protest when he pulls away and opens a double-doored fridge about the size of a smart car. He retrieves a milk bottle and begins to chug, such a boy.

"They're about three sizes too small and have spikes," I say, watching his Adam's apple bob.

He shrugs and tilts the bottle toward me in offering, but I decline with a shake of my head. "Laundry day—I live trim on the boat."

"That explains the uniform. I think I could do a capsule wardrobe someday—"

"You don't think I do spikes?" he interrupts.

"Nope."

"You sure you don't want some?" He tilts the milk toward me again. "Who doesn't want milk when they're about to get their cookie?"

Oh. My. God.

After chugging again like a man, not a boy, he has the gall to reach out, pull me to him, and wipe his milk mustache on my shoulder.

"Hey! This is vintage, sir!"

Without warning, the bottle hits the counter and he grabs the back of my thighs, placing me gently on the marble island. My wrap dress parts for him almost up to my waist. "As long as these dresses are part of your capsule wardrobe, I support you," he growls, mouth skimming up my neck creating tingles in all the places.

My legs wrap around him as if they're meant to be there. All thoughts of Declan's wardrobe, of Kind Klub and Corrine Woolwright evaporate. They'll still be here tomorrow.

I'll tell him soon, pinkie swear.

"I'll dry-clean it for you. It'll need it after I roll it into a ball and chuck it somewhere you can't find it. Why don't you think I can do spikes? I want to know!" He begins aggressively tickling me and I squeal.

"Ah, stop!"

"No, don't think I will. Not until you say I can pull off spikes, studs, grommets, mesh tank tops, leather—"

"Declan Lorden, you're a lot of things but there's not one edgy, punky, spiky bone in your body," I declare, knowing full well this is only going bring me more agony via tickling.

His eyes light on mine as if I've issued war.

"Hold on, Stewart," he says, tossing me over his shoulder.

I holler with shock, as he walks through the house, me clinging to him giving him ample opportunity to squeeze at my sides and make me shriek. "Mr. Uniform?" I laugh. "Mr. Button-down and Sweater Combo? And I need to explain why I don't think you do studs and spikes?" Goading him is one of my favorite things to do, I realize, even now I can't stop.

"You have so much to learn about me. *Pause over*, by the way." He smacks my backside, opening the door to Lenny's guest room, carrying me over the threshold and tossing me quite irreverently on the bed. I bounce a few times, riddled with laughter.

This is Declan, my Dec, and our pause is officially over, indeed.

CHAPTER
Twenty-Five

HE DOES EXACTLY what he said he'd do with my dress and silences my laughter as he tugs at the belt still knotted at my waist. It falls open, and he pulls one arm slowly through a sleeve. His fingers trail lightly across my skin leaving goose bumps in their wake. I gulp while he does the same with the other arm. Painstakingly gentle, peeling the dress from my body, leaning over me as I sink into the bed and breathing hot breath all over my skin until I'm left in a bra and panties.

He's panting just as hard as I am. "We're going to take this slow, okay. I want to savor every moment, alright?"

"Okay," I breathe, happy to let him take control.

With a satisfied smirk, he moves lazily up and down the length of me, dropping kisses as apologies for the past few weeks of torture we've put each other through. My skin is hyperaware of his touch, each kiss sending shock waves through me. It's impossible to hold back a whimper when his mouth sucks through the silk of my bra.

"First, I'm going to—" he says, ever the one in charge, but I stop him.

"Wait, what about Len?" My throat barely gets the words out like tires down a gravel road.

"Their bedroom is on the other end of the house," he replies, equally gruff. "Please, don't make me wait any longer. I will, if you need me to, I swear I will…"

He's being almost reverent with the way he's touching me. Sifting fingers through my hair that's splayed across his pillow, it's still surprising to me that a man with such a nonchalant exterior can be so tender, so sweet, so careful.

In answer, I pull him to me so that we fully fit together, skin-to-skin. The hard length of him pressing through his sweatpants into my center as my legs wrap tightly around him. My body begs to rock, to find friction. "I really don't know how I got here, Declan. In your arms, in your room, in your bed."

He moans softly into my ear when I arch my hips, trying desperately to feel more of him. Telling him with my body how much I want him but with my words that, yes, I'm a little nervous.

What is this going to mean? What will this make us, in the morning? Yes, he apologized. But a little part of me is scared. Scared of what will happen if I give myself to him and he bails again. He's not the only one with a heart that can get obliterated.

With a grunt he rolls off me, leaving me instantly cold without him. He kneels beside the bed and opens a side table drawer, pulling out a leather-bound notebook. Not what I expected. Not at all. "Would you like to read all about it? About how much, and how long I've loved you?"

How much, and how long?

All I can think to say is, "I'm naked, in your bed, and you want me to read a book?" But inside, my heart is hammering.

"Waiting for you has been the pleasure and the pain of my teenage *and* adult life. I'm savoring this. And journaling sort of saved me. Got me through the worst of my moodiness—don't laugh—in my school-age years. And a lot of it is about you." He stops to push hair away from his face, considering what he says next. "I'm trying. I'm trying to be open, and maybe if I can't *say* everything, you can read it."

Yearning rockets through my core when he unceremoniously tugs the backs of my thighs to the edge of the bed. Parts my knees so that he's sitting back on his heels between them, picks up an ankle and begins kissing with delicate nips. He opens the journal with his other hand.

"Get out of town, Lorden," I mock-laugh, and then abruptly stop short when he bites into the sensitive flesh behind my knee, then licks it better.

"I'm all too serious, I assure you, love." He stops, chest heaving, and hikes up my ankle to rest on his shoulder, kneeling between my thighs.

One hand holds the journal after he flips haphazardly to a page, the other gently rubs my thigh, my calf, the pad of my heel with heart-breaking affection.

He whispers to me as he tenderly kisses my ankle. "Take this one, senior year of high school on a particular *salty* day: *All she sees is him. George gets all the smiles, and she even touches him. She acts like it's an accident, but I see the way she brushes her elbow against his arm every chance she gets. My idiot brother is oblivious. I would do so many things for just one of those touches…*"

My voice is shaking. "Give me that. That's not what it says."

Without comment he tosses me the notebook and drags his tongue up my calf, all while gently pulling my panties down my thighs. His low, grateful groan is all it takes for me to lift and help him rid me of them. There's not one hint of hesitation in my body, not one ounce of embarrassment at him seeing me naked for the first time. Seeing his thoughts on paper makes it impossible to worry or care.

I thumb through his journal burning under his touch and struggling to read. The feeling of his deft fingers and reading his passion-filled words is driving me crazy. One finger then two dip inside as I gasp and shiver in the low light of the room.

I arch my hips and press into his hand when his thumb finds that delicate point, letting out a moan because it feels so good it almost hurts.

"Fuck, Holly," he growls in response.

On the page, his handwriting is everywhere. Doodles of dragons. Dates spanning the past almost two decades. There're entries about D&D games, entries about George, and fights at school. And I do see my name, *a lot*.

Oh God, it's so, so good.

His free hand reaches up to pull at my bra so that the straps fall down and my breasts are exposed, pushed up as if in a cupless corset. He greedily massages them, palming me and rubbing his thumb across the peaks, back and forth, back and forth. I don't even try to hold back the noises his touch elicits. He's everywhere at once, as if he can't bear for it to be any other way; fingers thrusting gently at just the right angle, that merciless thumb circling. In a rush of skin he pushes himself up my body, his hands still working me, but now his warm mouth finds my breast, licking and sucking as if he might never have the chance again. He has to have it all, right now. It's so Declan.

I hear myself say his name on an exhale and he kisses me in return. Both of us are becoming more sure and more greedy, biting and opening our mouths as we kiss, feeding off each other and the intensity of the moment.

When he breaks the kiss, I moan in protest. He's dragging this out to a point my body can't take. I need him so badly.

"Shh," he commands, his mouth moving in a slow trail down my stomach until he licks straight down my center, finding that same spot his thumb has primed so well.

I gasp, wriggle in pleasure under his sure touch, and beg him to keep going. "Don't stop."

"Never, love," he breathes. "Keep reading, I want you to know."

It's an effort to focus, but I flip to a page simply titled Prom Dress. My senses are almost to the point of combustion. He's everywhere. In my mind and all over my body. It's all-consuming as I read his words and writhe under every lick and every swirl of his tongue:

It's blue. I'm shocked. I would have thought she'd go for pink, or red, or even purple. She bought it with her grandmother in the store today, and then had it pinned for hemming. I like her dark hair with that purple sweater she usually wears when it rains. I had thought I'd prefer purple. But she chose a blue prom

dress and for some reason, that makes me love her even
more. She'll stand out from all the other blush dresses,
but then, she always does...stand out.

That does it. "Declan, I...this is..." I manage through a final moan
of sheer pleasure as I break into a thousand pieces, his mouth and his
words working through my system faster than anything else I've ever
experienced. A small scream escapes me, then a breathy, reverent
whisper of his name.

He peeks up at me, clearly proud of himself but also looking
slightly worried. He nods to the journal still in my hand. "Please don't
say creepy," he breathes, smiling a wolfish smile. "It's over a span of
many years. I didn't write about you daily, I swear. I did have a life.
But you were always on my mind. And every day I saw you in the
store I noticed another little thing you did that I loved. I couldn't help
it. It was the best, most pure torture of my life."

Officially done with reading, I toss the book to the side, push to my
knees, and launch myself at him. He catches me in his arms and spins
so that he's pressing me down into the soft mattress.

I run my fingers through his thick hair. "You've loved me for that
long, huh?" I ask, gazing up at him.

"Yeah," he says, unabashed and adorably honest. He turns his head
to kiss my palm.

I trace my finger down the strong bridge of his nose. "I'm gonna
reward you for your loyalty and devotion *so hard.*"

He bites his bottom lip, taking a deep breath and exhaling slowly.
"Yeah?" His eyes turn hungry again.

"Yeah," I say, pushing his sweatpants down his waist with my
hands, then farther down his legs with my feet.

He tugs them off and tosses them to the ground.

"Protection?"

"On it." He moves to the bedside table again, making quick work
of ripping the top of the foil packet.

When he's ready, hovering above me, he takes each of my hands and kisses me on the inside of my wrists, then places my palms on his chest. He waits for me to move and I can tell it takes effort on his part.

I don't hesitate, pushing my hips up so he can lean in, can sink deep into me. I've been waiting for this in more ways than one, and I don't want him to take his time.

But of course, he does. It's slow. A slew of expletives are lovingly hurled around the room in his low, devastating voice as he braces on his elbows.

"Are you okay?" he asks, framing my face with his hands. He pushes all my hair back from my face, kisses each temple and the tip of my nose.

"I feel amazing, beautiful, strong, and brilliant," I gush, delirious from the way his body is affecting mine.

He huffs a laugh. "I can't disagree."

"It's because of you. You make me feel like this."

"I've never wanted anything so bad, Holly. It was torture, but it was worth it."

My hands are in his hair, pulling lightly. Asking for more.

Within seconds he's moving, quick and hard and I'm crying out. He seems to understand I'm begging for *more*. He pushes deeper and our hips begin to pound against one another as our mouths frantically attempt kissing, but it's more like biting, nipping and sucking, and sharing breath. It's almost painful because neither one of us is willing to let him pull all the way out. I don't care if I'm bruised tomorrow, I want him as close as I can have him, as much as I can have him, and as hard as I can have him. I want to melt into him so we can never be separated again.

"*More, more, more please.*" This time I say the words aloud in demanding gasps as a pressure begins to build deep inside and I've got no idea what to do with it.

He laughs a little, pulling me to him while simultaneously pushing up onto his knees. It's one swift movement, so I don't lose him for a second. His large hands are splayed behind my back, gripping me to him as I straddle his lap.

"Push up on your knees a little," he tells me, moving his hands down my body and planting them firmly on my hips to guide me.

I do as he says, then sink slowly down with the weight of his hands, widening my knees as far as I can so that he's completely buried in me again but much, much deeper. "Dec—" I whine, needy and wanting and finding even more torture in this new position.

"I know, love. I know."

He tilts his hips and I gasp into his mouth. Every pleasure receptor in my brain goes off in an explosion. He groans and pants as he continues moving deeper than I ever thought was possible.

This is it. It's all over for me.

My head falls back, *so close, so close*, until his mouth finds my breasts again, and he squeezes them together—greedy, greedy, greedy. We both fall apart.

CHAPTER
Twenty-Six

I WAKE up the next morning in Dec's bed, at Lenny's house, and wonder at how much my life has changed for the better.

"Morning, sunshine," he hums into my ear.

"Coffee," I croak.

"Not a morning person, huh? Well, because I am a gallant lover, I will procure said coffee for you, milady."

Gallant lover, indeed. I know this now to be fact. "Do not tarry, boy!"

"Old English while lying naked in bed. That's the hottest thing that's ever happened to me. Except for everything that happened to me last night."

Happened again and again and again. *Thrice!* But I keep that little exclamation to myself. He already knows how good he is, no need to puff him up further.

I roll over to face him in the doorway, trying to stretch out and look sexy. I have no idea if I've accomplished it, but he smiles wide and I'm satisfied.

"By the way," he says, as he backs out the door. "Dinner tomorrow night? With my family? We just got confirmation. Dad's going to sign the contract, selling to Len and me. George is going to Zoom in for the occasion. I want you to be there. And maybe, another sleepover?"

There are no words to describe the feeling I get when I hear this. "You know I can't say no to that. I'd love to. Now, coffee!"

We all need to be in the office soon, so it's my turn to borrow from Lenny's closet since my sad little dress is indeed scrunched into a ball and in need of dry-cleaning. While David is in the adjoining shower and Len's shaving at a mirror, I poke through his collection.

"This is convenient, but it's still annoying I can fit in your clothes."

"I'm a lean queen, what can I say?"

I slip out of a blazer that is a little too big in the shoulder, but not by much, and continue my perusal.

"Hey, you know David's coming in with us today? He wants to check things out."

"Really, why?"

"He hasn't scheduled any big shoots for a while, taking some time off to fully recover, but he wants to get out. He's had a side project going that he won't tell me about. I think it's got something to do with why he wants to tour the store today."

"Can I wear this Gucci T-shirt? Maybe with your kilt? I think I can cinch it enough at the waist, do that front roll and tuck thing. It'll look good with my leather jacket and boots I had on last night."

"Tell me again, why can't you just wear your dress to work today?" He raises a parental eyebrow. "Did he rip it off you?"

"La, la, la, la!" I plug my ears and yell at him. "Please don't ever ask me about my sex life with your nephew!"

He holds his hands up, laughing. "Okay, okay!"

"I just really want to wear this T-shirt. It's iconic, and I could never afford to spend eight hundred dollars on a white T-shirt."

"Uh-huh. I'm happy for you, and yes you can borrow the Gucci but don't wash it! I'll take it to my cleaners, with your dress," he laughs. "And you know, it's not about the T-shirt, babe. It's all about the person wearing it. A nice white Hanes and well-fitted jeans do the trick just fine, for anyone, any day."

"Lenny Lorden, I do declare, you've changed."

"My heart overflow-eth, so my closet doesn't need to. But I mean, it will anyway."

"If you've got the heart, you don't need the label. Your words to God's ears."

"And you've got the heart, doll. What you're doing, starting something new… I'm proud of you."

"Len, I got it. Don't make me cry."

He shakes his head and speaks around a toothbrush in his mouth, "You *need* to tell him."

Instead of crying because his words mean as much to me as if they were coming from my own father, I kiss him on a baby-butt smooth cheek. "I will. Just not yet, things are finally good between us, and we need to focus on this last push for Lorden's. Thanks for being my style Yoda. And for everything over the years. We've really taken care of each other. I think I'm going to like these slumber parties."

"Speaking of slumber parties."

"Nope. Not talking about it."

"After a solid year of gushing about George, I get nothing about what goes on under my own roof with my own nephew and my own bestie?"

"I am not about to jinx this. Not even to give the juicy, juicy details."

He pulls me into a tight hug. "I think we've both evolved," he says, planting a kiss on the top of my head. "But take it from me, honesty is the best policy. Tell him."

The store is slow to wake this morning. We all do our best dog and pony show for David's sake, but the tension is easy to read. Nothing is normal. We can't expect a normal day because no one knows what the new normal looks like.

Lenny makes his morning housekeeping announcements with Declan by his side. And be still my beating heart, he cracks a smile for employee benefit. He's trying. I can see how they're going to run this company together. Len will be the microphone, the hype man, and Declan will be the muscle, the strong silent one who watches and plans.

David beams at Len as he wraps up, clapping along as employees scatter.

"Is it fun watching your man at work?" I ask him.

"He's done so much for me, I really want this to work for him. You know he's been in his brother's shadow his whole life."

"I didn't know how bad it was until recently, but yes, I know things were strained."

"Afraid to be himself, fully himself in this store. In this business. And why? It's fashion! It's clothes! It's shopping, excess, gratification. Art! Everything he's really good at," he laughs.

"Exactly," I say, smiling and shaking my head. This really is the beginning, for both of them, of a great life.

"So, I'm going to let you in on a little secret." David purses his lips, *tea* on the tip of his tongue. "I reached out to all of our friends to come shop today, you know, doing my part to save the store."

I turn to him, genuinely moved. "David, that is so sweet of you. Every sale counts. I'm sure he'll appreciate it."

The operator booms overhead, "Lorden's Pine Street is open for the day. Let's make it a great one!"

"I don't think you understand, Holly. I reached out to *all* our friends." He nods toward the doors.

O.M.G. How has no one noticed there's a huge line outside the Cosmetics entrance?

"David?"

His gaze happily follows mine. "Our community is very supportive. Lenny is a big deal in Seattle's LGBTQ+ scene. He's got a shit ton of fans and friends alike. And I bought a round of drinks for everyone at Guys and Dolls and asked them to pitch in. It spread like wildfire through the socials: #SaveLenny, #SaveLordens. And you remember Amanda? That friend of his you helped?"

"Of course," I say, half focused on him, half trying to count the people that have started funneling through our doors. Wide-eyed employees scatter to begin helping, and I swear I hear registers ringing sales already.

"Well, she posted a video talking about her appointment with you. About how helpful you were accommodating her size, all while treating her like your own friend. It's trending. What was her hashtag…" He snaps his fingers. "#NoSizeShame."

"Oh. My. God. David, you've created a movement!"

"I didn't create the movement, you did."

Declan appears at my side. Somehow, he's pressed through a crowd that has turned into a happy, sparkly, shopping mob. "Do you know what the hell is going on?" There's a terrified but ecstatic smile on his face.

Lenny pushes through the crowd next. We all pull into a tight circle near the MAC counter. "Dec, we have a party on our hands. I don't know where these beautiful people came from, but they are ready to spend." He catches someone's wave and says, "Morning, Josh." Looking back at us with curious eyes he continues, "I see a lot of familiar faces… Hey! Can we get the sound system set up?"

"David did this for you. For you guys," I gush, hoping I didn't just ruin some grand reveal.

Declan claps David on his back, while Lenny grabs him by both cheeks and gives him a slow, meaningful kiss. When they part, both of them have tears in their eyes.

"Thanks, man," Declan says, giving David's shoulder a squeeze. "Can I teach you how to ring on a register real quick?" He jumps on his walkie-talkie before David can answer, *Antonio, we need the sound system set up in Cosmo STAT, over.*

"Excuse me, do you work here?" A stunning six-foot man with a raffia Prada tote taps me on the shoulder. "Can you help me find the MAC Fix Plus?"

"I do work here, but you do not want my help with makeup." He has the most gorgeous rainbow eyeshadow I've ever seen. Like YouTube tutorial quality. "Here's someone who can help!" I grab a MAC employee and they take off.

The rest of us move farther out of the crowd and into the aisle. Shoppers of every walk of life, of every color, every gender, gender fluid, and nonbinary, and every costumed state of dress have filtered throughout the first floor. When I glance at the escalator going up, it's packed. Like a rainbow materializing right in the middle of our store.

"We're swamped. Like apocalyptic shopping is going down in this store right now," Lenny says, pulling David in for a bear hug.

"Well, good news, I'm absolutely up to work a register. I've been dying to be initiated into the family business." David looks at Declan with a delighted put-me-to-work expression.

Everyone's got arms around everyone now, my neck in the crook of Declan's elbow as he looks seriously at David, so serious we all pause in our odd little football huddle. "David, you're one of us now. *That's how we win, not fighting what we hate, but saving what we love.*"

I turn my head so that my cheek grazes his bicep. "Hey, that's *The Last Jedi.*"

"Sure is."

"Repeat after me," I say to David, full of brazen energy and ready to fight all day via good old-fashioned retail sales. "Fold, tissue, bag, smile!"

"Fold, tissue, bag, smile!" David repeats enthusiastically.

"Consider yourself trained, soldier." I throw in a wink, for good luck.

Antonio is fast. We break our huddle as the music cranks up.

CHAPTER
Twenty-Seven

THE NEXT DAY, the *Seattle Times* leaks news of Lorden's possibly closing its doors and reporters camp out on the street. The Saturday shopping extravaganza went viral on every social media platform, Lorden's started trending, and the company has been a topic of debate in every business journal and on every local podcast.

Unfortunately, all of this has outed the family for what they are, a long line of billionaires who stand to lose everything. But Seattle can smell a comeback. The papers are citing rumors of the company making a big change that could save the store. Everyone loves an underdog in a tuxedo, right? Declan is worried that they've been tipped off, that they'll know Louie is finally selling his shares and handing the business down to the next generation. He wanted to make a grand announcement, but either way, he, Lenny, and George who they've kept up-to-date, will be owners after tonight. Grand announcement or no, Lorden's will soon be theirs.

The dinner party is being held at SkyCity on the top of the Space needle. The Lordens rented the entire restaurant for the evening, a classy move considering Louie is making his family beg for the right to buy his business. It can mean only one thing, a celebration. Louie and Mira will hand over the keys to the castle and Lenny, Dec, and

George will run the company under the Lorden name for another fifty years.

And after that, when all the dust has settled and we have our happy ending, I'll tell Declan I've taken a job with Kind Klub. That, yes, I'm leaving Lorden's but not leaving him. I don't ever want to leave him, if I'm honest. It's scary to feel that way, so soon after we've fought hard to figure out our feelings but exhilarating at the same time. Kinda like the free fall of a roller coaster; it's scary, it's fun, and no matter what anyone says you know it's a little dangerous too.

The work day goes quickly. We sell, we bag, we smile. We do everything we can to turn a profit. Then it's time for the dinner party of all dinner parties.

When the elevator doors open, I'm met with an endless view of downtown Seattle, lights a-twinkle in the hustle and bustle of five o'clock, as if from a bird's perspective. Floor-to-ceiling glass walls surround us in a gentle curve and the restaurant slowly spins in the sky, revolving as if it's the center of the universe. Tonight, it feels like it is. We're immediately ushered by gloved staff to a dressed table bathed in candlelight.

I drop Gran's clutch, nestling it into a burnt orange velvet booth. A long, dark wood table covered in votives flickers. Everything is glowing. Ornate chandeliers cast a golden hue over us and even though my heart is fluttering for Declan and what's to come, I feel so content, as if I'm baking in the sun and basking in the word *happy*.

"It's our first family dinner together," he says, catching me off guard.

With a cheeky smile I prop my hands on the waist of my structured black Bottega cocktail dress—the last of the gratis I'm going to see from Lorden's. "The first of many firsts."

I can't wait to tell him I've signed with Corrine, for both of us to have something to celebrate tonight. Together.

Molly and Angel are going to be much happier when I'm gone and they're back to receiving the brunt of the designer prizes for top seller. I still can't believe I sold so much, so quickly. Something I wasn't sure I could do at all, and then I did it exceedingly well. It'll be hard saying goodbye to Jenny when she's only just come back, but

I know via hourly email check-ins she's had enough of maternity leave. When the news of Pine Street possibly closing first broke, she blew up my cell and was eternally grateful when I assured her that Declan and Lenny had secured a deal and she had a job to come back to.

"Tomorrow's Monday." He sticks his hands in the pockets of a gray suit, complemented by one of his starched white button-downs. A Burberry tie picks up the burgundy of his glasses, making him look effortlessly geek-chic.

"And?"

"And it'll be my first day owning my own company." He beams. "I can't believe we did it."

"You did it."

"But I never would have without you in my corner. What's that saying about a good woman being behind every great man?"

"Um, a really old sexist saying?"

"That's my point. I think they stand next to each other, propping each other up. Partners. A united front. Sure, we're always going to press each other's buttons, but now, we do it for pleasure." His hands roll down my bare arms, wrap around my waist, and knot at the small of my back.

"So, what's your master plan, Lorden? Other than being devoted to my pleasure, of course."

"Of course." He winks, wrapping me up tighter. Then he whispers his business plan in my ear, "Lenny and I are going to take the lead for Lorden's, keep store one open, and let George run Hawaii as well as taking over product development—"

"He is?"

"Yup. Spoke to him yesterday. I mentioned your idea about a new product, something akin to the soup, and he likes where your head's at. Told me I was a moron for letting you get away."

"You got me back." He looks into my eyes and I look into his. Now is the moment, he's almost asking without coming out with it in words.

Are you leaving to work with Corrine?

But I can't tell him now, not before everything is finally settled for him. "I like it when you whisper sweet business models in my ear. Tell me more."

"More shop talk?" He gives me a full-faced smile, one that makes me want to cling to a bicep and swoon.

"It's sexy."

"In that case, Len and I will head up technology and general corporate functions. We've got teams to lead us in industry needs. The board will want their say, but it'll be ours, not my parents'."

"Does that feel good?" This time I literally grab his bicep, and I swoon like the heroine on the cover of a smutty novel.

"Holly, my parents will be here any minute."

"Just trying to live up to my title of micro-risk taker." I lightly slap his chest, then step back to give the man some breathing room. He's right, Mira and Louie will be here soon. "I mean, does it feel good to run things?"

"You know I like being in control. Feels fucking great."

"Such a powerful dungeon master." I wink.

"You're placating me, but I don't care, I know you like it." He sweeps me back into his chest and pulls me from the table toward the windows. I'm not scared of heights in the least and apparently, he's not either. We both come so close we almost press our noses to the glass.

"All that down there," I murmur. Endless possibilities.

"Yeah."

"For a while, it felt like I wasn't a part of it. A part of anything of my own, you know. I didn't really believe in myself. You helped me overcome that fear."

"Holly, you helped me overcome so many things. And now we've got each other."

"And the whole city at our feet." Instinctively, I wrap an arm around his waist. This feels right, as if we've finally put all the puzzle pieces together and now we can just be. There are no more surprises, we've talked through everything like adults. We're going to make it, Declan and I.

"I know we can't sail around the world now, with everything going on. And I've got no boat. But I want you to know, I want you—"

He's about to say something that I'll feel down into my bones, but a pesky waiter has chosen this moment to hover about a foot away from us. He finally speaks when Dec looks at him annoyed over my shoulder.

"Can I get you something to drink, Mr. Lorden? And for you, miss?"

"I'll have a whiskey neat. You?" He looks down at me.

"Champagne, please."

"Champagne please, and you may as well leave the bottle on the table. I'm sure we'll all have a glass. We're celebrating."

"Very good, sir."

"Thank you," we both say, looking at each other instead of the waiter.

"You were saying?"

"Move in with me?"

"You're homeless!"

"We'll find a place together, if that's something you'd want?" He hedges and I love that he's used to getting what he wants, but with me, he wants to know what I want.

"What about my cottage? I know it's all granny style, but I keep telling myself one day I'll renovate, maybe add a garden out back...."

"If you'll have me, I'll pay rent. I'd like to make up for every day I pretended I wasn't mad for you."

"Dec, I don't know what to say, except that I'm mad for you back." And I am. The ways his eye can read my thoughts, the way his body feels paired with mine, the way we work together. It's all of it, together, that makes me crazy for him.

"Just think about it. And if it's too soon, I get it. I'll wait. I'm sure Len and David'll keep me a bit longer. Or I can get an apartment. I just wanted you to know I want you, Holly Stewart. Every day. I've been spoiled since we were kids, having you in my life, even if it was only to drool over you—"

"Torture me—"

"It wasn't that bad!"

"No, it wasn't. I think I loved hating you, a little."

He smirks. "And I'm not willing to give it up now. Not now that you kiss me instead of throwing daggers at me across the aisles of my store."

I'm bursting, like a starlet wearing two pairs of Spanx to the Oscars. I'm about to explode, I'm so happy. And because I can't think of anything to say, I grab his cheek and kiss him—happy, sloppy, silly.

He laughs and then kisses me in earnest, making my heart stop. "That's a yes," he murmurs through a smile.

Lenny makes a grand and boisterous entrance when the elevator doors open, pulling David toward our table. "Looks like the party has already started. Aren't we the ones who are recently engaged? Shouldn't I be the one getting all the candlelit kisses and public displays of affection?"

He's wearing a black suit—a woman's suit, the smooth silk tailored to his body in a way that makes it hang so elegantly from his frame. He has what he calls *base* makeup on: the foundation, the powder, contour, blushed cheeks. He must have a show later tonight, where he'll painstakingly add dramatic eyes and lips.

Dec and I detach, reluctantly, with a promise of what's to come later between us.

"Pour yourself a glass of bubbles, it's all about you and your fiancé now, I promise. I won't steal your thunder, but let's just say, good thing you're not planning on a long engagement. Holiday, right?"

"A Jewish-Christmas-wedding mashup is the theme, I believe. Honey?" David looks lovingly at Len.

"He thinks he doesn't like it, but he's going to love it," Lenny says. "A merry-mazel wedding!" He nods to a waiter who hands him a flute of champagne with a flourish.

"So, spring next year is open. Good to know." Dec's eyes heat and flick to mine.

I cough on a mouthful of champs in response.

"Tonight isn't about *us* though," David puts in, shrugging out of a worn denim jacket that is probably the bane of Len's existence but because he loves David, he's keeping his mouth shut. "It's about these two, and continuing the family legacy. Well done, boys!" He boisterously claps for them. I love David.

I join in shouting, "Bravo, bravo!"

The elevators ding and open again, and we're all assuming it will be Louie and Mira, but my heart drops to my knees. It's George.

His face erupts into one of the biggest smiles I've ever seen him wear. He's forgone the suit I'm so used to seeing him in for khakis and a button-down chambray. And he's tan. So tan, I think he must be officing outdoors at the Hawaii store.

"Hi, family," he offers sheepishly.

The men are stunned so I step in, "George! What a surprise!"

This kicks Dec and Len into gear, and they both move to George and wrap him in a double hug.

"What the hell? I talked to you this morning," Declan says aghast. They clap each other on the back as they embrace. "Welcome back, brother," he adds, then moves back to me, wrapping an arm protectively around my waist. "You didn't say you were coming in…"

"Wanted to surprise everyone. Holly, how are you?" George asks, coming to stand with us at the edge of the table.

"I'm really good. It's great to see you. How's Hawaii? You're so tan!"

"Incredible. I can't describe it. The change of scenery sorta set me free in a way. You know?"

"I do. Actually, I think I do."

"Seeing anyone?" Lenny asks, about as nonchalant as a bulldozer. "This is David, in the flesh, by the way."

"Hey man," George and David shake hands. "Nice to meet you in persona instead of through a screen via chat."

"Same, glad you could make it."

"So," Lenny prompts again, "Tell us all about getting *laid* on the big island."

"Met a coffee bean farmer on Oahu. He's trying to start-up a sip and see, like a winery, to view the plants, the harvest, the beans, then sip the coffee."

"You're kidding, I would love something like that," I gush, so pleased to see George and hear him speak as if he's found a whole new wonderful life already.

"Yeah, it's his passion project. Declan told me you two are—"

"Together," Declan puts in.

I look at him but words don't come. What do I say?

The look that crosses George's face is unreadable, maybe a little sad, but understanding. "Meant to be, that's what I say. All of this is perfect. Absolutely the way it was supposed to end up."

"Thanks, George."

Louie and Mira finally arrive in all their Armani and Dior glory. I swear Mira has so much glittering jewelry on she would sink like a stone in Lake Washington but her grace and class save it from looking crass; she resembles a queen.

We sit as white-coated waiters dispense the first course, lobster bisque, by placing filigree-edged soup bowls with lumps of lobster meat in front of us. A tiny carafe of bisque is poured on top of each bowl and we are told *bon appétit!*

"So, Dad, what do you make of Dec's numbers the past few months? Increase upon increase. Epic, right?" George is ever the diplomat, starting this off on a positive note.

Louie crumbles crackers into his bisque and I'm struck by how normal he is, despite his designer suit, gold watch, and country club air. "Hell of a come up. I tell you, I'd nearly lost hope with this one, but he pulled it out of his ass at the last minute."

The table exchanges glances while Mira purses her lips.

"It's more than that," Lenny pipes up, and I catch a glimpse of David's hand as it moves to Lenny's knee under the table.

"What's more?" Louie dishes out a leveling glare. There's still unspoken hurt and anger between these two. I'm not sure if it's ancient history or something to do with tonight's plan. I'd gotten the feeling they'd hashed things out after Lenny followed Louie out of the office that day, in tears, and then the lawyers started putting together a fair deal for the transfer of shares within the family.

Maybe not...

Lenny sits up straighter in his chair and speaks as the mouthpiece he'll be when he partners with Declan. "It's enough to keep the company going until we can put together new strategies and business models. Numbers are up companywide as we've begun implementing what Pine Street has been doing across all full-line stores."

Louie slurps his soup. "These pop-ups, dressed up *mall kiosks* in the middle of my stores, are not going to save our hides in the long run. That's why I've made my decision, and taken the company in a different direction. Mira and I—"

"Don't drag me into this, not when you went behind my back. Lied to me. Told me you had everything under control," Mira says in a low tone. "You know I wanted the kids to have the business."

"Wait—" Lenny tenses, and the whole room stills with him. A soup spoon clatters but I'm not sure whose.

"You're not selling to us? Is that what I just heard Mom say?" Declan's forearms come down hard on the table and I cringe.

George's face goes as white as the linen napkin in his lap. "Dad, what is this? You told me to fly in for a celebration. You told me this was going to be, and I quote, 'a momentous evening.'"

"This announcement is momentous. I've sold the company, *privately*. The deal went through about forty-five minutes ago. It's done and you boys stand to inherit enough money that you and your kids and your kids' kids don't have to worry about being successful or making a dollar for the rest of your lives!" He smiles at the table and when there's no response, goes back to his soup.

"But that was *your* worry, Louie," Lenny spits. "You were worried about the money. Always about the profit and the lifestyle and the more, more, more of it all. You were so worried you wouldn't make it and you wouldn't make our dad proud, and look at what you've done. You've betrayed all of us!" He's breathing hard, David is holding his hand now. Lenny's voice drops a few octaves as he finishes, "Because you're so fucking *scared* you're going to fail."

"What the hell, Dad?" Declan demands, albeit not poetic but to the point.

"What about Lenny's shares?" George asks.

"My inheritance was much smaller when our parents passed. The lion's share went to the eldest. They assumed it would keep the company safe from rash, immature decisions."

"Still, he couldn't have sold privately without full ownership." Declan stands, eyeing his father. "What did you do?"

"He sold his shares to me years ago. How right our late parents were, may they rest in peace," Louie booms.

"That's not true," Lenny starts.

"Think about it, brother. Think long and hard."

Realization washes over Lenny's face. "That night in your office after one of your parties. I signed some documents. You said it was a business maneuver."

"You cashed the check."

"I wanted to believe you. I did believe you." He shakes his head. "I want to say I'm shocked but you know what, I'm not."

"Just because you recently decided to pull yourself out of a bottle and dry out doesn't mean you can blame me now. All you talk about is that man and that wedding of yours."

David doesn't even flinch, he's a rock. It crosses my mind this may not be the first time he's found himself in a wrongfully accusatory position.

"I figured of all of them, you'd be the most pleased. You can just... go. Go live your life."

"Exactly how you've always wanted it. Go away. Go away and live my life the way I want. Not the way you deem fit. Not a life you want any part of. So much so, you coerced me out of my own company."

"You still get paid, the same salary and commissions. I made sure of it."

"So I wouldn't notice what you did. I get it now. You're a very good liar, and an exceptional cheat."

"I said I'll stand by you. Haven't I always? God dammit, what else do you want from me?" Louie booms.

To his credit, Lenny keeps his composure. "Not in the ways that matter. You certainly don't trust me, we've learned that. You don't respect me. You don't even like me. Sure, you pummeled a few kids at Vohs for giving me shit. You tolerate my lifestyle. But have you ever come to a show? Have you tried to get to know my fiancé?"

"Honey, stop. It doesn't matter," David hushes him, calmly.

"It sure as hell matters to me." Lenny stands from the table and David stands with him without hesitation. "I'm sorry, to you both." He looks at Declan and then even more meaningfully at George. Then back at Louie before continuing, "If you treat your sons the same way you've treated your brother all your life, you are going to die a very lonely man. Mira, you're a saint." With that, he turns to David who wraps an arm around his fiancé. "Let's go."

They make their way to the elevators and there's a horrid sixty seconds of waiting until the doors finally open and they disappear.

Apparently, no one knows what to say next so we all sit in the eerie quiet on top of the world. The waiters smell their only chance to keep the dinner moving and retrieve soup bowls wordlessly while simultaneously plunking down steak knives. Not the smartest move at this point.

Declan fumes in the chair next to me. I wait for what he'll do next, but the chef appears at the head of our table. He's as round as he is tall, with dark hair and a crisp white coat. "This evening we have a bone-in Wagyu steak with steamed mushrooms accompanied by family-style lobster mashed potatoes and creamed spinach."

The moment is more than awkward. I begin to clap and say, "Sounds delicious," because I feel bad for the guy having to present to a table of angry energy, but I stop after no one else joins in. The chef nods politely and rolls back into the kitchen.

Declan cuts into his steak with a vengeance as if he's imagining his father's heart on his plate, but he doesn't attempt to speak. No one does. Everyone begins eating as if we're just going to go on in silence for the rest of our lives.

It's ridiculous.

A one-hundred-and-nineteen-year-old Seattle business is dead.

Declan knows his legacy has just slipped from his hands. "I'll never speak to him again," he whispers beside me, staring down at his plate. "I'm only sitting here now for my mother." He nods at George who nods back at him in solidarity.

Louie grumbles about ungratefulness as he shoves back from the table and goes to stand by the windows with a full glass of wine.

It's unbidden, the image of my father that comes to me. He was just home from work, still wearing scrubs and I run to the door and fling myself at him before he's had time to prepare. We both fall back. An armful of manila folders crashes to the floor and flocks of paper birds in the form of charts and graphs scatter around us.

I know I've done something wrong. I know I've made his difficult job even harder for him. But all he does is wrap me up in his arms and hug me so hard I think I might pop.

Reaching under the table, I take Declan's hand in mine. "I'll support you," I say on an exhale. "You deserve so much better, you all do."

CHAPTER

Twenty-Eight

"WHERE ARE WE GOING?" I ask.

Streetlights glow around us as the city goes about its business. Seattle is oblivious to the fact that it lost a retail juggernaut tonight.

Declan closes my car door and then lets himself into the driver's side of his sleek black car, sinking into the seat beside me.

He pulls the tie from his neck and chucks it in the back seat. "Guys and Dolls. Len's got a show tonight."

"I'm proud of you for not storming out. I know you wanted to." The force of his acceleration presses me into my seat as we move into traffic.

He downshifts on a sigh. "Turns out the whole we-make-each-other-better relationship cliché is not so cliché. Like I said, I did it for my family. And to show them there's more to strength than brute force. But I'm not letting go of a company with my name on it. I have to do something to stop my father."

We hold eye contact at a stoplight until it changes. "Can I ask you something?"

"Anything," he says in a guttural tone, all vengeance and spite.

"Have you ever thought maybe there's something else for you?

Other than Lorden's? You never seemed…" I break off because I'm not sure I should be pushing him right now.

"Say it."

"Happy."

He grimaces. "I wasn't. My brother was living a life that I wanted, and he didn't even want it. I want to run Pine Street. I want to take Lorden's to the next level. Do you know how many times I've gone to Louie about new marketing strategies? Our online presence? Fucking Amazon headquarters are down the street from our flagship store, but do you think he'd take a meeting with them to potentially grow, learn, partner? I saw what was coming and I had ideas on how to fight it, or at least keep up to coexist. But no. I wasn't George in a three-piece suit—"

"Neither was George."

"He tried to be. He almost caved to the pressure." He gives me a meaningful look.

"But you talked him out of it. Out of staying and conforming to what Louie wanted. You gave him your spot in Hawaii—"

"He thought I wanted Hawaii, and I did. But I knew he *needed* Hawaii. So, both of us refused the job trying to do right by the other. When we finally talked it out after the putting contest from hell, we realized we were both trying to take care of the other. In the end, I convinced him he needed to go or he'd end up with a wholly unauthentic life here."

"You sweet little porcupine."

"I'm a what?"

"You know what I mean, you're all prickly on the outside. But you don't mean anyone any harm." I reach over and squeeze his thigh. He kisses the crown of my head and we drive.

We pull up at the nightclub just as a show is letting out. A gaggle of the most eclectic humans exit a skinny side door in a brick wall on Washington Street. At Guys and Dolls there's the first show around 10:00 p.m. that kicks off the night. That crowd will dwindle, then around one in the morning, the second show begins and usually goes on until the sun is up. I've always wondered how they get around liquor laws.

Inside the bar, employees are turning tables while patrons staying for both shows stand at the bar. The heels of my shoes stick to the floor and I try to ignore how different this place smells without a buzz—a mixture of puke, sweat, and stale booze.

Declan grabs my hand and pulls me toward the dressing rooms in back. I've never seen him at one of Len's shows, but he seems to know where he's going.

All manner of nudity is on display in a hallway turned dressing room. Some old lockers line one wall with a bench adjacent. It's a typical high school locker room scene except here, there are mostly wigged men in support garments, some still in sequined or feathered dresses and only their hose caps, and a few are putting everything they've got on full display with zero shame.

As we maneuver through the crowd, a DJ's voice filters in announcing the second show before cuing up an old rap song. Lenny and David are at the far end of the room, sitting in front of a set of mirrors lined with bright bulbs. He's changed into street clothing but still has a full face of Gaga makeup. Tonight, he was *House of Gucci* Gaga.

"How was the show?" I hedge.

"Let off some steam. You know, I hated moving from the late show to the early bird, but I just couldn't keep up with the young'uns coming up. This way, I'm still a star." He shrugs as he collects makeup from the table and drops it into a Fendi tote. There's only sadness in his voice.

"He was phenomenal, as usual," David says, taking Len's bag from him. "You should see him get swarmed when he steps offstage, the *young'uns* all want his secrets."

"We need to talk." Dec's voice is gruff and emotional. It's enough to make his uncle pause. "I'm sorry I missed the show, but I wanted to stand my ground with Dad."

"You were planning on coming tonight?" I ask.

"Surprised? I've seen almost all Len's shows. And yes, half the time I saw you here and didn't have the balls to say anything."

"Declan Lorden, you did stalk me." I make googly eyes at him. "We would have fought the whole time and missed the shows anyway."

"You think? Something makes me wonder had I just done a tequila shot and grabbed you by the neck, after soliciting consent of course, but no, you're right. We would have bitten each other's heads off."

But still, I wonder. If I'd kissed Declan at the holiday party all those months ago…

"I don't want to talk tonight." Lenny holds a manicured hand up. "I can't, Declan. I'm sorry, I can't fight Louie anymore. I love my brother, but I don't know if I can forgive him for this. We don't even have the capital."

Declan squeezes my hand and I squeeze back. "That's what I'm getting to, just listen, please. When I sold my boat, the man who bought it was buying it for his wife. A fiftieth anniversary present, guess they're going to get to sail around the world. It's a little bitter-sweet for my taste, but I knew what I was doing and wished them the best."

Poor sweet boy. Sold his life's passion to fulfill his life's goal, and it all backfired in his handsome face.

"I'll help you get it back. Your boat, now that Louie has fucked us."

Declan shakes his head at his uncle. "That's not what I'm saying. It just made me think about getting married." He glances at me and my cheeks heat. He rushes on, "The guy said he could still remember what his wife looked like when she walked down the aisle, was going on about how she made him wear a tux in August and he sweat buckets but seeing her happy in a big white dress was all worth it."

"Sounds like my kind of guy," David says.

"You want to see me in a big white dress?" Len chides.

Without hesitation David replies, "I want to see you in anything." He wraps an arm around his fiancé's back.

"It got me thinking. About you guys getting married, all the plans you're making, all the shit you're buying, all the *money* you're dropping." Declan raises a knowing eyebrow, directed mostly toward his uncle.

"Um, on the most important day of our lives," Lenny cuts in while David lets out a good-natured laugh in agreement. "The theme is a merry-mazel wedding. It's two religions in one. That ain't cheap to accessorize."

"Yeah, yeah. But then I thought, M.O.B.," Declan prods.

"Neither one of us have mothers living," David says good-naturedly.

"Mother of the bride," I murmur under my breath, beginning to put together what Declan's saying. "The sale. My sale with the Louie pens…" I trail off.

"Exactly. We do a shit ton in bridal, despite not having much of an inventory or offering in the space. We have a dozen dresses listed online, that's it."

"You want to expand into bridal." Lenny nods his head and stage-rubs a nonexistent villain beard. "Genius!"

Dec's smile now is all pride but not the kind that's unattractive, the kind that's earned, shared, and celebrated with equals. "A roughly sixty-billion-dollar-a-year industry, yes I do."

The room has mostly cleared now, but a few performers take note as Declan launches into his closing argument. "I think we try to take a bigger piece of the pie, just like the stylists do. We take our M.O.B.'s, I know they're difficult, but we win them over with stellar service and we get their daughters in to dress shop. We get all the bridesmaids. Do you know what it costs to rent a tux?"

All three men's faces are blank because I'm sure they've owned tuxes since they were two; the Lordens because that's who they are; David because he's just that cool.

"I called around." He laughs at them. "If a guy spent about a hundred bucks more, he could own a tux from us."

"Oh my God, Declan, this is a great idea." Beaming at him, I pull him to me and plant a fat kiss on his cheek. *I'm so proud of my man!*

"Problem: How do we leverage this fast enough to try to find the buyer, and extend the same deal to them we were going to have with Dad? We could put down the earnest money, and pay them back plus interest, over the next five years, maybe? Sweeten the pot. That makes us full owners, just like we planned."

"I don't know who would take that kind of deal. We were banking on Louie and Mira going for it because they're family," Lenny muses, more serious than I've ever seen him, even with the Gaga makeup still intact. In fact, the Gaga face makes him look even more formidable.

"I can be very persuasive when I want to be. Let's cross that bridge when we come to it."

Declan's right, we can worry about that part later.

"You need a media blitz," David says, matter-of-fact as a Beyoncé pushes past us, winking at Declan before she sashays out the door. "To raise a mint in a hurry."

"Like?"

"Eye candy." Len has already picked up David's train of thought. "Some sort of social media campaign no one can ignore. Something that would equate to sales, foot traffic in all our stores, and online fast..." His mind is going into production mode. I see the styling, lights, and the blocking happening in his eyes.

"I could shoot the campaign for you. A big wedding shoot, a bunch of B-roll. I've got a videographer buddy who owes me a favor. You put it everywhere: TikTok, Insta, YouTube, morning shows."

"All with links to buy," I add in, as my mind whirls and the plan materializes. "We get it in influencer hands. I have some leads from Kind Klub and a bunch of other pop-ups we've worked with. They've all got big followings across all socials. We can work them into a deal, sponsor a few of them." Giddy energy is running through me. This is it —we can win back Lorden's.

"Your wedding would be perfect." Declan's on a roll, thinking out loud.

David shrugs his shoulders, but Lenny's face is stricken as he clutches nonexistent pearls. "I've waited my whole life to plan the wedding I want. I can't pull it off in a matter of days. I can't give up a merry-mazel wedding!"

"I get it. I don't want you to give that up." Declan takes a deep, thoughtful breath.

You don't grow up in era of social media and not know there's a simple solution here. "We just need a prop wedding," I say. "Fake it."

Two men and a Gaga look at me in unison, like, *it's easy to come up with one of those?*

"I can cheat a lot with the photos. It's the perfect time of year to do it outside, spring. That means cheap location," David offers.

"A fake wedding. We can't afford models. Who…" Lenny stage-whistles and makes big eyes at his nephew.

Dec takes my hand and falls to one knee in front of me for the second time in my life, "Wanna marry me, Stewart?"

My mouth drops as a gush of butterflies throw a party in my chest. The room erupts with applause and my eyes meet his.

He's kidding, of course, but those words do things to me. "Of course, I'll marry you," I say, pulling him up into the best bear hug I can manage. "I'll even ask Gran to come. Do we need a whole wedding party? A cute little grandma in a floral shift?" I direct my question to David, not sure what his vision is or how big this production needs to be.

"Absolutely. You sell dresses for grandmas, right? We need the entire wedding party so we can show you're a full-service, one-stop bridal destination. And with the Lorden's name behind it."

"Even if we pull this off, pull powerhouse, life-changing numbers off in weeks so that Lenny can use his portion of the profit to put down on the offer, how do we find the buyer?" Declan is holding my hand again, letting his thumb rub little circles on the inside of my palm.

"Leave that to me," Lenny says, packing his things more quickly. "Dick and Oscar, *stop laughing, Holly,* are ruthless. There'll be a paper trail even if Louie won't be forthcoming. And when we find them, we're all going to have to be very convincing and hope this whole fake wedding is a roaring success."

"I can't wait to see what you look like as a bride," Declan whispers. The warmth of his breath in my ear and the scratch of his stubble on my cheek does some very, very honeymoon-ish type things to my heart.

Lenny snaps his fingers at us and we jolt out of our fake engagement glow. We all head for the doors. He's right. There's not one second to waste.

CHAPTER
Twenty~Nine

OUR MASTER PLAN is going to take a few days, and in the meantime, we can't let Lorden's grind to a halt.

It's Saturday and I've got Birkenstock popping up to do hand-painted designs for anyone who buys a pair. The crowd they draw is substantial. It takes me an hour to get lines regulated and cash wraps properly staffed to handle the influx of sales in addition to spring traffic on a beautiful weekend morning.

The sun is out, shoppers are making purchases, and the city is humming with life. It's as if the whole world is as ready for a change as I am.

Taking the escalator two steps at a time in my combat boots and holding on tight just in case, I race up the stairs to pull my last appointment for Corrine. I know we'll be talking about more than just her spring wardrobe. This is our last appointment together. On Monday I'll be a full-time Kind Klub COO.

And I haven't told Declan yet. There hasn't been a moment or the right time, and the longer I wait the more I realize I'm not giving him much time to acclimate. And he likes to be in control and does not take change well. But I've got the weekend, and I'll still be Team Lorden's because I'm Team Declan and I don't think that'll ever change. He'll have me in his corner always, if he wants me. We'll continue to fight together. And I get to fake-marry him.

"Holly, there you are," she says, thirty minutes later. She's as elegant as ever in a cream twinset and the white Mother jeans I sold her.

"Good morning, Corrine. Jordan and Jameson doing well?"

"Good, good. My room is ready?"

"Absolutely, follow me."

The fitting rooms are unusually quiet for a Saturday morning, but I like it. I'm taking every opportunity I can to soak the store in. I'm going to miss it.

"Is there anyone else back here?"

"Not at the moment. Dorian has a customer he's helping in women's shoes. I'm manning the cash wrap while he's gone, but it's been a slow morning in our department so far. All the traffic is down-stairs with Birkenstock."

"I saw that. Pop-ups have really been working, haven't they?"

"Just another draw to brick-and-mortar. A reason to get off your couch and a website and come into a store to shop in person. It's my last week. I'm trying to make it count."

"And you've let the powers that be know you're leaving?"

How does she know? "Not exactly," I hedge. "Things have been a little wild around here, lots of unknowns. Lots of balls in the air." I actually mime juggling until I can force myself to stop. "There hasn't been a good time to mention it. But I will. I've already discreetly given my appointments and clients to the other stylists on the team. Jenny is out on maternity leave, but I've spoken to her at length and given my two weeks. It'll be a smooth transition."

"Hmm. Well, smooth may be a stretch." She sits and removes a quirky pair of Golden Goose sequined sneakers I sold her that *I'd kill for* myself. "I've got a proposition for you."

"What do you mean?"

"I've been thinking about your role with my company, and I'm thinking we may need to change your title."

Leaning against the frame of the door, I watch as she slides her feet into a pair of timeless mules. "How so?" I haven't even started and already her demands are rolling in.

"I recently acquired a department store. A rather large company. I need a general manager." She eyes me down in the mirror. "I've been going over potential applicants for days, but I keep circling back to you. You already know so much about the industry, and I could find someone else for Kind Klub."

My skin chills. A lump forms in my throat, but I manage to ask, "What company did you acquire?"

Please don't say it, please don't say it.

My head is suddenly empty. I'm hot and spinny and pray I don't faint while praying harder that her answer isn't what I think it—

"Lorden's, of course."

I might be sick.

With zero regard for personal space, I heave myself into the room and collapse on the bench already covered in jackets and blouses. With my head between my knees, I fight for air.

It's quiet for so long, only the sound of rustling garments in the background, and I finally look up.

She regards herself in the mirror while tossing a Fendi wrap around her shoulders, totally clueless to my turmoil. Or at least, that's the way she wants it to appear. I have a feeling she knows exactly the position she's put me in.

"How could you—"

"Louie called me himself, knew I'd do right by the business and try to save it. Most would tear it apart piece by piece, selling for a swift profit."

"Like in *Pretty Woman.*"

"Exactly," she smirks.

"Corrine, please. I can't take Declan's job. I can't be the manager of a company with coworkers whose family tree built it to be what it is working below me."

"Need we have this conversation again? You must take what you want from this life, Holly. No one is going to give you a free ride or a leg up if you're not willing to reach for it first."

"But is there a line? One you don't cross in business, when it becomes personal."

"For love or money? Is that what this boils down to for you?"

"If it does, I wouldn't pick money." I hold my chin up as I say it, ready to take whatever stern words she might throw at me.

"Interesting," is all she says, looking me straight in the eye. I think the next words out of her mouth might be *you're fired*. But she turns back to her own reflection and simply says, "Can I try this in smaller size?"

She holds up a gold dress. It's perfect for her and I knew she might need a smaller size when I pulled it for her, but I've already checked and the company is sold out. I've gone a step beyond that and contacted the designer, who's also sold out. "No, Corrine. That's the last one, it's sold out everywhere. I guess it's just not meant for you." With that, I walk out of the room, closing the door quietly behind me.

At home, I pace the worn cottage floor. The rosettes on the walls and the hum of the TV in the background bring me no peace. I've already texted Len, letting him know he can call off the search for the buyer. Dick and Oscar (those really are ridiculous names) are putting together paperwork to make Corrine an offer, but she won't let go of this new boon in her treasure trove easily.

And she wants me to be the manager.

There was no way I could have this conversation in the office, so I fled the second my shift was up. Texted Declan to come over when he was off the clock.

When there's a light knock on the door my heart jumps out of my throat and flops like a fish on the carpet. Every gut instinct I have says this is not going to end well. But there's no way to avoid it, I have to tell him everything.

"Hey, you," I breathe nervously.

He's standing on my doorstep in his Jordans and dark denim.

"Why do I get the feeling you're about to give me bad news?" It really is annoying that he can read my face that well. In seconds.

"How'd planning go?" I stall.

"Planning went fine. You'd think this really was my wedding the way Len's carrying on. How was the store today? Your appointment with Corrine go okay?"

This is going to be a lot to drop on him. He's going to have questions for me and I'm not sure I have the right answers. I know him now. Know how passionate he is about the store. And how defensive he can be because of the way he grew up, the way he's been treated by people he trusted his whole life.

I pick through my brain for gentle ways to start while he plops on the couch and picks up the remote.

"We found a pretty little gazebo near the marina in Lakewood," he says, totally relaxed. "David likes the idea of a wedding on the water. My idea." He winks, and when I respond by twisting my hands in my lap next to him, he reaches over and takes one, folding my hand into the warmth of his. "Hey, what's up with you? You still want to fake-marry me, right? It's kind of weird, considering you hated my guts on a primordial level a few months ago, but maybe we can think of it like a dry run."

Oh my God, he did not just say that to me right now.

"Declan..."

"Like a really over-the-top rehearsal? Because someday... Your ring is going to be the size of a flea. I'm going to be company poor for a while but—"

"Dec, stop."

He tries to pull me to him, but I can't let him.

"No, I want you to know that's how I'm thinking of it. I thought you were going to marry my brother one day and I'd have to go live in Alaska or something. But you're here with me. You're mine. George is happy, dating. Lenny's engaged. My dad is a dick, an even bigger dick than I thought, but *we're going to get our company back...* And I can't fucking believe how lucky I am." He takes my face in both his hands. "I've changed because of you. This whole thing with my family and the company...that dinner at Sky City would have crushed me. I think I would have given up everything if I hadn't learned from *you* how to fight. Holly, I lo—"

"Mrs. Smith is the buyer."

He pulls back. "What?"

"Corrine bought the business. She owns Lorden's."

He leans farther away from me and I wonder if he realizes how immediately he put physical distance between us. "You can't mean... What do you mean? Corrine? Our Mrs. Smith?"

"Yes. There's more."

"Did you tell her we want to buy her out? She's tough. I respect her as a businesswoman, but we'll make it worth her while."

"I took a job with Kind Klub," I blurt. He's already spinning, but I have to get it all out. "I was just waiting to tell you..."

"Wait, what? So, Corrine did make you an offer?"

"I took the job before I knew she bought Lorden's. I was waiting for the right time to tell you. I gave Jenny my two weeks, gave my clients to Molly and Angel. Today was my last day."

He doesn't move. Just stares ahead, glossy-eyed, chewing his bottom lip. "So, everyone knows but me."

This is a mammoth mistake. I hadn't thought of it that way. "Dec, I'm not the enemy here. Just listen, it's crazy the way it's all happened so fast and there was hardly time to tell you in the middle of every-thing that's been going on with your family and the store."

He takes a deep breath, in through his nose and out through his mouth. "What does she want you to do?"

"Well, that's the thing. She wanted me to run Kind Klub, but then she bought Lorden's and it changed."

"Changed to?"

"My title would be manager, of Lorden's."

He huffs a laugh that evolves into a short coughing fit. "Exactly what you wanted, right?" He looks at me with watering eyes, and his tone turns cold. "Corporate? Climb the ladder?"

I grab his knee and shake him, willing him to look at me. "It all happened today. Today, she said she wanted someone else for Kind Klub. That I already know so much about how the Lorden's brand functions, how the business works on a store level, and I know the industry."

"Is it still only about a title for you?" He stands, moving out of my grasp as if it's too painful. "I assume this means you're not going to help us buy it back?"

This is all going so wrong. "*I said no*," I plead, trying to make him see that I am not the bad guy here.

"It's not about the job, Holly. You know what the worst part of all of this is, Stewart?" He paces as much as he can in the tiny cottage. Back and forth, back and forth, running into chairs and chintz.

"Don't be angry." It's all I can do not to follow him around the room. I sit tight and try to keep my composure. "Of course, I'll beg her to sell you back the company. I'll do everything I can to make this right."

"The worst part of this is that you lied to me. I'm not angry. I'm—"

"I didn't lie. Don't say that!" I yell, jumping to my feet.

He drags a hand through his hair slowly. "A lie of omission, right. That's what it was, keeping all of this from me? You asked me to try, to be nice, to be honest, but you don't do the same."

"I only found out about Lorden's hours ago," I fight back.

"Holly, I don't give a shit if you take my job. I'd work for you. I think you're *fucking amazing*, brilliant, *damn* strong, and insanely fascinating. You'd do a great job running a company. Lorden's, Kind Klub, whatever. The part that hurts is that you didn't tell me. You didn't trust me. And you hid it from me while others knew. While I was out planning a fake wedding that like an idiot I was *wishing* was real."

"I don't know why I didn't tell you, I just couldn't. I wanted to stay at Lorden's and work for your family forever. Work my way to the *top*. If the terms were different, might have been a great step for me. If we still hated each other, none of this would matter."

"But we don't hate each other, do we, Holly? You lied to me, just like Louie lied to my mom. I knew we'd end up like my parents, and here we are."

"That's *fear* talking. We are different. I made a mistake, just like you did." The tears that burst from my eyes are epic. They are a full-on monsoon of pent-up emotions.

Instead of running like I know he wants, he sits tight on the couch, his entire body rigid and unmoving with what I can only assume is sheer determination. "So, what now?" he grits.

"You're so upset," I breathe. Because he is, and I can't believe it's all my fault. I'm the one who's making him hurt.

"Rightfully so."

I deserve that, and it hurts almost as much as seeing him sit so distraught and aloof on my couch.

"You don't have to stay." If he feels like he can't leave, and he's sitting here in pain because of me, I'll never forgive myself.

He stands, crosses the room, opens the front door silently, and just stands in the doorway. His back is to me so long I wonder what it is that's stopping him from walking away.

He turns toward me, and I move to fill the gap between us, wanting to reach out and touch him but knowing I can't. "Do you remember what I said, that night in the café when I asked if you were sure you wanted *me*?"

"You said if we went much further, there'd be no turning back for you." I remember it, crystal clear.

"We've just begun, so I know this is a selfish ask, but I can't help what I want."

"Anything." In this moment, I have no idea what he'll say, but I feel like I'd give him anything.

"I want all of you, or I can't live with any of you."

"Dec, what are you saying?"

"I swore I'd never walk away from you."

"You're not. This is how arguments work, if you need some time you say so."

He nods with a jerk of his head, his entire body ridged. "Right now, I'm going home and I don't know where we stand, Holly. You wanted so much from me, and all I'm asking for is the same in return. Partners. No secrets."

"Dec—"

"We've got a lot to accomplish in the next week. I need to be focused on saving my company, with your help, I hope. You think about it, okay? And let's talk after the wedding." His smile is small, sad, and I can read the exhaustion in his eyes. The last thing I want to do is let things simmer the way they are, but then he meets my eyes again and says, "Give me some time to sit with this. Do that, for me."

All I can do is nod and agree, resisting the urge to ask him to shake on it, which makes me close the door and crumble into a puddle of tears.

CHAPTER
Thirty

"WE NEED THE BRIDE! Where's the bride?" David shouts from a cedar gazebo near the lake.

"She's here somewhere. I saw her lugging that monstrosity you call a dress into the marina restrooms," Lenny replies.

I can hear them shouting through a moldy air vent in said bathroom. Molly and Angel are zipping me into a marshmallow-of-a-dress with baby-pink sparkles. With multiple layers of tulle, the skirt is easily the width of a car (Angel is drooling over it) and the bodice is a satin-wrapped dream with cap sleeves. I love this dress, but I can barely walk.

The linoleum in the bathroom is yellowed and we're all breathing through our mouths to avoid the smells. "Something borrowed," Molly says, pushing a few of her pastel-colored bracelets on my wrist with my watches. It makes for quite the arm party but looks intentional, eclectic, unique. "These also count for old and new, because one is old and one is new."

"And I've got your something borrowed," Angel says, fastening a small baby blue Chanel choker around my neck. "I want this back. And clearly it's blue, so…"

"You guys!"

They hug me.

"Thank you." Even though the tradition isn't necessary, it means something.

"Yeah well," Angel says, "When Lorden's finally goes under, we want jobs with Kind Klub."

"You weren't supposed to tell her!" Molly swats her arm. "Congrats, by the way."

We hear Lenny shout, "It's show time!"

"Time to go, ladies," Angel says, as she and Molly push me out the door toward the gazebo where Lenny and David are still going at it.

"Yes, the dress is over the top," Lenny says. "but it'll be perfect on film. Remember *Funny Face*, Audrey Hepburn? All the tulle floating on the wind like a cloud? And I chose a *second dress* look for her to change into, so you'll get your modern Barbie doll shots! I've even got a surprise up my sleeve that'll make for good video footage if we still have light to work with."

The fact that a *second dress* is par for the course these days in bridal only adds to our potential profit. Plus, it's the one I'm really looking forward to. As for the surprise, I've got no idea what Lenny's talking about and I hope there's not too much more on the shoot itinerary. I've barely spoken to Declan over the past few days, per his request, giving him the space he asked for while he, Lenny, David, and I focused on pulling off this media charade. But I've done quite a bit of thinking.

This fake wedding is going to be horribly uncomfortable.

"Has anyone seen my bouquet?" Angel asks while holding up part of my dress so I don't trip and fall flat on my face.

Molly holds two bundles of pink peonies in the air. "Got it!"

"I can't believe you're getting married," Angel squeals, "I mean, first Jenny has a baby—tiniest flower girl ever! Have you seen that little nugget out there? And then, Holly gets married!"

"You know this isn't a real wedding, right?" Though I have to admit, it is a little confusing. The flowers, the guest list, the rose-petaled aisle, you could shoot a CW sitcom outside right now.

We make our way down a small gravel walk where the gazebo sits just to the side of the shoreline. That's when my eye catches on the boat, tied off on the dock closest to where our wedding party is already politely sitting on white folding chairs.

It's Declan's boat, and it was not there this morning during the staged still shots with David. The man who bought it must have a slip here. This is going to crush Declan.

Once we're on grass, cream flower petals make a carpet for an aisle. There are a few boaters and maintenance people who stare at a bride about to take her first steps into her new life; Molly, Angel, and I look like the real deal. Everyone is waving, smiling, and wishing me congratulations.

"Holly, you look stunning!" Jenny is a little sweaty and holding an adorable baby in the crook of her arm. Her husband is just next to her in the last row of chairs set for the ceremony guests.

"Thanks for coming," I say, dancing on my feet at the back of the aisle.

"Are you kidding? We wouldn't miss Penelope's first photo shoot. Your photographer promised to send me some prints for her baby book." She nods toward David, in torn-up denim and a safari-style button-down with all kinds of caps and lenses tucked inside, as he heads down the aisle snapping pictures as he goes.

"He's the best."

"I really hope this scheme works for them." Unable to use her hands because they're full of baby and binkies, she nods toward the front again where Lenny is telling wedding guests where to sit and how to pose.

"Holly, we need you up here!" Len shouts.

"Okay, here goes nothing," I say through smiling teeth as David points his camera at me from afar.

"We're going to miss you, Holly."

A string quartet begins to play. A camera and microphone on a boom loom over my head. David's videographer buddy is just off to the side working another larger camera with a monitor on wheels. The wedding march swells on spring air, boats rock in their slips, guests stand, and I resist the urge to burst into tears because I've got no idea where I stand with Declan Lorden. When I see him at the end of the aisle, I might faint, I might vomit, I might fall to his knees and beg him to forgive me.

I do want him to forgive me. As for how we work the rest of it out, that's anyone's guess.

"You really do look beautiful. This all feels so real, doesn't it?" Jenny looks up at me suspiciously. I haven't budged, as Penelope coos. Word about Declan and me has traveled and surprisingly, I think the whole store is rooting for us to get back together or stay together —*whatever*.

The smile stays plastered across my face, and I don't have the heart to contradict her.

Finally, I take a step, and then another. The crowd seems to relax. I had them on the edge of their seats for a moment. As if I would be a runaway bride. *Make a commitment and stick to it!* Gran's and the General's voices ring through my ears.

As I make my way down the aisle, Gran gives me a small wave, Bernie salutes, and I salute him right back. I spot a smartphone in Gran's hand; the General's face on the screen draws tears to my eyes. Salespeople from the store sit scattered throughout the rows of chairs. Alice and Dorian both give me little waves and round out the bride's side.

On the groom's side I laugh out loud when I take in what looks like the entire Guys and Dolls nightclub. Dec's D&D buddies are here in full regalia as well—elf ears and capes, but understated enough that I think it will only add flavor to David's shots. Mira sits in the front row. I'm surprised to see her, but I'm not surprised she's alone.

Angel and Molly take their positions as bridesmaids at the front and I'm so happy to see Amanda standing in the middle wearing a cream silk suit with a baby-pink blouse that has an enormous bow tied just under her chin. Her makeup is done to perfection. She could easily be a bride herself.

"You're gorgeous!" I say to her.

"Your doing. You styled the officiant look for this wedding."

"I am good, aren't I? Thanks for doing this. It feels weird, you know? Like real but not real?"

"Honey, you make a beautiful bride. Don't worry about the rest too much. If there's anything I know to be true, it's that everything has a way of ironing out in the end. And if a few wrinkles remain, well, that's what makes it real. Wrinkles make it real. Just don't tell the woman who does my filler I said that!"

Amanda is an ordained minister, which is why Lenny thought to ask her to be in the shoot in the first place. I can tell she's the real deal as she turns to a marked page in a fat, leather-bound book. I'm sure she puts every couple she works with at ease.

"Where's the groom?" David hollers as he wraps his way around the wedding party and starts shooting up the aisle again, coming straight at me.

I smile as brightly as I can.

"Holly, tone it down, this isn't picture day at school," he laughs.

I do and he snaps a few more shots. Lenny whispers in my ear, "Just be yourself. Declan is on his way. He's been…struggling today. He's gonna die a small death when he sees you. You really did a number on him."

"I didn't mean to. I was trying to protect his feelings, but it totally backfired. And I may have been a little scared to tell him, too."

"Perhaps it's time to do some groveling? Lord knows I've done my fair share. Let me know if you need any tips."

"Is that his boat in the slip behind us?" I ask, turning my head to gaze out at the water.

"Yes. You know he sold it because he was terrified, he felt helpless. He could have come to me, gone to Mira. Fear makes us do silly things, don't ya think?"

"We need the groom," David yells. "Declan, get down here!"

"I'm coming." I hear his voice, but I don't see him. He's not coming from the marina in front of us.

That's when I notice the eyes of all our guests start to track something behind me.

It's Dec, he's appeared on his boat and is hopping off to the warm wood dock. He's James Bond, jogging toward us from the water in a tux. He makes his way up a small grassy hill as if I'm watching a movie; the man I've come to know so well and care for deeply is headed right toward me and, *surprise*, I'm wearing a wedding dress!

Except none of it is real. This is all pretend.

He jogs straight to me, charging across the front row of chairs to where I'm standing under a pergola. "I need to talk to you."

"Okay, everyone, here's the plan," David hollers to the crowd, then turns to Declan and continues before I can answer, "Declan, I need you to go down the aisle and come back up, I haven't gotten solo shots of you yet."

"I just need one minute," he replies, holding his ground and looking as if he's seconds away from reaching for me. I wish he would. I've missed his arms like I'd miss food, or breathing, or sunlight, or sequins.

My pulse is racing at the sight of him and the illusion of our wedding. It's playing tricks on my senses, making me believe that whatever our differences are we can work them out. I wish this moment was real. That things would have gone so much differently from day one between us. That he hadn't messed up. That I hadn't messed up in return.

"No time. The light is perfect and we still need to get party shots."

I've never seen David be pushy but apparently, this is professional photographer David and he's not taking no for an answer.

"We'll go through a bare-bones ceremony." David ushers Declan away from me and down the aisle while raising his voice to explain more details to our crowd of extras. "Our officiant is going to hit all the important beats so I can get the shots and we'll work through vows etcetera to get the video we need, probably about five minutes' worth. Then, the families of the bride and groom, those of you who have been tapped to play certain parts, will head down to the boat where we'll have the party scene. If you have any questions, just, I don't know, grab one of us on the way. Yeah? Oh, and enjoy the champagne, it's real. No one needs to pull out their SAG cards to have a good time. Here we go, let's have a wedding!"

The guests whoop and catcall, and I swear this suddenly feels so real I shed a tear that my dad's not here to give me away.

David calls his shots, asking Declan to slowly make his way down the aisle just as I did so he can capture the moment. His glasses glint in the sun and his tux is so fitted my mind wanders to everything I know first-hand is underneath it. When Declan comes to a stop in front of me my hands are shaking and so are his. Amanda begins her bare-bones ceremony and a knot forms in my throat.

Yes, I hear you inner monologue, I did withhold important information from him! And yes, you exasperating Jiminy Cricket, I do see how that could hurt someone, especially someone with trust issues!

He reaches out immediately to brush a tear from my cheek. I hear David say, "Perfect, Dec. Keep doing that. Can you join hands?"

His hands wrap around mine. I have to break the tension, the silence between us. "Are you sad about your boat? What were you doing down there?"

I've missed you.

His face twists into a pained smile. "Lenny. He bought it back as a surprise for me, wrote it off as a marketing investment. Instead of a jet, now we have a boat."

"That's great," I choke on a sob building in my throat.

"I made a rash decision, a rash mistake. I thought it was the only way. Sometimes I do things without thinking them through. *I'm working on that.*"

My face brightens when I realize what he's really saying, *I'm sorry.*

"I can relate," I awkwardly laugh. *I'm sorry too.*

His smile warms. "Holly—"

But Amanda breaks in, "I think we should do rings now. Repeat after me..."

"We don't have any rings," I say, knowing this part can be fudged on film.

But Declan pulls two rings from the breast pocket of his suit. He hands them to Amanda, David's camera *click, click, clicks.*

My gaze shoots to his and he gives me a knowing, sideways smile that causes my heart to gallop. They're two identical gold bands. Simple. Timeless. "It's taking everything in me not to make a *'my precious'* joke," he laughs nervously.

Amanda hands me a ring first. "Holly, repeat after me."

I cut a look to her and then back to Declan. "Okay." My voice cracks with nerves and the crowd knowingly chuckles.

"Declan, I give you this ring as a symbol of my love."

She gives me time as I take Dec's hand, repeat the words, and push the ring up his finger and over his knuckle. She gives me the second part of the vow and I take a breath, repeating the words, "As it encircles your finger, may it remind you always of my enduring love."

I say every single word as if I mean it because I wholeheartedly do.

He smiles.

"Now Declan." Amanda hands him a ring. "Repeat after me."

Declan nods and repeats her words just as I did, finishing his vow in a low thoughtful voice, "As it encircles your finger, may it remind you of my enduring love."

I startle at the feel of cold metal as he slides the ring on my finger.

"In the great state of Washington, for the sake of company and a wild media campaign, I now pronounce you work husband and work wife. You may kiss your beautiful bride."

The sound of David's camera clicks away as my lips find his.

CHAPTER
Thirty-One

BEING on Dec's boat is surreal. I change quickly in his cabin, inhaling the sweet scent of him I've been yearning for and lying to myself, trying to believe I didn't. I don't need help with this dress. It's a second-skin-thin, asymmetrical silk number by Amsale. The dress has slinky spaghetti straps and the hemline cuts from my right knee in a slash down to my left ankle. Lacing up my combat boots, I wonder if anyone will try to talk me out of the way I've styled my *second dress* look.

Outside, the party scene is covered in hydrangea blooms, traditional saucer-style champagne glasses, blue-striped cushions, and high white sails. The boat is polished to perfection, probably what kept Declan from our ceremony.

Bernie and Gran teeter over to me, holding on to each other on the slightly unsteady deck of the boat. "Congratulations! Everything was fabulous!" Gran says. She holds up her smartphone. I wonder who gave it to her. "And your mom loved it."

"Hello, Holly. Didn't want to miss the big day. You look beautiful. I'm proud of you," Mom says from the screen. Then she turns. "Yes, I'll be there in five."

"Presidential emergency?"

"Thankfully, no. But I do have to get back."

"Thanks for coming, Mom. It means a lot."

"Talk soon, honey. I, uh, love you."

"I *loveyoutoomom*," I blurt, because we don't say it often. Maybe Declan's not the only one still working on himself. Maybe we all are. Maybe that never stops, no matter how old you are or where you are in life.

"We're so happy for you." Bernie releases Gran only to pull me into a timid hug, then reaches back for her and they're a unit once more.

Gran uncharacteristically dabs Bernie's pocket square to the corners of her eyes.

"Gran, you know this is a fake wedding. I didn't actually marry Declan Lorden. Can you imagine?"

She eyes me with the sneaking suspicion of the Irish. "I can. Can you? Nice of him to make sure your mother was able to attend your wedding, wasn't it?" She hands the phone to me and I stare at it dumbfounded.

Does everyone know how in love with him I am? Did I? Maybe not, not until this very moment, but since the escalator incident I knew I was attracted to him. And then, the gala, all those heated hallway interludes, our little not-date in Lorden's, and that night in his bedroom in Lenny's house, and—

"David needs us on the bow of the boat. Holy shit, you look amazing!" He appears behind me, as if we have some sort of telecommunication ability. "The other dress was stunning, I mean, you're beautiful in anything. But this dress…this one looks like you." He pauses. "Like you're my bride."

"Dec." I turn to him and gaze into his eyes. My hair whips around my head, coming loose from the elegant chignon I felt was the perfect throwback.

"I wanted to talk to you before. I'm sorr—"

"I'm sorry," I rush to say before he can finish. I'm a big girl, I know when it's my turn to apologize. "I didn't want to hurt you."

"I didn't want to hurt you," he says, pushing his glasses up and taking a deep breath then letting it out slowly. "How is this going to work?" He pulls a tendril of hair that's gotten stuck in my lip gloss from my lips. My skin burns where his fingers touch.

"I told Corrine I wouldn't take the job with Lorden's because I would *never* do that to you. She said she respected me for holding my ground. I took the job at Kind Klub because that's the job I wanted."

"And I appreciate it," he says, wrapping me up in his arms and sheltering me from the wind. "But if you went back to her and signed on the dotted line tomorrow, I'd support you. None of this matters, Holly, don't you see? You are the only thing I've ever truly wanted, that I honestly don't think I can live without. I've tried."

We've had such a rocky start, how can we trust each other with our hearts? How is a fake wedding going to win them back their store? How can he and I move forward when we're about to go in different directions? He'll continue to fight for Lorden's and I'll go work for Kind Klub.

How is this all going to end?

"I shouldn't have lied to you. I should have been honest from the start and told you everything. I was only trying to save your feelings—"

"I know," he cuts in. "No matter what, I want you. And this time, even if you tell me to leave, I'm not budging. I'll do better. Are you all in, Holly? No secrets but partners, always? That's not what I grew up with, but I know it's what I want."

"I am." I smile, just for him, pulling back and looking deep into his eyes so he knows I mean it. "Shake on it?"

He chuckles and holds up his left hand, flashing his ring finger. "We're married, remember. I think that trumps a handshake."

"You think we can do it? Our start was not the best."

His hand lifts to my cheek, fingers grazing down my skin. Under the sun as the boat gently rocks, he leans in and bites into my neck, gently kissing and licking it better. "I don't think we had that bad a start."

"That's not what I mean, and you know it," I whisper, snuggling into him and kissing a spot just behind his ear, under his jaw. Smelling him again, it smells like home.

"We're married, love, and I take my commitments seriously." His tone should be light. It's a joke of course, we're not really married. But instead, there's only sincerity and gravity in his words. "We're just going to have to work hard with each other, at each other, for each other."

I pull at his hips, wanting him closer and warring with myself over how not to drag him into his tiny bedroom.

"I don't know what to say."

"Then come take wedding pictures with me. We're going to want to remember this for the rest of our lives."

We do. We take beautiful photos with wedding guests and just the two of us as the sun begins to sink into the water. There's even a cake. We cut it, and feed each other like morons smiling from ear to ear.

"Did you get what we need?" Len breaks an intense moment, one where I think I might rip off Dec's tux and have him there on the bow of the boat for all to see. That's how much I want him right now.

"Got it, in the can, that's a wrap." David pulls Lenny to him and they commence their own make out session.

When Len looks over at us, I blush, caught gaping at the happy, frisky couple. I'm grateful he's found his partner for life. "What? You guys aren't the only ones with steam!"

We laugh and come together while the party goes on around us.

"I think we've pulled this off," Declan says, gripping me even tighter. He inconspicuously pulls at the short side of my hem until his warm palm wraps around my thigh. I shudder and lean into him, letting him know I want the same thing and I want it *yesterday!*

"There's still one more shot I want. Follow me." Lenny is all mystery, as only a man of the stage can be.

The four of us push through the small crowd of friends and family on the skinny deck of the boat until we're at the stern. He hands Declan a white T-shirt, and then the same to me.

"Put them on."

"Why?" Declan asks, looking around. "You want us to get naked right here?"

"There's no one at the marina and the party guests can't see back here. Anyway, they're into their cups. Just turn and put them on."

"You better do it fast, I'm losing the last of the light," David says, swinging his camera around his shoulder and taking it in hand.

I don't think, I just duck as best I can behind David and pull the white T-shirt over my head. Pulling my arms out of my dress and letting it fall underneath. Thankfully, the T-shirt is large and comes close to my knees. "Boots on or off?" I ask.

"Off," Len answers.

Once I'm decent I look up to see Declan in the same white T-shirt, except his fits him much better, hugging the muscles in his arms. He's got on tight black boxer briefs and it's all I can do not to let drool puddle at my feet.

"Okay, you two, now act like you just got married."

We scoot together and awkwardly put our arms around each other. "I don't get it." Declan shrugs when David's shutter noticeably doesn't click.

Lenny starts a short pace across the teak boards. "You're just married. *You did it!* This is the fun part. The part where you get to live the rest of your lives blissfully in love. You know each other, you've fought and you've made up, you've made mistakes and you've forgiven each other, you've been sick, you've been well, you did the party and the tux and the dress and the guests, and now it's just you. The finale. The end."

We look into each other's eyes. And he's right. This is the end. This is the end of the road for me, and the beginning of everything new.

"I love you, Holly Stewart." As a wedding gift, he gives me the widest grin I've ever seen him wear.

"I love you, Declan Lorden, nemesis o' mine, king of the dorks. I love you more than I thought I could ever love anyone."

"That's it. That's good." I hear David, but his voice barely registers.

Dec's hands are in my hair and then his lips crush mine. It's as if we've both been patiently waiting for the resolution we knew would come. Because it had to.

"Now, jump off the boat you crazy kids!"

"The water is still freezing!" Declan shouts back, wrapping his arms around me and speaking over my head.

"Losing light, you better do it fast!"

Lenny cups his hands around his mouth to amplify the words he hurls at us with the passion of a community theater director. *"This is the shot! The no-fear, walking-into-the-line-of-fire-together, forever, no-looking-back-because-we'll-always-have-each-other- shot!"*

"You in?" Dec looks down at me. His palms slide up my arms where goose bumps have popped from the breeze coming off the water.

"Why not?" I shrug, laughing into his shoulder because he's as crazy as his uncle. Declan is not just one thing, he's so many things wrapped up together; emotion, heart, strength, passion.

"Wait, your watch." He takes my wrist and begins removing both watches. "This is a very cute choice, by the way. The one I gave you is waterproof, but just in case."

"I couldn't pick just one."

"And I love that about you, a two-watch woman, fascinating. Did you like the inscription?"

My face must tell him I don't know what he's talking about.

"Come on, Stewart. I was trying to woo you!" He holds it up to show me.

Time stops when I'm with you, love, Dec.

Well, that's it then. I'm totally and completely gone for him.

After handing the watches to David, he picks me up, like a good groom who's about to carry his fake bride over the threshold. He walks me back a few feet, David following us and clicking to capture every move. Lenny stands off to the side, a look of pure amusement on his face.

He plops me down on my feet. "We're going to run for it, then jump. Together."

"What?"

"We're in this together, love. Ready: one, two, three!" He grasps my hand and sprints.

I follow his lead, and we jump.

Epilogue

LAST NIGHT, I was rocked to sleep in the hull of a small vessel; a lullaby I'm surprised I've grown so fond of.

"What time is it?" Declan asks. He's pressed down the length of my back, his chin resting on the crown of my head.

I reach out, not far, and grasp my phone from the tiny floating table beside our bed. "Nine."

"Uh-oh, time to get moving." The spring in his step every morning is in direct conflict with my slow burn wake-up routine, and he loves every minute of antagonizing me.

"No." I roll fully to my front, letting my cheek sink into a memory foam mattress that is small but mighty, which only gives him ample opportunity to smack my bum. "Hey! Declan Lorden, I just woke up."

"Okay, okay. I'll start coffee and eggs, but then let's get a move on. You've got a big day and so do I."

When the double doors click shut, I roll to my back and look up at the low, wood-cladded hull of the boat. It's taken some adjustment, it hasn't all been sunshine and rainbows, but I wouldn't change it for the world. Still, I'm keeping my granny cottage and renting it. We'll see if I ever go back, but I'd be crazy to give up real estate like that in Capitol Hill and all of my and Gran's memories. For now, I've got everything I

need right here. Even my needlepoint, which is a hobby made for traveling and small spaces. My current WIP is a pillow for Dec that says
High Maintenance, High Return. I'm even adding sequins.

A quick brush of teeth, a change into jean shorts, and a tank later,
"Smells good," I say.

"Eat." He drops a plate of eggs in front of me.

"Coffee first," I demand.

"You've become addicted since I've introduced you to the 100
percent pure Kona cup of coffee."

"Snob."

"Look who's talking, Miss Two-Hundred-Dollar-Jean-Shorts!"

"I'll never go to Starbucks again. And these will last a lifetime."

He huffs a laugh. "Famous last words."

"No really, this is it for me. I love the tiny houseboat life. One pair
of shorts, one little black dress, one pair of heels, my boots and this
coffee. Where did George say he got it?" I gobble down my eggs and
follow him out onto the deck with a warm mug in hand.

"That farmer he met came into a crop of trees on Kauai. He's into
nano-roasting. It's tech-coffee."

"It's. So. Gooooood," I moan.

His eyes fire up. "Glad you like it," he says as he begins a daily
maintenance routine in hot-as-hell short red trunks that he knows are
my Kryptonite.

"I wish I had time to go with you."

"You've got to make deals and run empires, remember?" *Later,* his
bright blue eyes promise.

Around us, the island of Oahu looks lush and green. The water
here is so blue, it looks like I've just squeezed it from a tube of paint.
"Why do you get to go play on a coffee bean farm, sip dark roast with
your brother and the farmer, and I have to be door-to-door salesgirl?"

"His name is Ron, and George wants me to see the plants. He's
obsessed with them *and* the farmer. What can I say?" He shrugs his
tanned shoulders before pulling anchor. "They're Typica plants with
red berries, along with the new trees. I think he called them Katuai?
Very special. Haven't you seen them all over his Instagram?"

"I want to see the Typica. Wander around in a straw hat with the nene birds and the waterfalls." I'm whining, I know, but we've only been here two days and I want to do more exploring.

"Didn't Corrine say she was happy with your progress? You're doing great building the brand."

"Yeah, and she loves the surf angle. We even talked about numbering boards for Kind Klub. It works with surf culture. A no-brainer."

"That's why she gets the big bucks, folks!" He gives me a mock round of applause and moves on to his next morning task, coiling thick rope with his muscly arms.

"You think George's idea will work?" I follow and ogle him, which he enjoys, I think.

"That's why he wants me to see the plants so badly. And to possibly draft a contract with Ron. He thinks taking Lorden's into the coffee business is also a no-brainer, as you would say. We've already got the E-bar in all our stores. A Hawaiian blend manufactured with local growers to sell by the bag is not only going to help these farmers, but it's going to be damn profitable for us. It's a win-win for everyone. Corrine was tough, holding us to a two-year payoff deadline in order to make the deal. We've got to increase sales, more than we've done with the bridal push even, and this is it. I can feel it. George is over the moon that he gets to basically be a coffee bean farmer."

"I have seen his Instagram. He wears the straw hats and looks totally smitten with Ron."

"Time will tell. Len is happy too."

"Did you get ahold of him?"

"He's updating the board weekly back home, keeping all the players in the loop. Can you imagine Lenny in weekly board meetings?"

"I bet he's really playing it up, like a role onstage."

"Absolutely. He even had some of George's power suits tailored to fit."

"And David?" Almost immediately after our fake wedding, David's shoot went viral. The Lorden boys were able to strike a deal with Corrine because of it.

"Are you kidding? He's great. Do you know how much publicity he got from the wedding shoot?"

"Yeah, my mom contacted me asking for his number. Did I tell you that?"

"No?"

"The First Daughter is engaged, and guess who they want as their official wedding photographer?"

"Get out. Len and David at the White House, that's poetic. You know, I wonder, if you hadn't said no to the job, would Corrine have agreed to sell the company back to us? Would any of this have happened? Would you and I..." He breaks off as sincere emotion crosses his face.

"Hmm," I muse, setting my cup on a small table with sunken cupholders, everything slides on a sailboat. "Guess it's a good thing I did. I don't think we really worked well together."

I let out a yip as he pulls me to him so fast I lose my footing, but he's there, wrapping me up with those arms that pull in sails day in and day out as we move from island to island on our fake honeymoon that we turned into a work trip. "You and I work just fine together, last time I checked. Should I check again?" His hands wrap around the backs of my thighs. He doesn't even have to lift me, I jump into his arms and wrap my legs around his waist. My favorite place to be, plastered to him.

His mouth is on my neck, moving up to bite my earlobe. I let out a raspy breath and I think I say his name. In return, he walks a few casual paces to the captain's chair where he gently places my rear right in the center of the wheel. He presses his hips firmly in between my legs; everything he is, pressing deep into my center making me squeeze tighter around him.

Oh. God. Sometimes, I can't take how much he wants me and how much he shows it.

He pulls back, looks deep into my eyes, then comes so close we touch noses, but he doesn't kiss me. "Promise me, this is it. You and me? Those few days before our wedding..." He quirks a brow and cracks a smile, he really enjoys acting like it was real, so much that we both keep our rings on. "When we weren't speaking, when we weren't together, it just felt wrong. We're lucky everything has worked out, but we'll have more bumps in the road. My family is difficult, things with my dad are still strained."

I put a finger to his lips and stop him. I want more than anything for him to mend that bridge, if that's what's right for him.

"It'll get better," I say. "Your mom is on your side, she'll help. You'll find a way to work out your differences. I don't think he's a bad man."

He takes a deep breath in, chews that lip, and exhales slowly. "But only if he accepts me for who I am. Like you did. Flaws and all."

"We're all flawed, Declan. And we're all *scared* of what our flaws make us do, of what we might not accomplish because of them, of what we stand to lose."

We've hashed it all out, but I know he still feels guilty about what happened between us. So do I. Which means we've both spent every day trying to make the other one happy, which seems to be the key to everything.

"I know who you are. Maybe in the beginning I didn't understand, but I know what's in here now." I tap on his chest, just over his heart. "You're stuck with me. And if they can't see what an amazing man you are, you'll still have me. I'm not going anywhere."

"Thank God."

"Oh!" A random thought pops into my head.

He chuckles, eyes squinting at me, halo of sun over his head, "What?"

"What if Lenny and David got married in Hawaii?"

Salty air whips around us as waves slap against the hull of the boat. "If anyone could talk him out of a merry-mazel holiday wedding, it's you, and I'd be grateful. I hate Seattle winters."

"Let's bring them home some straw hats and try to convince them."

"Yes, let's."

Acknowledgments

Taking a chance—any chance—requires guts and loads of support. I might never have published if it hadn't been for my buddy Taylor, who insisted I couldn't let Sink or Sell sit in a drawer. Or two of my oldest friends, Kayce and Shanna, who were kind enough to chat with me for hours discussing my first attempt at writing a novel all those years ago. Gina was my first critique partner, and when she read Sink or Sell, she said, *"This is the one, girlie."* My buddy Erica who I met through Writing With The Soul said, *"It's not just a love story, it's a love everyone and everything story!"* I met Amanda through a MadCap Critique Partner matchup and she gave thoughtful suggestions that made my characters stronger and cheered me on through giggly comments.

A big thank you to Mrs. Waters, my high school English teacher, who gave the assignment to write our own vignettes based on *The House on Mango Street* by Sandra Cisneros. It was my first A+ (admittedly, a bit late in the game as it was senior year), and it changed my life.

As for my family, they're all over the pages of this book. The General, Gran, and Declan are all inspired by the most important people in my life. The people who raised me, and the people who unconditionally love me. I am eternally grateful you're mine.

Lastly, I wouldn't be where I am today without my experience in retail and as a Personal Stylist. Thank you to the driven women who inspired me, eclectic customers who gave me a chance, diverse coworkers who educated me, and all-around gorgeous people I've been privileged to know over the years. You taught me to be strong, that kindness goes a long way, that I can do anything I set my mind to, and most importantly that style is about confidence— that's the real beauty.

About the Author

Margaret Rose majored in English with an emphasis on creative writing, dabbled in philosophy, and has a concentration in theater. Before becoming an author, she worked as a personal stylist, secretly drafting novels and begging her friends to read them. Now, she enjoys wearing sweatpants just as much as sequins and watching her kids chase their dreams while she chases her own.

Connect Online at Margaretrosebooks.Com.

CPSIA information can be obtained
at www.ICGtesting.com
Printed in the USA
BVHW031932170223
658758BV00010B/71/J